TIMEBOUND

RYSA WALKER

TIMEBOUND

SKYSCAPE

SKYSCAPE

Published by Skyscape, New York

ISBN-13: 9781477848159
ISBN-10: 1477848150
Library of Congress Control Number: 2013909113

This book is dedicated to
ELEANOR AND THE UNCLES

∞ Prologue ∞
Chicago—October 1893

The heel of my white kidskin boot ripped a six-inch gash in the hem of my skirt as I whipped around the corner. Behind me, the footsteps halted for just an instant, and then continued, faster than before. I ducked into the next corridor, silently cursing the gods of 1890s fashion. Had I been in my usual shorts and T-shirt, I would have been out of this wretched hotel long ago. A solid kick to the head would have rendered the good doctor unconscious and the side of my neck wouldn't be screaming in agony.

I darted across the hallway and took a left at the next intersection, hoping that the doctor would assume that I'd taken the quicker, easier turn to the right. Three doors down, I jiggled the knob on the off chance that it was unlocked. No luck. I pressed myself as close to the door as possible and pulled out the medallion. The center glowed, surrounding me with soft blue light. Even though I knew he couldn't *see* the light, I felt exposed. How many women had he lured into this confusing maze of corridors during the past year? Were any of them still alive?

The faint yellow glimmer of his lantern vanished briefly into the opposite corridor and then appeared again as he reversed course, heading straight toward me. I tried to steady my hands so that I could focus on using the medallion to bring up the interface, but it was hard to concentrate with my heart pounding and my neck on fire from the acid.

The navigation display wavered briefly, and then blinked out. I fought down a rising wave of panic and was about to try again, when the door behind me opened and I fell backward into the room. A hand covered my mouth, trapping the scream before it escaped my lips. Another hand with a white folded cloth moved toward my face.

It all clicked then. The horrors inside this hotel were not the work of just one insane man. Dr. Henry Holmes must have had an accomplice. And thanks to CHRONOS and this stupid medallion, I had landed right in their path.

∞ 1 ∞

I do not require life to be neat and orderly. Anyone who doubts that should dig around in my backpack, where you will likely find a half-eaten candy bar that has been there since Iowa—a state we moved from nearly a year ago. I've changed schools five times since kindergarten. I spend half of each week with my mom and half with my dad, where I sleep on the sofa and share a ridiculously tiny bathroom. I'm not high-maintenance. I can *deal* with chaos.

Some things, however, should happen in the correct order. Shoes go on *after* socks. Peanut butter is applied *after* the bread comes out of the toaster, not before. And grandchildren are born *after* their grandparents.

Most people never give much thought to that last point. I certainly hadn't—at least not until my grandmother showed up last April. Because that one little element was out of order, my entire life changed. And I'm not being melodramatic here. Having your existence completely erased has to qualify as a life-changing event, by anyone's definition.

Before my grandmother's sudden reappearance, I hadn't seen her for more than a decade. There were a few yellowed photographs of the two of us in an old album, but to me she was simply someone who sent money for birthdays and Christmas—and someone my mom doesn't like.

"This is *so* typical," Mom said as we stepped off the subway. "Mother breezes into town and demands an audience. Never mind that we might have other plans."

I didn't have other plans and I was pretty sure Mom didn't either. But I also knew that probably wasn't the point.

A slightly chilly breeze greeted us as the escalator reached street level and we stepped onto Wisconsin Avenue. Mom raised her arm to hail a taxi, but it pulled over to take another passenger.

"The restaurant is only a few blocks away," I said. "We could be there by the time—"

"These heels hurt my feet." She glanced around, but seeing that there were no other cabs in sight, she gave in. "Fine, Kate, we'll walk."

"Why did you buy heels in the first place? I thought you didn't care about her opinion."

She scowled at me and began down the sidewalk. "Could we move it, please? I don't want to be late."

I really wasn't trying to annoy her. We usually get along very well. But on any issue involving her *own* mother, Mom is unreasonable. The birthday and Christmas checks I mentioned earlier? They go straight into my college savings, even though Mom usually says I should make my own financial choices and deal with the consequences.

The previous night, she had actually talked to her mother for more than five minutes—a record, at least to my memory. I only heard Mom's side, but I was able to put the pieces together. My grandmother was back from Europe, she was ill, and she wanted to see us. Mom argued but finally gave in. The negotiations then proceeded to logistics—location (neutral turf), cuisine (vegetarian), time of the meeting (seven thirty), and so forth.

We reached the restaurant a good ten minutes early. It was a trendy, mostly vegetarian spot, with large paintings of vegetables on the exterior walls that reminded me of the illustrations in one of Dad's well-worn cookbooks. Mom breathed a sigh of relief when we entered and she was able to confirm that we had indeed arrived before my grandmother.

I took the chair facing the bar. The young guy behind the counter making mixed drinks and smoothies was cute, in an artistic, moody sort of way, with long hair pulled back in a ponytail. Even if he was a *bit* too old for me, at least I'd have a pleasant view while they argued.

When my grandmother arrived a few minutes later, she was not what I expected. For one thing, she was more petite than she'd appeared in photographs—my height or a little shorter. Her gray hair was almost a buzz cut, and she was dressed casually, in a bold print tunic and black knit pants that looked, I thought enviously, a lot more comfortable than what I'd been forced to wear. And she didn't look ill. A bit tired, maybe. Sick? Not so much.

Mom apparently agreed. "Hello, Mother. You're looking *surprisingly* well."

"Don't scold me, Deborah. I didn't say I was going to expire before the end of the week." Her words were aimed at Mom, but her eyes were on me as she spoke. "I needed to see you and I needed to see my granddaughter—all grown-up and so pretty. School pictures did not do you justice, dear." She pulled out her chair to sit down. "I'm quite hungry, Kate. Is the food good?"

I had been so certain that she would call me Prudence that it took a few seconds to realize the question was for me. "It's not bad," I responded. "They have decent sandwiches, and it's not *all* vegetarian. Some okay fish, too. The desserts are good."

She smiled, placing her purse on the empty chair next to her but keeping her keys out and setting them on the table next to her napkin. Attached to the ring were two very ordinary-looking keys and a very *un*ordinary blue medallion. It was wafer-thin, about three inches in diameter, and emitted a glow that seemed unusually bright in the dim room. It lit up the back of Mom's menu and

I could see tiny blue dots reflected in the silverware. The light reminded me of a glow-tube necklace I'd won at the Montgomery County Fair a few months back, but this was much brighter and more elaborate. In the very center of the circle was an hourglass. The sand still flowed from one side to the other, even though the medallion was lying flat on the table.

Mom either hadn't noticed the strange item, which seemed impossible, or else she was ignoring it. If Mom was ignoring it, the last thing I wanted to do was stir up a hornet's nest between the two of them by calling it to her attention. I decided to follow her lead, at least for the time being. As I turned back to my menu, however, I saw my grandmother watching my reaction to the light and smiling softly. The expression in her eyes was hard to place, but I thought she looked . . . *relieved.*

Everyone tried to keep the conversation light during the first part of the meal. The weather and food were both safe zones, but we had explored these from every possible angle within the first ten minutes.

"How do you like Briar Hill?" my grandmother asked.

I dove into the new topic eagerly, sensing another safe zone. "I love it. The courses are more challenging than anywhere else I've been. I'm glad Dad took the job."

My new school has a very generous policy that grants free tuition to the children of faculty members. They even offer small cottages for faculty members willing to live on campus, which is why I crash on Dad's pull-out sofa three or four nights a week. The mattress is lumpy and you can feel the iron bar if you roll too far toward the middle, but I consider it a fair trade for the extra hour of sleep on school mornings.

"It definitely sounds like a good opportunity for you—and Harry tells me that you're doing very well."

"I didn't know you and Dad . . . spoke much." I wanted to know, even though I suspected this might lead the conversation into treacherous territory. "That's why you knew to call me Kate?"

"Yes," she said. "But you've also signed the thank-you cards for your birthday and Christmas presents as Kate for the past several years."

Duh. I had forgotten about that. "I'm sorry if it hurts your feelings. Really I am, but—"

"Why on earth would my feelings be hurt? Prudence was an awful name forty years ago, but I named your mom, so it only seemed fair to let Jim name the other twin. He named Prudence after his mother. She was a sweet lady, but I still think it was a dreadful handicap to put on a small, defenseless baby."

Mom, who had of course done the same to me as a small, defenseless baby, took the indirect reproach silently, and my grandmother continued. "I'm pretty sure that Prudence isn't considered a cool name for a sixteen-year-old. And I have to admit I'm flattered you chose my name instead."

I was now thoroughly confused. "But I thought . . . aren't you a Prudence, too?"

Both of them laughed, and I felt the tension level at the table ease the tiniest bit. "No, she's a *Katherine*, too," Mom said. "Prudence was named after my father's mother, but her middle name was Katherine, after *my* mother. So you are Prudence Katherine, as well. I thought you knew that."

Major sigh of relief. I had worried all day that if I insisted on being called Kate instead of Prudence, it would hurt my grandmother's feelings. The name was an ongoing point of contention between Mom and me. I'd even asked to legally change it when I started school at Briar Hill the previous January so that there would be no chance that the damaging info would leak out to potential enemies. But Mom's eyes had watered at the mere suggestion, so

I dropped it. When you're named for an aunt who died much too young, your options are limited.

I pushed a too-mushy piece of zucchini to the side of my plate and glanced pointedly at Mom before replying. "I've never heard anyone use her name, so how *would* I have known? You always say 'your grandmother.'"

My grandmother wrinkled her nose in distaste.

"Do you prefer Nana?" I teased. "Or maybe Gran-Gran?"

She shuddered. "No, and most *definitely* no to the last one. How about Katherine? I've never been one for formal titles and I'm Katherine to everyone else."

I nodded once in agreement and Mom gave me a reproachful look that suggested I was getting far too friendly with the enemy.

The waitress brought Mom another merlot and refilled our water glasses. I was surprised that she didn't even glance at the odd medallion as she approached the table—it isn't something you see every day. The glow turned the water a shimmering baby blue as it streamed from the pitcher. I thought she'd at least look back over her shoulder as she left, the way you do when you're curious about something but don't want to seem rude or, in this case, jeopardize your tip. But she headed to the kitchen, stopping only to chat for a moment with Cute Guy with Ponytail.

We had gotten most of the way through our entrees when I accidentally hit another conversational landmine. "Is your hotel nearby?" I asked, thinking perhaps I might be able to finagle a visit somewhere with a nice indoor pool and sauna.

"I'm not at a hotel," Katherine said. "I bought a house. Not far from your school, actually."

Mom paused, a forkful of risotto halfway to her mouth. "You . . . bought . . . a house."

"Yes. Connor and I have been camping out there for the past few days, but the movers are finally finished and now we just need to get things organized. Harry pointed me toward a very nice realtor."

"Harry." Mom's mouth tightened and I had a feeling that Dad was going to be on her list for a while. She continued, enunciating each word very precisely—the tone of voice that usually came just before I was grounded. "So you've been in town for several weeks, and you didn't bother to call *me*, but you *did* call my ex-husband, who was kind enough to find you a realtor. *And* keep it a secret."

"I wasn't sure how *you* would react to my decision," Katherine said. "Harry, on the other hand, likes me. And I asked him, as a special favor, to keep things quiet. I'm sure it's been tough on him. Secrecy really isn't in his nature." I mentally agreed on that point—Dad is a wide-open book in most respects.

"Okay. So you bought a house." Mom set the fork back down with the risotto still uneaten and pushed her chair from the table. I was worried that we were about to make a dramatic exit, but she just said, "I'm going to the ladies' room. When I get back, maybe you can tell me exactly who Connor is."

As soon as Mom was out of earshot, Katherine leaned forward, pushing the glowing blue circle toward me. "They can't see it, dear. No—that's not quite right. They see the *pendant,* but they don't see it as we do. What color is the light for you? Blue, right?"

I raised an eyebrow. "Of course it's blue."

"Not for me. I see a lovely shade of orange. A bit like an orange Creamsicle."

"It's *blue,*" I repeated. I'd never seen anything more vividly blue in my life.

She shrugged. "I don't understand the physics of it. But I have only known a few dozen people in my lifetime who really *see* this light, and each of us sees it a bit differently."

Katherine paused and glanced over her shoulder to see if Mom was headed back, before slipping the medallion into her purse.

"We can't discuss this in any detail right now—there's so much you need to know."

The urgent tone of Katherine's voice was setting off alarm bells in my head. But before I could ask exactly what she thought I needed to know, she reached over and grabbed my hand, holding it between both of hers. "But I do want you to know this, Kate. Those were *not* panic attacks."

I blinked, surprised that she knew about the two episodes that had shaken me so badly. The "counselor" Mom had taken me to see back in February, just after the second occasion, called them panic attacks, probably triggered by my move to a new school in the middle of the school year. That didn't make sense. If I were going to have a panic attack, it would have been during the five months at Roosevelt High, when I was adjusting to metal detectors and security guards after two years in sleepy, middle-of-nowhere Iowa. It also didn't explain the episode while we were still in Iowa, although I suppose *that* could have been triggered by sheer boredom.

Both times, I had been gripped by the sudden and powerful sense that something was very, very, horribly wrong, but I couldn't pinpoint what that something might be. My body kicked into full "fight or flight"—heart pounding, hands shaking—and nothing around me seemed *real*. During the last attack, I ran out of class and straight to my locker. I called Mom, interrupting a meeting. She was fine. Then I went to Dad's office. He wasn't there, and I wasn't sure of his teaching schedule, so I ran up and down the halls, stopping to peer through the rectangular windows at the door of each classroom. Several raised eyebrows and annoyed stares later, I found him. He was fine, too. I sent a text to my best friend, Charlayne, although I knew she was in class as well, and there was no way she could respond.

And then I went to the girls' bathroom and puked up my lunch. The feeling that something wasn't *right* had persisted for days.

I was just opening my mouth to ask how Katherine knew about the panic attacks when Mom returned to the table, a small, tight smile on her face. I know that smile well—Dad and I refer to it as the "Let's-See-You-Explain-Your-Way-Out-of-This-One-Look," and it never precedes anything pleasant.

"Okay, you've bought a house. In Bethesda. With someone named Connor."

"No, Deborah. I bought a house in Bethesda by myself. Connor is my employee and my friend. He is a wonderful archivist and a whiz with computers, and he has been a great help to me since Phillip died."

"Well, that's better, I suppose. I thought perhaps you'd moved on as quickly after Phillip's death as you did after Dad's."

Ouch. My eyes darted toward the bar, in the hope that Cute Guy with Ponytail was there to offer a distraction, but he was nowhere in sight. I then looked at the chair next to me—anything to avoid catching either set of eyes at the table. Sharp pinpoints of light from the medallion were shining out from the tiny holes in the weave of Katherine's bag. It looked like an ice-blue porcupine sitting in the chair, and between that silly image and my already-frayed nerves I struggled to keep a straight face.

It seemed for a moment that Katherine was going to let Mom's snarky comment pass, but she finally gave a long sigh. "Deborah, I don't want to hash through old history with you, but I'm not going to let you toss out snide remarks in front of Kate without giving her my side of the story." She turned to me and said, "I married Phillip three years after your grandfather died. Clearly, your mother felt that was too soon. But Phil was my friend and colleague for many years, and I was lonely. We had fifteen good years together and I miss him very much."

I decided the safest course was just to smile politely. From my perspective, three years was a pretty long time.

"Why don't we focus on the issue of the house then, Mother? Why buy a house if you're so ill? Wouldn't it make more sense to check into an extended-care facility?"

I thought that was a pretty cold statement, but I kept quiet. Katherine just shook her head, and then reached for her handbag.

"I have my library to consider, Deborah. They don't have much space for books in old-folks' homes. And I'd like to *enjoy* the time I have left. Shuffleboard and penny-ante poker aren't on my to-do-before-I-die list."

She opened the purse and blue light flooded the table. I watched Mom closely. I could see light reflected in her eyes, but her expression didn't change at all. I didn't understand how it was possible, but it was clear that she really couldn't see the light from the medallion.

"Here's the situation in a nutshell. I have a brain tumor. It is inoperable." Katherine didn't pause for reaction but continued, her voice brisk and emotionless. "We've tried chemotherapy and radiation, which accounts for the lack of hair." She ran her hand across the top of her head. "I'm told it would have been considered chic a few years ago. The *bad* news is that I probably only have a year—a bit more if I'm lucky and a bit less if I'm not. The *good* news is that with a few exceptions, the doctor says that I'll be able do pretty much anything I want in the time that I have left."

She pulled a long envelope from her bag and removed the contents—several sheets of paper, very official looking. "This is my will. I inherited a substantial sum when Phillip died. Everything I own goes to Kate, including the house. If I should die while she is still a minor, Deborah, I am asking you to be executor of the trust until she turns eighteen. There is only one stipulation. You must continue to employ Connor so that my work goes on. Kate will be free to change that once she is of age, but I hope he'll be allowed to stay as long as he wishes. If you decide that you do not want to be executor, I will ask Harry.

"I also have one *request*," she added. "I would not want to make this a requirement. The new house is huge and is less than a mile from Kate's school. I am hoping that you'd both be willing to move in with me." Katherine stared for a long moment at Mom, who had flinched visibly at the suggestion, before continuing. "If you'd prefer to stay closer to the university, Deborah, then I'll make the same request of Harry. Either way, Kate would be with me for part of each week and that would give us time to get better acquainted."

Katherine pushed the papers toward Mom. "This copy is for you." She squeezed my hand, then stood and picked up her purse. "I know that you need to think about all of this. Please, finish your dinner and have dessert, if you'd like. I'll take care of the check on my way out."

And then she was gone, before Mom or I could say a word.

"Well, she hasn't lost her flair for the dramatic." Mom picked up the legal document by one corner, as though it might bite. "I do *not* want to move in with her, Kate. And don't look at me like I'm evil incarnate. If you want to fulfill the 'one year in a haunted house' clause in your grandmother's will, you'll have to work it out with your dad."

"Now who's being dramatic? Me staying there isn't part of the will. She said it was just a request. And I don't think you're being 'evil'—but jeez, Mom, she's dying. She's not a monster and she seems very . . ." I paused, looking for the right word. "Interesting, I guess. And maybe if you spent some time with her, you two could work out your differences so you won't feel guilty when she's dead."

That earned me a dirty look. "Kate, I'm not in the mood for amateur psychoanalysis right now. There's a lot that you don't understand, and probably won't understand until you're a parent. Truthfully, I'm not sure I want you even visiting her, much less staying there. She's manipulative and selfish, and I don't want you getting hurt."

"I don't see how you can say she's selfish when she's leaving us a lot of money. At least, I assume it's a lot of money."

Mom glanced down at the envelope. "I think that's a pretty safe assumption. But I hope that I've taught you that money isn't everything, Kate. There's such a thing as giving of *yourself* when someone needs you. Time, attention, sympathy . . ."

She finished the last of the wine in her glass before continuing. "I was always closer to my dad than I was to Mother, but I needed her really badly after the accident. I lost my father and I lost my twin. I barely got a chance to say good-bye to Dad—and Prudence was just *gone*. No good-bye, nothing. I felt so alone. We both suffered the same loss, but Mother closed herself up in her bedroom and I hardly saw her. She came out for the funeral and then went right back into the bedroom."

Mom ran her finger thoughtfully around the edge of the empty glass. "Maybe that's why I was drawn to your dad. Harry was the first person I ever knew who understood that kind of loss."

Both of my dad's parents were killed in an auto accident when he was only five; he was lucky to have survived the crash himself. No one I loved had ever died, and both Mom and Dad had always been there, physically, when I really needed them. But I could definitely sympathize with feeling alone. After each of the "panic attacks," I felt as though no one understood what I was going through. I was furious that Mom and even Dad tried to dismiss them as normal and explainable events, when I knew without a doubt that they most definitely were not.

"I've always believed," Mom continued, "that a mother should worry first about her child, not about her own needs. But I probably don't always put that into practice as well as I should, either. And . . . I don't want you to look back twenty years from now and be as angry at me as I am with her.

"I don't want to live with my mother and I don't want her money. But," she added, "you'll be an adult soon, and you're old enough to decide for yourself. I won't stop you from seeing her if that's what you want. You and your dad can work out the rest of it. Does that sound fair?"

I nodded. I had been expecting her to mull things over for days or even weeks, and was surprised to actually have a decision. "You want to split a dessert?"

She smiled. "No way, kiddo. I want my *own*. I need something big and gooey, with lots and lots of chocolate."

∞ 2 ∞

"You're late, young lady." Dad shoved a bowl of vegetables into my arms the second I walked in the door. "We're going to have to hustle to get the jambalaya ready before Sara arrives. The knife is on the table. Chop-chop."

I rolled my eyes at the lousy pun, even though I really don't mind them. If Dad is making bad jokes, it means he's in a good mood.

We both like to cook, but on school nights there's rarely time for more than soup and sandwiches. On Sundays, however, we go all out. Usually Dad's girlfriend, Sara, joins us to sample whatever gastronomic experiment is on tap for the week. Unfortunately, the kitchen isn't really designed for anything more adventurous than microwave pizza. There's barely room at the counter for one person, let alone two. So I sat at the kitchen table chopping the "holy trinity" of Creole cuisine—bell peppers, celery, and onions—while Dad stood at the sink doing his share of the prep work.

The envelope with Katherine's will was on the far side of the small table so that it wouldn't get spattered as I chopped the vegetables. I glanced over at Dad as I pushed the last bits of celery into the bowl. "Mom said to tell you hello. So did Katherine."

Dad's smile twisted a bit. "Ouch. How deep am I in it this time?"

I grinned and began slicing the pepper into narrow ribbons. "About chin-deep, I'd say. Katherine said that you helped her find a realtor."

"I gave her the website of someone that Sara knows and said he might be okay. That's hardly aiding and abetting the enemy." He returned to the ham he was chopping. "So is she going to buy a place here?"

"She's already bought it. Walking distance from Briar Hill, so it must be pretty close by. I thought you knew."

He chuckled. "No. I think Katherine decided that my life might be easier if I knew less rather than more about her plans. But I will say I'm happy she's back." His eyes, the same deep green as my own, darkened. "How is she?"

"You know she's sick, then?"

"Yeah. She told me in her last email. Really sad. I've always liked Katherine, despite your mom's feelings about her."

I stacked the thin strips of green pepper and turned them around to start dicing. "To look at her, you wouldn't think she was dying. Her hair is super short—she said it was from the treatments. I can't remember what she looked like before, though, except for some really old photos." I paused for a moment. "Did you tell her about my . . . panic attacks . . . or was that Mom?"

"Um . . . that was me. I hope that's okay? She emailed me a while back and asked how you were doing. I was worried about you and I wondered if maybe your mom went through something like that when she was your age. I guess I could have asked your mom directly, but getting that sort of information out of Deborah is like pulling teeth."

"It's okay," I said. "I just wondered. Did she tell you about the will?"

"No. Didn't know there *was* a will. Is she trying to get your mom to take money again?"

"Well, not exactly." I slid the diced peppers into the bowl with the back of the knife and started on the onions. "Katherine says she's leaving everything to me, including the big house she just bought. A lot of other stuff, too. And unless Mom has a serious change of heart, I think you're going to need to be executor or guardian of a trust or something like that."

Dad narrowly missed slicing his forefinger. He set the knife down carefully on the cutting board and pulled up the other chair, wiping his hands on the dish towel. "A trust?" I handed him the envelope, and he was silent for a moment as he glanced through the legal documents. "I didn't even know Katherine had enough money to buy a house, especially around here. I thought maybe she'd be looking at a townhome or something. Sara's friend owes me a beer—hell, a six-pack—for sending him that commission."

"There's more," I said. "Katherine wants me to move in with her—well, Mom, too, but I think she knew what *her* answer would be. She knows I'm here part of the week and with Mom the other, so she said if Mom said no, she would ask you instead."

"That's a condition of the will?"

"No. But I want to do it."

Dad looked at me for a long moment. "Are you sure, Katie? I doubt the next few months will be easy ones for your grandmother. And this may sound a little cold, but the closer you get to her, the more it will hurt when she's gone. I mean, I care about Katherine, but my first consideration has to be you."

"I know, Dad. But I think she's lonely." I considered mentioning the medallion to him, but I wasn't sure he would believe me. He wouldn't think I was *lying,* but he might start worrying about whether I had a screw loose. And even though she hadn't sworn me to secrecy or anything, it seemed like a breach of faith to talk about what I had seen with anyone else before Katherine had a chance to tell me more. "I want to get to know her. Before it's too late . . ."

He sighed and leaned back in his chair. "What does your mom say?"

"Mom won't move in with her, even on a part-time basis. But other than that, she says it's up to us. And you could stay here on the days I'm with Mom so that you can spend some nights with Sara . . ." Dad's face turned a deep shade of red and I mentally kicked myself. I'd realized months ago that Sara stayed over on the nights I was with Mom, but that probably wasn't the smoothest way of letting him know that I knew.

"Um. Right." He stood up and went back to the cutting board. "I think I should have a chat with your mom before we discuss this further. Since I'm in chin-deep already, I'd like to avoid making things worse. But if she's really okay with this and you're sure it's what you want . . ."

Once the jambalaya was bubbling fragrantly on a back burner, Dad picked up his cell phone and the will and went into the bedroom. I pulled my astronomy book out of my backpack and tried to read the assignment, but concentrating wasn't easy. I kept expecting to hear raised voices coming from the bedroom—although that was probably silly since Dad never yelled, and it would be pretty hard to hear Mom over his cell even if she was screaming at the top of her lungs.

I had just gotten up to give the pot a stir when Dad returned. He handed me the will and a small scrap of paper, on which he'd jotted a phone number.

"That went better than I expected. Your mom seems kind of . . . subdued, I guess. And she says this decision is up to us . . . just leave her out of it as much as possible. The only time she got angry was when I suggested that *she* might want to think about spending some time with Katherine. She told me to mind my own business. Not in polite terms, either."

He pulled the plates from one of the small overhead cabinets—a complicated process that required him to first move the cereal bowls and a small colander. "Sara will be here any minute. Why don't we all have dinner and then you can call your grandmother with the news? I just hope she bought a place with a nice big kitchen."

∞

I was up well before dawn on Monday, with much more energy than I usually have in the early mornings. I showered and dressed, and then tapped on Dad's door. He was awake, but he didn't look happy about it. "You need to hurry, Dad, or we'll be late."

He yawned and stumbled toward the shower. "Patience, grasshopper. It's a five-minute walk."

When I called her with the news the night before, Katherine gave me directions to the house and asked if we would stop by for a quick breakfast before school. "I know it won't give us much time to talk—*really* talk. I just want to see you. I'm so happy you're going to be staying here. And I want you to meet Connor—and Daphne, too, of course."

I didn't have a chance to ask who Daphne was before she hung up, but I found out the second that Dad and I walked through the front door of the huge greystone house. A large Irish setter jumped up, placed both paws on my shoulders, and gave me a long, wet slurp on the side of my face. She had big dark eyes and little specks of gray on her auburn muzzle.

"Daphne, you beast, get down! You'll knock Kate over!" Katherine laughed as she pulled at the dog's collar. "I hope you aren't afraid of dogs, dear. She's really a sweetheart—just doesn't think before she leaps. Did she hurt you?"

"No, she's beautiful! She's so light for such a big dog."

"Yes, well, she's mostly fur. And she's a bit overexcited, I'm afraid. She's been cooped up in a kennel while we were moving in.

She's so happy to have a whole new house and yard to explore that she's acting like a pup again."

Katherine closed the door behind us. "Harry, it's wonderful to see you. Come, put down your things and let's head to the kitchen so that the two of you can make it to class on time."

The kitchen was a big, open space. The first tentative rays of sunlight were shining through the sliding door, which opened onto a small patio. At the far end of the room was a large bay window with an upholstered seat that looked like the perfect place to curl up with a good book on a rainy day.

"Harry probably remembers that I am the world's worst cook," Katherine said. "I decided it would be better to feed you bagels than to torture you with a grandmotherly attempt at blueberry muffins. There's cream cheese, fruit, orange juice, and coffee. And yes, Harry, I do have the kettle on for tea. Earl Grey or English breakfast?"

I looked toward the counter where she was pointing, and at first glance I thought there was a lamp behind the big bagel box. Then I realized it was the medallion, shining as brightly as it had in the restaurant.

I was surprised to see Dad stop looking through the bagel options and pick it up. "You still have this!"

"Oh, yes," Katherine said. "That goes everywhere I do. My lucky charm, I guess."

"This really brings back memories for me. Katie, I'm sure you can't remember this at all, but you were totally fascinated by this when you were a baby. Every time Katherine came to visit, you'd crawl into her lap and stare at it. I don't think there was anything you liked better. You would smile and laugh like this thing was the best toy in the world. You used to call it . . ."

"Blue light," Katherine said softly.

"That's right," Dad said. "We weren't sure what you were saying at first—it sounded like 'boo-lye.' Even after you knew all of your colors, you still called this your 'blue light.' When your mom or I would correct you, you would get all serious and say, 'No, Daddy, that's a *blue light.*' We finally gave up." He tousled my dark hair, the way he'd always done when I was small. "You were such a cutie."

He set the medallion back on the counter and I picked it up for a closer look. It was amazingly lightweight for its size. I could barely feel it in the palm of my hand. Curious, I brushed the glowing center with the fingers of my other hand and felt a sudden, intense pulse of energy. Small beams of light shot up at random angles from the circle and the room seemed to fade into the background. I could hear Dad and Katherine talking, but their conversation sounded like something on a radio or TV playing in a distant part of the house.

The kitchen was replaced by a swirl of images, sounds, and scents flashing through my head in rapid succession: the wind blowing through a field of wheat, large white buildings that hummed softly and seemed to be perched near the ocean, a dark hole that might have been a cave, the sound of someone—a child?—sobbing.

Then I was back in the wheat field and it was so real that I could smell the grain and see small insects and specks of dust suspended in the air. I saw my hands, reaching toward a young man's face—dark, intense eyes staring down at me through long lashes, black hair brushing my fingers as I traced the contours of his tanned, muscular neck. I could feel a strong grip at my waist, pulling me toward his body, warm breath against my face, his lips nearly touching mine—

"Kate?" Dad's voice cut through the fog surrounding my brain as he grabbed the hand holding the medallion. "Katie? Are you okay?" I took a deep breath and put the medallion down, clutching the counter to keep my balance.

"Um . . . yeah." I could feel the blush rise to my cheeks. I was pretty sure that this was exactly how I would feel the first time Dad saw me kissing someone—which was very nearly what had happened, or so it seemed. "Just dizzy . . . a bit."

Katherine pushed the medallion toward the back of the countertop. Her face was pale, and she shook her head once, almost imperceptibly, when I caught her eye. "I would imagine she just needs her breakfast, Harry." She took my arm and led me toward the breakfast nook.

It was a good thing, too. I was feeling very shaky on my feet. I'd never had any sort of hallucination, and the sounds and images had seemed so real, like I was actually experiencing them firsthand.

Dad insisted that I stay seated while he brought me a bagel and some juice. He had just returned to the table and was starting another "Do you remember . . ." story, when a tall, red-haired man of indeterminate age appeared in the doorway.

"Good morning, Katherine."

"Connor!" said Katherine. "I was just about to ring you to say our new housemates have arrived. This gentleman is Harry Keller. And this is my granddaughter, Kate."

"Connor Dunne. It's a pleasure to meet you." He shook Dad's hand briskly and then turned to me. "And Kate—I'm glad you're here. We have a lot to do."

"You need help with unpacking?" I asked.

Connor cast a quizzical glance at me and then looked back at my grandmother.

"Connor," she said. "Relax. We'll have plenty of time to discuss arranging the library once Kate and Harry have settled in. Have a bagel and enjoy the morning sunshine. You'll be happy to know they actually had the pumpernickel this time."

She turned to Dad. "Connor has worked with me for the past two years and I simply couldn't manage without him. He was helping me digitize the collection, but we were only about halfway through when . . ." She paused, as though searching for the right word. "When we decided to move."

"Do you have a lot of books?" I asked.

Dad snorted as he slathered some cream cheese on his bagel. "Katherine's collection puts Amazon to shame."

Katherine laughed and shook her head. "I don't have nearly as many books as *that*—but I do have a lot of volumes that you won't find there or much of anywhere else."

"What kind of books?" I asked. "Come to think of it, I don't really know what you do . . ."

"I'm a historian, like your mother." She paused. "You're surprised that Deborah would go into the same field that I did, aren't you?" I *was* surprised, but I didn't think that would be a very polite thing to say. "Deborah fought it, but I'm afraid it's genetic. She had no choice. She studies contemporary history, however. Most of my research deals with more distant eras . . ."

Connor chuckled softly, although I really didn't get the joke, and then grabbed a couple of bagels from the box and headed for one of the two staircases in the foyer. Clearly, he was a man of few words and a big appetite.

"And I'm a researcher more than a teacher," Katherine continued. "I haven't taught since your grandfather died."

"Grandfather and Prudence?" I regretted the words immediately—it had to be hard talking about the death of a child, even many years later.

But if it bothered Katherine, she didn't let on. "Yes, of course. And Prudence."

After breakfast we were given the grand tour, with Daphne padding up the stairs behind us. It was a very large house, with one curved staircase going up to the right and another, the one that Connor had followed, going up to the left.

"The living quarters are on this side. You each have a small suite of rooms—we can redecorate if they don't suit you." We walked down the hallway a bit and she pointed me toward a suite that was about the same size as our entire cottage at Briar Hill. Then she disappeared down the corridor, chatting with Dad.

I stepped into the main room in the suite, which was painted a very pale blue. The canopy bed in the center was white wrought iron, with scrollwork and a blue and white gingham quilt. It looked much more comfortable than Dad's sofa bed. I sat on the edge of the mattress and looked around. There was a private bath and dressing area to the right of the bed and a sitting area to the left with a sofa, a desk, and two tall windows that looked out over the back gardens. It was beautiful and spacious, but I was also glad that I wouldn't be leaving my small nook in the townhome behind entirely. I liked my glow-in-the-dark stars, my clutter, and my skylight, and I wasn't sure that this room would ever feel like it was *mine* in quite the same way.

"So . . . will it do?" I jumped slightly, startled to find Katherine at the door. My expression was apparently answer enough, because she didn't pause. "I sent your father up to the attic to check something for me. Hopefully, he'll get distracted by the chaos there and we'll have a few minutes to talk. We have more work to do in the next few months than you can possibly imagine, my dear." She sat down on the edge of the bed, placing a ziplock bag that contained a small brown book between us. "So much depends on you and your abilities and we haven't even begun to test them. I just thought we had more time."

"My *abilities*? Is this related to the medallion?"

Katherine nodded. "It is. And to your so-called panic attacks. I'm sorry you had to go through that alone—I know it was scary."

I made a small sick face. "It was awful. I felt like something was wrong—really wrong. But I didn't—*don't*—know what it was. Every inch of me just . . . I don't know . . . *screamed* that something was out of place, out of kilter. And it's not like it ended. It's more that it faded. Whatever was wrong was still not . . . fixed, but I became accustomed to it, maybe? That's not right, either." I shook my head. "I can't explain it."

Katherine took my hand. "The first time was on May 2nd of last year, correct? And the second began on the afternoon of January 15th?"

I raised an eyebrow. "Yes. Dad told you the *dates*?" I was surprised to know that he even remembered the exact days.

"He didn't have to. I felt it, too. But I had an advantage in that I understood immediately that I was experiencing a temporal aberration."

I could feel my eyebrow beginning to arch upward, but I tried to keep my expression neutral. It was so nice to have someone believe they weren't panic attacks, but what on earth did Katherine mean by a *temporal aberration*?

"And unlike you," Katherine said, "I had the medallion. You must have been frightened half to death." Her blue eyes softened. "You look like her, you know."

"Like my mom?"

"Well, yes, a bit—but more like Prudence. They aren't identical twins. Your eyes are your father's, however. There's no mistaking that green." Katherine's thin hand reached out to tuck in one of the stray dark curls that always seem to escape any hair band or clip.

"Deborah's hair is a much tamer version—you have Pru's wild head of curls. I could never get the tangles out . . ."

After a long moment, she smiled and shook her head, back in the present now. "I'm wasting time." She lowered her voice and spoke quickly. "Kate, it is going to happen again. I'm not sure when there will be another temporal shift, but I suspect that it will be soon. I don't want to scare you, but you're the only one who has the ability to set this right. And you must set this right. Otherwise everything—and I do mean *everything*—is lost."

Katherine pressed the book into my hand as she stood to leave. "Read this. It will give you more questions than answers, but I think it's the quickest way to convince you that this is all very real."

She reached the door and then looked back, a stern expression on her face. "And you absolutely must not hold the medallion again until you are ready. It was careless of me to leave it on the counter like that, but I had no idea that you would be able to trigger it." She shook her head briskly. "You very nearly left us, young lady, and I'm afraid that you would *not* have found your way back."

∞

Dad and I made it to class with only a few minutes to spare. He'd chatted on the way there about a telescope that was mounted in Katherine's attic, left by the previous owners. It was too bright in the DC area *now* for the thing to be of much use, but back when the house was built, he said, that wouldn't have been the case. I nodded in the right places but barely heard his words.

I had a hard time focusing in class that day. Too many things were racing through my head for trigonometry or English lit to be of much interest. One minute I would remind myself that Katherine *did* have a brain tumor and her comments could be the result of too much pressure on the hippocampus or whatever. Then I'd remember the sensation of touching the medallion—the roaring sound, the scent of the field, and the warmth of *his* skin beneath my hand—and I would know beyond all doubt that my grandmother was telling the truth, which led to the question of how on earth she expected me to fix things. And then, two minutes later, I was back to doubting the whole experience.

When the final bell rang, I stopped by Dad's office to give him a quick hug and then walked the half mile to the Metro station at a rapid clip, hoping that I'd make it to karate class on time for a change. I sank into an empty seat on the train and automatically put my backpack next to me to discourage unwanted company, just as Mom taught me to do when riding alone. The car was pretty empty, anyway—just a girl filing her nails and listening to her iPod and a middle-aged man with a legal file full of papers.

The trip rarely took longer than fifteen minutes this time of day, and I usually just put on my headphones and zoned out, watching the graffiti on the buildings for the first mile or so until the train submerged below ground. Some of the artwork has been there for years, with new layers piled on top of the older, faded images. Occasionally a building owner would paint over a wall, but the artists were soon back, drawn to the fresh blank canvas. Only a half dozen or so buildings remained blank for long. Some, like the tire warehouse, had built tall fences topped with razor wire around the wall that faced the tracks. The Cyrist temple we passed was also clean—a dazzling, pristine white like all of their buildings, which were repainted regularly by church members and, rumor had it, guarded by large and aggressive Dobermans.

Today, however, I was too distracted to pay much attention to the urban artscape. I carefully removed the book Katherine had given me from its ziplock bag. The cover had clearly seen better days, having been patched at least once with binding tape like the older books at the school library. It looked like a diary of some sort, and this was confirmed when I opened it and saw the handwritten pages inside.

The paper was in remarkably good shape compared to the cover. It wasn't yellowed in the slightest. My first thought was that newer pages had been bound inside the old cover for some reason, but as I ran my fingers across the lined paper and took a closer look, that seemed unlikely. The pages were a bit too thick, for one thing—even thicker than cardstock. The weight of the book suggested that it should contain at least a hundred pages, but I did a quick count and there were only about forty individual sheets.

I tentatively bent a corner down and was surprised to see the odd paper pop back up, unwrinkled. I tried to tear a small piece from the edge, to no avail. A few quick experiments later, I had determined that you couldn't write on the paper with ballpoint pen, pencil, or marker. Water beaded right off, even though the surface didn't feel laminated. Chewing gum stuck momentarily, but it peeled up quickly and didn't leave any residue. Within a few minutes, I had decided that the stuff was just plain indestructible—except for fire, perhaps, but I couldn't try that on the Metro.

I then began to examine the writing on the pages, and I noticed that only the first quarter of the diary had been used. Each of the written pages, except for the first, appeared to begin in midsentence. There didn't seem to be any continuity at all from one page to the next. It was most definitely an odd little book. The only thing that looked normal about the diary appeared inside the cover, in very faded ink.

Katherine Shaw
Chicago, 1890

The train was nearing my stop. I slipped the book back into the plastic bag and then paused, sensing that I was being watched. That probably wasn't too surprising given that I had been trying to systematically mutilate a book—strange conduct, even by subway standards.

I glanced up and saw two young men, now seated at the very end of the subway car, three rows away. I didn't recall anyone getting on at the last stop, and although I had to admit that I had been a bit preoccupied, I couldn't shake the feeling that they had just appeared out of nowhere. They were facing me, so I could see them clearly. One of the two was a bit overweight, about my age, with dark blond hair and sallow skin that looked like he rarely ventured outdoors. The emblem on his rather worn T-shirt reminded me of an album cover, but I couldn't place the band. His eyes darted down to his lap and he began writing on a small pad as soon as I looked in their direction.

The other guy was tall, several years older, and very handsome, with longish black hair. I felt a slow flush spread to my cheeks as I recognized the dark eyes that I had seen when I touched the medallion. My hands tingled slightly as I remembered the warmth of his skin beneath them, the feeling of his hand at my waist, and the warmth that had rushed through my body at his touch. I couldn't imagine how he had stepped out of my hallucination and into the Metro, but I was absolutely certain that this was the same guy.

He looked a bit older now than when I'd seen him earlier, and his expression was an odd mix of sadness, fear, and the same longing that I remembered from my vision. He gripped the seat cushion and didn't look away, even when the other guy elbowed him sharply. I was the one who finally broke our locked gaze.

The train began to slow almost immediately after I glanced away, and I quickly looked up again. The doors hadn't opened yet, and only a second had passed, but both of them were gone. I walked toward the bench where they had been seated and put out my hand, half expecting to encounter a solid form—or lose a finger—but the space was empty. I was almost convinced that I had simply imagined them, but two indentations in the orange vinyl subway cushion were gradually smoothing out, just as they always did when a rider left. I brushed my fingers along the edge of the cushion that the tall young man had clutched so tightly and found that it was still warm from his hand.

∞ 3 ∞

I arrived at karate class a few minutes late and slid into my usual place beside Charlayne. For the next hour we practiced our routines, and the physical activity pushed the events of the past few days from my mind—almost. I was usually able to take Charlayne, probably because I'd had an additional year of classes, but I was flipped twice that afternoon and soon would have a nice, colorful bruise on my right thigh from a rather wicked clip by Charlayne's foot.

We kept on task until class ended. As we headed out the door, Charlayne turned toward me. "So? What's up? You haven't answered any of my texts . . ."

I still wasn't sure how much I really *could* explain without Charlayne thinking I had totally lost my mind. So I opted for a lame shared joke. "Let me explain . . . No, there is too much. Let me *sum up.*"

Charlayne rolled her eyes. I could quote *The Princess Bride* pretty much start to finish. "Okay then, sum up, Inigo Montoya. What happened?"

I knew Charlayne well enough to be certain that she'd get the full story out of me eventually. If she thought I was keeping even a hint of a secret, she wouldn't rest until she'd convinced me to cough up every juicy detail.

"Okay, here goes. My grandmother is dying, she's leaving me a big house, a lot of money and my dad and I are going to move in with her for the year. I've inherited a special ability from her that she needs to teach me how to use in order to save the world as we know it. Or something like that. And I very nearly shared a kiss with what I think may be a ghost who disappeared into thin air on the Metro."

"You nearly kissed someone on the subway? Was he cute?" Leave it to Charlayne to zero in on the kiss. Having three older brothers meant that there was a constant stream of guys at her house, and she kept several of them dangling on a string at all times. It was her goal in life to ensure that I lived up to my personal romantic potential, but so far her matchmaking efforts had been unmitigated disasters.

"Yes, he was cute," I answered. "And I didn't almost kiss him on the subway. It was in my grandmother's kitchen—or in a wheat field somewhere. Both, I think."

There was a long pause, while Charlayne just stared at me. "Okay. I know you well enough to know you wouldn't lie to me, Kate. So that leaves insanity, heavy drugs . . ." She paused. "Or you're telling the truth. I'm going to need more than the 'let me sum up' version to figure this one out."

"We can figure it out together then, because I'm not entirely sure myself." I pulled the diary out of my backpack. "I'm really hoping this will help."

∞

Mom wasn't the slightest bit surprised that we wolfed down pizza, then grabbed sodas and headed back up to my room. That's what we *always* do when Charlayne stays over. She also wouldn't have been too surprised to see us hunched over books, since we often do homework together. She might, however, have been a bit confused if she had peeked in and seen us side by side, holding a lit match to a single page of what appeared to be a very old diary.

I blew out the match. "Okay. You can't burn it either."

"But the fire does make it smell kind of funny," Charlayne noted. "And the cover—you can burn the cover, write on it, whatever. That's weird. Why wouldn't they make the cover at least as strong as the pages inside? The cover is supposed to protect the book."

"True." I thought for a moment. "But . . . have you ever slipped a different book jacket around something that you *wanted* to read in order to make your mom or your teacher think it was something you were *supposed* to be reading?"

"Well, yes. But . . ."

"Maybe the writer was trying to make other people believe this was just a plain diary. Look at the date inside the cover: 1890. This doesn't look to me like something that should have been around in 1890."

"Doesn't look to me like something that should be around *today,*" Charlayne said. "Can't you just call your grandmother and ask?"

"I could. But she did say that this would probably give me more questions than answers. I get the feeling she wants me to dig around a bit and see if I can figure it out on my own."

Charlayne reached over and scratched at a small nub that was sticking out of the fabric on the spine. "What is this? There's something stuck in the cover." She had to tug a bit but eventually pulled out a small bright yellow stick, about twice the thickness of a toothpick, with a pointed black tip. "It's a tiny pencil."

I took the stick to look at it more closely. "It looks like a pencil, yeah, but—look, I can't scratch anything off the pencil lead. I think it's a stylus. Like the one on my mom's old PDA. You've seen them. You just tap the screen, like this . . ."

I took the book and tapped the tip against the first page. The lines of handwritten text started scrolling slowly upward. "Aha. It's not a book. It's some sort of portable computer."

Charlayne looked puzzled. "But why?" she asked. "Why not just carry a laptop, or iPad? This doesn't make much sense."

"Unless it's 1890 and you don't want to attract attention." I closed the cover and it once again looked like an old diary. "Unless you don't want people to know that you aren't one of them."

"Weird. I've never seen anything like this technology. How would your grandmother have something like this? You said she's a historian—like your mom, right?"

I flipped open the diary again and ran my finger across the name printed on the inside of the cover:

Katherine Shaw
Chicago, 1890

"It *could* be a coincidence that my grandmother's name is Katherine, but I don't think so. And yes, she's a historian, but I'm beginning to suspect that being a historian means something very different to her than it means to my mom." I turned to a random page and tapped the top edge with the stylus thingy and watched as the text scrolled downward, stopping at the beginning of the entry.

May 15, 1893
Chicago, Illinois
We arrived around sunrise and merged with a crowd coming from the train station. The calculations were correct, although the area was not as isolated as we might have hoped. The city is packed and we landed near the entrance to the most popular attraction, so another entry point might be advised in the future.

People from all over the world have flocked to Chicago to see the new wonder—an enormous wheel surrounded by closed carriages that will carry

passengers high into the sky as it spins. It will not open for another month,
but a large crowd is always present to view the giant wheel, created by Mr.
George Ferris. The hope is that it will be magnificent enough to outdo the
marvel of the previous Exposition in Paris—the fabulous tower of Monsieur
Eiffel.

I presented my letter of introduction to the Board of Lady Managers
this morning and it was accepted without question. Background request on
"the Infanta." Several of the women were discussing her upcoming visit to
the Expo.

"What's that?" Charlayne pointed to a small star in the margin. I shrugged and tapped the symbol once with the stylus. Nothing. I tapped twice, and then a small information window opened on top of the handwritten page:

Infanta Eulalia (1864-1958): Daughter of Queen Isabella of Spain and
Francis, Duke of Cadiz. Full name: Maria Eulalia Francisca de Asis Mar-
garita Roberta Isabel Francisca de Paula Cristina Maria de la Piedad.
Expressed progressive views on women's rights in her later writings. Cau-
tion: Infanta's visit will ruffle feathers of Chicago society. Was often
found eating bratwurst or smoking a cigarette at German Pavilion when
scheduled to attend official functions. Spouse found most evenings on the
Midway Plaisance.

"That doesn't make sense," Charlayne said when we'd finished reading the entry. "If Katherine had the answer here, why did she make a background request?"

"I don't know. Maybe she added it later?" I closed the pop-up window and we returned to reading the diary entry.

I am spending the afternoon at the Woman's Pavilion where the World's
Congress of Representative Women is scheduled to begin its session.
The Woman's Pavilion is viewed as something of a wonder in itself—it was

designed by a female architect, Sophia Hayden. Saul may attend later in the day, as there are scheduled speeches on the topic of women in the ministry, but he will spend most of his day at the other end of the fairgrounds, attending a planning meeting for September's Parliament of the World's Religions.

    P.M.

    Saw only a few activists; either have not arrived or (wisely) opted to skip this session. The welcome addresses were even longer in person than they seemed in print. I thought the introductions of the various foreign dignitaries would never end.

    Submitting speeches and crowd view of Midway Plaisance.

CHRONOS File KS04012305_05151893_1 uploaded.

CHRONOS File KS04012305_05151893_2 uploaded.

Personal File KS04012305_1 saved.

I tried tapping each entry with the stylus, but there was no reaction and no little symbols appeared in the margins. "If the files are linked, I can't figure out how to open them. I'll have to ask Katherine later, I guess."

"The second set of numbers . . ." Charlayne pointed at the file names. "Those are the date of the entry, right? May 15th, 1893."

I turned a few pages and clicked the top, scanning quickly through the entries. Each of the pages that had been used contained the entries for an entire year. Most of the entries contained a CHRONOS file upload, and the last numbers always corresponded to the date. There were usually several sets of daily entries and then a gap of a month or so. Most were written in Chicago. The last two were from New York, on April 21st, 1899, and San Francisco, on April 24th, 1899.

"The KS must be her initials," Charlayne said. "And . . . the first group of numbers also follows the format for dates, but . . ." She reached out for the diary and I gave it to her, along with the little stylus.

After a few seconds, a frown creased her forehead. "It's not working."

She pulled the stylus along the edge of a page, just as I had done, but the text didn't move. It looked like a static page of handwritten text. "Maybe there's a dead battery or something?" she asked.

I took the book from her and slid the stylus along the margin and, once again, the page shifted.

Charlayne looked a bit annoyed that she couldn't make the diary work, but she shrugged. "Maybe it's just sensitive—like the touch pad on my brother's laptop. That never works for me, either."

I scanned back through the entries, and Charlayne was right about the dates. The first two digits for each entry were always 01 through 12, and the second two digits were always between 01 and 31. "So we seem to have someone trying to blend in with the crowd in the 1890s by disguising a high-tech device as a handwritten diary. And we have two sets of dates, one from the past and one from the future. If we're reading this correctly, and if this isn't some elaborate forgery, this would suggest that these are entries about the 1890s recorded by someone in 2304 and 2305."

Charlayne nodded. "If this isn't some sort of elaborate forgery, then yes. I'm not ruling out elaborate forgery, however."

I gave her a tight smile. "You weren't on the train today. Those two guys just vanished."

"Are you sure you didn't just scare them off with the Ice Princess stare, like you did Nolan?"

I tossed a pillow at her head and she ducked, laughing. Nolan, a friend of Charlayne's brother, was the victim in her most recent attempt to fix my love life. Nice guy, really cute, with nothing in his head other than soccer. I could have been friendlier, in retrospect, but I didn't see the point in leading him on, especially when it was clear by the time we'd finished our pizza that Nolan and I were a total mismatch.

I put the diary back into the ziplock bag and tucked it into my backpack. "We need to sleep. I have at least a thousand questions to ask Katherine after school tomorrow anyway, and it will just add to the list if we keep looking through this diary. And if you show up with bags under your eyes tomorrow, your mom will never let you stay over on school nights."

It was a long time before I fell asleep, however. Each time I tried, the vivid sensations from the medallion came flooding back to the forefront of my mind, and a pair of disturbingly passionate dark eyes followed me when I finally slipped into dreams.

∞

Morning came much more quickly than either Charlayne or I wanted. I inhaled a breakfast bar as I ran to the Metro, which was so packed that I had to stand. The crowd thinned out as the train headed away from the city. I sank into the first open seat, plugging my iPod into my ears to muffle the subway chatter.

I didn't see the pale, pudgy young man at first, probably because he was behind me. A few minutes after I sat down, however, I caught a glimpse of the left side of his face in the security mirror. I shifted slightly to get a better view. He was wearing the same shirt as the day before and didn't seem aware of the mirror or of the fact that I had spotted him. I glanced around to see if the tall, dark guy was near, even pulling out my hand mirror on the pretext of fixing my hair, but I couldn't locate him. Pudgy, however, was clearly watching me.

The next stop was not mine, but I stood just as the last of the passengers were leaving and headed for the closest door. Before I could reach the exit, Pudgy was right beside me. I felt an arm around my shoulder and something cold and hard digging painfully into my ribs as the last few passengers getting off at the stop pushed past me.

He spoke in a low whisper. "Give me the backpack and you can walk away. I don't want trouble. Just pull it off your shoulders and give it to me."

Normally I would have just given it over, no questions, no hesitation. Lesson one of self-defense is that you don't argue with the man holding the gun. But the diary was in there.

Pudgy's face was suddenly inches from mine and I felt a crushing pain in my toes as his heel ground into them. He whispered into my ear, "I can shoot you and be gone before anyone knows what happened."

"Doors closing. Doors closing," the automated voice chimed. The sound of my pulse echoed in my ears as Pudgy pulled me toward the door, slipping the foot that had just mangled my toes between the subway doors to keep them open. I glared at him, then slid the backpack from my shoulders and handed it over. He squeezed his chubby frame through the door, pushing me backward into the train, hard, and then disappeared in a flash of blue light.

I fell against two other passengers. One had on earphones and must have missed the entire exchange—he just looked annoyed at my clumsiness. But the woman had clearly been watching. "Are you all right?" she asked. "Should I call security?"

"Kate!" The voice from behind me was deep and the slight accent unfamiliar, but I knew who it was before I turned. My first instinct was to run—not that there was really anywhere to go in a closed subway car—but as he moved closer, I glimpsed a familiar blue light shining through the fabric of his shirt. He reached out to take my arm and pulled me toward a seat a few aisles away, out of earshot of the woman who had offered to help.

I sat, then whirled to face him. "Who the hell are you? Why are you following me and why did your friend take my pack? And how did you get *that* from my grandmother?" I poked the spot on his shirt where the light of the medallion showed through.

He paused for a second, processing the barrage of questions, and then gave me a small, slightly crooked smile. "Okay—I'll answer them in order. I'm Kiernan Dunne," he said. "I was not following you. I was following Simon. I'm not supposed to be here. Simon—the guy who took your bag—is *not* my friend, Kate. And this key," he finished, pointing at the medallion on his chest, "is not from your grandmother's collection. It was my father's."

He raised his hand and I flinched instinctively. His eyes grew sad and his smile faded as he moved his hand, more slowly now, to brush the right side of my face with his fingertips. "I've never seen you this young." He reached around and pulled the band loose from my hair so that it fell to my shoulders. "*Now* you look more like my Kate."

I opened my mouth to protest, but he held up his hand and continued, speaking more quickly now. "We're close to your exit. Go straight to your grandmother's house and tell her what has happened. At least you still have this." He touched the black cord around my neck. "Keep the CHRONOS key on you at all times."

"CHRONOS key? I don't have . . ."

"The medallion," Kiernan said, again touching the cord.

"I don't *have* a medallion." I pulled the cord out of my blouse. At the end was the clear plastic holder that contained my school ID, a Metro pass, a few pictures, and two keys—one for Dad's cottage and one for the townhouse. I flipped the holder around so that he could see the plain silver keys through the back. "And these are the only *keys* I have. Could you stop talking in riddles?"

The color drained from Kiernan's face and panic filled his eyes. "Was it in the bag? You should keep it *on* you."

"No," I repeated. "I don't *have* a medallion. Until now, I thought there was only one, and to the best of my knowledge it's at my grandmother's house."

"Why?" he asked. "Why in bloody hell would she send you out with no protection?"

"I don't know how to *use* it! Yesterday, I nearly . . ." I blushed, thinking back to the scene in the kitchen. "I saw *you* when I held it. Why? Who are you?"

The train began to slow. Kiernan closed his eyes and rubbed his first two fingers against his temples for a few seconds before looking up and shaking his head. "I didn't plan for this, Kate. You're going to have to run. Take a cab. Steal a car. Whatever you do, get to her house as quickly as you can and *do not leave.*"

He moved us both toward the doors and then turned, pulling me toward him. "I'll try to stall them—but I don't know exactly what they're planning, so I have no idea how long you have."

"How long before wha—" My question was silenced as his lips met mine, gentle, but urgent. My body was swept with the same sensations I had felt earlier when I held the medallion—heart pounding, unable to breathe, unable to move, unable to think.

After a moment he pulled away, a small smile lifting the corners of his mouth. "This wasn't supposed to be our first kiss, Kate. But if you do not hurry, it will almost certainly be our last. Run. Run, *now.*" As the train decelerated, Kiernan reached into his shirt and closed his hand around the medallion. The dark green band that he had pulled from my hair was now on his wrist. And then he vanished.

The subway doors chimed open and I ran.

There was, of course, no cab outside the station. A glance at the schedule told me that a bus wouldn't arrive for twenty minutes, and I wasn't sure that I could run over three miles in my current state. On top of everything else, my toes hurt like hell from being stomped by Pudgy. I hobbled three blocks in the opposite direction to the Marriot and, after a panicked look at the empty cab stand, was relieved to see one just pulling up to the curb.

I slid into the back and gave him the address.

"You got money hidden somewhere, kid? 'Cause I don't see no purse or no wallet and this is rush hour."

"This is an *emergency*. It's just off Old Georgetown in North Bethesda and I need to get there as quickly as possible. My grandmother will pay you."

He looked as though he planned to protest further, but something in my expression must have convinced him to start the cab and pull back onto the main road. He drove as fast as traffic allowed, which was often only slightly faster than I could have run. I clenched my teeth in frustration.

"Sure you're not runnin' from the cops or something?" he asked, peering back at me through the rearview mirror. "You look like you're runnin' to me."

"I was *running* to catch a cab to take me to my grandmother's house. She's . . . sick, okay?"

"Yeah, right." He took a left at the next corner and then said, "Okay, Red Ridin' Hood. I'll get you to Grandma's house ahead of the Big Bad Wolf. But she better have some money in *her* basket or I'll be calling the cops myself."

I rolled my eyes at that lame bit of witticism and settled back in the seat. I wasn't sure why Kiernan thought I was in danger, but there was no mistaking the fear in his eyes. I touched my hand to my lips, remembering his kiss. It wasn't just *our* first kiss, but my first kiss ever. Even with my total lack of experience, I could tell that there was strong emotion behind it. He knew me, somehow, from somewhere or some time, and he cared about me. As confusing as it was to think that I had a past (or was it a future?) that I didn't remember, I couldn't doubt that Kiernan was desperately afraid for me. I clutched the edge of my plaid skirt as the cab inched a bit closer to Katherine's house and, hopefully, toward some answers.

∞

I was out of the cab before it came to a full stop. I ran to the door and banged on it frantically. Connor's face appeared moments later.

"Where is Katherine? Let me in."

"Yes, of course!"

"Can you pay the cab? He stole my bag."

Connor looked confused. "The driver?"

"No—a guy on the Metro." Daphne was barking loudly, and Connor held her collar to keep her from dashing out the door.

"Yes, yes, I'll pay him. Take Daphne." He grabbed shoes from the hall closet. The driver began honking, inciting Daphne to ratchet up her noise level as well. "Katherine! Come down!" Connor called as he headed out the door. "Kate is here."

Katherine appeared at the top of the stairs a few moments later, pulling a robe over her nightgown as she hurried down to greet me. "Kate! Why aren't you at school, dear? You look frightened. What on earth? Sit down, please." She motioned toward the sofa and slapped her hand against her thigh. "Daphne! Outside!"

She led Daphne to the kitchen door and I sat down, trying to catch my breath. I peeled off my shoe to inspect the toes that had been crushed by . . . Simon, Kiernan had called him, although I still thought of him as Pudgy. Two of the toes were a deep angry red, and one toenail had been squished so badly that it was ripped down to the quick. I gritted my teeth and pulled off the nail fragment to keep it from snagging on my sock.

Connor reentered the house just as Katherine came back in from the kitchen. I saw a soft blue glow through the threads of his jeans pocket and was relieved to know that he had a medallion. It hadn't occurred to me that he, too, might be in danger.

He sat down in the armchair across from the sofa. "Did you find out who robbed her?"

"*Robbed?*" Katherine exclaimed. "Kate, what happened? Are you okay?"

"I'm fine," I said, pulling my sock back on carefully. I slipped off my other shoe and slid them both under the coffee table. "Some guy on the Metro now has your diary, however—and my iPod and textbooks. I'm sorry, Katherine. I would have tried to fight him off, but the Metro was crowded and . . . he had a gun. Or something that felt like a gun, poking into my side."

"Don't be silly," she said. "You did the right thing. I have several other diaries here and that volume is backed up in the computer system."

Connor nodded. "We can track the original, too—so we may be able to get it back. I doubt a mugger will be too concerned with looking at an old diary, anyway. And he won't be able to activate it."

"Does this happen often on the Metro?" Katherine asked.

"What?" I shook my head. "No—I mean yes, people get mugged occasionally. I never have—the Metro's safe, really. But this wasn't just somebody grabbing a random backpack. He *knew* what he was doing. He *wanted* the diary. He saw me with it yesterday. And I think he had a medallion—like yours."

Katherine looked at Connor skeptically, then back at me. "Are you sure? I don't think—"

"No, I'm not sure about the mugger. But he did vanish into thin air—twice. And I *saw* a medallion under Kiernan's shirt—" I stopped as Connor and Katherine simultaneously drew in sharp, startled breaths.

"His name was Kiernan?" asked Connor. "How do you know that?"

"Yes. Kiernan . . . Dunn or Duncan, I think. But he was *not* the mugger. He's the one who told me to run. Dark eyes, dark hair, tall, and . . ." I trailed off, sure that I was blushing. "Why? Do you know him? He wanted to know why I wasn't wearing a medallion. He told me to get here, to your house, as fast as I could, that something was about to happen, but he would stall them if he could, to give me time."

Connor and Katherine exchanged another look. "Kiernan Dunne was my great-grandfather," Connor said after a moment. "And I find it unlikely that he would be doing anything to *help* us."

I had forgotten that Connor's last name was Dunne, and I can't say that there's much resemblance between the two of them, except perhaps around the nose. And Connor was at least thirty years older than Kiernan—or, at any rate, at least thirty years older than the Kiernan who kissed me on the Metro. I sank farther into the couch.

"Maybe you should start from the beginning," Katherine suggested.

I recounted my steps from the time I left Katherine's house on Monday morning until the cab brought me back to her doorstep. I glossed over a few bits—I wasn't sure how she would feel about Charlayne reading the diary and our experimental efforts to determine its composition, and I most definitely was *not* ready to share the kiss. It wasn't something I wanted to discuss in front of my grandmother, or for that matter, in front of someone who claimed to be the great-grandson of the guy who had kissed me. Things were weird enough without complicating matters further.

When I finished my summary, I turned to Katherine. "Whether you believe Kiernan's information or not, there's a lot going on that I need to know about. And I think perhaps my dad should be in on this. Or mom . . ."

I felt a bit like the accused claiming my right to an attorney, but maybe that wasn't so far off. I didn't know either Katherine or Connor well enough to feel that I could completely trust them, and Dad—well, he's my dad, and I know whose interests he'd put first. And while my relationship with Mom is a little more complicated, she would do the same.

"Kate . . ." Katherine hesitated, apparently looking for the right words. "I admire you for wanting to keep your parents informed—and yes, Harry would be far more likely to understand than Deborah—but perhaps you should wait until you've heard my story. Then, if you want to talk to Harry . . . that's fine."

She reached up and pulled the chain around her neck, allowing her medallion to fall in front of her dark red bathrobe. The blue light altered the color of the robe near the medallion to a peculiar shade of purple. "But you must keep in mind, Kate, that your parents will never see this pendant as anything other than an odd piece of jewelry. If either of them held it for more than a few moments, they might feel a strange sensation—as Connor or anyone else with the recessive version of the gene does. They might notice a slight change in the color. But neither of them will ever see this as you or I do. And it would take time to convince them of what we can see and experience directly."

Something about that statement nagged at me, but I focused on her key point that pulling Dad into the discussion would take time. I couldn't shake the sense that time was short—the urgency in Kiernan's voice had made that clear—and I wasn't entirely sure that we could afford to wait until Dad was there and had been filled in on everything. And even though Katherine and Connor seemed to doubt the sincerity of Kiernan's warning, I did not. It might have been my first kiss, but I trusted the instinct that told me Kiernan was on my side—whatever side that might be.

∞ 4 ∞

"I was born in the year 2282," Katherine began. My face must have shown doubt because she quickly added, "I'm not going to waste time trying to convince you of what you already *know,* Kate."

"Before my birth," she continued, "it was decided that I would be a historian. My parents had saved a bit and, as I understand it, my grandparents and a childless aunt also contributed some funds, so there were several chosen gifts from which my parents could select. Everyone is allowed one—and *only* one—chosen gift. Initially they were distributed by lottery, but money has a way of opening doors in any society. All things weighed together, I'm not unhappy with their purchase."

Connor returned from the kitchen with three mugs of black coffee that looked much too strong for human consumption and a large box of cookies, which he clearly would have eaten all by himself had Katherine not nodded in my direction. He gave up three gingersnaps—grudgingly, I thought—and propped his feet on the short table positioned between his chair and the couch.

Katherine continued. "Had my family been less well off or less inclined to invest in my future, I might have been given special aptitude for healing or for music, or some other trade or craft. My father's chosen gift was chemistry. My mother's chosen gift was logic, and she worked for many years at CHRONOS—programming the computers that were used to track historical missions and analyze the data they collected."

I took a sip of my coffee, wishing for some milk to cut the burned taste. "What exactly is CHRONOS? I saw that in several diary entries."

"Chrono-Historical Research Organization and Natural Observation Society," Connor said through a mouthful of cookie. "Proving that future Americans are just as willing as their ancestors to contrive a title in order to get a good backronym."

"At any rate," Katherine said, raising an eyebrow at him, "my mother loved her work at CHRONOS—no surprise, since she and everyone else of my time are, quite literally, *born* to love their jobs. But I think there was some small element of wanderlust in her soul. The chosen gift she selected for me meant that I would see different times and places—"

"But," I interrupted, my voice a bit hesitant, "what about free choice? I mean, what if you'd rather have been a chemist, like your dad? Or a baker? Or . . ."

Katherine smiled, but it was a tired smile. I could see that it wasn't the first time she'd dealt with these questions. "Yes. But there is much to be said for making some adjustments before birth. How much time is wasted today training children to perform a variety of skills that they not only will never use but would never even *consider* using? I remember your mother complaining that she would never need to know the square root of anything, and while I forced her to do the math homework nevertheless, we both knew she was correct.

"Don't get me wrong—people still learned about subjects beyond their occupation. We still had hobbies and avocations. But we all knew the general route to our primary destination when the journey began, and we didn't regret the destination, nor did we have any desire to change it. After all, our genetic makeup ensured that we would be far better at our jobs than anything else we attempted—and far better at our jobs than others, who did not have that chosen gift, could ever be."

"So everything you are was determined before you were born, by this . . . enhancement?"

"No. The only thing that was changed before my birth was my *chosen* gift. I have some natural gifts from my parents—my mother could sing beautifully and I can carry a tune quite well. Like you, I have my father's eyes, although you're lucky—Harry's eyes are far more striking."

Connor leaned forward and squinted a bit, staring me straight in the eyes. "Very . . . green." Unsure whether it was intended as a compliment, or whether Connor even bothered with such niceties, I simply nodded.

"I also have some residual effects from the chosen gifts my parents received. Like my mother, I'm good with computers." Connor snorted derisively and Katherine amended the statement. "Or rather, I'm good with computers that are not centuries before my time. I am more than happy, however, to let Connor handle the archaic piles of nuts and bolts that *he* refers to as a computer."

Katherine stopped to take a sip of her coffee and turned back to me. "I do understand your . . . concern . . . about free choice, but let's set that aside for the time being, okay? I didn't devise the society in which I was born any more than you devised this one, and I'm perfectly willing to admit that it has its flaws. The point I wanted to make is that the gifts of the parent—all gifts, chosen and natural—are passed along to the child. I inherited some from my mother, some from my father, and I *acquired* one specific, chosen gift that I passed on to your mother and that she clearly passed on to you, given your reaction to the medallion."

I was getting increasingly confused. "But Mom can't see the light on the medallion."

"That doesn't mean the trait isn't there. It's just recessive. It might not even be the reason she's interested in contemporary

American history. She was exposed to it enough through Jim. He was one of those professors who always had historical anecdotes on the tip of his tongue. In your case, however, the trait is dominant."

"Why do you think that?" I asked. "Just because I can see that blue light? I mean, I like history, but I like a lot of subjects. I haven't decided what I want to do. I could just as easily settle on math, you know—or a foreign language. Or law."

"It's not just a matter of *interest*, Kate. For many of the specialized trades and professions, a chosen gift—the genetic 'enhancement,' as you call it—carries with it the ability to operate specialized equipment used in that profession. I saw you in the kitchen yesterday. You were born a CHRONOS historian, whether you want to be or not, just as I was.

"I won't bore you with all the mundane details of my job," she continued, "but unlike your mother, who must study her field through documents and artifacts, I traveled to the sites where history was made. I specialized in women's political movements, mostly American, mostly nineteenth century, although I took a few side trips into the twentieth century to follow long-term trends. I learned history by watching Susan B. Anthony, Frederick Douglass, and Lucy Stone argue, both publicly and privately, while I was disguised as someone from their era.

"In order to ensure"—she glanced at Connor and made a wry face—"or at least *try* to ensure the sanctity of the timeline, CHRONOS allowed only a limited number of historians. There were thirty-five active historians when I joined in 2298. I took the place of the thirty-sixth, who was retiring. This key is the portable unit that allowed us to return to headquarters when our research was complete. And the diaries were our link in the field—a quick way to get an answer to any question that hadn't been answered in preliminary research.

"The important point for now," she said, "is that the altered gene structure allowed me—and through inheritance, allows *you*—to activate the CHRONOS key. Or the medallion, as you call it. When I was in training, I would hold the key and eventually 'see' the surroundings of the set coordinates to which I would be transported. There are a certain number of destination points on each continent, established in areas that we know have been stable points throughout the period we're examining. For example, one stable point in this area is a corridor in the Senate wing of the U.S. Capitol that escaped destruction in the War of 1812—it is a geographic stable point between 1800 and 2092."

"What happens in 2092?" I asked.

Katherine's mouth tightened into a firm line. "The corridor ceased to be a stable point."

"Don't even bother to push on that," Connor interrupted. "She'll go all 'need-to-know' on you."

"To get back to the medallion," Katherine said, "it allows the user to scope out the territory, make minor temporal adjustments if needed, and determine the best time to make the jump."

"So how did you wind up here—now? Did you just decide to stay in the past? Or was there an accident of some sort?"

"It certainly wasn't an accident," Katherine answered. "It was made to look that way, however. Your grandfather—Saul, your biological grandfather—sabotaged CHRONOS and stranded the teams at their various locations. I was scheduled for a jump to Boston 1853, but . . . let's just say I was forced to make a last-minute adjustment. Saul had . . ."

Katherine paused, phrasing her words carefully. "Saul had fallen in with some bad elements in our society, and I'm quite sure he planned to follow me. He was always a black-and-white sort of person. Either you were friend or you were foe, with no gray area in between. He considered me a traitor, and he would have killed me and—although he wouldn't have realized it—your mother and Prudence along with me, if I had not ducked into 1969 at the very last minute."

∞

Over the next hour, I learned how Katherine had started a new life in the 1970s. She emerged in an abandoned barn about a mile outside Woodstock, New York, in mid-August of 1969, taking the place of a music historian friend who had hoped to see Janis Joplin and Jimi Hendrix at the festival. Dressed in the height of fashion for the 1853 destination for which she'd been scheduled, Katherine was somewhat overdressed for a rock concert. Hoping to get at least some usable data for the friend whose slot she had taken, she removed the pins from her hair, stashed the elaborate gown, gloves, and button-up shoes in her carpetbag, and headed for the concert in just her silk chemise, pantalettes, and a black lace choker. She was still a bit more fully covered than many of the young women at the concert, but after a few hours in the mud and heat, she said, she managed to blend into the crowd.

"I returned to the stable point—the barn—several times over the next few weeks and tried to contact headquarters. But I could see nothing—just a black void with occasional bursts of static. I tried to correspond using one of the diaries that I had packed, but it vanished. It was as though everything from my time no longer existed."

"So why didn't you go back to the day before you left?"

Connor nodded. "I asked that, too."

"You've both seen too many movies, I'm afraid. I couldn't just zip from one location to any other point in time. The CHRONOS key allowed me to emerge at one preprogrammed stable point and then return to CHRONOS headquarters when my work was done. No side trips allowed.

"Fortunately," she continued, "CHRONOS historians followed the Boy Scout motto: 'Be Prepared.' If we could not contact headquarters, we were to find a way to blend in and lie low for a year or two. And, after that point, if we still had no contact with home, we were to give up and try to create normal lives in our new time and place."

Using a safe-deposit key stitched into her undergarments, Katherine had retrieved the contents of a box initially set up in 1823 with the Bank of New York. She selected the best option from the array of identities inside, invented a husband who had died in the war in Vietnam, and over the next few months secured a university research position.

She had tried to find information about a few of the other historians whose destinations had been the relatively recent past, including Richard, the friend who swapped places with her and landed in 1853. "I would love to know how he managed to blend in after arriving in the bell-bottom jeans and rather loud shirt he was wearing at the time. He would have been perfectly dressed for Woodstock—but I'm sure that he looked rather ridiculous for 1853. Richard was always clever, however. I eventually learned that he edited a newspaper in Ohio for the next forty years, married, had children and grandchildren. That wasn't protocol—we were told to avoid having children at all costs—but I would imagine that was a bit hard if you were stranded in the 1850s and wanted a normal life."

She sighed. "He died in 1913. It was strange to read that he had grown old and died so long ago when I'd seen him just a few weeks before. He was a good friend, although I think he'd have liked to be more than that. If I hadn't been so fixated on Saul . . .

"Anyway," she continued, shaking her head as if to clear it, "I sent a letter to the granddaughter who was Richard's caregiver before he died. I told her I was writing a history on nineteenth-century journalists and her grandfather was one of the people I was researching, and I was surprised when she asked me to visit in person. When I arrived, she went straight to her china cabinet and pulled out a CHRONOS key.

"She said that her grandfather had always been a bit psychic and he told her that one day when she was in her seventies, a woman named Katherine might come asking questions. If that happened, Richard said that she should give me that old medallion and his diary, because I'd know what to do with them.

"I packed Richard's key away with my other belongings when I married Jimmy, a few months later. He was a young history professor, and I was a newly widowed research assistant, six months pregnant with your mother and Prudence."

She smiled softly. "Jim should have been born in an era where knights-errant rescued damsels in distress—when he met me, he became a man with a mission. I was reluctant to marry so quickly. CHRONOS members were told to wait at least a year before making the decision on how to best assimilate. But I knew better than the others that this was, in all likelihood, something worse than a mere technical glitch. Jim and I were married before the girls were born and they were, in every sense other than biological, truly his girls. I could not have asked for a more devoted husband and father."

"So Mom doesn't know?" I asked. "I mean, even after the accident, you didn't tell her that Jim wasn't her father?"

Katherine looked a bit surprised at the suggestion. "Do you really think that I *should* have told her? She was angry enough at me as it was—telling her a different lie about a father killed in Vietnam was pointless. And telling the truth would just have convinced her that I was insane. I did the only thing I could do after Jim died—I tried to get her sister back from Saul. And I failed."

∞

Her comment explained so many other things that I found myself unsurprised that Prudence was alive—or at least, that Katherine believed Prudence had survived the crash.

"It never occurred to me that *either* of the girls might be able to activate the key," Katherine continued. "There had only been a few generations of CHRONOS historians and . . . well, it's not as though we carried CHRONOS equipment around in public. If the children of historians had ever shown an ability to activate the equipment, it wasn't something I'd been told.

"I kept my key in my jewelry box. I'm not sure why. I wouldn't have left my family if it had suddenly become active, but I guess it was just a memento—a reminder of a world that seemed almost unreal to me by that time." She paused for a moment. "And I knew that Saul had made a jump. He was stranded, too. He thought that destroying the stable point on the CHRONOS end would mean that he had free rein—that it would allow him to go from one stable point to the next, from one time to the next, without limits. And it might have worked, but . . . I still don't know what happened that day. Wherever, *whenever* Saul landed, however, I'm quite sure he blames me for wrecking his plans."

Katherine toyed with the chain around her neck. "I never imagined that the key would be dangerous to the girls. Prudence found it a few months before she disappeared. She and Deborah were looking for old items to use as costumes for a school play. I don't know how long Prudence held it or what she saw. I do know that she and your mother got into a rather nasty fight because Prudence insisted the medallion was glowing green and your mother couldn't see it—she was convinced it was another of her sister's little jokes."

She was quiet for several seconds. "So what did you do?" I prodded.

"I did what most mothers would have done—I took it away, yelled at both of them, and said I was tired of their silly arguments. I refused to take either side or to discuss the issue when Prudence raised it later." Katherine's blue eyes dimmed a bit and she looked down at her hands. "That was a mistake. I know that now. I think she saw something that . . . troubled her. Maybe it was the same black void that I still see when I try to activate it—but I don't think so. She started having nightmares and was moody. Well, she was always a bit moody, but . . . more so . . . after."

A tear slid down Katherine's face, dropping onto her sleeve. "I thought she was getting past it. Then, a few weeks later, I was going to walk into Georgetown with Deborah to buy her some new shoes. It was a Saturday and Jim was taking Prudence to her violin lesson, which was on campus. Prudence had this sneaky look on her face as she got into the car, but I assumed that was because she was wearing a lot more makeup than I usually allowed—Deborah said she had a crush on her violin instructor. As they pulled out of the drive, Prudence gave me a sassy grin and held up something that looked like my CHRONOS key, glowing a soft orange . . .

"We only had the one car—so following them was out of the question. If it had been a decade later, we would have had cell phones. I could have called and told him to come right back so that I could take the damned thing away from her.

"Instead, I ran to my bedroom and dug through the dresser drawer where I'd hidden the key, and to my surprise, the key was right where I'd left it. I decided that Prudence must have found a similar piece of costume jewelry, and Deborah and I headed downtown as planned. But something kept nagging at me—hadn't Prudence said the medallion glowed green for her? So why would she have bought costume jewelry that was *orange*? Still, I couldn't think of any other explanation.

"And then I remembered the box in the attic," she said. "We ran back to the house—Deborah was furious, of course, that I had changed my mind after a half-mile walk. Anyway, I found the old trunk with my items from before Jim and I were married—and sure enough, it was open and Richard's key, the one his granddaughter had given me, was gone."

Katherine heaved a sigh, then stood and walked into the kitchen. After a few minutes, I heard her let Daphne in. The dog was apparently sensitive to her owner's mood, because she was far more subdued than I had ever seen her. She padded softly over to the couch and sniffed around in Connor's lap, looking for ginger-snap crumbs, apparently. He fished a cookie from the bottom of the box and tossed it into the air. Daphne caught it with a snap of her jaws and stretched out at my feet, anchoring the prize between her paws and nibbling at the edges.

I was about to follow Katherine into the kitchen, but Connor shook his head. "She'll be back soon," he said. "It's difficult for her to talk about this."

I nodded. "My mom, too. But I think I know the rest, anyway. Mom said Prudence was never found, and her dad died that evening at the hospital. They don't know why he lost control of the car. I don't think Mom even got to talk to him, so I guess he never woke up?"

"He spoke to Katherine. He was in and out of consciousness, and—"

He cut off the sentence as Katherine appeared in the doorway, looking frail and tired. "Jim only spoke for a few seconds. He said, 'She was there and then she was just gone. The car . . . I lost control.' And then he grabbed my hand so tightly and said, 'Where did she *go*, Katherine?' And then Jimmy was gone, too. Not literally, like Prudence, but . . ."

She ran one hand across her short gray hair and leaned against the wall. "The nurse and Deborah were both in the room. I'm sure they assumed he meant that the river had pulled Prudence away—that he was confused about the order of events. But I saw the look of disbelief in his eyes, Kate. I *knew* what he meant. She disappeared—and seeing someone vanish from the seat next to you when you've never seen anything of the sort . . . well, I'm not too surprised that Jim forgot about the road."

Katherine fell silent after that. I didn't know what to say, and I was relieved when Connor shifted the conversation. "Maybe we should focus on what happened to Kate this morning. Can you tell us any more about the guy who took your bag?"

"My age, maybe a bit older? Kiernan said his name was Simon. He had a black shirt, with something like a band logo on the front, but I didn't recognize the band. A bit on the chubby side . . . looked like a hard-core gamer."

"A gamer?" Katherine asked.

"Out of shape, pale, rarely sees sunlight," Connor said.

"Yeah," I said. "He was writing something—kept looking down at his notes. I got a better look at the other guy, actually. Kiernan. Tall . . ."

"Wait . . . ," Connor said. He held up his hand and headed for the stairs. "I may be able to save you some effort there." When he returned a minute later, he was carrying two very old photographs, in identical black frames. He handed one of them to me. "This was taken in 1921."

It was a formal photo of a family with four children, the youngest boy seated on his mother's lap. The man was middle-aged, tall and dark with a well-groomed beard. He was looking directly at the camera and I recognized his eyes instantly. I glanced at the woman sitting in front of him and felt a sudden, irrational twinge of jealousy that his hand was on her shoulder. In his other hand he clutched a large, ornate book, perhaps a family Bible, with a ribbon that hung from between the pages.

I handed the photo back to Connor. "It's him. I'm sure."

"The second boy from the right," he said, "the one standing next to the mother? That's supposedly my grandfather, Anson. I think he was eleven, maybe twelve. The man, as I noted earlier, is Kiernan Dunne, my great-grandfather. Based on the genealogical research that I've done *recently*, Kiernan was a prominent Cyrist Templar in Chicago until his death in the late 1940s. He came over as a child with his parents to work on one of the Cyrist collective farms that sprang up in the Midwest during the mid-1800s."

I looked again at the picture that Connor held, unsure which bothered me more—that I had been kissed by a married preacher or that he had died more than half a century before I was born. I could still feel the sensation of his lips on mine and his hand on my face, and I could see his smile as he loosened my hair.

I shook my head to clear it, and Connor thrust the other picture into my hand. "I have always believed, however, that *this* young man is my grandfather Anson." He pointed to a boy, a bit younger, in another family photo. In this picture, there were three children and a different mother. They were dressed less formally, seated outside in front of a large farmhouse. The man was tall and dark, with a slightly longer beard, and he looked less serious, with just a hint of a smile. The eyes were identical.

"Kiernan had a twin?" I asked.

"No," said Katherine. "At one point, these were two copies of the same photograph. The second one has been in my possession and under the protection of a CHRONOS field continuously since 1995, when Connor's mother allowed me to make a copy of the original for my research on the descendants of the various CHRONOS historians. The first one—the more formal portrait—is actually the original photograph that I made this copy from in 1995. Connor obtained it from his sister by mail last May. Except I don't guess you can really call her his *sister*, since—"

"Wait, you're losing me here." I had no idea what a CHRONOS field was, but there was no way that these photographs were from the same original. "They're not the same photograph at all. Different people and different locations . . . how could the second one be a copy of the first?"

"In the stories I remember," Connor said, "my great-grandfather was a farmer—not a minister, and certainly not a Templar." I noted the disdain in his voice and was about to inquire further, but he went on, pointing out the differences in the images. "The mother is not the same in this photo. There are slight differences in the children." Connor nodded toward the staircase. "I can trace the male line in my family on current genealogy sites, but the names are different. My mother never married my father. I was only able to attain that photograph by pretending to be my—what would you call him? He seems to be the version of me in this timeline. My half brother? Half self?" He looked at Katherine, his eyebrows raised in a question.

Katherine just shrugged. "We're beyond my level of understanding now. I'm just a historian. I used the equipment, but I didn't invent it. We were told that the system was safeguarded against this type of—aberration—but Saul . . ."

"Saul," Connor said with a sneer. "I spend my time now trying to figure out exactly what that bastard has changed and how we might change it back." He crushed the cookie box, with a bit more force than seemed necessary. "And every day, I see a few more of his bloody temples dotting the landscape."

∞ 5 ∞

Dad had been telling the truth when he said that Katherine had a lot of books. They lined three walls of the very large library that took up most of the left wing of the house. It looked like a normal library in most respects, at least normal for the type of library that I had seen only in movies, with a rolling ladder connected to each wall and books stacked from floor to ceiling.

There were, however, some distinct differences. Along the vertical edge of each block of shelves, a bright blue tube—the exact shade of the CHRONOS key—ran from bottom to top and then extended across the ceiling to meet in the middle, where they formed a large blue X.

My gaze drifted toward the computers. Dozens of hard drives were stacked on metal shelves. There were three workstations, each with large dual monitors. To their right was an odd apparatus that I couldn't identify—except for the objects in the very center. Two CHRONOS medallions were seated in some sort of casing, from which they seemed to be connected to a series of cables. The top of the case was tinted glass, which partially dimmed the blue light. A thick rope of twisted cables attached to the casing ran four or five feet from the computer station to bookshelves and connected to one of the bright blue tubes.

"What . . . is all of this?"

"This, Kate, is what makes the house a *safe* house," my grandmother said. "You have no idea how difficult it was to move all of this to a new location, especially given the need to keep everything protected during the voyage. It would have been much easier to bring you to Italy, but I suspected that would be impossible to arrange with your mother.

"Connor has devised a rather ingenious system here. The signal from the CHRONOS keys is amplified and the protection extends, more or less, to around twenty feet outside the house."

Connor added, "For now, we just keep one of the other keys on us if we need to go outside that perimeter. I'd like to add the entire yard to the safe zone, but that will require using a third key—and I'm worried that extending the protection that far could overload the system."

"What do you mean—protection?" I suddenly flashed back to Kiernan's question on the Metro. *Why would she send you out with no protection?*

"From the temporal distortions," Connor answered. "Any thing and any person within these walls—or anyone wearing one of the keys—is not affected by a temporal shift. Katherine and I, for example, clearly remember that the second picture you saw is the correct one. It has been shielded along with most everything else in this house. But the first picture that you saw and . . . the people and things outside the protective area . . . have all been changed."

"So why didn't the first picture change back when you brought it here?" I challenged. "If this is, like, a safe zone, shouldn't it show the reality you know?"

Katherine shook her head. "It doesn't work that way, Kate. It wasn't protected when the temporal shift occurred. Think of this as . . . a lead apron, like you've worn at the dentist. You're shielded when the apron is on, but it isn't going to undo any damage that might have been caused if you were exposed earlier. The documents we have here, that we've always been protecting—including the ones that are digitized on these servers—all of those are preserved. Anything that we bring in from the outside, however, might have been changed. Actually, it *will* have been changed, unless it was in constant physical contact with someone wearing a medallion. But it won't be altered further once we have it here."

"That . . . makes sense, I guess. Okay, I've seen . . ." I paused to count. "Five medallions, including the one Kiernan had. I'm assuming Simon . . . the guy who mugged me . . . must have one as well. Where are they coming from? Have you learned to replicate them?"

"No, the additional keys and diaries that we have here are ones that I've collected," Katherine said, sitting down at one of the computer stations. "Before Prudence disappeared, I hadn't expended much effort trying to track down what had happened to my former future colleagues—other than keeping an eye out for Saul, because he could have landed anywhere, anytime.

"After Prudence was gone, I locked myself in a room and spent the next several weeks trying desperately to get some sort of signal from the CHRONOS key. I think I came very close to disappearing into that void—that black hole is still the only thing I can see in the medallion."

I hesitated. "Do you think that's where Prudence went? Into that . . . black hole?"

"I thought it was likely, at first, although I didn't want to admit it to myself. The other possibility was that Saul had found us and that he had taken Prudence. Either way, I was determined after that point to collect every single one of the remaining keys, because I didn't want to think of anyone else disappearing in that fashion. Twenty-three CHRONOS historians were stranded and each had a key. Most, fortunately, were headed for relatively modern eras—only four were before the fifteenth century. Several were traveling as a team, as Saul and I had done often. Twelve were handling North American history—since CHRONOS is located in North

America, there is a bit of a local bias. Six were in Europe and the rest were scattered around the globe.

"To date, I have located ten keys and a few diaries, in addition to the diaries that I had packed for my last jump. Many of the keys were passed along by family members as an odd heirloom, a strange piece of jewelry. Most people were eager to get rid of the things, which they believed to be haunted—either they or someone else said it glowed or moved, or it just gave them a bad feeling. One of the researchers who was investigating Nazi Germany—he actually destroyed his CHRONOS key and the diaries he had with him. I spoke with him briefly, just before he died, and he said he had not wanted to take any chances that they might be reverse-engineered by the Nazis, as highly unlikely as that might have been.

"In retrospect, he made a wise choice. Had I not known that Saul, wherever and whenever he was, would have no scruples about misusing the technology, I would have destroyed every single one I found. I'm glad I didn't destroy them, however, because about three years after the accident, I noticed the first change."

Katherine turned toward the computer and clicked a folder, and a file, and then an image opened. It was a scanned replica of a yellowed document with a list of names, separated into columns labeled *Ladies* and *Gentlemen*. Printed at the top were the words *Woman's Rights Convention, Seneca Falls, New York, 1848.*

"A framed copy of this document was on the wall of my office at the university from the time Prudence and Deborah were two or three years old, so they had both seen it many times. One hundred people—sixty-eight women and thirty-two men—signed the Declaration of Sentiments from that convention. But if you look carefully, you'll see there are now one hundred and one names. There's another name here, near the bottom of the middle column—Prudence K. Rand. And that name began to show up in other documents as well."

"But . . . why Prudence *Rand*? Mom's last name is *Pierce*."

"I can only assume that Prudence decided to sign this document *after* she met her father—Saul Rand. She was clearly trying to send me a message, but I'm still not sure what she intended to say. Did she want me to rescue her or was she just . . . telling me that she knew my secret? What hurt most was not knowing . . . Did she know I couldn't reach her? Did she know I was trying?"

∞

Katherine and I went back to the main floor, leaving Connor in the library with the computers, where he was investigating to see whether there was anything going on outside of the ordinary that might have prompted Kiernan's warning. Something had been nagging me all through the previous conversation, but I couldn't quite put my finger on it. It finally hit me when we were seated in the kitchen, a few minutes later.

"Wait, wait, wait . . . before, earlier this morning, you suggested that all *three* of them had this recessive version of the CHRONOS gene—Connor, Mom, and . . . *Dad*?"

Katherine nodded. "It's stronger in your father, I believe, than in Deborah. One of the nastiest arguments I ever saw between the two of them happened just after your second birthday party. I was visiting and I wore the medallion. Deborah never much cared for it—but I wanted to see your reaction. As Harry said yesterday, you were fascinated and kept calling it a 'blue light.' Harry casually remarked that the medallion seemed to have more of a pinkish glow. Deborah was *furious*. She thought I'd told him about her argument so many years ago with Prudence, and I guess she thought that we were having a good laugh at her expense. Poor Harry. He didn't have a clue what she was going on about and couldn't understand why she kept insisting that it was a plain bronze pendant, not pink, not green, not blue."

Katherine sighed heavily. "As much as Harry loved—and perhaps still loves—your mother, I've always wondered whether he'd have been better off if I'd never pointed him in her direction. Deborah has her good points and I love her dearly, but I think she inherited a touch of her father's temper and—"

"Wait," I interjected. "Mom and Dad met at some sort of historical thing. A Renaissance fair or something like that. He was selling jewelry. He took the place of a friend because she was sick."

"Close," she said with a little smile. "Harry took the place of a young lady who was quite happy to accept one hundred dollars and have someone *else* spend eight hours in the heat and humidity—although I don't think Harry ever knew I paid her. He was doing it as a favor to *me*. And I told him that if he met Deborah, it would be unwise for him to let her know we were acquainted. He had seen her picture and said she was pretty—and I explained he'd be starting out with two strikes against him if she thought I knew him or that there was the slightest possibility that I might approve of him."

I stared at my grandmother for a long moment, then got up and walked to the window, watching as two squirrels chased each other up and then down the large willow in the backyard.

"Katherine . . . is there anything else that I *think* I know about my own life and my parents that is totally incorrect? The way I heard it, Mom didn't even introduce you to Dad until they were married."

"Well, that's actually true—it's just not the whole story. Your mother didn't introduce us; I first met Harry when he was about eighteen. His adoptive parents had always told him that they would help him find out about his biological parents if he had questions. I was the most logical person to point him toward. His biological parents, Evelyn and Timothy, were also CHRONOS historians and were stranded in 1963—they were studying events surrounding the Kennedy assassination. I contacted them after my arrival in 1969. They were living in Delaware. They had a friend who put in a good word to help me get the research job in New York, where I met Jimmy.

"We exchanged Christmas cards a few times. I remember them once including a picture of a small boy who would have been your father. And then I heard nothing from them. People lose touch— and that happened even more often before your Facebook and email, and . . ."

Katherine refilled her coffee cup, stirring in a bit of cream from a small porcelain pitcher on the table. "After Jim's death, I started looking for CHRONOS keys, as I told you before. In looking for Evelyn and Timothy's keys, I learned of their deaths, and eventually found out that Harry had been adopted by a couple outside of Milford. I introduced myself to the Kellers as a friend of Harry's mother who had just heard about her death, which was true. I said the keys were keepsakes from a sorority Evelyn and I had belonged to in college. The Kellers hadn't seen them, but I left a card with them in case they remembered anything.

"Later, when Harry began college here in DC, they suggested that he look me up. He had started wondering more about his biological parents and what they were like. His memories of them had faded and . . . well, I'd known them, so I met with him and we talked. I couldn't give him the *full* truth, obviously, but what he really wanted to know was what his parents were like as individuals. I had worked with them for several years and I could give him that—anecdotes, little descriptions of things they had done."

Katherine sat in the window seat, adjusting the cushion a bit. "We hit it off quite nicely and . . . well, I noticed that he was drawn to the medallion when I wore it. It isn't vivid for him—the light is faint, not neon and glaring like it is for us. But it was enough that I started to think that maybe he and Deborah might—if they were to get together and . . ."

She trailed off and I just stared at her, unsure what to think. "You set my parents up hoping they would have a kid—me—so that I could . . . what? Go on a quest to find my long-lost aunt?" At one level, I could understand, but I was also beginning to feel a bit angry, even used. "Did you not understand what an unbelievable long shot that was?"

Katherine stood and put her hands on my shoulders, staring directly into my eyes. "Of course it was a long shot, Kate. But it was one that I had to take—can't you see that? And the inescapable fact is that it worked—you're here and you . . . well, I've never seen someone who was able to lock on to CHRONOS equipment instantly, like you did yesterday. It was nearly three months before I could see anything other than a blurry vision, and you . . . from what you've said, you were practically there—wherever *there* was—five seconds after you grabbed the medallion."

I shook off Katherine's hands. I couldn't help but feel that Mom had been right to warn me. *She's manipulative and selfish.* "Don't you think they had a right to decide for themselves—to let fate take its course? My parents clearly weren't meant to be together or they still *would* be. Maybe they'd be happier if you hadn't interfered. They weren't chess pieces or puppets!"

"Perhaps they would have been happier, Kate. But their feelings, as important as they might be to you, and yes, to me as well, really aren't the issue here."

"Yes," I said. "Prudence. I know—this is about Prudence. But she's been gone for a very, very long time. I'm sorry for your loss and for my mom's loss, but I don't really know what it is that you expect me to do to fix things—and I'm not sure that I'm willing to help. Maybe I'm being a bit selfish here, but someone held a freaking gun to my ribs on the Metro . . . and I would think you'd be a bit more worried about what is happening in the here and now than—"

Katherine banged her hand against the counter. "You're missing the entire point, Kate! *Yes*, I would love to learn what happened to Prudence. I would love for *her* to know that I tried with all my heart to find her, to get her back. But that is not why I tried to get your parents together and it is *not* why I brought you here. The fact that Prudence could change that document you saw—not just my copy, but *every* copy and half a dozen other bits of history as well— *that* is the reason we have to worry. The temporal shifts—you felt them, you *knew* something was wrong, and everyone around you went about their lives as though nothing had changed. Like the problem was with *you,* right?"

I nodded once, still angry.

"But the problem was *not* with you. Changes have been happening for the past twenty years—the two that you felt were just rather . . . major." Katherine took several deep breaths, making an effort to calm down. "Despite having the chosen gift, despite the best intentions of the trainers at CHRONOS, Saul was very good at hiding his real views. He and a group of friends, two of whom were connected to CHRONOS, all believed that the technology was not being used as it should be . . . that it was in the hands of weak individuals who lacked vision. Why simply study history? they asked. Why not make history—*remake* history?

"I don't know where Saul ended up, but he figured out the same thing that I did, Kate—that parents with the CHRONOS gene can produce children able to bypass the safeguards. Like Prudence did. Like you nearly did yesterday morning. And based on what we are seeing, he has managed to create himself a small army of people who can move through time at his command. All I have to combat that, Kate, is *you.*"

Katherine had clearly hoped that this statement would make me understand, and to some extent, it did. But the enormity of what she was saying—that she seemed to be on the verge of asking me to single-handedly take on an individual she had just described as insane—scared me. "I want Dad in on this. You talk to him, we make these decisions together. Or I walk out of here and you're on your own."

"Agreed. We'll call him when school is out and—"

The clock on the microwave showed that it was 12:22 P.M. "No," I said. "I have class with him in about ten minutes. He'll worry if I'm not there anyway, and if I leave now, I can make it." There was a small voice in my head insisting that I should stay put, but I shut it out. All I knew at that moment was that I had to get away, to get out of the house so that I could clear my head.

I headed for the front door, grabbing my shoes from beneath the table and tugging them onto my feet. Katherine followed behind me, still talking, but I was no longer listening. I looked around for my backpack before remembering that it—and my books—had all disappeared into the past or future or some weird alternate version of the present.

"I'll see you after I talk to Dad." I closed the door behind me and was halfway to the gate when I heard Katherine running up behind me.

"Kate, come back!"

I turned just in time to see her stop, a few yards away from the house, pulling back suddenly like a dog wearing one of those radio collars when it detects the signal and is afraid of being zapped.

She was holding out the medallion. "Take this. I have another one. I just didn't have a chance to grab it because you left so suddenly . . . and I almost forgot about the boundary. The signal fluctuates a bit, but it's never farther out than the maple." She nodded toward a tree a few feet to her left.

"Don't remove the key for any reason," Katherine said. "Keep it on your person. And be careful. I don't know what the scene on the train was about and I have no idea what Kiernan's motives are, but I won't feel comfortable until you're back here."

Katherine looked pale and anxious. I could tell that the emotional morning had taken a toll on her. I took the medallion, putting the chain around my neck and slipping it inside my blouse. I was still angry, but I forced a smile for her sake. "Relax, okay? I'll be back this afternoon. With Dad," I added, as I headed for the gate. "If you're right, and it really *is* me against an army, then we're going to need all the help we can get."

I walked at a brisk pace, nearly jogging. I would have to check in at the front desk and make some excuse about missing morning classes, which meant I would probably be late getting to Dad's class anyway. My toes still hurt, but the exertion felt good otherwise and some of the tension I had been carrying began to melt away.

The morning had been a bit cool for mid-April, but the day was warming up and my hair was hot on my neck as I headed into the building. That reminded me of the fact that my hair was down, in violation of the Briar Hill dress code, and that reminded me of Kiernan. I could see my dark green hair band, vivid against the skin of his wrist as he vanished, looking like a knight carrying his lady's favor—a scarf or ribbon—into battle. I wiped that ridiculous image from my head and pushed open the door to the main office.

"Kate Pierce-Keller. I'm checking in late," I told the rather stern-looking middle-aged woman who was one of three who worked the main office at Briar Hill. The two who usually handled the front desk were much more personable, but they were probably at lunch. I waited while the woman pulled up the attendance log on the computer. "I don't have a note. There was an emergency this morning and I forgot to get my mom to write one before I left the house. I'll bring it tomorrow. And . . . I forgot to put my hair up. Do you have a spare rubber band?"

The woman raised her eyebrows and then rummaged around in one of the desk drawers. After a moment she found a large manila-colored band, which she held out silently toward me, along with a pink hall pass.

"Thanks."

I pulled my hair back into a loose knot as I walked down the hallway. I reached the classroom several minutes late and peeked in through the small window on the door, hoping to enter when Dad was between sentences and get to my desk with minimal disruption of the class and with as few people as possible staring at me. Dad was standing near the Smart Board, pointing at an equation . . . and then I felt the same gut-wrenching sensation that had hit me twice before.

I leaned forward, my arm inadvertently pushing down the door handle as I did. The door swung inward. If not for the fact that I have a decent sense of balance, I would have landed in a heap on the desk in front of me, but I caught myself and looked upward toward the spot where my father had been standing.

Dad was no longer there. He was no longer anywhere in the classroom. A plump, middle-aged woman was at his desk. The woman wasn't anyone I knew. Another stranger, a good-looking guy with dark blond hair, was in the desk where I usually sat, with a trigonometry textbook open in front of him. I was pretty sure he was new as well. The other faces in the class were familiar. They were, however, all looking at me strangely. I caught the eye of Carleigh Devins, a girl with whom I was friendly although not quite friends, and tried a weak smile—only to receive a quizzical look in return.

I couldn't breathe. I looked at the woman behind the desk, who was not Dad, and back at the guy who was sitting in what was usually my desk. I opened my mouth to say "Wrong class . . . ," but it came out as a hoarse whisper. Then the classroom began to spin and I slid to the floor.

∞

As I came to, the first thing I noticed was a chubby, pale hand with a faded pink lotus tattoo patting my arm. After a moment, my eyes began to focus and I followed the hand up to the face of its owner, who was apparently the teacher. She and the tall blond guy who had been occupying my desk hovered over me anxiously. I looked around the room again. This was definitely Dad's classroom, and with the exception of the blond guy, this was my trig class.

"Are you okay?" the woman asked.

I wasn't. The dizzy sensation was much the same as it had been during the previous two time shifts, although it seemed more subdued this time. Perhaps that was due to the CHRONOS key? The wrenching sensation in my gut was worse, however, and that was definitely due to the fact that Dad had just vanished in front of my eyes.

"Wrong class. I'm okay—really. Sorry for the interruption."

But . . . what if Dad was sick today? And she was a substitute? Even though I knew it was probably wishful thinking, I needed to go to the cottage and check it out.

I pushed myself upward and the blond guy helped me to my feet. "I'm Trey. You're new here, right? Careful . . . you still look a bit unsteady. Maybe you should sit down."

"Sorry," I repeated. "I need to go." I was still feeling a bit dizzy, but I pulled away and headed out of the classroom.

"Wait," the teacher called. "You shouldn't be up so quickly. Trey, follow her. Make her see the nurse."

And so, as I hurried down the hall, Mr. Tall Blond and Handsome followed, only a few steps behind. "Wait, where are you going? The nurse's office is this way."

"I'm fine."

I continued out the building exit, with the guy still following me. He grabbed my arm. "Hey, be careful. You don't want to faint again on these stairs."

"Look, it's Trey, right? You seem nice enough, but please, go away. I have to find my dad."

"Your dad?"

We continued across the parking lot, toward the soccer fields. "He's a teacher here," I said. "Harry Keller? We live across the campus, near the edge. In one of the faculty cottages. That's where I'm headed. Please, just let me go."

He released my arm. "Okay, we can go to the cottage if you want, but then we go see the nurse."

"No—I'll just lie down. I'm fine. I should have eaten lunch . . ."

I kept walking, and so did he.

"Sorry, no can do. I told Mrs. Dees you would see the nurse. I can't go back to class until . . ." I turned to glare at him and saw that he was smiling—a wide, friendly grin. "Listen," he said, "I don't know what game you're playing, but unless you enrolled today, you're not a student here. I would *definitely* have remembered you. I haven't been here long myself, so I keep an eye out for newbies—it's a bit hard to fit in with those who have been here since seventh grade. And I'm pretty sure there's no Harry Keller on the faculty."

I shook my head. "He has to be . . . and if you think I'm not who I say I am, why don't you trot back to teacher and tell her to alert security?" I picked up my pace. "If I'm not a student, I shouldn't be here."

"Right," he said. "But where's the fun in that? You don't appear to be a dangerous terrorist and, besides, you *did* faint back there. So why don't you tell me what's wrong? Maybe I can help."

"You can't. Go back to class."

"I don't think so. Come on—I have the choice of going back to trigonometry or walking across the school with a beautiful girl on a warm spring day. Which do you honestly think I'm going to choose?"

I looked at him in amazement. He was actually trying to flirt with me when I was right on the very edge of losing it. For no reason I could explain, tears rushed to my eyes and I was caught between laughing hysterically and crying. I sat down in the middle of the soccer field and put my head in my hands.

"Oh, hey! No, I'm sorry," he said. "Don't . . . don't cry. Really . . ."

I kept my head down for a moment to pull myself together, taking deep breaths. "I'm okay," I said. "It's just been a bad, *bad* day." When I looked up, he was sitting on the field in front of me, his face level with mine. His gray eyes, which had little flecks of blue, were full of concern and he gave me a tentative, sympathetic smile. He reminded me of a big friendly puppy and I wasn't sure how I was going to shake him.

I remembered my school ID and tugged the cord out of my shirt. It was there, beneath my Metro card. I pulled it out, holding it up for him to see. "I really am a student, see? I have proof."

He leaned forward to read the ID. "Prudence Katherine Pierce-Keller. Cool monogram—PKPK. Hi, Prudence. I'm Trey."

I grimaced. "It's Kate, please."

Laughing, he pulled his own ID out of the gray messenger bag that was slung over his shoulder and handed it to me.

"Lawrence A. Coleman the Third," I read. "What's the *A* for?"

"Alma. My great-grandmother's maiden name."

"Ouch."

"Yeah—granddad is Larry; dad is Lars. No good versions left—not that I really like the first two—so Mom went with Trey." He held up three fingers. "You know, for being number three."

I nodded and got to my feet, handing him back his ID. I put my own ID back into the holder and took out one of the keys. There was a small white tag attached, on which someone in the school administration had written the number 117 and the name Keller. "This key, Trey, fits the front door to that last little house over there. My dad, Harry Keller, lives in that house, and so do I for the better part of each week."

He was walking beside me again. "If this key fits," I continued, "you can go back and tell Mrs . . . Dees?" Trey nodded. "You can tell Mrs. Dees that I'm fine. Just a silly girl who should have eaten her lunch. Deal?"

"Deal. But not until you're inside."

"Fine," I agreed. "I'm going to open the door, heat up some leftover jambalaya that's in the fridge, and take a very long nap."

I sighed, aware as I walked up the front steps of the cottage that I was saying all of this as much to reassure myself as to convince Trey. I really *needed* to open the door and see that Dad was there, that Mrs. Dees was a substitute because he'd come down with a cold or something else, and that I'd just imagined him being in the classroom. I kept telling myself that Katherine and Connor were crazy, or maybe the past few days were just one extended bad dream. I held the key out with shaky hands and, with Trey watching, finally managed to insert it in the doorknob.

To my immense relief, it opened. I turned back toward Trey and gave him a huge smile. "See! I told you this was my—" I stopped suddenly as I saw his face, then followed his gaze inside the open door.

Everything in the cottage was wrong. The couch where I slept had been replaced by two overstuffed chairs. A braided rug was on the floor. And then I saw what Trey was staring at—a framed photograph of Mrs. Dees with two small children, next to a large white mug that held pens and pencils. The red letters on the mug read *#1 Grandma.*

"No!" I backed out of the doorway. "The key fit! You saw it, didn't you? It fit!"

Trey closed the door, making sure it locked. I sank onto the front steps, and after a moment he sat down beside me. "So . . . you want to tell me what you think is going on?"

I looked at him. What difference would it make? It wasn't like he would believe me. I tugged the CHRONOS key out of my blouse. "What color is this?"

His gaze shifted from me to the medallion. "Brown, bronze— not sure what you'd call it. It looks old."

"Well, it's bright blue for me. There's an hourglass in the middle."

"Blue. Really? I can see the hourglass, but . . ."

I raised my eyebrows. "You see an hourglass in the middle, and the sand is moving back and forth?" Trey shook his head. "I didn't think so. If I hold this in my hand for too long, my grandmother says that I'll vanish to some point back in time. Or forward, maybe. It nearly happened to me yesterday."

His expression didn't change, so I went on. "Someone is altering reality . . . changing things. When I first looked in at the classroom this morning, my father, Harry Keller, was standing at the Smart Board. My desk—*your* desk now—was empty, because I was just arriving at school. And then, in an instant, I saw all of that change."

There was sympathy in his gray eyes, but I could tell he didn't believe me. Of course he didn't. He would have to be crazy to believe what I was saying. He probably thought that I was mentally unbalanced, and I wasn't sure I could argue against that theory successfully. "Someone—apparently my grandfather—is changing history. My grandmother says I'm the only one who can stop it, because I inherited the ability to work this piece of equipment. Some other people inherited the ability, too, but apparently they're all on the Dark Side." I put the house keys back in the holder and then tucked both that and the medallion back inside my shirt. "I was coming back here, to school, to pull my dad into this nightmare . . . I don't want to make decisions about how to handle this alone. I've felt these time shifts twice before, but it was just . . . a bad feeling. No one ever disappeared."

I sighed, staring down at my shoes. "And the key *fit,* damn it. I was so sure . . ."

"But . . . wouldn't the key fit either way?" Trey spoke softly, the way you might around someone who was unstable. I recognized the slightly condescending tone, and resented it, but I couldn't really blame him. "I mean, even if everything you've said is somehow true, if they hired Mrs. Dees instead of your dad, it . . . would be the same key to the cottage. Right?"

I closed my eyes but didn't answer. Duh—of *course* it would be the same key.

After a few minutes I stood up and gave Trey a weak smile. "I know you need to alert security now, but would you give me a few minutes' head start to the Metro? Please?"

"Where are you going?"

"I'm going to try and find my mom—she's in DC. And then . . ."

"Okay." He stood and brushed off his pants. "Let's go."

"What? No!" I said, beginning to walk away. "No, no, and no. *I'm* going, Trey. *You* go back to class."

He shook his head firmly. "That would be very irresponsible of me. You're either in trouble, in which case I might be able to help, or else you're crazy, in which case someone needs to keep an eye on you. I'm volunteering, at least for the rest of the afternoon."

I headed across campus in the straightest path to the Metro station. "You have school. You can't just ditch. Don't you have *parents?*"

He shrugged, matching his stride to mine. "My dad would— *probably*—say I'm making the right choice. He's not going to complain either way. My mom might disagree, but she's on assignment in Haiti for the next few months, and I don't think the school will be giving her a call. Estella—she lives with us—*will* chew me out for ditching class, but the school won't leave messages with anyone but parents. So you're stuck with me."

I was torn between angry and amused. Trey was nice and, I had to admit, very cute, but I needed to focus on the problems at hand. Maybe I could lose him in the crowds at the station?

Thinking about the Metro, however, brought a wave of anxiety. Suddenly the idea of having someone along, after the experience I'd had that morning, didn't sound so bad.

"Okay," I said, "you can come. But in the interest of full disclosure, you should know that I was mugged on the Metro this morning."

He gave me his crooked grin again. "Damn, girl, you *have* had a bad day."

∞

We had to wait about fifteen minutes for a train, but the ride into DC was short. Trey attempted to make conversation. My brain was on autopilot; I managed to nod in the right places, though. His mother worked with the State Department, and she traveled a lot. His father worked for some international firm—something that sounded vaguely financial to me—and they had just returned from two years in Peru, where he had attended a school for the children of diplomats. When I asked about siblings, Trey laughed and said his parents hadn't been on the same continent often enough to manage a second child. They had decided that he and his dad would stay in DC so that he could finish up high school at Briar Hill, which his dad and grandfather had both attended. Estella, who had worked for his family since Trey's dad was a kid, kept them organized and fed.

When they returned from Peru in December, Briar Hill told his dad that Trey would be admitted into the senior class in the fall, so he had been studying at home through a correspondence course in the interim. But a space opened up unexpectedly in January and he was able to start during the spring semester. It sounded like the same slot I'd taken when Dad accepted the job.

I gave him my own two-minute bio—or at least the version that had been true an hour ago—and we talked music and movies for a few minutes. Or, rather, Trey talked while I listened and nodded.

As we headed up the escalator into the sunlight, I stopped and closed my eyes, taking in a deep breath to steady myself.

"Are you okay?" Trey asked.

I shook my head. "It's only a few blocks to the townhouse, and I . . . I don't think she'll be there. And I'm scared." It felt odd saying this to someone I barely knew, but Trey was so friendly that it was hard to stay distant.

"Well," he said, "we cross that bridge when we come to it, right?"

When we arrived, I didn't even have to try the key. I stared up at the windows of the house as Trey opened the mailbox and peeked in—all of the mail was addressed to someone named Sudhira Singh. But I had known as soon as we'd rounded the corner that Mom didn't live there. Pink ruffled curtains with tiebacks would never be in any house where Deborah Pierce lived. If such curtains had come with the place, they would have been down and in the trash before the first box was out of the moving truck.

I seemed to have lost every bit of energy I possessed, and it was all I could do to move from the steps in front of the townhouse. Trey took charge and steered us toward Massachusetts Avenue, where we found a coffee shop. He sat me at a booth by the window and came back with two coffees and two blueberry muffins. I promised to pay him back, but he just laughed, saying coffee and muffins made me a cheap date, relatively speaking.

"So why do you think this time-shift thing made your dad and your mom . . . disappear?" he asked. "You said it happened twice before, and no one vanished. Why this time?"

"I don't know. I haven't really stopped to think about that." I paused for a moment, going over what I knew in my head. "There were two photographs at my grandmother's house—her friend, Connor, said they used to be identical copies of the same family portrait. One had been kept in a protected area—an area shielded from time shifts by one of these medallions. The other photo wasn't. When I saw them today, they were portraits of two different families, headed by the same man."

I took a sip of my coffee before continuing. "Something must have shifted the course of the man in the photograph's life—two different paths. And yes, Connor and Katherine could be mistaken or lying—one picture might be Photoshopped, or the men could be twin brothers, I don't know . . . But I'm pretty sure the man in both of the portraits is the same man I met on the Metro this morning, just after I was mugged. Only this morning, he was about twenty years younger than when the picture was taken in the 1920s."

"Wait," Trey said. "You met the guy in the photos? This morning?"

I nodded. "He warned me that something was about to happen. And I watched him disappear while he was holding a medallion just like this one."

I gave Trey a weak smile. "All of this sounds just as crazy to me as it does to you. But to answer your question about why my mom and dad have vanished, I think something was changed in the past. Something that affected my family."

I relayed the story my grandmother had told me, realizing as I spoke that there were huge gaps in what I knew. I explained about CHRONOS and how Katherine had escaped into 1969. "If I had to guess," I concluded, "I'd say that Saul finally caught up to my grandmother in the past. If she never had my mother, then I was never born and my father . . ." I shrugged. "There would be no reason for him to be at Briar Hill. Or something else changed and my mom and dad, and maybe me . . . ? I have no idea how this works. Maybe we're all still in Iowa . . ."

Trey stood up from his side of the booth and motioned for me to slide over. He squeezed his tall frame into the seat next to me and removed a small laptop from his messenger bag. "Then that sounds like the place to start—let's find your parents. Is it Debra or Deborah? And how do you spell Pierce?"

I looked at him skeptically. "You *believe* me? You actually believe all of this?"

He took a bite of the muffin, chewing it slowly as he considered his answer. "No," he said. "Don't be offended, please. You said yourself, it's crazy. I don't believe that reality has shifted and that the medallion around your neck will cause you to disappear.

Although I have to admit that it made me nervous when you were holding it in your hand earlier, so maybe I don't entirely *dis*believe you, either."

"So why help me?" I suspected it was, in part, because he found me attractive. Trey was a nice guy, but if not for that little fact, I was pretty sure that he would have decided that his obligation to help ended at the Metro station.

He finished off the muffin and then replied. "The important thing is that I do think *you* believe what you've told me. And I'm sure you have parents somewhere and I'd like to try to help you find them. Please eat something, okay—otherwise, I'm going to have to carry you on the way back to the Metro."

"Why not just take me back to my grandmother?" I asked, a bit defensively, taking a bite out of my muffin. I felt like a lost kitten that he was feeding and keeping out of traffic while he searched for my owner.

"Well, first, you haven't told me her name or address," Trey said. "And second, that's not what you want, right?"

I shook my head. "No. I mean . . . not until I know."

"Okay, then—we look for your mom and dad. Let's start with a Google search . . ."

Twenty minutes later, we had established that Deborah Pierce did not exist—or, at least, she had never taught history at either of the colleges where she had worked. I knew the login and password to access her university website, because Mom always used the same password for everything. The password was irrelevant anyway, since the system had no record of user dpierce42. We tried a search for several academic articles that she had written, but there was nothing listed.

It was hard to imagine a world in which my mother didn't exist—had *never* existed. I bit my lower lip and took a few deep breaths, pushing down the fear that was building inside me so that I could focus on searching for Dad. He wasn't listed among the faculty at the Briar Hill website, something that didn't surprise either of us. Then we moved to a general web search. There were a lot of Harry Kellers, including one who had been a movie director back in the 1950s. I asked Trey to narrow the search to Delaware and to include my grandparents, John and Theresa Keller. Their address hadn't changed and I felt a surge of hope.

"Try adding something called the Math Olympics. My dad was on the team in high school—it's something he always puts in a bio. I guess it's to establish his math geek creds."

"Or maybe to inspire his math geek students," Trey said with a smile. He adjusted the search criteria and a few minutes later I was staring at Dad's photograph. He had a beard, which I had seen him wear only in a few pictures from his college days, but it was definitely him. He was teaching at a boarding school about an hour away from my grandparents' house in Delaware.

I grabbed Trey's hand and squeezed it hard. "We found him. That's my dad!" I thumbed through the three pictures I carried in my ID holder. One was of Mom, who didn't like having her picture taken and therefore looked a bit annoyed. One was of me and Charlayne after a belt ceremony at karate. The last picture was of Dad, taken the previous Christmas with the wok I gave him. I showed the picture to Trey.

He nodded. "Yeah, it's the same guy. And it's pretty obvious you're related, even in the online photo—you have his eyes. And your smile is the same, too."

I reached over Trey to scroll down and read the rest of the bio, laying the picture on the table beside the laptop. But as soon as I moved my hand away, the picture vanished.

Acting on reflex, I tried to grab what was no longer there, knowing as I did that it would make no difference. One second the photo was there, a splash of color against the polished black marble of the table. And the next, it was gone.

"Son of a—" Trey's mouth was open, and he pulled away, moving toward the edge of the booth. "Kate, did you see that?"

We were both silent for a moment. "I don't think I'm going to keep that muffin down," he mumbled.

Without thinking, I pulled the CHRONOS key from under my shirt and held his hand against my chest so that we were both in full contact with the medallion. After a few moments the color returned to Trey's face. "Do you remember what just happened?" I asked.

Trey nodded. "Yes. We found your dad. And then his photograph—which was *right there* by the salt shaker—just disappeared." He looked down at his hand, which I was still holding against my chest. "I'm not complaining or anything—not at all— but why are you holding my hand . . . there?"

I blushed, but I didn't move it off my chest. "I'm beginning to think that it could be rather . . . dangerous . . . for me to lose contact with this medallion for even a moment, Trey. If my mother doesn't exist in this . . . time . . . then I don't either, right? But I also remember what it was like when the temporal distortions happened and I didn't have the medallion. I felt . . . like you looked, just a few minutes ago. Faint, queasy, panicky?"

"Yeah . . . it's getting better now. But there's a part of me that insists the picture was never there. It's not just that I don't think things should be able to vanish like that, but more that I remember two opposite things at the same time, if that makes sense?"

"None of this makes sense," I said. "What I can't figure out is why you saw the picture disappear at all. I don't think you have the CHRONOS gene since the medallion looks ordinary to you . . . but Connor—that's my grandmother's friend—said that anyone who wasn't wearing a medallion wouldn't realize that anything had changed, when there was a time shift."

"Maybe it's enough to be touching someone who's wearing a medallion?" Trey suggested. He moved his shoulder and his knee slightly, which had been brushing against me all along due to the small booth.

"Maybe," I said. "But . . . you believe me now, right? That what I'm telling you is real?"

Trey made a slightly sick face. "Yes. I'm going to have to go with Sherlock Holmes on this one—'When you have eliminated the impossible, whatever remains, however improbable, is the truth.'" He stared at the spot where the picture had been. "I would have said that the things you described earlier *were* impossible, but I've just seen an example with my own eyes. I could try to pretend it didn't happen . . . I might even make myself believe it . . . but I know better."

"That's why I'm holding your hand on the medallion," I said. "I'm scared that if you take your hand away, you'll forget . . . that you'll stop believing me." Tears came to my eyes and I blinked them back. "I know that sounds incredibly selfish, but I really, really need someone to believe me right now."

His grin was back, just a bit shakier. "Okay, but I think we're going to find it difficult to finish this search with our hands in this position. And people are going to stare if we try to walk down the street this way. Maybe . . . if we just sit really close?" He put his left arm around me and very slowly pulled his right hand away, while I watched his face for any changes.

"See?" he said. "I still remember. We're both fine." He tapped the touch pad to pull up the rest of my dad's bio, his arm still around my shoulders. "And I could definitely get used to browsing this way."

I gave him a sideways glance, but didn't disagree. My entire body had stiffened when Nolan, Charlayne's latest matchmaking candidate, had put his arm around me at the movie. Being next to Trey, on the other hand, felt natural.

"Is there an address at the bottom?" I asked.

"I think so. But Kate . . . maybe you need to finish reading the bio."

I scanned the three paragraphs quickly. The bio included the same bit that Dad always added about the Math Olympics, the same college data and interests. Some additional facts, however, brought me back to reality—the new reality. "Harry lives with his wife, Emily, and two children, in a faculty house overlooking East-wick Pond."

∞

It was just before 4 P.M. and the traffic was beginning to pick up as we left the coffee shop and turned onto Massachusetts Avenue. We held hands even as Trey collected the laptop and stowed it in his bag, probably looking like a lovesick teenage couple who couldn't bear to be apart for even a second. And within a few minutes, we looked like a lovesick teenage couple having an argument.

"He will still know me, Trey. He *will*. He's my dad; how could he not know me?" I had already said this several times, but Trey didn't seem convinced. I wasn't entirely convinced myself, but I also wasn't willing to acknowledge any other possibility.

We waited for the walk signal and Trey pulled me toward a bench that curved around the small park at the center of Dupont Circle. Several people—a few of them homeless, judging from the bags and blankets surrounding them—were seated at the stone chessboards nearby, intent on their games.

"I'm not sure, Kate. I know you want to see him—and I'm more than happy to take you if you really think that's best." Trey put his finger on my chin and pulled my face in his direction, forcing me to look at him. "Listen. It's a ten-, maybe fifteen-minute walk to my house from here. We're over near Kalorama. And it's a two-hour drive, give or take, to Delaware. If we leave now, we'd get out of the city before rush hour and we could probably be there before dark."

He held up one finger as I moved to get up from the bench. "But . . . hear me out. I have no doubt that, in your timeline, your father loves you dearly. To *this* Harry Keller, however, you're going to be a stranger. Maybe we should go to your grandmother. Or at least call her before we go? You said that she believes you can somehow . . . fix . . . this. Shouldn't we concentrate on that?"

I sighed. He was being logical, and I knew on some level that he was right, but . . . "I *can't* call Katherine. I don't have her number. It was in my phone, which was in my backpack, which was stolen. The number would be brand-new, and I can guarantee it's unlisted anyway, since she's worried about being tracked down by my grandfather."

As I said this, I pushed away the nagging fear that the CHRONOS keys had, for some reason, not protected Katherine and Connor. I had to focus first on finding Dad. "Maybe we should go there first, but I think she'd try to stop me from contacting Dad. And I need to see him, Trey. Even if he doesn't know me, I'll convince him. I need to see that he's real, that he exists. I can't . . . I can't do that with my mom. She's not here . . . I don't think she's anywhere."

Maybe it was the rising panic in my voice. I'm pretty sure I didn't convince him with the strength of my argument because the reasons didn't even sound logical to me. All I knew was that I needed my Dad, that he was only two hours away, and Trey had offered to take me to him.

"Okay." He gave me a sad smile and took my hand, pulling me up from the bench. "We go to Delaware. I don't think it is going to help, but I've known you—what?—right at four hours, now. I'm willing to admit I could be wrong."

∞

Trey's family lived in a three-story house perhaps a bit smaller than the one Katherine had bought in Bethesda. It was in a quaint neighborhood, with row houses, the occasional single-family home, and a few small embassy buildings. Trey said it had belonged to his grandparents, but they had retired to Florida years ago, and he'd lived in the house for most of his life—at least during the times his family had been in the States.

We entered through a side door that opened into a large kitchen with pale yellow walls. "Estella?" Trey called as he opened the door. "It's me." A large gray cat who had been sleeping in the afternoon sunlight stretched and slinked over to Trey for a greeting. "Hi, Dmitri. Where's Estella?"

I bent down to stroke the cat's ears and he purred in response, rubbing against my legs.

"Hmm. Estella's usually here. She must have stepped out to the market. Probably just as well, since she would have a thousand questions about you, even if I just said we were going to the movies. She's a bit . . . overprotective." Trey left a note on the desk for his father, telling him he was helping out a friend, and attached another note to the fridge, explaining to Estella that he wouldn't be home for dinner.

At Trey's suggestion, we found my dad's number through directory assistance and called to be sure he wasn't away on vacation or something. It was Dad's voice that answered the phone, and it was all I could do to keep from talking to him, but Trey pulled the phone from my hand and said he'd dialed the wrong number.

Trey's car was parked in a garage behind the house. It was an older model Lexus, dark blue, parked next to a much newer, similar Lexus in black. "This one is Mom's hand-me-down," he explained, "but Dad added the Bluetooth for my phone and music." He grinned. "I convinced him that it was a safety issue—so that I can focus on the road and still call home—but I really wanted it because this car only had a CD player. It needed a serious music upgrade."

The ride to Delaware was uneventful. Traffic wasn't bad once we got out of the city. I kept my hand on Trey's shoulder, so he could have both hands free to drive. Although my seventeenth birthday was fast approaching, I hadn't yet gotten my own license—there seemed little need since the Metro went most places I wanted to go and the only car to which I had access was an old clunker that Dad used almost exclusively for trips to the grocery. Trey had apparently been driving for a while, however, and seemed very comfortable behind the wheel.

He was hungry, so we stopped to grab some food at a McDonald's near Annapolis. We were through the door and halfway to the counter before we realized, simultaneously, that Trey had dropped my hand to open the door.

"Trey?" I said. No response. He was looking at me quizzically, his head tipped to the side.

I waited a moment and then grabbed his hand again, and practically screamed his name. "Trey?"

"Exactly who *are* you?" he said. "And why are you holding my hand?"

He broke into a grin before the last words were out, and squeezed my hand. "Joking!" I tried to pull my hand away, but he wouldn't let go. "I'm sorry, I couldn't resist."

I punched his arm with my free hand.

"Ow! Okay, that hurt, but I guess I asked for it." Trey pulled me around the corner, holding my wrists together to avoid another punch. "I'm sorry, really. I didn't intend to drop your hand . . . but I was thinking about it earlier, and it doesn't make sense that I would forget. I mean, unless there is another temporal shift, or whatever you call it, I don't think my memory would be affected."

I glared. "Then why didn't you say that earlier?"

Another grin. "Would you have held my hand for the past three hours if I had? Really, Kate—I was going to suggest that we test the theory after we sat down to eat."

"Test it how?"

"Well, if I had forgotten, the worst that could have happened is that you had to pull out your Metro pass so I could watch that vanish, right? Or one of your earrings? I mean, if the picture disappeared, those things should, too. And if a disappearing photograph convinced me in DC, I think a disappearing Metro card would do it in Annapolis."

I shrugged, and then nodded. I was still annoyed, but it was hard to stay mad at Trey.

"Also," he said, "judging from the way you've been shifting around in the car seat the past twenty-five miles or so, I suspect you need to use the facilities as badly as I do. And a joint trip to the bathroom might have been pushing the limits of familiarity for both of us."

I couldn't argue with that.

∞

I spent most of the next hour staring out the window and trying to decide what I was going to say to Dad when I saw him. The area looked a lot like Iowa—flat patches of farmland, broken up by the occasional small town. Chaplin Academy was just outside one of those towns and I wasn't any closer to figuring out what I was going to say when we arrived.

There was a security gate at the entrance, and I leaned over Trey, holding up my school ID for the guard's inspection. "I'm Kate Pierce-Keller. My . . . my uncle, Harry Keller, teaches here. We're driving through, so I wanted to tell him hello." I was terrified that the guard would try to take the ID from me to inspect it—at which point I had no idea what I would have done. I couldn't risk everything in the ID holder disappearing. The guard, however, was a friendly sort who leaned in the window to glance at the ID and then gave us directions to the faculty housing area.

I had worried that it would be difficult to find Dad. We didn't have an exact address and I thought we might have to go door-to-door until we found a helpful neighbor. But I saw him before we even located a place to park. He sat at a wooden picnic table near the pond, a book in his hand, watching two boys—one around five and the other a few years younger—who were riding Big Wheels across the grass. The area was green and lush, with a large willow near the pond. I could see the back entrances to several small, neat-looking houses fifty yards or so behind the table, most with grills on the patio and a few with sandboxes or plastic playhouses.

I sat motionless, just staring at him. After a minute or two, Trey came around to the passenger side and opened the door, kneeling down to look at my face. "Do you want me to wait here at the car or come with?"

I thought for a moment. "Would you mind going with me?" I asked in a small voice. It would undoubtedly be a more personal conversation than anyone should have to witness on such short acquaintance, but I could feel my knees shaking and I hadn't even stood up yet.

"Not at all," Trey said. He reached out his hand to help me from the car and continued to hold it as we walked toward the picnic table. "For moral support," he said, squeezing my fingers gently.

I gave him a grateful smile. I had never felt so vulnerable.

"Mr. Keller?" I said. Dad looked up and closed the book, holding his place with his finger. The cover of the paperback was an autumn mélange of yellow, orange, and brown, with the image of a rabbit in front—*Watership Down*, a book that he had read to me years ago. One of our favorites.

"Yes?" He furrowed his brow a bit and glanced at our school uniforms. I realized they probably weren't the same on this campus, if uniforms were even required. "Do I know you?" he asked.

I sat down on the other side of the picnic table, with Trey beside me. "I hope so." I had rehearsed twenty different ways to start this conversation during the ride and now the only thing I could think to say was, "I'm your daughter. I'm Kate."

His look of utter shock made me instantly wish that I had taken a different track. "I'm sorry! That's not how I wanted to begin this . . . I mean . . ."

Dad shook his head adamantly. "That's not possible. I'm married . . . only for the past ten years, but . . . Who is your mother?"

"Deborah," I answered. "Deborah Pierce."

"No." Again, he shook his head. "I never dated anyone by that name. I'm sorry, but your mother was mistaken."

"Oh, no, it's not like *that*," I said emphatically. "I'm . . . I already know you . . ." I did the only thing I could think of—I pulled the CHRONOS key from inside my shirt. "Have you seen this before? What color is it?"

Dad looked at me now as though I were stark-raving mad, and possibly dangerous. He glanced at Trey, although it wasn't clear whether he was looking for a possible ally or sizing him up as a threat. "No, I haven't . . . and it's sort of pink." He glanced again at the medallion. "It's an unusual object—I'd remember if I had seen it."

I reached into the plastic holder and showed him my school ID—Prudence Katherine Pierce-Keller. Then I pulled out Mom's picture. "This . . . this was my mom." He clearly noticed the past tense, because his eyes softened.

Dad looked down at the photo for several moments before raising his eyes to meet mine again. His tone was gentle when he replied. "I'm very sorry for your loss . . . Kate? Is that it?" He glanced over at Trey. "And who is this?"

Trey turned toward him and put out his hand. "Trey Coleman, sir. I'm a friend of Kate's—I drove her here from DC."

Dad leaned forward and shook Trey's hand. "Hello, Trey. I'm sorry you came so far to be disappointed. If you had called, I could have saved you the . . ." He trailed off as the youngest of the two boys came running over and propped his foot up on the bench of the table.

"Daddy, fix my shoe, please. The sticky part came loose again . . ."

He reattached the frayed Velcro on the tiny shoe and pulled up the sock. "You need new sneakers, don't you, Robbie?"

"Mm-hmm." Robbie nodded, looking shyly at the two people talking to his father. His eyes were the same deep green as my own. I could tell from Dad's expression, as he glanced at me and then back at the boy, that he had also noticed the similarity.

My father ran his hand through his son's light brown curls and I drew in a sharp breath. The gesture was so familiar, but the hand was always on my head, the smile was always for me. "Go play with your brother, okay?" he said. "Your mom will be home soon and we'll have pizza."

"Yum!" Robbie cried as he ran off. "Pizza!"

When Dad turned back toward me, I pushed Mom's picture forward. "This is the only photo I have of my mother." I pulled my hand away, hoping fervently that my grandmother had at least a few pictures of Mom. The photograph vanished, just as Dad's picture had earlier, in the café. I felt Trey's body tense up and wished I'd had the forethought to tell him to look away.

Dad was staring at the spot where the picture had been, a stunned expression on his face. I reached out and took his hand. "I'm sorry. I know this is hard, but I need to make you understand."

I spent the next several minutes telling him everything that had happened to me over the past few days. I told him about living with him in the cottage at Briar Hill, adding little details about his life and personality that I hoped hadn't changed with a new marriage and a new family. I told him everything Katherine had said about his real parents and the accident, about my grandparents, and I explained Katherine's theory on what was happening with the temporal shifts. Dad didn't speak until I finished.

Finally, he met my eyes, his expression sad and distant. "I'm sorry . . . but I don't know what you expect me to say or do. I can't explain how you know the things you know. And I can't deny what I just saw here. And seeing your eyes—it's like looking in the mirror."

"You believe me?" My voice was unsteady.

"I guess. I don't really know, to tell you the truth." His voice shifted, becoming a bit angry. "But either way, this timeline you've told me about . . . that's *not* my world, Kate. You are a lovely young lady and I do not want to hurt you. In whatever reality you know, you could well be the center of my universe." He stopped and nodded toward the kids, who were now chasing after something in the grass. "But those two little boys, and their mother, who will be home any minute now with pizza and groceries—*they* are my life. I can only assume that, in your world, John and Robbie do not exist and Emily—well, who knows if I ever meet Emily?"

My lower lip began to tremble and I bit down hard to steady it. Trey put a protective arm around me.

"I would like to be able to say that I wish you luck in . . . whatever this is that you are planning to do," Dad said. "But that would be a lie. How can I look at my two kids over there and do anything *other* than hope you fail?"

∞ 8 ∞

I don't really remember going back to the car. Trey helped me inside and pulled the seat belt over me, snapping it into place. "I'm sorry, Kate. I'm so sorry." There were tears in his eyes. He gave me a soft kiss on the forehead and drew me into his arms. At that point, I broke down, sobbing against his shoulder. I held on to him tightly. As much as I hated to seem needy or weak, after a day in which I had lost my mother, my father, and in every way that mattered, my own existence, I desperately needed the human contact.

He held me for several minutes and then I pulled away. I was still crying, but I said, "I'm okay. We need to go."

"You don't sound okay, but yeah . . . let's get out of here." He rummaged around in the console and found some napkins from a fast-food place. "Sorry, I don't have any Kleenex," he said. I took the napkins, dabbing at my eyes and nose.

I glanced back at the picnic table. The youngest boy was in Dad's lap trying to get his attention, but Dad continued to stare at the car as we drove away. He looked miserable and I felt a surge of guilt for putting him through what was, in the end, very unnecessary pain.

I was glad Trey wasn't the type to say I told you so, but I acknowledged the fact anyway. "You warned me. I should have listened."

We drove, without saying much, toward DC. Somehow I dozed off, my head against Trey's shoulder. When I awoke we were on the Beltway, a few miles from the turnoff to Bethesda. Trey was singing softly to an old Belle and Sebastian song. He had a nice baritone voice, and the car was dark, except for the dashboard lights and headlights on the highway. I had the urge to close my eyes and stay in the moment, not thinking about anything else that had happened.

"I'm sorry, Trey," I said, sitting up. "You've been wonderful to chauffeur me all over two states, and I thank you by falling asleep." I noticed that his sleeve was damp—had I been crying in my sleep? Or yuck—drooling?

"No apology necessary," he said. "I think you needed to shut down for a while. I was going to have to wake you pretty soon, though. I don't know where your grandmother lives, except that you said it's near school."

At the thought of Katherine, I felt another wave of guilt. I glanced at the clock on the dashboard. It was nearly nine o'clock. I knew my grandmother had to be frantic, and although I was still a bit angry, it was less at Katherine than at this faceless, future grandfather who had reached out from someplace I couldn't even imagine and snatched away my entire life.

I should have gone back to Katherine's house, rather than trying to pull Dad into this. Brief images flashed through my mind—the two boys running by the pond, Robbie crawling into Dad's lap—and suddenly I felt protective of them.

"Trey, what if he's right?"

"What if who is right?"

"My dad . . . Harry. I mean, I'm going back to my grandmother's and she says that I'm the only one who can set this straight—who can fix the timeline. I don't know what that means, what she wants me to do, or if I even *can* do it—but what if I succeed and those little boys don't exist when I'm done? How can that be a good thing? Maybe Harry is better off there—with Emily, with *that* family. And who else exists in this timeline but not in the other? Who has the right to say that the other timeline is better?"

Trey thought for a long time before he answered. "I don't know, Kate. But someone—apparently your grandfather—is going to a lot of trouble to change things, and he sounds like he doesn't much care who ceases to exist in the process. You, on the other hand, are actually bothering to ask that question, even though you didn't create this problem. So I'd trust your judgment more than I would his if someone has to pick and choose between timelines—do you follow my meaning?"

"I guess so, but . . ."

"No, let me finish. You told me earlier that you're pretty sure that *you* don't exist in *this* timeline. And based on what we've both seen, I think you're correct. Sooner or later, something will separate you from that medallion and I think you'll pop out of existence just like those photographs." He reached over and took my hand. "And if that's true—well, I've decided I don't really like this timeline."

That nearly made me cry again, a clear sign that the day had pushed me well over my emotional limits. I cleared my throat and nodded toward the windshield. "We're almost there. Turn right at the next intersection."

I looked ahead nervously as he turned onto Katherine's street. Although I didn't want to mention it to Trey, I was very worried that we would round the corner and there would be a For Sale sign in front of the greystone house, with no evidence that my grandmother or Connor had ever been there.

I breathed a huge sigh of relief when I saw the lights on in the house both downstairs and upstairs. I could see the many shelves of books that lined the library through the upper windows and the pale blue glow of the CHRONOS equipment. It seemed like days since I had stood in that room. "Thank God they're still here."

Trey pulled the car up next to the curb. "You were worried?" he asked as we got out. "I thought you said the medallions were protecting them."

Daphne began barking from the backyard as we approached the house. "I did, but yes, I was worried. You could put everything I understand about all of this into a thimble and still have room left over. And, with the exception of meeting you, anything that could go wrong today has, so . . ."

I had just raised my hand to ring the bell when the door opened in front of me and Katherine pulled me into a hug.

"Oh my God. Kate! Where have you been? We thought . . ."

"I'm sorry, Katherine. I had to see if—Mom, she's gone. I can't find any trace of her, now or in the past. And Dad . . ."

Katherine led me inside. "I know. We felt it, too." I saw a slight mental guard go up on Katherine's face as she saw Trey, who was just behind me in the shadows of the porch. "Who is this with you?"

I reached for Trey's arm and pulled him forward. "Trey, this is my grandmother, Katherine Shaw. Katherine, this is Trey Coleman." I can never remember whether the older person is introduced first or last, but formalities seemed a minor point given the situation. "Trey has been . . . wonderful today. I'm not sure I would be here without his help."

We walked into the living room and I collapsed onto the couch, tugging Trey down beside me. "Trey knows everything—well, he knows as much as I do. I don't know if that's a problem for you, but it was kind of unavoidable."

Katherine sighed and sat down in the armchair across from us. "I tried your cell phone, but . . ."

I gave a wry laugh. "Did you get a message saying the person you're calling is outside the service area? The phone was in my *backpack* this morning." I patted the sides of my skirt. "No pockets. Your number was in the phone—I didn't have it written down. And since the phone was on Mom's plan, I doubt there's any record now of that account."

"What took you so long? We had almost given up hope."

I glanced at Trey. "He drove me to see Dad. Who is now in Delaware."

"Oh, Kate. I wish you had just come back here. What happened? You didn't try to *explain* to Harry, did you?"

"Yes, I did."

"And?"

"Disappearing photographs are pretty convincing."

Trey nodded. "It worked for me."

Katherine gave Trey a skeptical look. It was clear she thought there might be other reasons he was easy to convince.

"Dad believed me," I said. "But it didn't matter. He has a life. A family. Kids."

I stopped, realizing how bitter my voice sounded, and waited a moment before going on. "Could you please tell me exactly what happened today that changed my entire life to the point that my own father doesn't know who I am? To the point where my mother simply doesn't exist?"

Katherine nodded. "I *will* do that, Kate. But I expect your friend needs to be getting home. It's a school night, correct? We can talk about this afterward."

"We can talk in front of Trey—" I began.

"No," said Trey. "It's okay, Kate—really. I *do* have school tomorrow and my dad will be looking for me." I started to object, but I knew he was right. I just didn't want to be alone. And I knew that I would feel very alone after he left, even with my grandmother and Connor nearby.

Katherine stood up, moving toward the kitchen. "It was nice to meet you, Trey. If you'd wait here a moment . . . I'm sure you incurred expenses driving to Delaware."

"Not necessary, Mrs. Shaw. It was my pleasure."

"You have my thanks then, Trey. Kate, I'll go make you a cup of tea. You look like you could use it."

"Walk me to the door?" Trey asked when Katherine had left the room.

I nodded and we stepped outside, onto the front porch. Trey pulled me into a hug, then stepped back and studied me closely. "Don't look so glum." He tucked a stray piece of hair back behind my ear and gave me a soft, quick kiss on the side of the mouth. "You get some sleep, okay? I have to go home and finish my trig homework." He smiled. "Hey, there's a bright side for you—no homework."

"I don't actually mind homework. Well, most homework."

"Really?" he asked. "How do you feel about other people's homework? I'm seeing great possibilities in this relationship." I laughed and sat down on the wooden porch swing as Trey started down the steps. "Oh, wait . . . I don't have your number. Will your grandmother sic the dog on me if I just come back to see you tomorrow?"

"If she does, I'm pretty sure the worst Daphne would do is lick you to death. I'm just . . . I guess I'm worried that something will happen—another shift—and you'll forget I exist." I could feel myself blushing. "I mean . . . I quite literally do not have another friend in the world right now."

"Not a problem," he said. "If your grandfather changes the world again, just find me at the school and take off a sock or something. I'll see it vanish and you'll have me eating out of your hand again in five minutes flat."

And then he was gone. I stood on the porch and watched as his taillights receded down the street, thinking that, if he had to go home, it was actually quite nice to have someone exit in the normal, gradual way.

∞

Katherine was waiting in the kitchen with a cup of herbal tea brewing on the table. "Are you hungry? There's a pie in the fridge . . . cherry, I think . . . or I could make you a sandwich."

I shook my head and sank into one of the chairs in the breakfast nook. I glanced around at the big kitchen where Dad had looked forward to cooking and was almost in tears again.

"I don't think it's entirely safe for us to be outside the house for the time being, at least not for an extended period." She sat down opposite me. "I sent Connor out to the store, however, as soon as we realized what had happened. I can't guarantee his taste, but there's a nightgown and a change of clothes in your room that should fit you, along with a toothbrush and other necessities."

I gave her a weak smile. "Thanks. It occurred to me on the way back from Delaware that I don't even own a hairbrush."

"We also placed one of the laptops in your room. It will take a few days to get all of the other financial details back in order, but the credit accounts are all in Connor's name and they are apparently still active, so you can go online and have whatever you need delivered."

I stared down at my tea. The scents of chamomile and lavender drifted up from the cup. "How did you know? I mean, I know you felt the temporal shift, but how did you know that Mom . . . Dad?"

"Connor has a program that monitors relevant information on the internet. He checked, as he's done after every temporal shift, and Deborah . . ." Katherine paused for a moment, and her voice was soft when she continued. "Saul has taken both my daughters from me now, although I'm quite sure that Deborah just . . . doesn't exist in this timeline. I can only hope that Prudence, wherever she is, is protected by a CHRONOS key."

I took a sip of the tea, which was still quite hot. "So he's killed you, right? At some point in time?"

"That's the assumption we're going on," Katherine said, nodding. "The question, of course, is when and where?"

"That's what Trey and I were saying in the car—"

Katherine broke in. "Do you really think it was wise to pull that young man into this problem, Kate?"

I waited a moment, measuring my words before I spoke. "Maybe not. But I didn't have much time to stop and think today. I just met him, but to be honest, I trust him more than anyone else I know right now . . . including you." I could tell Katherine was hurt by my words, but if we were going to make this work I had to be truthful.

My elbows were propped up on the table and I put my forehead into my hands, rubbing my closed eyes. Despite the nap in the car, I couldn't remember ever feeling so utterly exhausted.

"I love you, Katherine," I said as I looked back up at her. "I *do.* You're the only family I have left now. Whatever you say I have to do; I'll do it. I don't see that I have an option, really. But . . . Mom's gone. Dad . . . well, he's someone else's dad now. Charlayne . . . my other friends . . . I'm guessing they've never met me. I *need* a friend right now, if you want me to keep my sanity."

Katherine's lips tightened, but she nodded. "If you trust him, that's enough for me." She got to her feet. "Connor is in the library. Shall we go up and—"

"No," I said. Katherine looked surprised, and I continued. "Tomorrow, first thing, I want to know the *why* behind all of this. And then we can move on to how you believe I can change it. But for now, I'm going to finish my tea and then I'm going up to bed. I can't think anymore."

∞

I fell onto the bed immediately, hoping exhaustion would take me away as it had in the car. It was soon clear, however, that it would be a while before I could sleep.

To my amazement, Connor had picked out pajamas, jeans, shorts, a few shirts, and even underwear that I actually might have bought on my own. The jeans were a bit too large, but that was better than a pair that I couldn't get into. The pajamas were a soft green flannel that might have been too warm in Dad's poorly air-conditioned cottage, but they were just right in this new room. There was a selection of toiletries in a drugstore bag, along with a brush, toothbrush, and disposable razor. Also a bottle of Tylenol PM. The shampoo wasn't my usual brand, but it smelled nice and he'd bought conditioner as well. Either Katherine had given Connor a list, or he had aspects to his personality that I wouldn't have imagined.

I took two of the Tylenol, hoping they would help to relax my head. Although I'm usually a shower person, I ran a hot bath, pouring a few capfuls of the shampoo under the tap to make bubbles. Slowly and somewhat painfully, I removed the cheap rubber band from my hair, again remembering the image of Kiernan with my green hair band on his wrist.

I slipped into the big tub, wincing at first when the hot water hit my smashed toenail. Closing my eyes, I slid under the water and allowed my hair to float out around me. I've loved that sensation since I was a small child—the feeling of weightlessness, of being surrounded by warmth. I stayed under for as long as I could, and then floated to the surface. Each time a thought about my mother or father appeared, I resolutely pushed it aside and submerged myself again to clear my mind. I refused to think of Mom as dead. If Katherine said that I could fix this, then I would make it happen.

I tried to focus instead on the few pleasurable aspects of the day. In the past, I had generally avoided guys at school, preferring to concentrate on my books. The two boys I'd been on dates with were nice enough, but I had few common interests with either of them. With one guy, the feeling was clearly mutual after our first evening out, and I found a polite excuse when the other boy asked me for a second date.

In the space of this single traumatic day, I had gone from a girl who had never been kissed at all to one who had been thoroughly and passionately kissed by Kiernan—I still felt a bit dizzy thinking about it—and who had been given just enough of a kiss by Trey that I was now very curious about how it might feel if we really and truly kissed.

Twenty minutes later, I dried off with a fluffy blue towel. I then wrapped another towel around my hair and pulled on the new pajamas. The big bed looked plush and comfortable—far nicer than my twin bed at home or the sofa at Dad's. I would, however, have gladly traded it for either of the other options. After drying my hair for a few minutes with the towel, I crawled under the covers, turned out the lamp, and curled up on my side. And much, much later, I slept.

∞ 9 ∞

I was awakened by a light tap at my bedroom door. "Kate? Are you awake?" I opened my eyes to unfamiliar surroundings, and it took a moment before I realized where I was.

The clock on the nightstand indicated that I had slept away the better part of the morning. "I'll be down in a minute, Katherine."

"No rush, dear. I just wanted to be sure that you were okay."

"I'm fine. I was just really tired, I guess. I'll be down in a few."

I splashed some water on my face and pulled on the jeans and shirt Connor had bought the day before. My hair was a chaotic mess. Usually I would have just pulled it back, but I only had the rubber band and I shuddered at the thought of trying to get that out of my hair again. So I spent several minutes trying to work out the assorted tangles that always developed when I went to bed with wet hair.

A few minutes later, I walked down the stairs. Katherine and Connor were apparently in the library. I heard a whimper and a tap on the screen door in the kitchen and went to let Daphne in. There was a new addition to Daphne's collar—one of the CHRONOS keys had been sewn onto the top. I was confused for a moment, but then it occurred to me that, in this timeline, Katherine wouldn't be around to own a dog, and Daphne would belong to someone else.

"I guess you'd just disappear in the backyard without this, wouldn't you, girl? Or is another version of your tail wagging in someone else's kitchen?"

After several minutes of hugs (from me) and kisses (big wet ones from Daphne), the dog was calm enough for me to scavenge around the kitchen for some breakfast. I was glad to find Cheerios, a banana, some milk, and a half-full pot of coffee. Katherine must have made it, since it was far more palatable than the stuff Connor had produced the day before.

I had almost finished the cereal when Connor walked in. "Thanks for making a department store run for me yesterday, Connor. You chose well."

Connor nodded curtly, pouring more coffee into his mug. "You scared Katherine half to death. And she doesn't need the extra stress."

I took the last bite of Cheerios and looked at him for a moment. "I'm sorry. I was preoccupied with the discovery that my parents no longer exist."

He caught the sarcastic tone and turned to face me. "All the more reason to get yourself back here to safety, rather than driving all over the countryside with your boyfriend. I'm not sure of the range on that medallion, you know. If you trip over a gap in the sidewalk, and it swings away from you, you'll like as not be just as gone as your mother. Finish your food and get up to the library. There's work to do."

I fought a childish urge to stick out my tongue at his retreating back.

Reluctant to give Connor the satisfaction of following him quickly, I took my time with the last bit of coffee and then stopped by my room to brush my teeth. I sat down at the desk chair and looked at the new laptop. I thought of checking my email before remembering that the account I had would no longer be active. Daphne rested her auburn head on my knee. "I guess we should go see what the grump wants us to do, right, Daphne?" The setter waved her tail back and forth and I gave her another hug.

I looked up to see Katherine in the doorway of the bedroom. Her skin had a bit more color than the evening before; like me, she had apparently managed to get some sleep. "I take it you slept okay?" she said.

I shrugged. "It took a while. But I seem to have made up for it this morning."

"Connor was worried about you as well, Kate. If he was a bit gruff, it's understandable."

"He's always a bit gruff. I think it's just his nature."

Katherine nodded slightly. "I suspect that wasn't always true, but he has as much at stake as any of us here."

"I know," I said. "It's not easy to lose your entire identity . . ."

"It's more than just his identity, Kate. He also lost his *family*—and I don't just mean that his sister is different or that he has a brother now. Those are minor details for him. His wife—she died about ten years ago, a brain aneurism totally unrelated to all of this. But his children disappeared during the time shift last May. He was already working with me, and . . . they were both off at college. His son and daughter—they both ceased to exist, just like your mom. For whatever reason, when we trace the records back, Connor never met his wife in this timeline."

I was silent. I glanced down at my outfit and realized that Connor's taste in clothes was probably attributable to experience—he knew firsthand what teenage girls needed, because he'd shopped with one as a single dad, not that long ago.

We left my room and walked around the curved hallway overlooking the living room until we reached the library on the opposite side of the second floor. Daphne, who was loyally padding along behind us, gave a whimper as she realized where we were going, and she reversed course, heading to the stairway.

"Poor Daphne," Katherine said. "She really doesn't like the library. We're not sure why—she shouldn't be able to see the lights from the CHRONOS equipment. Connor thinks maybe the medallions make a sound that bothers her when they're active."

Connor was at the far side of the room, engrossed in his work. Katherine sat down at one of the terminals and I grabbed a nearby chair, pulling my bare feet onto the edge and resting my chin on my knees. "So what are you doing and how can I help?"

Connor glanced in my direction, then came over and handed me three diaries. They were similar in size to the one that had been in my backpack, although the color and condition of the covers varied. "You can start going through these. We're trying to pinpoint exactly when Katherine is killed. While we're doing that, you need to become familiar with each of the expeditions. I assume you have a basic familiarity with the history of rights movements in America?"

He walked away without waiting for an answer, so I spoke instead to Katherine, placing the diaries on the desk beside me. "Civil rights? Like Martin Luther King?"

"Yes," said Katherine, "and women's rights. There are other categories as well, of course, but my research career focused on abolition—anti-slavery, that is—and women's rights. I studied the movements in a broad sense, looking at changes over the course of several centuries. My very first research trip was to a Quaker village in the early 1700s. Are you familiar with the Quakers?"

"A little. I knew someone in Iowa who was a Quaker. He was in my karate class. One of the guys in the class thought it was funny that someone who was supposed to be a pacifist was into martial arts, but he explained that there was no contradiction, since karate is about trying to avoid violence, not about using violence to solve problems."

Katherine nodded. "The Religious Society of Friends, often called Quakers, was the earliest religious group in America to both oppose slavery and to promote equality for women. The fact that women often traveled as ministers of that religion made it fairly easy for me to observe a community without being too conspicuous. During my first two jumps—one to 1732 and a later one to 1794—I was paired with the senior historian whose place I was taking at CHRONOS. After that, I did a solo trip to the 1838 meeting where the Declaration of Sentiments was signed. Many of those who signed it were Quakers."

"That's the document you showed me that now has Prudence's signature, right?"

Katherine nodded. "I took a few other solo jumps as well, but CHRONOS generally found that expeditions went more smoothly when historians traveled in pairs. The logical person to group me with was Saul Rand, since his specialty was religious movements. There were frequently overlaps between religious organizations and rights movements—not just among the Quakers but with many other denominations, too. Saul was only eight years older, so our traveling as a young married couple provided an effective cover. And eventually, the cover became very natural, because we *were* a couple.

"So" she continued, turning back to the computer screen, "we had twenty-seven jumps together, total." She tapped the mouse and pulled up a list of cities with a date printed next to each. "These twelve seem to be the most likely candidates for when my murder might have taken place. We can't really rule out my solo jumps either, although I'm not certain how much information Saul had about those."

"Why?" I asked. "Not why these specific trips—we can discuss that later. Why is Saul doing this? Why does he want to change the past? Why does he want to kill you?"

"Why *did* he kill me is the more correct question—or, technically, why did he have someone else kill me," said Katherine. "As I explained earlier, Saul is stuck in whatever time he landed and

I'd wager a great deal that it's a point in the future, not the past. He's using someone else—or, I'm beginning to suspect, several individuals—to change history for him. We know that there are two—the young men you encountered yesterday—but I don't think we can safely assume those are the only ones. I suspect that Prudence is one of them as well. We have evidence that she has, at least, made small changes to the historical record."

"I still don't understand Saul's personal motives. What does he hope to gain?" I could see Connor shaking his head in annoyance out of the corner of my eye and decided to address him directly. "You have to admit, Connor, if I'm supposed to help track down a murderer, it might be important to understand his reasoning."

Connor turned his swivel chair to face me. "Take any psychopath, sociopath, whatever label you choose. Scrape off the details and the motivation is always the same, Kate. Power. As much power as they can get."

"But why kill Katherine? Why didn't he just have Pudgy kill me on the Metro? Katherine can't use the medallion and she hasn't exactly hidden the fact that she has a terminal illness."

"That's a good point, Kate. I suspect it's personal," Katherine added. "The first time Saul planned to kill me—the time I escaped to 1969—it was because I was in his way. And, equally important, because I had ceased to find him fascinating, attractive, brilliant—all of the things I foolishly believed him to be for the four years we were partners. He failed to kill me then, and Saul never accepted failure lightly. If he has the means now to finish what he started back at CHRONOS, I suspect that he would do it simply on principle."

It was hard to picture Katherine as young and impetuous, and I still felt that we were missing some part of the overall picture, but I nodded. "What exactly made you change your mind about Saul?"

"I began to discover some . . . inconsistencies in his reports, and I observed several actions that were contrary to CHRONOS protocol. This was about the same time I learned I was pregnant. Many of our colleagues assumed that Saul studied the history of religion because he was a devout believer. He was certainly capable of giving that impression to people of a wide array of faiths. I knew him a bit better than most, and I thought he was attracted to religious history because he was a religious skeptic. Neither was true."

Katherine looked carefully at me. "Saul is a devout believer only in *himself*, and he was convinced that the religious faith of others, if manipulated skillfully, was an excellent path to the power he sought. He was studying religions of the world in order to pick up tips on how to build his own."

"How do you 'build' a religion?" I asked.

"Many others have done it with less," Katherine said with a wry smile. "Saul had an excellent tool at his disposal. I think his plan was to personally go back to various places and times in history and lay a trail of appearances, miracles, and prophecy—blending a variety of religions. Just as Christianity pulled in elements of pagan religions in order to attract followers, he would incorporate elements of Christianity, Islam, and other religions, laying the path for the reign of the prophet Cyrus . . . who would, of course, be Saul."

"Wait . . . you aren't saying he founded the *Cyrists*? That's crazy. I went to a service at one of the temples a few months back. I mean, I really didn't get into it, but they seem okay. Charlayne goes occasionally with Joseph, her brother. He's dating a girl who's a Cyrist."

I didn't add that Charlayne's parents were a bit nervous about how serious the relationship had become. Joseph would be required to convert if they decided to marry, and most Cyrists married pretty early. From the age of twelve, Cyrists wore a small lotus flower tattoo on their left hand as the outward symbol of chastity. Members took a vow of abstinence—total abstinence—until their twentieth birthday or marriage, whichever came first, and all marriages had to be approved by the temple elders.

I remembered a conversation with Charlayne's mom after we'd attended the temple's Sunday service. Her feelings were very mixed—she was suspicious of the Cyrists in general, but Joseph had always been her wild child, and after meeting Felicia he had totally straightened up his act. No alcohol, no drugs, and as far as she knew, no sex. His life revolved around work, college, and carefully supervised visits with Felicia, who at eighteen had two more years of abstinence to go. They had been dating for about six months and Joseph was ecstatic that he was finally allowed to hold her hand. Charlayne said Joseph's transformation was creepy, in a romantic kind of way. I didn't see how *creepy* and *romantic* could go together, but then Charlayne's mind sometimes worked in mysterious ways.

"Are you sure?" I asked. "I mean, they do have some odd beliefs, but that's true of a lot of religions. Isn't the vice president a Cyrist? I remember Charlayne talking about how Joseph had seen her at the temple pretty much every week in the months leading up to the election. This isn't some new cult that just appeared. The Cyrists have been around for centuries. Why would you think—"

Katherine gave me an exasperated look. "I don't just *think* this, Kate. I know it for a fact. Saul created the Cyrists. And whether they've been around for centuries depends on your perspective. To those—including yourself, Kate—who have not been under continuous protection of a medallion for the past two years, the Cyrists were founded in the mid-fifteenth century."

"Fourteen seventy-eight, to be precise," said Connor.

Katherine walked over to one of the shelves and scanned the contents for a moment, eventually pulling out a fat book. "Your textbooks probably devote pages to the history of the Cyrists and their role in various eras. Pull any book from *these* shelves, however, and you'll find no mention of Cyrists, their beliefs or their history."

She handed the book to me. It was a survey of American history written in the 1980s. I thumbed through the index and saw no mention of the Cyrist colony at Providence, which every history class I could recall studied along with the Puritans of Salem and the Pilgrims at Plymouth Rock.

"This is the correct history, then?" I asked.

"Correct is a relative term, but yes—that book gives a generally accurate depiction of the timeline before Saul started mucking about. We were very lucky to be able to preserve these books. If I hadn't found Connor when I did, the entire library would have been corrupted. And while you'll find no mention of the Cyrists in any of these volumes, Connor and I can give you a precise date for the *actual* founding of Cyrist International: May 2nd of last year."

"Ah," I said, comprehension dawning. "That's when . . ."

"Exactly. That was the date of the first temporal distortion you felt, when you were still in Iowa."

"That's so hard to imagine, though. I mean, I can remember seeing Cyrist temples since I was a kid. They're what, maybe ten percent of the population?"

"You'd have been close a week ago," Connor said. "As of this morning, however, the *CIA Factbook* says 20.2 percent—they gained quite a few adherents in the last time shift. Oh, and you mentioned *Vice* President Patterson?" He typed a few characters into the search window on his computer and clicked a link near the top.

The White House website opened to display a photographic slide show of Washington scenes, most including Patterson's trim figure at a podium or photo op. Connor tapped the screen lightly with the tip of his finger, partially obscuring Patterson's face and her perfectly styled auburn hair. "As you can see, she's had a promotion."

My jaw quite literally dropped at that. Paula Patterson wouldn't have been my choice for first female president by a long shot, but it was kind of cool to know that the highest glass ceiling had finally been shattered. "But how? Was the president killed, or . . . ?"

Connor shrugged. "Nothing so dramatic. Patterson just won the primary instead. She was very well funded."

I shook my head slowly. "That's . . . unbelievable. You're saying that nothing I remember, nothing I've learned in school, is real?"

"It's not that your *memories* aren't real," Katherine said. "You just experienced a different timeline than we did after the temporal disturbances you felt. To be precise, you aren't the *same* Kate that I would have encountered if I'd started this project eighteen months ago, as I had planned."

I took a few moments to digest all of this. It was hard to imagine a different version of myself, with different memories. And the Cyrist Temple was on the periphery of my life. How different would the timeline be for people who grew up with that religion or whose entire families had been of that religion for generations?

"Okay," I began. "Let's set aside how recently the Cyrists were created. Why do you think they're involved in your murder? I don't know a lot about the Cyrists, but I know they don't advocate killing people. I'm pretty sure they have specific rules against that."

"Of course they do," said Connor with a derisive snort. "All major religions have rules against murder. If they didn't, there would be few converts. Well, at least few converts that you'd want to be in the same room with. But that doesn't mean that there aren't plenty of people willing to kill in the name of their faith—that's true of most religions."

"So why build a *religion*? You mentioned power—it would seem to me that there are much more direct routes to power than building a religion."

"Perhaps," said Katherine. "But a minister from the 1870s—not Saul, but someone he studied—once preached to his congregations that 'Money is power and you ought to be reasonably ambitious to have it.' The Cyrists have capitalized on his advice. Above all other rules of the church, members are required to tithe. They are promised that their 'spiritual investment' will be returned to them many times over."

Katherine leaned forward, a sly smile on her face. "And it *is* returned many times over, if those members also follow the suggestions their leaders make for the *rest* of their investments. You can be quite sure that there are plenty of Cyrists who knew when to invest in Microsoft and when to dump their Exxon stock. They've managed to manipulate their portfolios wisely through every recession. Of course, the poorer members who can spare only the ten percent tithe are pretty much out of luck, but the others? They have, in their eyes, firsthand evidence that God will bring riches to those who believe.

"Cyrist International is a very wealthy organization, Kate. Much of the money might, admittedly, be under the control of other religious groups if the Cyrists hadn't . . . emerged. But either way, it has resulted in billions of dollars in the hands of someone with the ability to manipulate that wealth even further, by interfering in the historical markets."

"And Saul did all of this with just three temporal shifts?" I asked.

"We think that there were three major shifts," Katherine said. "The three that you've experienced. The first was when the temple was formed. The second—well, we haven't quite pinpointed the cause of the shift on January 15th. The third, of course, was yesterday. We originally thought it was a minor shift for the timeline as a whole, with a major impact on anyone whose life has been intertwined with mine since 1969, because it means I never switched places with Richard, never landed at Woodstock, and never gave birth to my daughters. Therefore, Deborah never existed to meet Harry, and you were never born."

Katherine paused, taking a sip of tea before she continued. "But we're seeing a lot of other changes, so I'm guessing that they timed this strategically. After all, these shifts must be as unpleasant a sensation for them as they are for you and for me. It would make sense to minimize the discomfort and do several things at once, assuming you have enough people with the ability to time travel."

The scariest thing to me was that some of this was beginning to sound logical. "Did you know what Saul was planning before you . . . ended up in 1969? Did you know that he was going to create this new religion?"

Katherine didn't answer, but took the stack of diaries that I had been holding from me and ran her finger along the spines, reading the dates that were embossed in gold. She shook her head and returned to the bookshelf, locating another small book, which she opened, tapping the first blank page three times. I saw her fingers move briefly on the page, as though she were entering a PIN at the ATM.

"The short answer is no," she said as she walked back to where I was sitting. "I didn't know what he was doing. But I did suspect he was up to something—something against CHRONOS regulations."

Katherine handed me the stack of diaries. "You still need to read my official journal," she said, "in order to become familiar with the missions. But perhaps this would be the best place to start. We were all asked to keep personal logs in addition to the official trip reports. This one on top is my personal journal."

Connor gave Katherine a look of surprise. I thought I caught a hint of annoyance as well, and guessed that this was one book in the library to which Connor hadn't been given access.

Katherine rummaged in a desk drawer and located a case, from which she pulled a small translucent disk, about the size and shape of a contact lens. She placed the circle in my palm. "Stick this just behind your ear, in the little hollow at the bottom. If you press inward, it will adhere to your skin."

I tried it and the device attached without a problem, but I didn't notice any change. "Is it supposed to do something?"

Katherine opened the journal and tapped the page three times. I watched as several tiny icons appeared, hovering above the page like a hologram. A volume icon was grayed out until I pressed it with my finger, and then I heard a faint hum. "You can pause, skip entries, and so forth using these controls. They are a bit different from the buttons on your iPod, but they should be self-explanatory."

As she handed me the journal, she held on to it for just a moment, as though she was reluctant to give the book over. "You can start from the beginning, but you're unlikely to find much of interest until the entries for late April." She paused, an odd expression on her face. "Try not to think too badly of me as you read it. I was young and in love, and that rarely leads to wise decisions."

∞ 10 ∞

It seemed too intrusive to listen to Katherine's personal journal while she was right there in the room, so I headed downstairs, grabbed a diet soda out of the fridge, and plopped down on the cushions in the big bay window. This wasn't exactly the type of reading I had been thinking of when I saw the spot on my first visit to the house with my dad, but it was, as I had suspected, a very nice place to curl up with a book.

Figuring out how to use the controls took a few minutes. Once I had worked out the navigation, I visually scanned several of the early entries for the year. Most of them were fairly basic. The book seemed to be a cross between a journal and a reminder calendar— a note about a New Year's Eve party Katherine had attended with Saul; a lover's spat with Saul, who wanted to request larger quarters now that they were living together; a brief but embarrassingly vivid description of their Valentine's Day celebration—the type of notes that someone might jot in a diary if she were too busy and too happy for a lot of introspection. Other than a rant about a coworker who had too little respect for personal boundaries, the entries made almost no mention of CHRONOS or Katherine's day-to-day work with the organization.

I noticed a gradual shift in the entries by early spring. Tapping the page three times, as Katherine had done, I pulled up the icons again. Once I had adjusted the volume, I pushed the play button on an entry registered as 04202305_19:26. The hum began again and then the words on the page shifted downward, making way for a small video window, like a three-dimensional pop-up ad. I could see a small, clear image of a young woman—pretty, with delicate features—seated at a desk, with a hairbrush in her hand. She was wearing a red silk robe. There was a bed in the background, piled with clothing that appeared to have been dumped from a large brown traveling bag.

The woman's long hair, which was still damp, was a honey-colored blonde. The blue eyes were familiar, as was the voice when she spoke, and I realized that I was looking at a much younger and very annoyed version of my grandmother.

We're back from the meetings in Boston. It was very nice to be able to take a decent shower and wash my hair after over a week of nothing but sponge bathing. Saul . . .

The younger Katherine looked over her shoulder at a door, and then continued.

Saul is at the club again. God, how I hate that place. He always wants to see Campbell and his other Objectivist Club buddies first thing after a jump these days. He didn't even bother to come home first.

We had an awful fight in Boston and I don't know what in hell he thinks he's up to. He's likely to get both of us kicked out of CHRONOS, but of course he doesn't think that anything he's doing is any of my business.

He was actually at the podium—at the damned podium!—when I entered the auditorium. I wasn't supposed to be there. I was supposed to be at a meeting of the New England Woman's Club where Julia Ward Howe was going to be honored, but they rescheduled the meeting because Howe was ill—and wouldn't it have been nice if they had mentioned that little fact in the newspaper accounts CHRONOS gave me?

So . . . I walked back to the church where Saul was supposed to be attending an annual meeting of Congregationalist ministers. He should have been observing—blending, for God's sake—but no. He's at the front, leading a discussion about prophecy and miracles. Several of the more practical ministers in the audience were looking at him as though he were mad—and maybe he is. The others were hanging on his every word, like sheep, so I think maybe he did something—something against CHRONOS rules, no doubt—to get their attention.

She stalked away from the camera at that point, and I could see her back as she dug through a pocket in the traveling bag and pulled out a small opaque bottle with a label that I couldn't make out. Katherine shook the bottle at the camera.

And this . . . I was looking for his tooth powder, since I forgot to pack mine and this was in his bag. Cerazine. Of all things. He knows we are absolutely forbidden from taking any out-of-timeline articles—including pharmaceuticals—on a mission. He knows better.

When I confronted him, he said that it was also prescribed for his headaches. How stupid does he think I am? Cerazine for headaches? That's total bullshit. I looked it up just now and exactly as I thought—its only purpose is as an anti-cancer agent. That's it.

Maybe his intentions were good. He mentioned before that he was pretty sure one of the ministers he'd met had skin cancer—I'm sure he was just trying to help. But he has to understand the risks . . . he can't just . . .

And yes. I know, I know—I should write this up in my mission report anyway, regardless of his good intentions, or I should at least talk to Angelo about it. I know that.

The anger seemed to be draining away, and Katherine sat on the edge of the bed, her eyes closed. She didn't speak for about twenty seconds, and then continued.

He swears it won't happen again—he apologized for putting both of us at risk. He picked me the prettiest spring bouquet afterward. He just stood there, face like a sad puppy, with the flowers in his hand, saying how he'd been incredibly stupid and how he loves me so much.

And he does. I know he does. So I forgave him and we spent the rest of the day making up. Saul can make it really easy to forget why you were mad at him in the first place, until he does some other stupid . . .

I just wish he'd think before acting sometimes. He's so impetuous, and CHRONOS rules are in place for a reason. He can't just make an impromptu speech or give a friend a bottle of Cerazine—you never know what difference even a tiny change could make in the timeline.

I just wish he'd think . . .

The video ended, and I scanned a few more day-to-day entries before clicking on the visual for 04262305_18:22.

Katherine was dressed in what looked like business attire, a form-fitting gray jacket with a light blue scoop-necked shell underneath and a string of small black beads around her neck. Her hair was pulled back and her eyes were pink and a bit puffy around the edges, as though she'd been crying but had tried to hide the damage with another application of makeup.

So much for these damned implants being foolproof. I was really hoping it was just a stomach bug I'd picked up on the mission to Boston last week. One hundred and sixteen days—which would mean it happened after the New Year's Eve party.

And now—I don't even know if I want to tell Saul. He lied about the Boston trip. That wasn't just a whim, and it wasn't the only time he's spoken at the meetings. I think he's using a different name and maybe that's why the CHRONOS computer checks haven't caught any anomalies. But I spent this morning in the library—near the bathrooms in case the nausea hit me again—and I found several references that have me worried.

There are some scattered mentions of a traveling minister named Cyrus in the late 1800s and an entire article in something called the <u>American Journal of Prophecy</u> from September 1915 on how, at a small church somewhere between Dayton and Xenia, Ohio, this Cyrus predicted the Dayton Flood of 1913 in vivid detail—nearly forty years before the actual flood. He even pointed to a boy in the congregation and predicted that his home would be destroyed and that they would find a pig floating down the city street in his automobile. In 1877, no one was quite sure what an automobile was, but the comment was documented in an editorial in the local paper, and sure enough Danny Barnes found a pig sitting in his Model T as it floated away down a city street after the 1913 flood.

And the article talks about the rumors of miracles—dozens of healings that Brother Cyrus supposedly performed in the Midwest. Tumors. Pneumonia. Arthritis.

This isn't my specialty, but you don't live and travel with a religious historian for nearly three years without picking up the gist of it. I've heard Saul mention Sister Aimee, Father Coughlin, and dozens of others—but nothing about this guy Cyrus. And I doubt it is a coincidence that the dates when Brother Cyrus visited these towns sync up perfectly with several of Saul's jumps.

Brother Cyrus is Saul. I'm positive. This is all wrapped up with that lunatic Campbell and the others at his club.

And I also don't think it's a coincidence that Cyrus is the name of Campbell's damned dog—that gassy old Doberman who snarls and snaps at anyone who comes close.

Katherine took a swig of something from a pale blue bottle labeled *Vi-Na-Tality*. She grimaced as though it was sour and then rubbed her eyes, slightly smearing her makeup, before she looked back at the camera.

I have to tell Angelo. I don't have any choice. My only question is whether to talk to Saul first—to try to reason with him. Maybe if he knows I'm *pregnant—maybe he'll realize this isn't a game, that our lives and careers shouldn't be jeopardized due to some academic wager with Campbell. Saul loves kids—I think he'll be happy. And then if we go to Angelo together . . .*

She shook her head and sighed.

They are going to kick him out of CHRONOS. I can't see any way out of that. But maybe if he tells them everything, they'll let me stay—even if we're together. And at least one of us will have a decent job—he could stay with the baby or maybe they'd just let him do background research.

She massaged her temples briefly and closed her eyes.

He'll be home soon. He's been with Campbell and his other idiot friends all day. I'm scheduled for a solo jump tomorrow morning at nine. I'm going to try to talk to Saul tonight, and then with him or without him, I'm going to talk to Angelo tomorrow.

If it wasn't for the baby, I'd say to hell with him. But if Saul ends up on a labor farm, this kid isn't going to see much of his—or her—daddy. And maybe things will go okay . . . there's so much good in Saul. I just can't believe that he'd . . .

A deep sigh and then Katherine leaned forward to stop the recording.

∞

A gentle rain had begun outside while I watched the April 26th entry, and I heard a light pawing at the screen door. The earpiece brought in the sound from the journal so clearly that almost all background noise was canceled out. Judging from the reproachful look that Daphne gave me, she had been scratching at the door for a while. I was repaid for my negligence with a secondhand shower as Daphne shook vigorously to rid herself of the rain that had collected on her auburn coat.

Connor had come in around twelve thirty, while I was watching the journal entries. He hadn't said anything—just grabbed a fork and a plastic container of some sort from the fridge—so I assumed that lunch, like breakfast, would be just me and Daphne.

There were several other plastic containers in the fridge, but I had no idea what they were or how long they'd been there. I poured a glass of milk and began to forage through the pantry, eventually coming up with bread and peanut butter. The peanut butter was smooth, rather than the extra chunky I prefer, and there was no jelly other than mint (yuck), so I sliced a banana on top of the peanut butter and switched the journal back on, watching while I ate.

The last entry in the diary was dated April 27th at 0217 hours. When Katherine reappeared on the screen, I drew in a sharp breath, nearly choking on a bit of sandwich.

She had taken off the jacket and was wearing only the blue sleeveless shell. Her hair, which had been pinned up neatly before, was in disarray. The necklace was gone, and the angry red line around her throat made me suspect that it had been ripped from her neck. Her lower lip was split, and she held a small white pad against her right cheek, which was swollen. When she spoke, her voice was small and flat.

Saul knows—I mean, he knows that I know. I didn't even get to the part about the baby—I didn't dare, not when he was screaming at me that way. Maybe I should have started with that part . . . maybe he wouldn't have— but, no. I don't want him to know about the baby. Not now.

I think . . . I think he's gone crazy. I've never seen him like this . . . so angry.

Tears were pouring down her face and she stopped to collect herself before continuing. The traveling bag I had seen on the bed in an earlier video was neatly packed, but the rest of the room had been trashed. A large tube-shaped object that might have been some sort of lamp was shattered and the painting that had hung above the bed was now on the floor, with a huge rip in the center of the canvas.

When I told him that we needed to just go to Angelo and tell him before someone else discovered the same violations that I had, he began raving that I didn't understand the good that CHRONOS could accomplish if we harnessed the tools that we had at our disposal to change history, instead of just studying what century after century of idiots had created through their mistakes and blundering. About how this was his destiny and that Campbell had shown him that people just needed a strong leader to help them create the world that could be and should be. He had a plan, he said—and he wasn't going to let a bunch of academic fools at CHRONOS determine the fate of humanity.

And all the while, he kept hitting me. Saul never hit me before. Even when he was really angry, he would hit the wall or break something, but never . . .

I finally lied—I told him that he'd convinced me. That I loved him and we wouldn't go to Angelo and maybe I could help him change things. Just to make him stop. But he got this cold look in his eyes. He didn't believe me. And then he left.

I don't know where he's gone, but I've bolted the door. If he comes back, I'll call building security. I'm going to try and get a few hours of sleep and then I'm going to CHRONOS Med so that they can . . . repair this.

She pulled the pad away from her swollen cheek and gently touched the area, wincing at the pressure. There was a small abrasion near the cheekbone.

I'll tell them . . . something. I don't know. Then I'm going to talk to Angelo. He usually gets there by eight when we have jumps scheduled.

But . . . I'm going to message him first. Tonight. And I'm going to copy Richard on the note. I'm scared of what Saul might do—and if something happens to me, somebody at CHRONOS needs to know why.

I had been so immersed in the journal that I didn't realize Katherine was sitting across the table from me, a cup of tea and some apple slices in front of her. It was an odd sensation to look up from the younger, battered face in the video and see the older version, calmly sipping her tea.

"I just reached the part where Saul left," I said. "What happened the next day? Could they really repair your face?"

Katherine laughed softly. "Yes. There were quite a few improvements in medical care, and a minor dermal injury like that was a pretty easy fix. If we were still in that era, I wouldn't have these wrinkles at such a young age, either. That's one—of several—medical advances that I'd love to have access to now."

"Could they cure your cancer?" I asked.

Katherine nodded. "There has been a lot of progress in cancer research in the past few decades, but there will be much more about fifty years from now—assuming we can repair the timeline. If I was a patient in 2070, or even a bit earlier, my treatment would have been a fairly simple course of medication—they'd have caught it much earlier and it would be a bit like curing a difficult bacterial infection today. Instead, my body gets pumped full of much more dangerous chemicals and radiation. And they *still* miss the target."

Katherine shrugged and then continued. "All of which matters not in the slightest in this timeline, since I'm dead already. The next morning, I visited CHRONOS Med and told them I fell down in the tub. I doubt they believed me. It was surely not the first time a woman had shown up with a similar story. But I didn't want to do anything that might alert the rest of CHRONOS about Saul until I'd had a chance to discuss the situation with Angelo."

"Who exactly was Angelo?" I'd given up trying to figure out the correct tense for these people. If he was in Katherine's past, I was going to refer to him in the past tense, even though he wouldn't be born for several centuries.

Katherine took another sip of her tea before she answered. "Angelo was our direct supervisor. He trained both me and Saul. He was a good man and I was, in many ways, closer to him than I was to my parents, because he . . . well, he had the CHRONOS gene, too. There were things I could ask him that would have been incomprehensible to my father or even to my mother. From the time I entered the program when I was ten years old, Angelo was the one who guided my studies. I understood the CHRONOS bureaucracy well enough to know that he would also be in very hot water over Saul's actions. I wanted his advice, but I also wanted to warn him.

"After I finished at the med unit," she said, "I went to costuming so that they could get me ready for the jump. It was around eight, and between wardrobe and hairstyling, they usually had me ready for a mid-1800s trip in about half an hour. But that day—I don't think it had ever taken nearly that long. Several of the costuming staff had arrived late and they were backed up. I sat there in a chemise with my hair half up for nearly twenty minutes. The plan had been to give Angelo a few minutes to check his messages and then we could talk, but it was after nine forty-five when I finally got there. I was just going to stick my head in and say we'd talk after I returned."

"You couldn't have delayed the jump?" I asked. "It seems like a pretty important conversation to put off for several days."

Katherine shook her head. "Not without a major upheaval. The jump schedule is set a year in advance. The crews put a lot of effort into getting things ready, and I'd already gone through costuming. And . . . you're thinking linearly again, Kate."

I was getting a bit tired of hearing that. "Sorry. Like most people, I'm used to moving through time in a single direction—forward."

"My point is that the trip would, for me, seem to last the four days that it was scheduled," she explained. "But I didn't return four days later—that would have been a waste of time for the jump crew. We all left and returned from our jumps in batches. It was more expedient to set destinations for two dozen jumpers once or twice a week than to keep track of a bunch of individual travelers. When I got back to CHRONOS, only an hour would have passed for the crew, Angelo, and even Saul, since he was one of the dozen who wasn't on the schedule. The first cohort—the day-trippers who didn't need as much prep—had gone out at nine thirty and were scheduled to return at ten thirty. The twelve in my cohort would depart at ten with a set return for eleven o'clock.

"So it really wasn't much of a delay for anyone at CHRONOS, and I kind of liked the idea of having a few days to myself, away from Saul, to think about exactly what I wanted to do. The idea of being a single mother and what it might mean for my career scared the hell out of me."

Katherine shifted her gaze and stared out the window for a moment. "I don't know what time Angelo got to the office," she continued, "but when I got there, the door was open and one of his mugs was shattered on the floor. He always drank this really horrid herbal concoction in the mornings and the room smelled awful— there was a large puddle of the stuff on the carpet.

"I opened the closet to get a towel, and there was Angelo, shoved to the back, on the floor. There was a ring of adhesive wrapped around his mouth and his nose—the stuff is sort of like duct tape, but stronger. It's been over forty years and I can still see his face sometimes—bluish purple and his eyes wide-open."

"He was dead?" I asked.

"Yes," she said in a small voice. "It was long past the point where the med unit could have resuscitated him. I've always wondered, however, if it would have been different if I had gone to see him before I went to costuming."

I gave her a sympathetic look and shook my head. "More likely, Saul would have killed you as well, right?"

She shrugged and pulled her sweater closer around her shoulders. "Either way, I felt responsible. I knew I needed to call security, but I was fully dressed for 1853, with just my bag packed for travel, and I didn't have a communicator on me—I couldn't exactly take it on a jump to the 1850s, so I'd left it back in the locker with my other belongings. I walked down the hall to find another supervisor, but they had either stepped out or weren't in the office yet. And then I saw Richard, coming out of wardrobe. He had on the most outrageous tie-dyed shirt and bell-bottoms that were nearly as wide as my skirt—and it was clear from his expression that he'd gotten my email. He was as devastated as I was when he saw Angelo.

"Richard said everyone was probably already in the jump room, which made sense. We usually gathered around the platform—a large circular area—for ten minutes or so before getting into place, chugging a last cup of decent coffee or whatever. Richard and I were actually late—we only had three or four minutes before the jump."

"But the crew would cancel a jump in case of a murder, right?" I asked.

"Yes. But they never got the chance to cancel it. Richard and I told the jump coordinator—his name was Aaron—about Angelo. Richard also mentioned that he had seen Saul a little after eight, outside the building with a few of his friends from the Objectivist Club. Two of them were part of CHRONOS—a middle-aged historian who was scheduled to retire in a couple of years and one of the guys in the research section."

She gave me a little smile. "But I'm getting sidetracked. At any rate, Aaron was calling in this information to security headquarters, which was two buildings over, and we were just about to tell the others, when Saul came into the room—although I don't think anyone realized it was Saul at first. I know I didn't. He was dressed in a burqa—you know, the Middle Eastern head-to-toe covering?"

I nodded.

Her face was pale as she continued. "He was holding our colleague, Shaila, right in front of him, with a knife to her neck. And there was something odd strapped to her chest—a small square box.

"Saul ordered Aaron to cut off the call to security and told everyone to get into their places for the jump. And, of course, we all did what he said—I mean, the others didn't know about Angelo yet, but some crazy person in a burqa was holding a knife to Shaila." She shuddered. "He was staring straight at me the entire time, Kate, with the same expression I'd seen in his eyes the night before, like he was wishing the knife was at *my* throat. Richard saw it, too, and I think that's why he moved into my spot on the platform. I don't know if Saul noticed we switched or not—he was in Shaila's space, still keeping the knife to her neck."

Katherine gave me a rueful smile. "And the burqa was a very smart choice on his part."

"Because no one could see who he was?" I asked.

"Yes, it definitely kept him from being immediately identified, except for me and Richard, and we might not have recognized him if we weren't already forewarned—just the eyes through that tiny space? But," she said, "that's not the only reason. With all of the rest of us, you could make an educated guess as to *when* we were headed. Maybe not where, at least not after the mid-1900s when fashions became more global, but you could generally tell the era within a few decades from the way we were dressed. The burqa, however—women have worn that in many countries for thousands of years. It was still worn in a few isolated communities in my era. Shaila studied changes in Islamic culture over time and I knew she'd made jumps that ranged from the mid-1800s to the mid-2100s. So who knows when or where Saul landed? He could have been fully dressed for any era under that wrap.

"And it all happened so *fast*," she added. "When Aaron pushed the button to launch the jump, Saul shoved Shaila face-first into the center of the circle. She hit the platform and the very last thing I saw was a flash of white light and a loud whooshing sound, before I landed, hard, in the cabin just north of the field where they were holding the Woodstock festival. A hard landing is not normal—usually you just appear in the new location in whatever position you started. If you were scratching your nose in 2305, you'd still be scratching when you landed in 1853. But I landed flat on my back on the dirt floor, with my hoopskirt quite nearly inside out. The thing Saul strapped to Shaila's chest must have been an explosive—and I can only assume it was a powerful one since no one, to my knowledge, has been able to connect to CHRONOS since."

∞

The apple slices were still untouched on Katherine's plate and I realized that my own sandwich was barely half eaten. I took a few more bites and then asked, "Why did Saul think that destroying headquarters would make him able to jump from one time to the next, if he hadn't done that before?"

"I wondered that myself," Katherine said. "We all knew that we couldn't jump between stable points, without a trip back to CHRO-NOS. In training, they said this was an institutional check—a way for CHRONOS to keep tabs on our temporal location. The medallion reads the genetic structure of the jumper as you depart and Saul must have believed, with headquarters out of the picture, that he'd be a free agent, so to speak. Without the anchor at headquarters pulling him back, he assumed that he would be able to travel between stable points whenever he wanted. But the medallions were locked to return to CHRONOS—the only thing he did was ensure that we couldn't use them at all. I wasn't pleased at being stranded in an earlier century, and I didn't know when or where Saul landed, but it was at least nice to know that his plan hadn't worked."

"Kind of poetic justice," I said.

"Right. All of that changed, however, when Prudence disappeared—or, I suspect, when Prudence found Saul, whenever or wherever he was. Once he realized that the CHRONOS gene could be inherited, then it was only a matter of time before he found a way to manipulate that knowledge to breed people who could go where he could not."

"Just as you did . . . ," I reminded her in a soft voice.

"No, Kate," said Katherine. She got up from her chair and walked over to the window, putting her empty cup and barely touched plate on the counter. "I introduced two lonely people who had something in common—sadly not enough to make their relationship last, but they *were* in love at one time. I think you know that, if you're honest with yourself. I never forced anything, but just hoped for the best. And I got incredibly, unbelievably lucky."

She paced back toward me, a touch of anger in her voice. "Saul, on the other hand, left nothing to chance. Did you know that Cyrist clergy are required to marry only people approved by the Temple hierarchy? That leadership of a temple is hereditary—and always subject to approval by the International Temple? Did you know that?"

Yes, I had known that—although the reasons hadn't really clicked until Katherine spelled it out directly. "So all Cyrist Templars carry the CHRONOS gene?"

Connor, who had appeared at the doorway, answered my question. "We can only speculate at this point. But it seems likely. We'd know a lot more if we had a copy of their *Book of Prophecy*— assuming, of course, that the damned thing actually exists. The

Cyrists use smoke and mirrors so often to fool their believers that it's hard to tell what's real and what's a lie."

I gave him a long, hard look and then turned to Katherine. "And the two of you really think that I can change all of this? That I can what? Alter the timeline so that the Cyrists never emerge?"

Katherine shook her head, then stopped and threw her hands up in frustration. "To be honest, Kate, I don't *know*. When you were a baby, I just hoped that someday you could help locate Prudence—if only to give her a message for me. To try and get her to come back to this time and let me explain. But then I began to see subtle changes in the timeline. And last May—everything became clear. Saul was putting his plans into action. I wanted to come back here, to see if you would help, to train you—but the cancer hit and I basically had the choice of fighting cancer or fighting Saul. I'm still not sure I made the right choice . . ."

"You did," said Connor, who had appropriated Katherine's apple slices and was munching as he spoke. "Your treatment bought us some time, and we have a much better chance of succeeding if Kate is trained by someone with actual experience."

"It also *cost* us a considerable amount of time, and we have a more powerful enemy as a result," Katherine countered with a sigh. "But either way, it's done and we'll have to play with the cards we've been dealt."

I was still mulling over the point I'd made to Trey in the car. Would I be happy in a timeline where I was a museum piece who couldn't leave the protection of a CHRONOS key without ceasing to exist? No, but . . .

"What makes you sure that the timeline you want me to help you 'fix' is the correct one?" I asked. "Wouldn't it be more in keeping with your training for me to go back and tell you what Saul is planning and have him arrested? After all, he kills at least two of your colleagues in the process. And how many changes happened because of his actions? Even if all of those historians stranded at various points in time did their best to avoid changing things, they must have made some alterations to the timeline. And like you said, if you hadn't been stuck here, you wouldn't be dealing with cancer right now."

Katherine flushed and looked down at her plate, a bit of guilt in her eyes. "You're right, Kate. That's what I *should* have you do. There *were* some minor changes to history—I'll admit that. A few instances where someone made a discovery that was a bit too advanced for their time, if you know what I mean.

"But," she continued, "those changes were miniscule compared to what Saul is planning. And I haven't been a CHRONOS historian for many years now. I've got a personal motive here. So do you. So does Connor. The timeline I knew for over forty years is the *correct* timeline for the three of us, as long as we can stop Saul. Being cured of the cancer would be nice, but I've lived a long time. I'm not willing to trade your life and the lives of my daughters, not to mention Connor and his kids, for an extra decade or so added on to my own life. Angelo and Shaila didn't deserve to die that way, but from my perspective, they've been gone a very long time, and from your perspective, they never existed at all."

Connor nodded. "Katherine and I have debated this over and over, Kate. I'm not sure there *is* a correct timeline here. I'm in this to get my kids back and hopefully to give them a nice, Cyrist-free future. I don't know exactly what the Cyrists are planning, but based on what Katherine has told me, I don't think a future with Saul in control is one that is good for anyone. It's tougher for Katherine because she lost friends, but it's pretty simple for me. I couldn't care less which timeline is *correct*, because I know which one is *right*."

∞ 11 ∞

I put the book down by the computer and rubbed my eyes. "This is the world's most boring version of the Travel Channel. And the History Channel. Combined. And I don't much care for either of those . . ."

Connor snorted. "You have real-time views of hundreds of spots in history, all around the world, and you're bored?"

The Log of Stable Points was as deceptively thin as one of the diaries that I had been reading, but it contained even more information. It was similar to watching a small video, but these were live webcams, as best I could tell. I used the visual interface to choose a date and time and then blinked my eyes to select, at which point the translucent "screen" in front of me would display the geographical location at that specific date, in real time. It might sound cool in principle, but . . .

"Have you actually *watched* any of these?" I asked Connor.

"No," he admitted, continuing to scan the document on his screen as he talked. "I can see text on the page, but the earpiece that you're wearing is what triggers your ability to hear and see the video. I've tried it and I get occasional sound and images that break up every few seconds. It gives me a stomachache. Katherine can't really pull them in clearly either—we think it's because CHRONOS still had a lock on her signal when the explosion or whatever it was happened. But she has described some of them to me . . ."

"Did she tell you that most of these videos are of a deserted alley? Or woods? Or a dark broom closet?"

"Would you rather appear suddenly in the middle of a crowd? On top of someone? In some of the eras you're observing, that would be a quick ticket to burning at the stake, you know."

"Yeah, well, I just spent five minutes watching a squirrel in a park in Boston. Supposedly on May 5th, 1869, but it could just as easily have been yesterday. He looked like a very modern squirrel to me."

"Then you wasted five minutes." Connor sighed. "Focus on the elements that are *constant*, Kate. The squirrel isn't going to help you locate that stable point when you start doing test jumps, unless it happens to be a stuffed squirrel."

I picked the book back up and was scrolling through to find something remotely interesting when Daphne began barking, followed by the doorbell. A few seconds later, I heard Katherine's voice from below.

"Kate, you have a gentleman caller."

I rolled my eyes. "How is it that a grandmother from the twenty-fourth century sounds like she's from a Charles Dickens novel?"

Connor shrugged. "Maybe both eras seem like ancient history to her. Could you tell me the difference between what they called a boyfriend in 1620 and in 1820?"

This time I gave in to the temptation to stick out my tongue, and Connor surprised me by actually laughing.

I had purposely avoided thinking about whether Trey would come by like he said he would, mostly because I didn't want to feel let down if it didn't happen. The previous day had been too devastating for me to get my hopes up about anything. Still, I was ridiculously happy to know he'd kept his promise, and it took a conscious effort to keep from taking the stairs two at a time.

I could hear Katherine's voice in the kitchen. "So kind of you, Trey. Connor will certainly be pleased—he has an insatiable sweet tooth." She turned as I walked into the kitchen, two iced coffee drinks in her hands. "I'll just take these upstairs and leave you two young people to talk."

"Hi, Kate." Trey was crouched down, petting Daphne, whose tail was wagging happily. "I see they found you something to wear besides your school uniform."

I nodded, hit by an inexplicable wave of shyness. Despite everything that had happened the day before, we were still only a few hours removed from being strangers. "Connor is a surprisingly good shopper, as it turns out." I took one of the two remaining drinks, both of which were topped with whipped cream and a drizzle of caramel, and settled down on the window seat. "Thanks. How did you know that caramel and coffee is my favorite flavor combination?"

"Well—the coffee part I knew from yesterday. Caramel was just a lucky guess." He sat down next to me and his smile faded a bit. "So . . . are you okay? I mean, that was some hellacious day you had. I was thinking about it on the drive home and, well, I was worried about you. Kind of wished I could call or text you or something, but . . ."

"Hold on." I walked over to the counter near the telephone and found a notepad. I jotted down the screen name and free email account I had set up that morning while I was ordering some additional clothes and other necessities.

"These are both active now," I told him. "No phone yet—we're going to get one of those pay-as-you-go things next time Connor goes out. Katherine and Connor had to do some creative banking yesterday once they realized what happened. She kept a lot of cash on hand and his accounts are still active—I mean, he still exists, it's just that some things are different. I'm beginning to wonder how long we have before someone out there figures out that we are, technically, squatters. The house is shielded from the time shift, but . . . if Katherine doesn't own it now, someone must."

"Yeah, you'd think," he said. "So did you get all of your answers? It looked like the conversation was headed toward choppy waters when I left."

I shrugged. "I actually decided I wasn't up to that conversation last night. But we've made up for lost time since I woke up this morning." I began filling him in on the day's events and revelations, then hesitated a bit when I reached the part about the Cyrists.

"What religion are you, Trey?"

"Uh—Presbyterian, I guess? We don't really go regularly—at all, to be honest. Actually, I've probably been to more Catholic services. Estella likes to have company at holiday mass. Why?"

"Just making sure I wasn't about to step on any toes. This is going to sound kind of crazy, anyway." I took a deep breath and then continued. "How much do you know about the Cyrists?"

"About as much as anyone who isn't a Cyrist, I guess. They're pretty secretive—but I've known a lot of members, both here and abroad. They're everywhere in Peru. Not quite as numerous as Roman Catholics, but it's a close call. I don't like it when they try to lecture me on 'The Way,' especially when they seem so genuinely worried that 'The End' is near. But otherwise they seem harmless enough. And they do a lot of educational work with the poor and other charities, so . . ."

I explained about Saul's creation of Brother Cyrus and the Cyrist International, and as I expected, Trey's reaction was pretty much the same as mine had been. It was hard to fathom how an organization that had, in our view, existed long before we were born could have possibly been formed in just the past year.

"But you know," he said, considering the possibility, "if you wanted to build a power base that was outside the scrutiny of the government, a religious organization gives you a lot of room to maneuver. And the Cyrists have an odd mix of liberal and conservative views—the purity pledge, and then women can be ordained, but they have to marry another ordained minister. Most of the temples are led by a family, with control passed down from one generation to the next."

He paused, pointing at the CHRONOS medallion on my chest. "So if you took that thing to a Cyrist temple, you're saying that they would see it the way you do? And that they could use it?"

I nodded. "The leaders of the temple, yeah. Or at least that's the theory we're going on. They'd be able to power the diaries, too." I walked over to the table, then picked up Katherine's personal diary that I been listening to earlier and opened it. As with Charlayne, Trey could see the scrolling text, but he couldn't make it scroll.

I pulled my hair back a bit and removed the small disk from behind my ear. "Want to try it?"

"Sure."

My fingers brushed the side of his face as I reached up to tuck the little disk into the hollow between his ear and jaw. He pulled my hand toward him once the disk was in place, pressing the skin of my inner wrist against his lips. "You smell wonderful."

I blushed, and tried to slow my pulse. "It's probably the jasmine soap . . ."

He smiled, shaking his head. "The jasmine is nice, too—but it's mostly you. And this is going to sound crazy, Kate, but I missed you from the moment I left."

"I missed you, too." I looked down, still a bit embarrassed. Trey tilted my chin up until our eyes met and then he kissed me, his lips soft against mine. I leaned into him slightly, thoroughly enjoying the tingle that pulsed through me at his touch.

It took several seconds for me to notice the gentle scratching at my knee. When I pulled away from Trey, Daphne took a step back from the two of us. Her head was tilted to one side, a quizzical look in her soft brown eyes.

Trey laughed and scratched her behind the ear. "I think we have a chaperone. Yes, Miss Daphne. I'll behave." He looked back at the diary. "So . . . what is this ear thingy supposed to do? I don't see anything . . ."

I gave him a half smile. "And now we know for sure that you don't have the CHRONOS gene. I was seeing a video of a much younger version of my grandmother, filmed in 2305, explaining in pretty graphic detail what she was going to do to a coworker who wouldn't stop using her tea mug."

"I just see a bit of writing and some squares, there . . . and there." He removed the disk from behind his ear and faked a sad look. "Guess I can't be part of the secret club then."

"You say that as though it's a bad thing." I took the disk and pressed it back into place behind my own ear. "If you could operate this, they'd put you to work memorizing half a million jump locations—or stable points, as they're called. I feel like I've spent the day in a rather odd history class. As I'm reading Katherine's historical diaries, every now and then I'll see a question that Katherine asked, like, 'Who is the Infanta?' or 'What is a simoleon?'"

"In SimCity, a simoleon is money," Trey interjected.

"Yes—it was slang for a dollar back in the late 1800s. Anyway, I couldn't understand why she was writing the question when the answer was right there on the page."

"Maybe they have like a 28G network in the future and they just texted her back?" he suggested. "Seems unlikely, but . . ."

"The answer is actually really simple, if you're not thinking in a straight line. See this button—oh, no, I guess you can't."

He made a face at me.

"Sorry!" I gave him an apologetic smile. "At any rate"—I pointed to a section of the display that he couldn't see—"when Katherine or the other historians pushed that button, the diary recorded the question. At the end of the trip, the historian returned at a set time, but the diary itself was set to return twenty-four hours prior to the time that the historian left on the trip. As long as Katherine made it back to CHRONOS as scheduled, each time she jotted down a question in the diary, a response would pop up because the question had already been answered by the researchers during that day before the trip began."

"Okay—that kind of makes my head hurt."

"Welcome to my world." I grinned. "The bad news is that I can't use that neat little trick. The date can be altered, but Katherine is pretty sure that the diaries are hardwired to return to the CHRONOS research department. She tried to send a message when she got stranded and the diary just disappeared. Poof. So when I go, I'll have to rely on the information that's already in the book or in my head."

"So you're really going to be . . . using that thing soon?" He gestured toward the medallion, with a note of concern in his voice.

"Yes, although Katherine says that it will be short local hops initially. There are a dozen or so stable points in the DC area and I'll just do a quick shift there and back—a few hours or maybe a day ahead. That sort of thing." I sounded more confident than I felt. "But even that's a little while out."

"And how exactly are you going to change things? How are you, all alone, supposed to be able to restore the timeline? I mean . . ." He shook his head slowly, a very skeptical look on his face.

I shrugged. "We'll figure out when they killed Katherine—and then I'll warn her and try to get her to return to CHRONOS headquarters before it happens. I'm sure they had—will have?—some sort of emergency return-to-base protocol. We haven't really gotten that far."

"You said the guy on the Metro—the one that mugged you—was armed."

"Yeah, I think so. At the very least, he wanted me to believe he was armed." I paused. I was torn between kind of liking the fact that Trey sounded protective and not wanting him to think I was *totally* helpless.

"But if the Metro hadn't been crowded," I continued, *"and* if I hadn't suspected he had a gun, I would have tried to flip him. I've been taking karate since I was five. I have a brown belt. Or at least I had one . . . I guess that disappeared, too."

"Really?" His voice was serious, but his eyes were clearly laughing. "Think you can flip me?"

"I *could*," I teased. "But on a marble floor? You'd crack your skull when you hit. And we would scare poor Daphne. She's still looking a bit concerned from . . . earlier."

"I want a rain check, then. You don't look like you could flip anything much heavier than Daphne. No offense." He grinned at me. "Prudence Katherine Pierce-Keller, time-traveling ninja."

"Oh, ho . . . funny." I laughed and then faked an angry look. "Lawrence Alma Coleman the Third clearly likes to live dangerously."

Trey's smile lingered for a moment and then his eyes grew serious. "No, Kate, not really," he said. "And I think I'd be happier if you didn't have to, either."

∞

The next few weeks fell into a pattern. I spent my mornings reading the mission diaries that seemed the most likely targets for Katherine's murder. In the afternoons, I would focus on memorizing the stable points, and by the end of the second day, I had begun trying to pull up visuals of local stable points while holding the CHRONOS key. On the occasions I managed to hold the focus steady, I could see a holographic display. If I moved my eyes carefully, the medallion picked up those movements and I could adjust the digital display to set a date and time.

Within a week, I'd become pretty good at locating the specific stable points and even setting the time display. I had also learned how to set a new location—in this case, two points within the house—although this was, Connor said, not something you wanted to do unless you knew for certain that those points would *remain* stable. Otherwise, you might materialize over an empty elevator shaft or in the middle of a busy freeway.

Katherine said I was making incredible progress, but I found it frustratingly difficult to maintain focus with the medallion. At first, while holding it, I found myself repeating what had happened in the kitchen, when Dad was there—I would zip through a series of scenes, overwhelmed by sensory input and the absolute clarity of what I seemed to be seeing and hearing. On several occasions, I was again in the field with Kiernan. Watching him, feeling his warm skin beneath my fingers, was downright unnerving and I immediately put the CHRONOS key down and moved on to a different task when this happened.

And even though it was probably irrational, as the days went by, I found myself feeling disloyal and a bit angry at myself when Kiernan's face appeared. Trey's visits were the only thing I had to look forward to, especially since Katherine and Connor were adamant that I wouldn't be leaving the house at all for the time being. Trey came by most evenings and on weekends as well, and we would work on his homework or he'd bring DVDs. There was no TV in the house, so we ordered pizza and watched the movies in my room on the computer—at least Katherine wasn't a prude and allowed us some privacy. Even Daphne had begun to relax a bit in that regard.

Trey was funny, smart, and handsome—everything I would have looked for in a boyfriend. (Although, as a little voice in my head that sounded a lot like Charlayne pointed out, I had rarely given guys with hair as short as Trey's a second glance.) It was wonderful to curl up next to him, watching the Man in Black and Inigo Montoya battle left-handed atop the Cliffs of Insanity, or laughing at Shrek and Donkey or some silly comedy Trey had rented. He was clearly picking movies that he thought would make me smile and, at least for a short time, help me escape my present reality. I eventually satisfied his curiosity about my karate skills by flipping him—after setting out a pile of cushions and making sure Daphne wasn't around to object. Trey then pulled me down beside him when I tried to help him up and discovered my own personal kryptonite—terribly ticklish feet.

If it hadn't been for anxiety about the rapidly approaching trial jumps and a hollow ache whenever I thought about my parents, I would have been happy. And there was also the gnawing fear each time I watched Trey drive away—the fear that he wouldn't be back, that another time shift would occur and he wouldn't even remember my name.

All of this—the happiness, the fear, everything—made me miss Charlayne. In my previous life, she would have been texting me five times a day to find out how things were going with Trey and filling me in on which guy she was dating, considering dating, and/or planning to dump. I had gotten very used to using her as a sounding board for my ideas. Talking to her always made me feel stronger and more capable, and with so much on the line, I really needed that kind of support.

One night after Trey left, I brought the laptop over to the bed and stretched out, pulling up Facebook so that I could look at Charlayne's page. I knew that only "friends" could view some sections but some of her photos were public. I thought it might make me feel better just to see her smile.

Charlayne's page wasn't there, however, and that had me puzzled. She'd joined Facebook about a year before I transferred to Roosevelt, and had been the one who'd convinced me to start posting. If this latest time shift was fairly localized, as Connor had said, then the only thing that should have changed in Charlayne's life was that she and I never met—meaning her page should still be active.

I Googled Charlayne Singleton and her address. Nothing. I removed the address and typed in Roosevelt High School. Still nothing, so I decided to try her brother, Joseph. He had played three sports last year, when he was a senior, and his parents had a scrapbook filled with newspaper clippings on a table all by itself in the living room. Charlayne referred to it scathingly as the Joseph Shrine, but her dad said that she'd been the loudest voice cheering him on from the stands.

Several hits popped up for Joseph Singleton in the DC area—mostly sports-related, but not at Roosevelt. It was the second link from the bottom, however, that caught my eye—a wedding announcement in the *Washington Post* "Style" section. "Joseph Singleton, Felicia Castor." The wedding had been held in February at the Cyrist temple on Sixteenth Street, the same church I'd attended with Charlayne a few months before. I scanned the article and read that Felicia's parents had been members of the Temple since they were children—not a big surprise—but the next sentence was a shocker. "Parents of the groom, Mary and Bernard Singleton, have been members of the Temple since 1981."

A picture of the bridal party appeared below the text. Joseph, tall and handsome in a resplendent white tux, beamed happily at the camera, his arm around his new bride. There were three bridesmaids, each clutching a small bouquet of flowers against her chest. The face at the end caught my eye and I clicked to enlarge the photo. Her smile was more subdued than the wild, exuberant grin I'd hoped to see on her website, but it was definitely Charlayne—with the pink petals of the lotus flower clear and distinct on her left hand.

∞ 12 ∞

My first test jumps went smoothly, despite the fact that I was terrified. I set two stable points within the house—one in the library, which was my departure point, and one in the kitchen, which was my destination. I had planned to do my first jump from the library to the kitchen at around noon, when I had been down there eating lunch, but Katherine suggested avoiding situations where I might encounter myself.

"Why?" I asked. "What will happen if I see myself? Does it disrupt the space-time continuum or something like that?"

Katherine laughed. "No, dear," she said. "It's just very tough on your brain. I'd wait a bit, until you're more accustomed to the process. It's not something you want to do regularly, anyway, and never for more than a minute or so. You have to reconcile two conflicting sets of memories and it always gave me the most awful headache. Saul *claimed* that he had no problem with it, but everyone else I knew dreaded the test where we had to go backward and engage a past self in conversation. We'd been warned that we would be totally useless for hours afterward and they were correct—it's a real sensory overload. I heard some lurid stories about the early days of CHRONOS, when they were testing the limits of the system. A few people became rather . . . *unhinged,* if you will, trying to reconcile several hours' worth of conflicting memories. One girl had to be institutionalized. Really unpleasant."

That sounded almost as bad as disrupting the space-time continuum, so I discarded any ideas I might have had about sitting down for a long chat with myself. I decided to jump backward about three hours, to a quarter after twelve, when Connor had gone down to the kitchen to fix a sandwich. I was so nervous that it took nearly a minute for me to pull up the visual of the kitchen and another thirty seconds or so to set the arrival time. Once I had it locked in, I followed Katherine's advice and blinked my eyes, holding the image of the kitchen in my mind. When I opened my eyes again, I was in the kitchen. Connor was by the fridge, stacking ham on a slice of wheat bread. The kitchen clock read a quarter after noon.

"And what are *you* staring at?" he asked, glancing down at his shirt as though looking for spilled mustard or mayo.

I smiled at him and then focused again on the medallion, pulling up the image of the stable point that I'd set near one of the library windows. The image was clear enough that I could see Katherine's reflection in the window, looking toward the spot from which I had just embarked. I concentrated to pull up the time display, which was stamped with my departure time, plus five seconds. I blinked, as before, and opened my eyes to find Katherine a few steps in front of me, with an elated smile on her face.

"I didn't think I would ever see anyone do that again." There were tears in her eyes as she hugged me. "You know, Kate—we might just have a shot at this."

∞

The next morning, as I was reading through more of Katherine's diary entries, I realized we were taking the wrong track in trying to pin down the murder date. "Why don't I just watch the jump sites around that time for a few minutes just before Katherine's scheduled arrival? We start with the last jumps, and the first one where she appears—that would have to be the trip during which she was murdered, right? Because she wouldn't have been alive to make any jumps after that."

Connor and Katherine gave each other an amused look. "Now that we have someone who can make the CHRONOS equipment work, that's an excellent idea," Katherine said. "This time, *we* were the ones thinking too linearly, I guess."

Katherine hadn't included the arrival time in the list of dates she had printed, so Connor went back through the diaries to pull out that information, pausing every few minutes to pull another pretzel rod from the clear plastic tub by his keyboard. I wasn't sure which was more amazing—that Connor was thin despite the constant munching, or that his keyboard continued to function despite the variety of crumbs that were collected between the keys.

When he finished the list, I scanned through and noticed that several of the dates were repeated or overlapped. "Why are the same dates here twice?"

Katherine shrugged. "There were a lot of different events going on. Sometimes a meeting held at one end of the fairgrounds conflicted with something else we needed to observe—especially on jumps where Saul and I traveled as a team or where we were gathering some information for another historian. We did that a lot in Chicago, because we were the resident 'Expo Experts' and almost anyone who studied American history—politics, literature, music, science, you name it—had someone or something they wanted us to observe. For example—you've heard of Scott Joplin?"

I nodded. "A piano player, right? Ragtime?"

"Correct," she said. "Richard—you remember, the friend who swapped places with me on that last jump? Well, he had information that Joplin led a band at a Chicago nightclub during the time of the fair, but there were no specifics. He would have had to spend a lot of time preparing for an 1890s trip, but it was a pretty simple matter for Saul and me to ask around, make a side trip to hear Joplin, and take back a recording for Richard to analyze. I also picked up some data for a colleague studying serial killers—there was a rather nasty one preyeing on young women during the Expo. And I got a brochure announcing Colored American Day at the fair for someone studying race relations."

She made a face. "That was an interesting one—the leaders of the Expo decided it would be a good idea to give away watermelons to commemorate the occasion. Frederick Douglass was there representing Haiti—he was consul general to Haiti at the time. Let's just say he was *not* amused."

I laughed. "I would imagine not. But wasn't it kind of risky to have several versions of yourself wandering around the same place?"

"Not really," she said. "There were thousands of visitors each day, so as long as we kept away from the area where our earlier selves were working, there really wasn't much chance of anyone spotting both sets of us. The CHRONOS costume and makeup department was also incredible. I saw myself on one occasion crossing the street, and I didn't even realize it was me until I was halfway down the block. And we generally kept a pretty low profile, observing but not really interacting much—well, I did, at any rate. Saul clearly had different ideas near the end."

The last jump before Saul sabotaged the system was to Boston 1873, when he and Katherine had quarreled. There were one or two other jumps to Boston, but most of the twenty-two jumps prior to that were all to Chicago, at various points during the year 1893.

"The Expo was in 1893, right?" I picked up the Log of Stable Points and began scrolling backward, beginning with the last entries on the list. "I really think it's going to be one of those dates. After all, it was the 1890s diary that was stolen on the Metro."

I started with Boston, however, since those jumps were the last two that they had taken together. There were seventeen stable point locations listed in the Boston area, but Katherine said that she and Saul had only used the one a few blocks from Faneuil Hall on their trips. The location, like many others, was a narrow alley. I pulled up the stable point and set the time for one minute prior to Katherine's scheduled arrival: 04181873_06:47—April 18th, 1873, at 6:47 A.M.

A large rat ran into view after a few minutes, which kind of creeped me out, and I nearly lost focus. A few seconds later, however, a man appeared—so close that I could have counted individual threads in the weave of his black coat. As he moved away, and his face came partially into view, it was clear that this was Saul Rand—above-average height, with dark brown hair, pale skin, and the same intense expression I had seen in the two images in Katherine's diaries. His beard was trimmed closely with no mustache, and my first impression was that my grandfather had been a slightly shorter, more handsome, but not very pleasant Abraham Lincoln, although that impression was at least partly due to the tall, black stovepipe hat on his head. Katherine was not with him.

Saul turned abruptly in my direction and I drew in a sharp breath as his eyes, narrowed and piercing, stared almost directly into mine, as though he knew I was watching him. I finally exhaled when I realized that he was just scanning the alleyway to make sure he'd arrived unobserved.

I tried the next-to-last jump and drew a total blank. The jump was either rescheduled or Saul skipped it, because although I waited several minutes, no one showed up, not even my good friend, the rat.

Since Katherine hadn't appeared at either of the Boston jumps, I crossed that city from the list and focused on Chicago. There were four stable point locations listed within the fairgrounds, and the one used for most of the jumps was labeled as the Wooded Island— a secluded, shady area, with floral vines and lush foliage. I could see a cabin of some sort about twenty yards away, with large animal horns scattered about the exterior and a few park benches along the pathway. No one appeared on the first date I tried, although I observed, through the cover of the leaves surrounding my vantage point, a few people strolling along the sidewalk in the morning light.

On the next attempt, however, I hit pay dirt. About fifteen seconds into the surveillance, my view was suddenly obstructed by two figures. As they moved away from the stable point, I could see that one of them was Katherine. I immediately felt two strong, conflicting emotions—relief that we'd found the correct time and dismay that I would soon have to dress in something like the ornate period costume that she was wearing.

The tall man from the 1873 jump was next to her. His beard was gone, replaced by a long handlebar mustache. He gave the surroundings another quick scan, as he had done on the Boston jump, and then grabbed Katherine's elbow to help her up the slight incline to the walkway. She held up the skirt of her gray dress. It was trimmed in dark purple and the outfit was topped off by a small hat with a ridiculously large lavender feather. As the two of them walked past the wooden cabin, a dark-haired boy of about eight or nine emerged from inside, a broom in his hand, and began to sweep away the leaves that had accumulated on the walkway.

I pulled my gaze sharply to the left to turn off the log display. The abrupt visual change from an autumn morning in the park to the interior scene of the library, where Connor was hunched over a computer and Katherine was replacing books on a shelf, was a bit disconcerting.

I carried the list over and put it on the table beside Connor, tapping the target date with my fingernail. "Found it. Chicago. A jump from April 3rd, 2305, to October 28th, 1893. Looks like it was the only jump to that date."

Connor nodded at first, and then shook his head, pointing to an entry near the top of the log with one of the pretzel rods he was munching. "Yeah, the only jump specifically to the 28th—but look, here's a two-day solo trip, October 27th to 29th, from February 2305."

"Great," I replied, rolling my eyes as I sank down into Katherine's desk chair. "So there will be two Katherines strolling around the fair to confuse me."

"Don't know what you're complaining about," he said, taking another bite of pretzel. "At least *you'll* get out of the house for a while."

Katherine took the list from Connor. "I remember those trips—there was a lot going on. The fair was scheduled to close at the end of October, and it was horribly crowded with visitors who had procrastinated but didn't want to miss out. There was a huge celebration planned for the last day, with fireworks and speeches, but the murder meant that everything was canceled."

"Murder?" I asked. "Oh, yeah—you mentioned something about a string of killings at the fair . . ."

"No, no. This was separate. An assassination, actually."

"McKinley?"

She shook her head. "President McKinley was killed at the next World's Fair, in New York, in 1901. This time, the target was the mayor of Chicago. Carter Harrison. A very nice man . . . good sense of humor. Saul and I spent most of the day with him on the second jump and I was sad to think that he would be dead before the day was over." She paused for a moment and then began to thumb through the stack of diaries on the desk. "Oh, right. That's the diary Kate had on the subway. Hold on, it will just take a second to access the backup file."

She grabbed the top diary and flipped it open, clicking a few buttons to locate what she needed. "Okay, here we go. The February jump was to view the reaction to the assassination and the final days of the fair—more general research for CHRONOS than part of my individual research agenda. Cultural research on the Midway, mostly. It was a nice little microcosm, with workers imported from around the world mixing with people from around the United States who had come to Chicago in search of work—the Expo took place in the middle of a major economic depression, you know."

She chuckled. "I was posing as a writer for a travel magazine—complete with a huge, heavy Kodak camera around my neck. They called it a portable camera, but I was always very happy to take it off at the end of the day. Cameras were the latest fad, especially among the younger fairgoers—the older folks called them 'Kodak fiends' because they would jump out and snap pictures without asking.

"It was a fun trip," she added, "but not very eventful, as I recall. I interviewed several people from the Dahomey Village and picked up a bit of information for a crime historian on a waitress at the German beer garden who had just disappeared. He thought she might have been one of the victims of the serial killer, but I never found any evidence one way or the other.

"The jump from April," she said, tapping the screen again, "was triggered by an event that caught my attention during an earlier trip—American Cities' Day, when about five thousand mayors from around the country visited the Expo. Mayor Harrison was scheduled to show a delegation of about fifty mayors and their spouses around the fair, prior to his big speech before the full assembly of mayors that afternoon. One of the individuals in this select group was the first female mayor in the nation, Dora Salter, also a leader in the WCTU—Woman's Christian Temperance Union. Prohibition? Anti-alcohol?"

I had a vague recollection of someone's ninth-grade history project about Carry Nation bashing up a bar with her ax, so I nodded.

"Salter was no longer an active mayor at the time, and I suspect that someone with a twisted sense of humor added her to that invitation list," Katherine continued. "Carter Harrison was well known for his gallantry toward the ladies, but he was a hard drinker and most definitely *not* in favor of the WCTU's anti-vice agenda. I thought there might be some interesting conversations between the two, so Saul and I blended into the group, with him claiming to be the mayor of a little town in Oregon and me as his wife. But it was really a waste of time—Salter turned out to be this meek little mouse of a woman and the two of them never even spoke after they were introduced."

"You have to wonder why she ran for political office if she was shy. Especially back then," I added, "when most women couldn't even vote."

Katherine nodded. "Women could vote in local elections in Salter's state—Kansas—but she didn't actually choose to run. Some of the men in the town added her name to the ballot as a joke, and they were very surprised to discover that most of the women and quite a few of the men preferred her to the other candidate. I do have to admire her for turning the tables on them and actually taking the job when she was elected, but that was apparently the extent of her activism for women's rights.

"A very disappointing trip overall," Katherine said. "Although I did finally manage a ride on the Ferris wheel. The line was always too long when I went on my few solo jumps, and Saul was never willing to wait for me when we went together—he is terribly afraid of heights. This time we were in the group with the mayor, however, so we were moved straight to the front of the line. A lot of people decided to wait on the ground, but Saul didn't want to look like he was a coward. So he was green the entire time and nearly hurled on the peanut vendor when we got off," she added, with a very satisfied smile.

∞

With the date and general location of Katherine's murder nailed down, we shifted the focus over the next few days to getting me ready—both mentally and physically—to attend the Exposition. The physical side of the preparations involved yards and yards of silk and lace and a corset that I loathed from the first moment it arrived via UPS. Katherine still had her clothes from the planned 1853 jump, but they were forty years out of date. That would hardly do in an era where fashions shifted with the whim of Parisian designers, even though it took several months for news of those changes to reach America from across the ocean.

"So why can't we just forget all this and let me go dressed as a barmaid?" I asked. "Or one of those Egyptian dancers I saw in the photographs? They looked pretty comfortable . . ."

Katherine sniffed disdainfully as she sat down at the computer and opened a browser window. "You've read enough about this era that you should understand their perceptions of class, Kate. You have no idea where you'll need to go and whom you'll need to speak with. A barmaid could never approach the group I was with that day without drawing unnecessary attention. If you're dressed as a lady, you can ask a question of anyone, regardless of their social class. The proper attire opens doors . . ."

Katherine ran a search for historical images of dresses from the 1890s and I was surprised to see that there were actual fashion magazines from that era available online. A publication called *The Delineator* even included tips on how to create the dresses, accessories, and hairstyles.

A local bridal designer came to the house the next day to help design my costume. She raised a well-manicured eyebrow at Katherine's insistence that the dress be reversible, with a different color fabric on the inside, and that it have two hidden pockets, one in the bodice of the dress and another in the undergarments.

This made sense from our perspective, since I might have to stay an extra day and couldn't easily walk around the Expo with luggage. I also needed quick access to the CHRONOS key, and Katherine was determined that I have a place to hide a spare medallion and some extra cash, just in case. However, a reversible dress with hidden pockets—heavily lined to contain the light from the medallion—made little sense for a costume party, which was our cover story. After a brief hesitation, the designer simply nodded, showing she was savvy enough not to question eccentric requests by someone willing to pay her outrageous prices.

My role in all this was to stand impatiently as the assistant took my measurements and then to endure repeated fittings, pin sticks, and admonitions to stand straight and stop slumping. The end result was an outfit that, while admittedly the height of 1893 fashion, was going to be hot, stiff, and a royal pain to wear.

When we weren't engaged in fittings, I read and reread Katherine's diary entries for the target dates, memorized maps of the Exposition, and combed through dozens of historical accounts of the exhibits and of 1890s Chicago. In addition to the accounts in Katherine's library, I pulled up documents from the internet.

On two different occasions, Trey rented documentaries about the Exposition and Chicago in the late 1800s. Several were about the Exposition itself, and they really brought the images and stories I'd been reading to life.

One of them gave me the creeps, however. It was filmed like a horror movie, but it was actually a documentary about Herman Mudgett, the sociopathic killer Katherine had mentioned. Posing as Dr. H. H. Holmes, a physician and pharmacist, Mudgett had killed dozens, maybe even hundreds, of young women during the time he lived in Chicago. Several of them were women he had married or simply charmed out of their money, but most were total strangers. He had the perfect setup—a building he owned near the Expo was transformed into the World's Fair Hotel, catering to female visitors. Some of the rooms had been specifically equipped for torture; in other cases, he piped gas into tightly sealed, windowless rooms through small holes he drilled into the wall, and watched through a peephole as the women asphyxiated. Then he dumped their remains into lime pits in the basement and, in many cases, sold their perfectly articulated skeletons to medical schools for a bit of extra cash.

We didn't make it all the way through that show. I'm not a big fan of horror movies, even of the true-crime variety, so I ejected the DVD when it became clear that the three little kids Mudgett had been watching for a business partner weren't going to survive, either. We spent the next hour watching a much more pleasant documentary about Jane Addams and her efforts to help Chicago's poor. I was still on edge, so we rewatched *The Princess Bride* to get my mind off the murders. And despite all of that, I had to sleep with the bathroom light on that night.

Most of the history that I read and watched was the same between the two timelines, except for a few references to Cyrist leaders who, like the leaders of all other major religions, had attended the World Parliament of Religions at the Expo in late September. And there were some other oddities, such as a picture of a smiling Mark Twain entering the tethered balloon ride with several young Egyptian dancers—although Twain had, according to Katherine's history books from the pre-Cyrist timeline, fallen ill upon his arrival in Chicago and never left his hotel room.

Even though I've never had a great passion for history, I found the reading more interesting than I would have imagined. It felt less like research and more like reading a tour guide in preparation for an upcoming vacation, even if it wasn't exactly a trip I would have chosen on my own.

I was also working on the practical side of things, perfecting short, in-house jumps with the medallion. I could now focus on a stable point and set the display in under three seconds. I even showed off for Trey a few times, popping up in the foyer when he arrived for a quick kiss, and then back to the library.

I also set an extra stable point in the living room and confirmed that I could, as Katherine had suspected, jump from point

A to point B to point C, without returning to point A first. The restrictions that had limited the CHRONOS historians to round-trip jumps were a safety feature mandated by headquarters, and not something that was hardwired into the medallion. Unlike Saul, Katherine, and the other original CHRONOS crew, I could travel when and where I chose, assuming the existence of a nearby stable point. We also *suspected* that I could travel back to a known stable point from a location that hadn't been previously set as a stable point, although Katherine wasn't keen on having me test that possibility. Connor couldn't think of any logical reasons why it wouldn't work, but Katherine insisted that we should consider that to be a last-resort, emergency exit option.

The next test, before attempting a long-distance jump, either geographical or chronological, was a short hop to a local stable point. The nearest location in the CHRONOS system that was easily accessible was the Lincoln Memorial—to the left of Lincoln's chair, outside the roped-off area, in a section that was somewhat obscured by shadows. It was listed as a stable point between 1923 and 2092. I was tempted again to ask Katherine exactly what happens in 2092, but suspected I would still be told that it was none of my business. The memorial was staffed from 8 A.M. to midnight—and was also more likely to have visitors during those hours—so we decided that a 1 A.M. arrival would be a safe bet. Katherine and Connor were both concerned that, this early in the training, I might get there and not be able to lock in the return location, so Trey had offered to be there with a ride home, just in case.

We scheduled my departure for Friday at 11 P.M. Trey was in the library when I left. I gave him a big, brave smile and said, "One A.M., Lincoln Memorial. Don't stand me up, okay?"

He squeezed my hand and said with a huge smile, "Our first date outside the house? I'll be there, don't worry."

Katherine pressed her lips together firmly, her eyes anxious. "No dawdling, Kate. I mean it. You come straight back, okay?"

"She will," Trey said. "We're just joking. No unnecessary risks, I promise."

She gave him a brusque nod and turned back to me. "You don't have to be in the exact same spot when you leave—the key has a reasonable range on it—but get as close as you can."

I released Trey's hand and pulled up the stable point. I had been practicing the location all day, and had watched hundreds of visitors climb the steps to the memorial, taking photographs and videos, but I now took the additional steps of pulling up the time display and locking in my arrival time by shifting my gaze on the display to the appropriate options and blinking once. It was almost like a mouse click, although I had to wonder what happened if you were trying to select and dust blew into your face. I glanced at the final control, then took a deep breath and blinked.

A warm evening breeze told me that I had arrived before I even opened my eyes. After looking around for a minute, I saw Trey leaning against one of the nearby columns. He was holding a brown bag and a large soda.

I walked toward him, breathing in deeply. "Oh, yum—I smell onion rings."

"Yes, you do," he replied. I had confessed a few days before that I really, really missed the onion rings from O'Malley's, the neighborhood bar and grill where Mom and I often ate on weekends.

I smiled and stood on tiptoe to kiss him. "Thank you. But you're spoiling me, you know. And two minutes—then I should head back. Not that Katherine would know either way," I admitted, "but we promised."

He sat the bag and soda on the steps and pulled me into his arms. "I know, I know. We'll eat fast—I'm going to make you share those onion rings. I even brought a mint, so if you eat neatly for a change"—he laughed as he blocked my punch to his arm—"*and* if you avoid breathing in their faces when you return, our secret is safe."

It was a beautiful night and the romantic glow from the lights and the reflecting pool made me wish we could do ordinary things like this all the time. I was feeling more and more like someone under quarantine.

Trey was apparently on the same wavelength. "Too bad we can't do this more often. Especially with your birthday this weekend . . ."

"And how did you know my birthday was this weekend?" I had purposefully avoided thinking about the day, knowing that it would only make me think of past birthdays, Mom, Dad, and everything else that was now missing.

He gave me a sly smile. "I have my ways. Think Katherine would give us a temporary furlough for a night out?"

I sighed. "I think we both know the answer to that. This will probably be our only night out for some time, unless you'd like to come with me to the World's Fair?"

"Chicago I could probably do," he said. "Eighteen ninety-three might be a problem, however."

"True," I admitted.

I hesitated for a moment, taking another onion ring from the bag. There was one thing I really wanted to know more about—and one person I felt I needed to see—before making the trip to Chicago.

"Maybe you could take me to church instead?"

"What?" Trey laughed for a moment and then stopped. "Oh. Charlayne?"

I nodded. "She's not the entire reason, but yes, I want to see her." I turned toward him. "I also want to see what they're up to, Trey. The Cyrists. I mean, right now, my main motivations for changing this timeline are personal—getting my parents back and being able to leave the house without this damned medallion. But Katherine and Connor seem to think that the Cyrists are . . ."

"Evil?" he asked.

"Yeah. I guess that's the right word. Granted, I've only been to one service at the Cyrist temple—and that was before the last time shift—but I just didn't get that sense. And, on top of that, I can't say I'm totally down with the idea of a future where many of the most important decisions you make in life are decided while you're still an embryo."

"I know," he said. "I can understand why they do it, but it doesn't leave much room for individual choice, does it?"

"No, it doesn't. I don't doubt that Saul's methods are evil—I mean, he pretty clearly killed Katherine to set this up—but what about the larger movement? I feel like there's so much that I don't understand. And, if the Cyrists as a whole are as rotten as Connor and Katherine believe them to be, I guess I want to try and get a better idea of what I'm up against."

Trey thought for a minute, and then nodded, giving my shoulders a squeeze. "When and where? They have something going on at the temples most days, but the main services are on Sunday mornings, right?"

"They are. Could you pick me up here around seven, before the guards arrive? If I get caught . . . sneaking out, I'll just act like I'm practicing a short jump. I do that enough that Katherine shouldn't think anything of it. And I've been to the temple on Sixteenth, so I'm at least somewhat familiar with the layout."

"Why do you need to know the layout?" he asked, a suspicious look in his eye.

I shrugged. "Well . . . I *mainly* want to see Charlayne and I'm *probably* just going to ask some questions, but I might need to . . . look around a bit. I don't know. I'm playing this by ear."

Trey frowned slightly and then leaned his head down to nibble on my earlobe. "It's a very pretty ear, too. Let's just hope we can keep it attached to your head. Those Dobermans look hungry."

I elbowed him. "They don't keep guard dogs on the prowl during services, silly. But if you're worried, we'll bring a few of Daphne's dog biscuits to bribe them."

The onion rings were now reduced to a few tasty crumbs at the bottom of the bag. I gave Trey a good-bye kiss and popped the mint into my mouth as I walked back over to the spot near Lincoln's chair. "I'll see *you* again in just a sec," I said, pulling up the library stable point with the medallion. "But you'll next see *me* tomorrow night for dinner—so drive safe, okay?"

Now that I wasn't nervous, I accessed the location quickly, and when I opened my eyes again I was back in the library, where Trey, Katherine, and Connor were staring at me, with slightly anxious expressions.

"Lincoln sends his best," I said with a grin.

A few minutes later, I walked Trey to the door, since he still needed to get across town for our meeting. "Unbelievable," he said, when I kissed him good night and slipped the last little sliver of the mint into his mouth with my tongue. "You taste like minty onion rings. I was going to surprise you, but it really doesn't seem like a surprise now."

"It was very sweet of you and it *will* be a surprise. Or *was* a surprise," I amended. "Take your pick."

∞ 13 ∞

Trey left around ten on Saturday, a bit earlier than his usual weekend departures. I wanted him to get a good night's sleep, since he would be picking me up bright and early the next morning at the Lincoln Memorial. I'm personally more of a night owl, and it would be easier for me to "sneak out" when Katherine and Connor were asleep, so I planned to head down to the kitchen around midnight. It would have been safer to make the jump from my room, but I was reluctant to add another stable point to the list. I wasn't exactly sure how to delete them and didn't really want to draw attention by asking.

I constantly found myself forgetting that my closet and dresser didn't hold the same contents as their counterparts in my old room, so it didn't occur to me until shortly after Trey left that I had no appropriate "church clothes." I sorted through the few outfits that I'd ordered online and selected the dressiest shirt in the bunch, which was a loose floral tunic, and a pair of slim black jeans. My only shoes, other than a pair of sneakers and a pair of sandals, were the black flats I'd last worn to school. I couldn't entirely remove the scuffed mark from where Simon had smashed my foot on the Metro, but they would have to do.

I put on a bit of makeup and some small gold hoop earrings, then pulled the sides of my hair back with a peach-colored clip that matched the blouse. The pocket copy of the *Book of Cyrus* that

I had ordered a few weeks earlier was on the nightstand, where I'd left it the night before. It was one of two core documents of the Cyrist faith—the other, the *Book of Prophecy* that Connor so wanted to get his hands on, was an internal document available only to higher-echelon members. Cyrist International was very protective of its copyright on the *Book of Prophecy,* and the few disgruntled members who had leaked sections of the book online or in exposés about the church's leaders had landed in the middle of costly lawsuits. In every case, the Templars had won.

The *Book of Cyrus,* on the other hand, would have lost any copyright battle, were it not for the fact that the scriptural sources it cribbed content from were well past the copyright expiration date. The short volume was a mishmash of quotes from the Bible, the Koran, and other religious texts, with a few original ideas added in here and there. I'd found it much more effective than a sleeping pill—five minutes of reading and my eyelids began to droop.

I tucked the small book into the back pocket of my jeans, slipped the CHRONOS key inside the tunic, and surveyed my reflection in the mirror. From what I remembered of the service I'd attended with Charlayne, I'd never be mistaken for a devout Cyrist—with or without the lotus tattoo—but I looked presentable enough that I might pass as a prospective convert.

At the last minute, I turned back. I'd gotten used to seeing the blue glimmer of the CHRONOS medallion through the fabric of my clothes on the rare occasions I ventured beyond the protective zone, but it occurred to me that I might actually encounter others who could see the light from the key once we were at the temple. I slipped off the tunic and began layering camisoles over the top. The first two were thin and I could still see the glow pretty clearly. I pulled a third from the dirty clothes hamper and added it, and then finally a black tank top—pretty much every item in my limited wardrobe. When I was finished, I could still detect a very faint blue, but it was masked by the floral pattern of the tunic and I decided it would have to do.

Sneaking out felt wrong. I'd never so much as broken curfew, although there had been a close call after a party at the house of one of Charlayne's cousins. If Katherine or Connor saw me headed downstairs, it wouldn't usually be a big deal—I often got the urge for a midnight snack, but never fully dressed and in makeup. I kept all of the lights off and was still nervous when I reached the kitchen. My hands shook slightly as I pulled up the Lincoln Memorial, locking in the location and setting the time for just over seven hours later.

Trey was waiting in the same spot as last time. He looked very handsome in a dark blue shirt and gray dress pants.

"What, no onion rings?"

"I have something even better planned," he said with a smile. "Services don't start until eleven, and I know that Katherine and Connor's culinary skills are . . . well, limited." That was putting a polite face on things—on the few occasions that he'd eaten a full meal at Katherine's, I'd been the one doing the cooking. "So what would the birthday girl say to a real home-cooked breakfast that she doesn't have to cook?"

My face fell. "Oh, Trey—I don't think we should. What if . . ." I didn't think breakfast at his house increased the chances of me getting caught—but I was terrified at the thought of meeting his family, and I could tell from the look on his face that he knew exactly what I was thinking.

"Dad is going to love you. Don't look so scared. It's too late to call and cancel, because Estella is already cooking. And you really don't want to cancel anyway—her *huevos divorciados* are *muy delicioso*."

"Divorced eggs?" My Spanish wasn't nearly as proficient as Trey's, but I was pretty sure that's what he'd said.

"You'll see," he said, laughing.

∞

Estella was well under five feet tall and very round, with vivid red curls that were clearly not part of the natural color palette of her native Guatemala. She gave me a quick up-and-down appraisal when she opened the door and, her judgment apparently complete, broke into a huge smile and pulled me down for a hug.

"Lars is in the shower—Sunday is his only day to sleep in—but he'll be down soon. I am sorry that Trey's mama is not here to greet you, but I welcome you for her. When she is back from Peru, she will be so happy to meet the young lady who has made her baby smile."

Trey's blush at that statement matched my own, and Estella laughed, leading us both into the big yellow kitchen. I was relieved that breakfast would be an informal occasion in the kitchen rather than at the long, formal dining table I had glimpsed from the foyer. Estella put us to work setting the table and slicing fruit as she scurried between fridge and stove, shooing Dmitri (who was clearly in search of his breakfast) out of her way and asking me a steady stream of questions as she worked. I answered as best I could, piecing together bits of my old life (Mom, Dad, and Briar Hill) and my new one with Katherine and Connor.

By the time breakfast was ready, Estella had managed to make Trey blush three more times. I learned about his first steps and an unusual encounter with the tooth fairy when he was six, and she had just finished telling me about Marisol, the first girl he'd had a crush on—"not nearly as pretty as you, *querida*"—when she broke off to greet Trey's dad. "Sit, *mijo*. I will bring you coffee."

Mr. Coleman was nearly as tall as his son. He had darker hair, but it was instantly clear where Trey had gotten his smile. The gray eyes were also the same, if slightly distorted by the horn-rimmed glasses that made him look a little bit like an older version of the lead singer from Weezer. "Kate!" he said, the smile growing a bit wider. "I'm glad to see that you're real. I was beginning to think

Trey had invented a girlfriend to keep Estella from trying to fix him up with girls from her church."

"Ha. Very funny, *mijo*." Estella slid a plate of *huevos divorcia-dos*—two eggs, one covered with green sauce and the other with red—in front of him. Trey was right; they were delicious. In fact, the entire breakfast was so good and Estella so insistent we eat more, more, that I was amazed Trey could actually live there and still manage to stay thin.

The four of us engaged in breakfast chitchat for a few minutes while we focused on our food, and then Mr. Coleman surprised me with a more pointed question. "So I understand you're off to do some detective work this morning?"

I gave Trey a startled glance and he jumped in to explain. "I told Dad that you're worried about Charlayne's sudden interest in the Cyrists."

Estella's expression gave little doubt about her opinion on the matter. "You are a good friend to be worried, *querida*. Those Cyrists are no good. Always going on about the riches God will give you here on earth if you are strong—never anything about how you should treat others. I watch that preacher on TV one morning—Patrick Conwell—all the time he asks for my money and says I will get it back ten times over. Same thing they say in Atlantic City. I don't trust him. Don't trust any of them."

"Charlayne has a good heart," I said, "but she can be a bit . . . easily influenced, I guess? That's why I'm concerned." I hadn't caught the televised worship services, due to the lack of TV at Katherine's, but I'd seen several segments from Cyrist ministers, including Conwell, the current Templar for the Sixteenth Street congregation, that were posted online. His smile was too polished and everything about him screamed fraud to me. When I'd attended the services earlier in the year with Charlayne, an older man had given the sermon, so I assumed that Conwell was his replacement in this timeline. The older guy hadn't been particularly memorable as a speaker, but he didn't give off the used-car-salesman vibe that I picked up from Conwell.

Mr. Coleman spooned some of the fruit salad onto his plate and smiled at Estella. "You know that I agree with you on philosophical grounds, Estella, but as your financial advisor, I have to tell you that your odds would be much better with the Cyrists than with any of the dealers in Atlantic City. I have several colleagues who are devout Cyrists and let's just say that their stock portfolios are very healthy—one might even say *suspiciously* healthy. I've never been one to buy into conspiracy theories, but . . ." He shook his head. "Not something I'd discuss too much in public—Cyrists have some pretty major political connections—but I ran a statistical analysis of their primary stock holdings last year. Just out of curiosity. If you're interested, Kate, I can show you next time you're here."

"I'd be very interested, Mr. Coleman." I was sure that Katherine and Connor would find that information useful, too, although I wasn't sure how I would manage to visit again before I left for Chicago.

Trey apparently had the same thought. "I'd actually be interested in seeing that research myself, Dad."

"Sure. I'll email you what I have after breakfast. But don't share it with anyone other than Kate, okay? I wasn't kidding about Cyrists having friends in high places."

Much to my embarrassment, Trey had leaked the news about my birthday, and breakfast concluded with *buñuelos*—wonderful little doughnuts covered in honey. Mine had a single candle in the middle. When we finished, I stood to help Estella clear the table, but she shooed me away with the same wave of her hand she'd used on Dmitri. "Go, go. You have places to be. I already went to early mass this morning and I have nothing else to do all day."

I glanced at the kitchen clock. "We probably do need to get moving, Trey, if we're going to find a parking space. Charlayne's dad had to park six blocks away last time."

Trey looked a bit surprised, but we said our good-byes and headed toward his car.

The temple was only a few miles away, and as we approached I understood why Trey hadn't been worried about parking. A three-level garage and several smaller Cyrist annex buildings now occupied two blocks to the north that had previously held an apartment complex, a few small shops, and several dozen townhomes. The temple itself, which had taken up a city block when I visited in early spring, now covered at least twice that. The surrounding area, which had been a bit run-down the last time I saw it, was dotted with upscale bistros, a Starbucks, and several other cafés.

"None of this is new, is it?" I gestured toward the garage and other buildings.

Trey shook his head. "The restaurants down the hill come and go every few years, but the rest of the area looks pretty much as it has for as long as I can remember. I thought you just wanted to get here early for some reason."

He pulled into the garage, which was still more than half empty, and we headed toward the temple. It was a beautiful morning, but there was a heavy quality to the air that suggested it would be hot and humid by midafternoon. Several families and couples were walking ahead of us in the direction of the temple. Most were in their Sunday best and I glanced down apprehensively at my jeans.

The temple itself gleamed in the bright sunlight, a behemoth of white stone and glass. The main building was much larger than I remembered, and gave the impression of being larger still due to its soaring steeple and its position at the crest of a hill. Perched atop the steeple was a huge Cyrist symbol—similar to a Christian cross, but with a rounded loop at the top and flared at the bottom, like an Egyptian ankh. It was also rounded on both sides so that—if viewed from the back—the horizontal bar looked a bit like an infinity symbol. In front of this, at the very center, was an ornate lotus flower.

We climbed the steps to the main entrance and followed several others into a spacious foyer that bore little resemblance to the building I'd entered with Charlayne a few months back. Just inside the door, we were welcomed by a security guard who asked us to remove our shoes and step through a metal detector. I was halfway through when it occurred to me that the machine might pick up the medallion, but the guard handed Trey back his wallet and keys and nodded us toward the main foyer.

The carpeted hall that I remembered from my previous visit had been replaced by a large vaulted atrium with polished stone floors and an arched entranceway leading to the main chapel. The morning sun beamed down on an immense white marble fountain in the center. On the left side of the atrium was a café, where several dozen people were chatting over coffee and muffins, and to the right, a Cyrist bookstore.

Trey and I wandered toward the bookstore entrance, where inspirational paperbacks by prominent Cyrist authors lined the shelves, along with a variety of Cyrist CDs and DVDs, T-shirts, and assorted souvenirs. Conwell's latest book, *Faith and The Way: Five Steps to Financial Freedom*, was featured in the main display. His bronzed face, with its long, aquiline nose, was a rather stark contrast to the carefully manicured silver hair and prominent white teeth. The combination had the odd effect of making him look both older and younger than the age of forty-seven that I remembered from his online biography.

A CD cover near the book display caught my eye and I tugged on Trey's sleeve. "That's it—that's what was on his T-shirt!" I whispered.

"Whose T-shirt?" he asked.

"On the Metro. Simon—the guy who took my backpack. It was really faded, but I'm sure that was the band logo." I picked up the CD and examined the cover more closely. In the center was an image of an eye, with the lotus from the Cyrist symbol superimposed over the pupil. "I don't know the band, though— Aspire? Have you heard of them?"

Trey raised his eyebrows. "Uh, *yeah*. You mean you haven't? They're not really my kind of music, but you couldn't turn on the radio without hearing one of their songs last year."

I gave him a weak grin. "Not in *my* last year. So another one for our list, I guess." We kept a running tally of the differences in the pop culture of the new timeline. Connor's computer program had tracked down the new political leaders that emerged after the shift (about a dozen) and had noted the general shifts in economic power and other things that could be viewed in terms of the numbers, but he and Katherine weren't really the type to keep up with the latest trends in music and entertainment. There were at least a dozen blockbuster movies from the past decade or so that I should have remembered but had never heard of, and several new-to-me celebrities and authors who all happened to be Cyrists. Going farther back, Trey had introduced me to a handful of "classics" that I was pretty sure you wouldn't have found on the reading list for any Western civ course before the last time shift.

"I think Aspire won a Grammy last year or maybe the one before," he added. "I wouldn't have said they were religious music, but then I can't say I've listened very closely to the lyrics."

A guy about our age walked over from behind the counter and asked if he could help us.

"No thanks," Trey said. "Just browsing for a few minutes before the services begin."

The guy, whose name tag identified him as Sean, glanced at the CD in my hand. "Are you fans?" he asked.

Trey shook his head, but I nodded and gave him my best smile. "I really like the new album. I heard some tracks online." I placed the CD back in the display. "I may come get this after the service."

Sean reached out and straightened the CD on the rack, although it really didn't look crooked to me. "Did you see them when they were here?"

I must have looked confused, because he glanced down at my hand, probably scanning for the lotus tattoo. "Oh, no," I said. "I'm not a member—yet. I've only been here once before and this is Trey's first time."

His smile brightened. "Welcome! We're always happy to have visitors." He pulled a cell phone out of his pocket and hit a button, then put it away again. "Yeah, Aspire was here about three months ago. It was members-only, otherwise we'd have had a mob scene. And even so, the auditorium was packed; you could hardly find a spot to stand." He stuck out his hand in Trey's direction. "What was your name again? I'm Sean."

Trey shook his hand. "I'm Trey, and this is K—" He paused for a split second and pretended to clear his throat, before continuing. "This is Kelly."

I wasn't sure why he'd used his own name and opted to give me an alias, but it looked like I would be Kelly for the rest of the morning. "Hi, Sean," I said. "It was nice to meet you. Maybe we'll see you later."

I pulled slightly at Trey's elbow to move us toward the main chapel, but Sean took hold of my other arm. "I'll turn you over to the Acolytes who are on visitors duty this month. They're on their way over now. They'll be happy to answer any questions you have and point you toward some of our social activities. You're actually in luck if you can stick around a bit, because there's an Acolytes lunch in the Youth Center just after the service this morning."

I sighed, hoping that my annoyance wasn't visible. The last thing I wanted was to be led around by a delegation of devout young Cyrists. Trey and I turned toward them as they approached and, with a small lump in my throat, I realized that one of the three girls in the group was Charlayne.

∞ 14 ∞

Her hair was longer, and my Charlayne would have considered the white skirt and pale yellow sweater set much too tame, even for church, but it was definitely her. She was laughing about something with the girl next to her as they approached and wasn't paying much attention, until her eyes landed on Trey. She gave him the quick but thorough up-and-down appraisal that I'd seen her give every guy she considered cute, and then she glanced over at me as if sizing up the competition. Yep, that part was 100 percent Charlayne.

And it gave me an idea. I whispered to Trey out of the side of my mouth, "The one in the yellow is Charlayne. Play along with me, okay? We're *cousins*. She's more likely to talk to us if she thinks you're available."

"You're pimping me out?"

I stifled a laugh. "Just for an hour or so. I know Charlayne—in any timeline. She just gave you her hot-guy appraisal and she'll talk to you if you're even a little bit nice to her."

He didn't have time to object before the flock of Acolytes descended upon us. Sean introduced Trey, who then introduced me as his cousin, Kelly. The slightly annoyed emphasis on the word *cousin* was noticeable to me, but apparently not to anyone else. Charlayne's smile brightened instantly.

After a few minutes of general chatter, we were whisked into the main chapel and seated in one of the first few rows. The circular room was arranged more like an auditorium than a standard church—there were even three elevated sections at the back that reminded me of box seats at a stadium or large theater, except for the fact that most box seats aren't encased in what I suspected was bulletproof glass. All three sections were lit, and two of the sections were occupied, mostly by older men and a few women in expensive-looking suits.

Just then, a door opened inside the third section and four muscular men, who looked like a security detail of some sort, moved in and inspected the room carefully, even looking under the seats. Apparently satisfied that the area was safe, they went out, and just a few seconds later Paula Patterson entered. It was still hard to think of her as the president, instead of vice president. She was followed by her husband, a somewhat older and rounder man, and her four sons, who were all in their teens or early twenties. Her daughter-in-law was the last to enter, accompanied by two toddlers, neither of whom looked too happy about being there.

I pulled my gaze back to the front of the auditorium, which featured a semicircular stage with a giant plasma screen. A large Cyrist symbol lit the center of the display, surrounded by pictures of Cyrist mission activities that changed every few seconds.

Tall stained-glass windows alternated with white stone panels along the exterior walls. A few of the windows showed scenes from the Christian tradition, similar to those I had seen in other churches—Noah's Ark, the Madonna and Child, and so forth. Buddha was in one frame as well, but over half were clearly based on Cyrist history. A good number of these depicted a tall man with short dark hair and a white robe, who was blessing children, curing the sick, and handing out gold coins to the masses. It was several minutes before the obvious fact dawned on me—this was my grandfather in his Brother Cyrus guise.

I sat down to the left of Trey. One of the guys from the Acolyte group plopped down on the other side of me. He continued chatting about the merits of the Baltimore Orioles' manager with one of the other male Acolytes, who was sitting in the row directly ahead, and didn't pay us much attention.

Charlayne was on Trey's right, flanked by the friend she'd been chatting with, who had been introduced as Eve. The girl was impeccably and very fashionably dressed and I suspected that her handbag alone had cost more than my entire wardrobe, even before the last time shift reduced me to a week's worth of clothes.

I knew it was petty to be jealous that Charlayne had another best friend in this timeline, but that didn't change the fact that I *was* jealous. I'd had few close friends in my life, and it stung a bit to see that I'd been replaced. I gave Eve a sideways glance and was comforted by the realization that her mascara was smudged and her nose too hooked to be traditionally pretty, although I suspected that would be cured by a trip to the plastic surgeon within a year or two.

Trey was also looking around at the windows, in between answering Charlayne's questions. He nudged me with his elbow and motioned very slightly with his head to the panel just behind me. A young woman stood in the middle of a garden, with her arms raised and eyes pointed upward. She wore a white sleeveless gown, belted at the waist, and at one end of the belt there was a large bronze medallion. Dark, unruly curls fell across her shoulders.

Katherine's words—*you look like her, you know*—echoed in my mind. She wasn't kidding.

Trey leaned toward Charlayne and said, "Tell me about the windows—they're so detailed. That one is Cyrus curing the sick, but who is the woman there"—he motioned toward the panel behind me—"and in the panel across the auditorium?"

I tensed a bit, unsure that it was wise to call attention to the window, but I wanted to hear Charlayne's answer as well. I had found only the vaguest mention of Prudence in my web searches.

Charlayne gave Trey her best smile, the one that I knew she practiced in the mirror. "That's Sister Prudence," she replied. "Prudence is an oracle, like Cyrus, but she's more . . . personal. I've never seen Brother Cyrus—none of us have seen him personally, except Brother Conwell and his family—so I don't know about the panels that show him. But the panels of Sister Prudence are a very good likeness."

"So the artist based the work on photographs?" Trey asked.

"Well, maybe. I think there are some photographs of Cyrus, although I haven't seen them. But I've seen Prudence here in the temple—she ordained Brother Conwell when he replaced his mother as leader of this region, about seven or eight years ago. I believe she ordains all of the regional leaders."

"Oh." Trey paused for a moment. "I didn't know she was alive. You don't usually see stained-glass windows of living people."

Charlayne paused for a long moment, as if carefully considering her next words. "We don't often speak of it outside the temple, but Prudence and Cyrus are both alive. Not just here"—she tapped her chest—"within our hearts, like the other prophets. They are alive. Eternal."

She nodded toward the window behind me. "That image, for example, was created nearly a hundred years ago—these windows were preserved from the previous regional temple in Virginia. My mother saw Sister Prudence when she was a small child and said she still looks exactly the same as she did back then." Charlayne smiled at me. "You look like her, you know."

I gave her a nervous smile in return and wished I'd thought to pick up some glasses or anything else that might have disguised my appearance a bit. Of course, I'd never thought we would run into stained-glass windows of my doppelgänger aunt. Trey adroitly shifted the conversation to some other area of Cyrist doctrine, distracting Charlayne's attention. Watching him, I realized he was much more skilled at role-playing than I was, and I wished, not for the first time, that he was coming along on my jump to the Expo.

I picked up the hymnal from the row of seats in front of us and began flipping through the pages. I'd attended church with my dad's parents when we visited them during the summers. It was a small, rural Christian congregation, of no specific denomination, and I'd always found the traditional hymns they sang comforting.

The background music that was playing as we waited for the Cyrist service to start was more modern, almost new age, but there were a few hymns in the book that were familiar to me—"There Shall Be Showers of Blessings" and "I Come to the Garden." Others were new, and still others were similar to older hymns but had altered lyrics. "There Will Be Many Stars in My Crown" had replaced an old hymn that I remembered singing called "Will There Be Any Stars in My Crown?" While I couldn't remember all of the words, the lyrics from the Cyrist hymnal—*you will know I am blest when my mansion's the best*—didn't really fit with what I remembered about the spirit of the song.

The incidental music trailed off just before Brother Conwell entered from the left of the stage. He wore a dark, well-tailored suit with a white mandarin collar and a long clerical scarf across his shoulders. It was gold brocade, with large, white Cyrist symbols on each end. A CHRONOS key hung from a white ribbon around his neck. I should have expected it, but for some reason the sight of the medallion, bright blue against the white and gold, caught me by surprise.

From the corner of my eye, I could see that Charlayne's friend was watching me and I hoped my expression hadn't been too telling when I spotted the medallion. She gave me a quick smile when I caught her eye, and I turned back to Brother Conwell, trying to keep my gaze focused on his face and not on the glowing blue disk resting just above his abdomen.

"Welcome Brothers and Sisters on this glorious spring morning." He flashed his beaming smile across the general congregation and toward the back of the auditorium. "We would also like to extend a special welcome to you and your family, Madame President. You have been missed greatly during the past few weeks, but I'm sure that your trip abroad has done much for the advancement of our great nation and of The Way."

Patterson gave a smile and a slight nod to the congregation. Conwell then raised his arms to direct us to stand for the opening hymn. The lights dimmed and a recessed section of the stage rose up gradually to reveal a large choir and musicians. The hymnals were apparently a relic from earlier days or else were simply placed there for casual reading before the service because the lyrics to "Morning Has Broken" began to scroll across the plasma screen, superimposed over serene images of nature.

Two songs and a moment of silent meditation later, Conwell began his sermon. It was fairly short and very similar to the Cyrist messages that I had read online, with a strong emphasis on self-improvement and at least half a dozen very explicit references to tithing in the half hour or so that he spoke. Conwell had a charismatic aura that was much more apparent in person than in the snippets I had watched online, and I found myself smiling at a few of his anecdotes, despite my predisposition to dislike him.

The responsive reading, however, was really creepy. I had read the Cyrist Creed online and it was printed on the inside back cover of my handy pocket copy of the *Book of Cyrus*. While it seemed a bit out there, it wasn't that different from stuff I'd read from other religions that believe they have a lock on divine wisdom and a reserved seat in the VIP section of the hereafter. There was just something about having the words chanted aloud by several hundred people that made them more . . . tangible, I guess.

The lights dimmed as Brother Cyrus moved to one side, and the backdrop lit up to reveal a group of individuals and families of various races and ages whose faces beamed as they exclaimed, "We choose The Way, so we are the Blessed," with those words floating across the bottom of the screen. The pictures shifted to a large offering plate overflowing with gold coins, which struck me as oddly similar to a leprechaun's pot of gold, and the caption changed to "As we give to Cyrus, so shall we prosper."

The same group of faces, now a bit more serious, declared, "We choose The Way, so we may be Chosen," just before the video slowly morphed into an apocalyptic background, with dead, blackened trees stark against a red sky—and the voices continued: "As humans have failed to protect the Planet, the Planet shall protect itself."

The screen then flashed back to the group of Cyrists, whose expressions ranged from determined to angry. "We choose The Way, so we are Defenders. Enemies of The Way will face our Wrath and Judgment." And then the last line of the Creed, "We choose The Way, so we may be Saved," showed the group with triumphant faces, standing before a lush and verdant garden—the earth restored, a virtual Garden of Eden. Trey was apparently unnerved as well, because his hand sought out mine for a brief squeeze before the lights came back up.

The service concluded with announcements—the quarterly executive meeting in the annex following the service, two upcoming weddings, and a retirement party—as young men at each end of the aisle passed the collection plate. That was another thing that I probably should have anticipated, but it wouldn't have really mattered since my very last dollar had vanished with my backpack on the Metro. I gave the guy on my left an apologetic smile as he handed me the collection plate and then passed it along to Trey. He put a rather generous donation on top of the stack of bills, checks, and envelopes, and was duly rewarded by the beaming approval of

Charlayne and Eve, who were already whispering to him about the youth meeting after the service.

I toyed with the idea of following Conwell, who was almost certainly headed toward the executive meeting that he had announced, but I wasn't even sure what I was looking for. A copy of the *Book of Prophecy* would be nice, but based on everything I had read online, the temple leaders didn't just leave those lying around. Tidbits were doled out to members and initiates; few had seen the actual book.

I suspected that there would be some interesting financial tips handed out at the executive meeting, but we stood zero chance of getting into that little soiree, especially if Patterson was attending. It looked like I would have to make do with what we could tease out of the Acolytes.

Trey and I followed Charlayne and her friends out of the auditorium, with Charlayne practically glued to Trey's side. I stopped off at the first ladies' room. Eve and one of the other female Acolytes did the same. I wasn't sure if they were following me or just needed to pee, since they entered the first two stalls inside the door and went straight to business. I entered the stall at the opposite end and took my time, hoping they would leave without me. They didn't, and there was a look of impatience on Eve's face as I stopped by the sink to wash up.

She turned to the other girl and said, "I hope there will still be some decent pizza by the time we get there." I smiled politely and followed the two of them out the door and down a long corridor, to a large and cheery sign welcoming us to the Youth Center.

The inside appeared to be a combination gym and recreation room, with several smaller rooms arranged along the outer walls for classes or meetings. Trey was seated at a long picnic-style table with Charlayne and the rest of the group that had sat near us during the sermon, and I saw that he'd not only saved me a seat but had also snagged me a slice of pizza and a diet soda.

I slid onto the bench. "Thanks." Eve and my other companion from the restroom gave a loud sniff, almost in perfect unison, and headed over to the collection of pizza boxes at the end of the table to see what remained.

"No problem at all, cuz," Trey said. I gave him a look suggesting that he was overdoing it a bit, and he flashed me a quick grin before turning back to Charlayne. "So I've read most of the *Book of Cyrus*, and it's really interesting and all, but I don't think it really gives me an idea of what Cyrists do. What you believe. My mom says that you don't accept everyone for membership—that not everyone is eligible to be Chosen. Is that true?"

Charlayne looked a little uncomfortable. "Well, yes and no. Anyone at all can attend our services—I mean, you're here today, right? And you could attend the Acolyte meetings and you could become a church member. Then, over time, we would know if you were Chosen. Not everyone is Chosen. You'd have to go through several years of classes, and you would find out whether you could open your mind to The Way. And you'd have to commit to our rules—they're pretty strict on some things—and then . . ." She shrugged.

"So is everyone here Chosen?" I asked.

"Oh no," she said. "We're still Acolytes. We aren't independent yet. Most of us are still in school and even after . . . there's no guarantee you'll be Chosen."

"But the Creed—'We choose The Way so we may be Chosen'—all of you repeated it in the service?"

"Yes." She nodded, with a patient smile. "'We choose The Way so we *may* be Chosen.' 'We choose The Way so we *may* be Saved.' We aren't assured that Cyrus will protect us, but those who choose The Way *may* be among those who will find mercy at The End. Those who are Chosen *may* be saved. Those who never listen, who ignore the warnings in the *Book of Cyrus*, have no chance at all."

I thought that it seemed like a pretty weak promise compared to other religions I had studied, but I nodded and returned her smile.

Trey took another bite of his pizza and then asked, "So how would you know? I mean, what tells you that someone is Chosen?"

"It varies for each individual. Most people are identified by their gifts—by the degree to which God blesses them once they begin to follow The Way. That's how my parents became Chosen. The members of the board and Brother Conwell examined their ledgers before they joined and compared it to their ledgers afterward, and decided that God had shown them favor."

Eve, who was now seated across from Trey, picked a piece of sausage off her pizza and gave me a sideways look. "But there are some who are identified by their talents—who can do miracles, who can prophesy. Sometimes they are Chosen very young. Brother Conwell, for example, was Chosen when he was thirteen. His daughter was even younger when she first read from the *Book of Prophecy*. They were predestined to be Chosen, so their names are written in the *Book* itself."

"I'm still a bit confused. Exactly what it is that Cyrus promises to save the Chosen *from*?" Trey asked. "From hell?"

The dark-haired boy next to Eve, who had been one of those arguing about sports before the service, laughed. "Cyrists don't believe in an afterlife. Your rewards are in this life. Cyrus can save the Chosen from The End. The world is going to end, you know—and pretty soon, based on the prophecies we've been given. The Chosen will live on, when everyone else dies. They will be the future."

That gave me a bit of a shudder and it must have shown in my expression, because Eve gave the boy a long, hard look. "Really, Jared. Is this a conversation we should be having at lunch? With visitors?" She turned back to me with a reassuring smile. "All of this would be covered in eschatology classes—the leaders know a lot more about The End than *Jared* does, believe me."

"The thing that I like to focus on," Charlayne said to Trey, "is that The Way gives us the tools for a happy and successful life here and now. And contrary to popular opinion, Cyrists *do* know how to have a good time. We're planning a trip to Six Flags next weekend if you're interested."

"That's a good idea, Charlayne," Eve said. "Why don't you give Trey the info about the trip? Get his email so that we can contact him. And Kelly, if you'll come back to the office with me, I can get the two of you a couple of membership kits that will answer a lot of your other questions. Our Acolyte meeting needs to start in a few minutes and that is, unfortunately, for Acolytes only, so . . ."

Charlayne gave Eve an annoyed pout. I wasn't sure whether she was irritated that Trey was going to have to leave or simply didn't like being ordered around, but she reached over and stacked our empty plates onto her own without comment. Trey joined her, gathering the soda cans to take to the recycling bin, while I stood to follow Eve.

I had assumed that she was taking me to one of the small rooms along the perimeter of the gym, but she headed toward the exit at the far side. I glanced back at Trey a bit nervously but followed her. We took a left into a hallway that looked to be nearly the length of a football field, lined on both sides with office doors and the occasional framed piece of artwork. I could see glass double doors opening to a side street at the end, just below a lighted Exit sign.

It looked like the street we had crossed when we were coming in from the parking garage—and I thought that Eve might be heading out to one of the smaller buildings I had seen. We had only walked a few feet down the corridor, however, when she pulled a small access badge out of her handbag and waved it in front of a reader next to a glass door on the right. The door beeped softly and she pushed it open, leading me into a second, more dimly lit hallway.

"We're nearly there," she said brightly. "Normally, we keep a few membership kits in the Youth Center, but . . ." She trailed off as we approached the last door on the left, which she again opened with her access badge, and then switched on the overhead light.

The room was a luxuriously furnished library, with shelves along three walls. The fourth wall was glass, with a stone fireplace in the center of the panels. The chairs in front of the fireplace looked out on a meticulously manicured garden enclave, enclosed by the white walls of the surrounding buildings. Two massive, well-muscled Dobermans were taking a leisurely drink from a smaller version of the white fountain that Trey and I had seen in the atrium of the temple.

Eve closed the door behind us and leaned against the edge of the large desk in front of one set of bookshelves. Another, much less ostentatious desk sat to the right and she nodded toward the small office chair in front of it. "You might as well sit, Kate. We may have a bit of a wait."

It took a second for the fact that she had said Kate, not Kelly, to register with me. "I'm sure Charlayne will keep your *cousin* entertained," she continued. "The silly girl was so flattered when I asked her to sit with me in services this morning. What I don't understand is why her name is even *in* your file. She clearly doesn't remember you at all."

I took a deep breath as she was chattering and began considering my options.

Option one—take her out while it was still just me against her. Eve was thin and had almost no muscle. I was pretty sure I could have her down quickly, especially if I caught her off guard. She was a good ten pounds lighter than me and I doubted she had martial arts training. The downside was that Trey and I would then have to make a fast run for the exit, and I had no idea which of the other Acolytes she had alerted.

Option two—pull the medallion out and hope I could get a lock on the location back home in the kitchen. Given that Conwell was strolling around with a CHRONOS key on his chest, I was reasonably sure that this was a stable point. That would be the best bet for getting me out of the building, but I wasn't willing to risk the chance that they might hurt Trey.

Option three—jump back to the kitchen five minutes early, convince myself that this trip was a very bad idea, and go back to bed. I could send Trey a text and cancel—his dad and Estella would be disappointed, but that was a small price to pay if it kept him safe. As tempting as this seemed, I kept thinking of Katherine's caution about the mental effects of reconciling even a few minutes of conflicting reality. Could I really handle five hours of dueling memories? And what about everyone else—would Trey and all of the other people I'd encountered have the same problem? I had to admit that I didn't know enough to risk it.

The first option seemed best, but I wanted to get a bit of info from Eve before making my move. I was curious—who were we waiting for and what had tipped her off about my identity? The self-satisfied smile on her face as she sat there on the desk suggested that she actually *might* be stupid enough to want to brag about how very smart she'd been to put all the pieces together.

I pulled the office chair toward me, then turned it around and straddled it, rolling slightly toward her perch on the desk and leaning my arms against the padded backrest. She wrinkled her nose at my unladylike position while I calculated how effective the chair would be as a weapon if I stood and brought the heavy base up hard and fast beneath her chin.

I was about to ask how she knew who I was, when I suddenly realized who she resembled. "So you're Brother Conwell's daughter? The one who was Chosen at such a young age?"

The smug expression faded for a moment, and then it was back. "Could be."

"Of course you are. You favor him nearly as much as I do my aunt Prudence."

"If you knew you looked like her, did you really think you could walk in here and no one would notice? Especially wearing a key of CHRONOS? Security called the office the moment you walked in."

I was very surprised she knew about CHRONOS, but I tried to keep a blank face. "I thought that might happen." I shrugged, hoping she was gullible enough to swallow the lie. "But it's probably for the best. Otherwise, I'd have wasted a lot of time trying to prove to you who I am. This way, we can get straight to business."

Eve raised her eyebrows ever so slightly. "Business?"

I nodded. "I've learned all I possibly can from my grandmother. From what I see, she's waging a hopeless battle and I don't like to be on the losing side. What I don't know yet is whether your side has anything better to offer. When will your father be here? I really should be talking directly to him, I think."

"The executive meeting is usually an hour or a bit more—I expect it will end on schedule since we don't like to waste Sister Paula's time." Her use of the president's first name was so clearly an intentional bit of name-dropping that it was hard to keep from rolling my eyes at her pretentiousness.

"Daddy doesn't know you're here yet—I don't like to disturb him when he's preparing for services, and I thought you'd be a lovely surprise when he comes in after the meeting. They can be so stressful." She pushed herself up to sit on the big desk, and crossed her legs at the ankle.

"But you aren't really in a position to bargain with anyone, are you, Kate? From what I've heard, you won't even exist if I take your key."

I gave her my best wicked grin. "I'd like to see you *try.*" That was only a tiny lie, since I was growing fond of the idea of wiping that perpetual sneer from her face. "But even if you succeeded, and I don't think you would, do you really believe my aunt—or my grandfather—would be happy with your decision? When I've come here freely, of my own accord?"

That one set her back a bit. "I can't see why they would care one way or another. From what I've been told, you've never met either of them."

"True," I admitted. "But for many people, blood is thicker than water. Are you aware that all four of my grandparents were—" I stopped. I wasn't sure exactly how much she knew about CHRONOS and the origins of Brother Cyrus, so I kept it vague. "Were originally of CHRONOS? This key isn't around my neck simply to ensure my continued existence. I activated it the very first time I held it."

She tossed her blonde hair back over her shoulder. "That's not possible. It takes months—years in most cases."

I arched one eyebrow and held her gaze as I reached into the collar of my shirt, pulling the medallion from beneath the layers of fabric. "How many Cyrists have blood as pure as mine, Eve?"

A flicker of doubt passed over her face. She eyed the CHRONOS key with an expression that bordered on lust, and it occurred to me that she had probably rarely been allowed to hold one. Katherine had located ten of the twenty-four that had been in the field when headquarters were destroyed. Even if the Cyrists had found all of the remaining keys, which seemed very unlikely, that left only fourteen, divided among the thousands of Cyrist temples. I doubted they would have more than one in any region.

"What color is it for you?"

"Kind of pink," she said, watching me warily.

"Really? My dad sees it as pink as well. It's blue for me." I gave her a little smile and centered the medallion in my hand, pulling up the display instantly. Eve drew in a sharp breath as the navigation control board appeared between us and then she lurched toward me.

I pulled my finger off the center. As the control panel vanished, I slipped the medallion back beneath my shirt and she relaxed. Her reaction answered one question, at least—apparently I *could* use the CHRONOS key from this office if I had to.

"Don't worry," I chuckled. "I haven't the slightest intention of leaving." I gave her what I hoped came across as a sympathetic smile. "Katherine—that's my grandmother—says she's never seen anyone able to activate the key as quickly as I did. Was I foretold in your *Book of Prophecy*? According to your criteria, I should be among the predestined. Or does it even exist? I've heard rumors . . ."

"It exists," she snapped. "Each Grand Templar has a copy. And you're not in it."

"Are you sure? I find it hard to believe that Cyrus wouldn't have foretold my arrival, wouldn't have known that I'd want to learn more." I pushed the chair a bit closer and lowered my voice a bit. "Or will they not let you read the entire thing? I've heard that the Chosen are only given little snippets of prophecy—like the paper inside a fortune cookie."

Her jaw tightened. "Most Cyrists only see the *Book* on the day they join the Chosen. I *live* here, however." Her glance drifted slightly over her left shoulder, to the shelves behind the desk. "I haven't read all of it—that would take ages—but I most certainly *can* read anything I want."

I gave her a skeptical look. "Well, *if* that's true and *if* you know where the Chosen are listed, then why not check while we wait? One less thing to be taken care of when your father arrives. I mean, either I'm in the *Book* or Cyrus made a rather large mistake."

"Cyrus doesn't make mistakes." She walked around the edge of the desk and searched the fourth shelf up, which was filled with large and ornately bound volumes. Her hand closed around a much smaller book, however, which I recognized instantly as a CHRONOS diary. The only decoration was on the front, where the words *Book of Prophecy* were engraved in simple gold letters, with a Cyrist emblem below.

She opened the book and then, after a few seconds, snapped it shut again, an annoyed look on her face. "We'll have to wait. I don't have the . . ." She paused, searching for the word. "Oh, the adapter thing . . . I can't remember what Daddy calls it."

"Oh," I said. "The little translator disk? I have one. Here . . ." I stood up and put my hand behind my ear, hoping that she would come closer before I actually had to remove it. She walked part of the way around the desk and then paused, waiting.

"Damn!" I said. "I dropped it again. These disks are awful— it's like trying to find a contact lens . . ." I leaned forward and a few seconds later, Eve took the bait and joined me, bending down slightly to examine the carpet.

I felt guilty beyond belief but reminded myself that I really had no choice. I pulled the office chair upward and swung hard. One of the wheels flew off and rolled under the desk as the pneumatic base of the chair connected solidly with the side of her head. Eve fell backward and hit her head on the desk with a resounding thump before she crumpled to the floor.

I waited a second and then touched her eyelashes to see if she was faking. There was no flutter, so she really was unconscious, but it was impossible to say how long she would stay that way. Or, I thought, glancing around nervously, whether there were security cameras hidden in the room.

That's when the barking began. I turned automatically to look and wished I hadn't because both Dobermans were staring straight at me through the glass, teeth bared.

I took several steps toward the door and then remembered the access badge. It was on the desk, next to the *Book of Prophecy*. I grabbed them both, stuck the book into the waistband of my jeans under my various layers of camisoles, and ran as fast as I could for the door.

The hallway was still empty. I hurried down it toward the door to the gym, hoping that Trey was still there and not wandering around the temple with the other Acolytes. I waved the badge in front of the keypad as I looked through the small window.

I could see several of the group still seated at the tables, but Charlayne and Trey weren't with them. The access pad beeped and I pushed hard to open the door, nearly hitting Trey and Charlayne, who had been about to open it from the opposite side.

"Hey, watch out!" Charlayne cried, jumping back. "See, she's fine, just like I told you." She moved toward me and looked down the hallway. "Where's Eve?"

"There were no kits," I said. "She's going to look in the main office . . ." I grabbed Trey's arm and pulled him out of the gym.

"How can she do that?" Charlayne asked. "You have her access badge."

I stared at her for a moment. She wasn't my Charlayne, not really, but I didn't like lying to her. "Eve's not your friend, Charlayne. I know you won't understand this, but she was using you to get to me. Take care of yourself, okay?" And then I threw the badge as far into the gym as I could. As I'd hoped, she gave me a confused look and then turned around to retrieve it.

I slammed the door behind us. "Run," I said, nodding toward the exit at the end of the corridor and grabbing his hand. "We have to get out of here *now*."

We were about a third of the way to the exit when a door opened behind us. I looked back over my shoulder, expecting to see an angry Charlayne at the gym entrance. Instead, I saw a *very* angry Eve, with a trickle of blood running down her cheek. She was leaning against the frame of the glass door for support. Two even angrier Dobermans were trying to push their way past her. Eve's legs gave out and she fell forward. One of the dogs yelped as she landed on him, but it didn't deter either of them from their target—me.

We were still a good sixty yards from the exit and I knew there was no way that we could get out before they reached us. Trey, however, might make it if I could create a diversion, especially since his longer legs covered the ground much faster than my short ones.

I yanked the CHRONOS key out of my shirt, still running, as Trey pulled me by my other hand, trying to speed me up. "We can't make it unless we split up, Trey," I said. "Get to the car. I'm going to jump back to Katherine's house. It's our only chance."

"No!" he said, pulling me harder.

"Trey, please! I'm sure Eve has called security—get *out* of here! I'll be okay." I let go of his hand and shoved him as hard as I could in the direction of the door, hoping that I sounded more confident than I felt.

Then I spun around to face 180 pounds or so of snarling teeth. The dogs were still running toward me, but when they saw the medallion, they slowed their pace and stopped barking. I touched my hand to the center. One of them whined softly, like Daphne had at the door of the library, and took a couple of steps back. The other one looked confused but kept coming toward me, his large teeth bared and looking much too sharp for my comfort.

"Back! Sit!" I said in my most commanding voice, which right then was about as authoritative as Mickey Mouse. The dogs weren't impressed with me, but they were still eyeing the CHRONOS key warily and moving toward me at a slower pace.

I was tempted to look back to see if Trey had actually left—I hadn't heard the door open, but the dogs were making it difficult to hear anything else. I didn't dare break eye contact with them, however. So I stood my ground, pulled up the display, and tried to lock in my destination.

"Good doggies," I whispered. They were only about ten feet away; I needed to hurry. "Stay . . ."

The larger and more aggressive of the two beasts apparently didn't care for the "stay" command because he began barking again and lunged toward me. I countered with a left kick to his midsection.

Unfortunately, his jaws connected with my thigh at about the same time my kick sent him sprawling. I screamed as his teeth ripped through my jeans and raked two deep grooves in my leg. My hands shook and the display flickered in front of me, but I steadied them before I lost the stable point entirely.

I heard Trey calling my name from a distance and footsteps running toward me. "I'm okay! Go back, Trey!" The alpha dog was once again on his feet, his haunches tensed and ready to spring. If I tried to block him, I knew I'd lose the stable point again.

A split second later, the dog was in the air, headed toward the arm holding the CHRONOS key. I did the only thing I could do—blinked my eyes and hoped for the best.

∞ 15 ∞

I don't remember screaming, but I must have, since it was a scream that brought Connor to the kitchen. In retrospect, a scream would have been a perfectly normal reaction to the fact that ninety pounds of vicious Doberman was so close that I could, very briefly, smell him and feel his breath, warm against the skin of my arm. After a moment had passed without teeth again puncturing my skin, I tentatively opened my eyes. I looked around the dark kitchen and then sank to the floor, pulling in ragged breaths and wrapping my arms around my chest in an effort to calm down.

Connor and Daphne were in the doorway a few seconds later. "What in God's name have you done, Kate?"

I gave Connor a weak smile as Daphne came over to nuzzle me. "Remember that book you wanted from the library?" I pulled the *Book of Prophecy* out from beneath my shirt. "Turns out the Cyrists release the hounds on you if you don't have a library card."

I could tell from his eyes that he was very happy to see the book, but the sentiment didn't reach the rest of his face. "You've got to be kidding me. Why on earth would you take such a chance just to get that? You're bleeding all over the damned floor."

He was right. It wasn't a *major* injury—I'd had one cut that was nearly this bad back when I was just learning to shave my legs. There were, however, twin two-inch furrows in my leg, just above the knee. A dark stain on the leg of my jeans was growing, and blood was dripping into a small puddle on the marble floor.

"I'm just glad Katherine didn't hear you—fortunately, once her meds kick in, she sleeps through anything," he said, shaking his head. "I'll get the bandages. You *stay there*," he added forcefully, and rather unnecessarily, since I was highly unlikely to be traipsing off on another adventure with a bleeding leg.

I waited, my face buried in Daphne's ruff, until Connor returned with a pair of scissors, a washcloth, antiseptic ointment, several gauze bandages, and a roll of medical tape. He pulled me up onto one of the kitchen chairs, cut away the leg of my pants, and began to clean the wounds.

"Ow!" I said, flinching from the washcloth, which he had apparently dipped in alcohol.

"Stay still. You're lucky this isn't worse than it is, Kate."

I shuddered as my mind flashed back to the image of the Doberman flying toward me. Connor didn't realize exactly *how* lucky I was, and I didn't think it was a good idea to give him the gory details. He didn't speak again, just finished cleaning the cuts and applying the ointment and bandage.

When he was done wiping the blood from the floor, he pulled up a chair and stared at me for several seconds. "So?"

I gave him a brief overview of my past few hours. When I was finished, I pushed the book toward him. "The book isn't why I went. I just had the opportunity to take it, so I did. I went to see Charlayne. I'm all on board with changing this timeline—I want my parents back—but, as far as the rest of it goes . . . well, the Cyrists have been around forever based on my memories. I guess I wanted to know if the Cyrists are really as . . . I don't know, diabolical . . . as you and Katherine seem to think."

"And are they?"

"Probably." I shrugged. "Fine, *yes,* they are. I think they're planning something big—or rather, Saul is. I don't suppose you can really pin it on the rank and file who think this is all predestined. You know the Creed, right? 'We choose The Way, so . . .'"

He nodded, and I continued. "Well, they take it a lot more seriously and more literally than I would have thought."

"Not surprising," he said. "The few Cyrists I've encountered, even in previous timelines, clearly drank the full cup of Kool-Aid."

"This one guy," I said, "he was an Acolyte, one of their youth members, and he was talking about the Chosen being saved. Not from punishment in the afterlife, but from some sort of disaster. He said that the Chosen would live, when everyone else died. That the Chosen would be the future . . ."

Connor was silent for a moment, staring down at the cover of the book, and then looked back up. "So—you jumped back here. Where's Trey?"

"Right this minute, he's asleep at home, with his alarm set so that he can pick me up at seven, at the Lincoln Memorial." I took in a deep breath. "But if you're asking about this afternoon, I *think* he got out. I don't know for sure. I told him to run, that I was going to jump back here—there was no way we could have made it otherwise. But when he heard me scream, when the dog bit me, he was running back toward me."

My lip was shaking and then tears started. "I made a mistake, a big one. We shouldn't have gone. And Connor—they know who I am. For one thing, I'm almost a carbon copy of Prudence. There are pictures of her—stained-glass windows—everywhere. And . . . I think they're watching the house." I thought back to what Trey's dad had said about Cyrists having friends in high places. "If they know we're here, that Katherine is training me, then I don't understand why they haven't just stormed the place. The Cyrist Templars clearly do whatever Saul and Prudence tell them to do, and we're just . . ."

He nodded. "I've wondered that myself. We have a security system, and it's not a cheap one. Daphne's also pretty good at warning about intruders, at least for people coming and going in the *conventional* fashion," he added, narrowing his eyes at me. "But it would be child's play for someone who was determined, who had money and skill on his side, to get in here."

I crossed my arms on the table and laid my head down for a moment, overwhelmed by the enormity of what we were facing and how little we knew. And there was a huge gnawing sensation in my stomach, fear that Trey might be in trouble and I wasn't—or rather, wouldn't be—there to help him.

"Connor, should I go back and fix it? Stop myself from going? Tell Trey not to meet me? I know what Katherine said about trying to juggle two different realities, but maybe . . ."

"No. We can't risk that, Kate. First, it wouldn't just be you juggling two sets of memories. It would be anyone in contact with a medallion during this time. Katherine would be okay, since she's been sleeping, but Daphne and I have both been here for what, fifteen or twenty minutes? And how long would it be for you—five hours? Six?"

His expression was still stern, but he squeezed my hand. "No. I know it's tough, but you're just going to have to wait. If you call him, it could change something—especially if he can tell you're upset or that you're hurt. He's a big guy and you say he was near the door—he'll be okay."

Connor stood up and walked over to the cabinet where Katherine kept most of her medicines. He hunted about for a few minutes, finally opening a prescription bottle. He filled a glass with water from the fridge and then handed it to me, along with a small red capsule. "Take this. It will help with the pain in your leg and should help you sleep. And," he added, "I'm not inclined to tell Katherine unless we have to . . . I don't want to worry her. So you're going to need to come up with some logical excuse for that injury."

I hadn't looked forward to telling Katherine that I'd been stupid enough to waltz right in to the lion's den just to assuage my curiosity about the Cyrists, so I was very happy that Connor was willing to keep my secret.

"That should be easy enough," I said. "Slipped in the shower, cut myself with the razor. It's all bandaged up now, so she won't be able to tell the difference. But . . ." I nodded toward the *Book of Prophecy*. "She will need to know about this, won't she?"

"I'll remove the cover and stash it with the other diaries we've collected, after I download the contents to our computers."

"But won't she wonder how you got the information?" I asked. "I know you've been trying to get this for a while . . ."

"It's just amazing what you can find at WikiLeaks," he said, with a totally straight face. "I don't know why it hadn't occurred to me to look there earlier. She'll believe me, Kate—I'll make it convincing. And once we're finished analyzing all of this data"—he grinned—"WikiLeaks may well be where this little book winds up."

Connor went upstairs to the library, presumably to work his magic on the *Book of Prophecy*. I took the little red pill he had given me and then I went up the other staircase to my room, carrying the rest of the bandages.

The pain medicine did begin to numb the throbbing in my leg after about half an hour—in fact, I felt a bit numb all over—but it was still a while before I could sleep. I kept hearing Trey's voice calling my name and seeing sharp white teeth flying toward me. And the chair hitting Eve's head, in slo-mo and vivid color. Despite her generally nasty attitude, I felt a bit guilty about that and hoped she was okay.

∞

I woke a bit before ten and ran a hot bath, easing myself into it in deference to the wounds on my leg. The area around the cuts was beginning to turn blue from the impact of the dog's muzzle, and it was annoying to think that the mongrel was probably relaxing in the sun right now in that little garden, several blissful hours away from our encounter. I consoled myself with the knowledge that he wouldn't be feeling all that good by this afternoon—I was pretty sure that the one kick I'd landed to his chest would leave a much bigger bruise than the one he left on my leg.

It was hard to comprehend that Trey and I were, this very minute, chatting with his dad and Estella. Despite the rumbling in this version of my stomach, which hadn't eaten for about ten hours, the other version of me was being stuffed to the gills with *huevos divorciados*, tortillas, and *buñuelos*. That thought made me even hungrier, so I reluctantly pulled myself out of the tub, rebandaged my leg, and dressed to go in search of breakfast.

I let Daphne in from the yard, happy to have some company while I ate my Cheerios. Judging from the dishes in the sink and the fact that I had to reheat the last bit of coffee in the pot, Katherine and Connor had eaten several hours ago.

They were probably already poring over the documents that Connor had miraculously located online, and I didn't look forward to joining them in the library. My ability to lie convincingly was already taxed to the limit; pretending to be surprised at Connor's discovery while simultaneously pretending not to be worried sick about Trey seemed a rather gargantuan task. The alternative, however—sitting by myself and thinking about Trey and this totally screwed-up day for the next two or three hours—was even less appealing.

As I had expected, they were both in the library. Katherine rose from a chair by the windows when I entered. She had one of the diaries in her hand, and I strongly suspected that it had, until last night, borne a cover reading *Book of Prophecy*. "Happy birthday, Kate! Connor has a—oh my goodness, Kate! Whatever did you do to your leg?"

I gave her my cover story and explained that it really wasn't that bad—and, to be honest, the big bandage did make it look worse than it really was.

She gave me a sympathetic smile. "You should be more careful, dear. I was lucky—I had all unsightly hair zapped away long before I was your age—but I do remember Deborah slicing her shin something awful when she was a bit younger than you.

"Anyway," Katherine continued, leading me toward the computers, "Connor has a wonderful birthday present for you—well, it's for all of us, actually."

I pretended to be surprised as Connor unveiled the *Book of Prophecy*, now downloaded into the hard drive for easy searching and installed on two of the CHRONOS diaries, just in case we wanted to do a bit of armchair reading. After glancing through the first few pages, however, I seriously doubted that I would be using the book to fill my light-reading needs.

The *Book* was barely organized—just odd bits of political and social "prophecy" juxtaposed with investment tips, aphorisms, and platitudes. And then, every ten pages or so, you'd get a nice long sales pitch about how those who followed the Cyrist Way would be rewarded beyond their wildest dreams. The *Book of Cyrus* might have been repetitive and plagiarized from every religious text out there, but at least there was some sense of poetry and it was reasonably coherent.

The *Book of Prophecy*, on the other hand, reminded me more of the infomercials that come on TV around 2 A.M.—when they know you're so loopy that almost anything will seem to make sense. It was hard to see why Connor had thought it would be important.

Reading it was diverting, however, in the same way that clicking links online, in a train-of-thought fashion, is diverting—those times when you end up so far from your original topic it's hard to remember what you were looking for in the first place. Still, I kept glancing at the clock every ten minutes or so, trying to think where the other version of myself was right that minute, and what Trey was doing.

At twelve-forty, I couldn't take it any longer. I left the library and headed back to my room. The disposable cell phone that Connor had bought a few weeks back was sitting on the desk next to my laptop.

I knew that Trey had turned off his phone during the service—or maybe he'd put it on vibrate? I just hoped that he had remembered to turn it back on after we went to the gym with the Acolytes. I sent him a short text, which seemed vague enough not to alarm him too much—"Run when I say run. Don't look back. I made it home OK"—and then stuck the phone in the pocket of my shorts.

Even if what Connor and Katherine had said about the problems caused by trying to reconcile conflicting versions of reality was true, I was already in the office with Eve or headed in that direction. I'd see Trey for only a couple of minutes before I made the jump, and surely that couldn't screw things up too much?

When I returned to the library, Katherine had gone downstairs, probably to scavenge about for some lunch. I sat down again in my chair by the window but couldn't bring myself to continue reading.

"I didn't know people literally chewed their knuckles," Connor said. "I thought it was just a figure of speech. Is the book really so suspenseful?"

I glanced down at my hands and saw that he was right. I'd lapsed into an old habit—my first two knuckles on my left hand were bright red.

"Obviously not," I responded. "You know why I'm nervous."

He gave me a little smile. "He'll make it out, Kate."

"I think so, too—*now*," I said defiantly. "I decided to buy a little insurance."

"What do you mean, *insurance*?" he asked.

"I sent him a text. About two minutes ago. Telling him to run, and that I made it back okay. It can't change much, I barely even see him between now and then, but I just hope he turned his phone back on after the service was over."

Connor chuckled softly, shaking his head. "It won't matter whether he turned his phone on or not."

"And why is that?"

"I left him a message before I went to bed, about four this morning. I told him to stay near the door of the gym and run when you said to run, and I promised him that you were safe here at the house. And I said *not* to let you know that I had texted him, under any circumstances."

"So that's why he was there, at the door! I was scared I'd have to hunt him down. But you said we shouldn't . . ."

"I said *you* shouldn't," he corrected. "But the more I thought about it, there wasn't all that much risk if I called him."

"You couldn't have told me? I've been chewing my damned knuckles off!"

He shrugged. "What was I supposed to do? Pass you a note? Katherine has been in here all morning. And speaking of . . ."

As he trailed off, I could hear Katherine's footsteps on the stairs. I picked up the diary and pretended to focus, while Katherine and Connor argued about the significance of some bit of "prophecy."

When the phone in my pocket rang about twenty minutes later, I jumped up so quickly that my copy of the book fell to the floor. Katherine muttered something about how I should be careful with sophisticated CHRONOS equipment, but I was already out the door.

As soon as I reached the bedroom, I answered the phone. I knew it had to be Trey, since the only other possibility was a wrong number, but I was still tremendously relieved to see his name pop up on the screen. And then it occurred to me—it might be Eve or some Cyrist security guard calling to say that they were holding Trey or that—

"Trey?" My voice was shaking. "Is it you? Are you okay? Where are you?"

There was a brief pause, but it was his voice that answered. "Yes, I'm okay. I'm a few blocks from the Beltway."

I sat down on the edge of the bed and pulled in a long breath. "I was so scared, Trey. I heard you running toward me and I didn't know if you turned around in time—or if Eve had called security. Did you get my text?"

"No, but I see I've got one waiting. I called as soon as I could. I got Connor's message this morning, but he said not to tell you. I'm not sure I would have agreed if I'd known what you were walking into. Are you okay? That dog was huge, and he looked like he was going straight for your throat."

"He was. He only got me the once, in the leg—not very deep because I kicked him pretty hard. I'm just glad you kept running."

He gave a wry laugh. "I don't think it would have mattered even if I'd waited. He hit the floor pretty hard and he was, uh—let's just say I don't think either of them had much experience with their prey vanishing into midair. I didn't hear them start barking again until I was almost to the parking garage—and they were behind the door, so . . ."

"Are you sure you're not being followed or anything?"

There was a pause, and I suspected he was checking the rearview mirrors. "I don't think so."

"Well, I'm not hanging up until you get here."

There was a long silence on the other end and my mind immediately kicked back into panic mode. Was someone else in the car with him? Was he still in danger?

"Trey? What's wrong?"

"Nothing," he said. "Really, Kate, I'm fine. I'll stay on the phone if it makes you feel better—but don't tell Katherine, okay? I promised I'd make a stop on the way over and pick up your birthday cake, and I think she was counting on it being a surprise."

∞

The birthday party was fun, despite the occasional lump in my throat when I remembered that this was the only birthday that my mom or dad had missed. We had pizza—I couldn't tell Katherine that Trey and I had eaten it just a few hours before—and Katherine opened a bottle of wine for a toast. She hesitated before pouring for Trey, although he assured her that his family had a very European view of wine consumption. Then she shrugged. "Given the fact that I'm not technically *alive* in this timeline, I doubt the authorities are going to be concerned about my corrupting a minor."

The cake was sinfully decadent, dripping with chocolate, exactly the way a birthday cake should be. Trey gave me several T-shirts with funny sayings and a gold chain made of delicate little interlocked hearts. Katherine and Connor's present was a small video camera, which we used to record the rest of the party, including some silly footage of Daphne trying to pull the little cardboard birthday crown off my head.

I still felt horribly guilty that I'd put Trey in danger. It was hard to shake the panicked feeling I'd had before he arrived. I think he was feeling the same—we both kept finding little reasons to touch and reassure ourselves that we were both really there.

Once we'd eaten and finished our celebration, Connor showed Trey the *Book of Prophecy*. At least Trey didn't have to fake his surprised reaction—he hadn't realized that I'd actually managed to get something substantive out of our adventure.

After a few minutes, we left Katherine and Connor to their analysis and headed up to my room. Trey pulled me close as soon as the door clicked shut behind us. After a very long kiss, he held me out at arm's length. "You scared the hell out of me, Kate. What happened in there? I mean, I knew *something* was going to happen, because of Connor's message, but . . ."

"She knew who I was. The only reason we got out of there at all is because Eve likes to impress her daddy. She wanted to surprise him by catching me all by herself."

"Her *daddy*?" Trey asked.

"Conwell," I said. He sat down on the couch and I snuggled up next to him. "It didn't hit me until we were in the office together—same eyes, same nose. She said that temple security detected the CHRONOS key when we arrived and sent a message up to Conwell's office. She was there when it came in. She didn't want to disturb Conwell before the service, and security had their hands a bit full with the executive meeting, so . . ."

I filled in the pieces of the puzzle he had missed—my escape from Eve, the Dobermans in the center garden. He lifted the edge of the bandage on my leg and winced a bit. "I guess it could have been a lot worse," he said.

"Yeah. We were lucky. I'm just so, so sorry for taking you into that," I said. "It was stupid and reckless and . . ."

He shook his head. "I'm the one who should be apologizing to you. You didn't know what we were getting into. I went in knowing that there was *some* sort of danger, because I was going to have to run—but I took Connor's word that you were okay. I didn't know you were going to get hurt. I should have told you . . ."

"You did the right thing, Trey. And maybe it will be worth it. Maybe there's something in that stupid book that will help us."

We spent the next few hours talking about other things, or nothing at all, just happy to be together and safe. It was clear that neither of us was especially eager to say good night, but I knew he had a trig final bright and early the next morning, so I pushed him out the door, reluctantly, a little after nine.

I watched him drive away and then, still a bit wound up, decided that a cup of herbal tea might help me relax for bed. Katherine was already in the kitchen, and the teakettle was beginning to whistle.

"You read my mind," I said, reaching into the cabinet for cups. "Is there enough water for two?"

She nodded, and I selected a bag of chamomile, adding a smidgen of honey to my cup along with the hot water. Katherine opened a bag of her usual evening tea. I don't know what's in the blend, but it smells vaguely like Italian sausage and I always try to avoid the steam rising from her cup.

"Since you're here," she said as she poured the water over her tea bag, "maybe we should take a few minutes to talk."

"Sure," I said, sitting down at the table. Something about her tone led me to think that this was not going to be a happy conversation. "What's up?"

"Two things. First, I have another gift for you." She reached into her pocket and pulled out a delicate silver bracelet with a single charm hanging from it. It was a tiny replica of an hourglass, about as long as my fingertip. It wasn't a functional replica—the two bulbs were actually tiny pearls and the edges were a flat green stone that looked like jade.

"The chain is new," she said. "The original broke long ago. The charm, however, is something that my mother gave me when I completed my CHRONOS training. A friend of hers made it especially for me, and I've never seen one like it. I always wore it when I traveled—a good-luck charm, I guess."

She helped me fasten the bracelet onto my wrist. "I think it is a fitting gift. Not just for your birthday, but because you're quite close to the end of your training, too—although yours has been a very compressed version, I'm afraid."

I smiled at her. "Thank you, Katherine. It's beautiful."

"I wanted you to have it anyway," she said, "but the gift serves a practical purpose, too. If you show this to me at the fair, I can promise that you'll get my attention—especially if you point out the chipped edge right near the top and remind me how it happened."

I hadn't even noticed the tiny imperfection—just a small chip in the green stone that was suspended above the pearls by a small silver casing. "And how *did* it happen?"

"It was one of my earlier jumps—a solo trip, without Saul." She paused for a moment, taking a tentative sip of tea, which was apparently still a bit too hot. "I'd been on dozens of jumps over the previous two years and you would think I'd have been used to seeing famous people. But as I was getting out of a carriage in New York City, where I was scheduled to attend the evening session of the American Equal Rights Association meeting—the one where they were debating whether the Fifteenth Amendment should include women?"

I nodded, vaguely remembering the discussion from history class and, more recently, from one of her trip diaries.

"Well," she continued, "I looked out and saw Frederick Douglass arguing with Susan B. Anthony and Sojourner Truth, all three of them just a few feet away, near the entrance to the building. And like a gawking tourist catching her first sight of the Statue of Liberty or the Capitol Building, I forgot what I was doing and somehow managed to slam the carriage door on my wrist."

"Oh, dear." I chuckled. "Sorry—I hope you weren't hurt."

"Not really—a minor cut from the door latch, but Mr. Douglass was carrying a handkerchief that he very kindly donated to the cause. That's one souvenir I would love to have had in my bag when I got stranded in 1969." She sighed. "But the main injuries were to my dignity and this little chip on the hourglass charm. I don't think I've ever told this story to anyone—not even Saul. I was worried that anyone at CHRONOS would laugh at me for being 'starstruck.'"

She took another sip of tea and glanced back up at me. "And now, the other thing." There was a long pause, and then she continued. "I'm worried about you, Kate. Not about your work with the medallion," she added quickly. "You've made truly unbelievable progress. I was nearly two years into the program before I could pull up the data as quickly as you do. You have a wonderful ability to focus."

"Then . . . what?" I asked.

Another pause as Katherine stirred her tea, clearly trying to decide how to phrase what she wanted to say. "It's about Trey, Kate. I'm worried that the two of you have gotten much too close, and certainly you know this relationship can't last?"

I was stung, and yet I couldn't help but feel that there was some truth in those words. I myself had questioned why Trey would be interested in me—he was handsome, smart, funny . . . and I was just me, just *Kate.* "I know," I said, looking down into my teacup. "He's really great, and I'm sure there are lots of other girls who—"

Katherine reached over and grabbed my hand. "Oh no, sweetie. No, no, no." Tears had risen to her eyes. "That's definitely not what I meant. There is every reason in the world for that young man to be interested in you. You are beautiful, intelligent, witty—why *wouldn't* he want to be with you?" She shook her head and smiled at me. "It's true that you may lack self-confidence, but . . . I seem to remember that being a rather common problem at age sixteen— excuse me, *seventeen.*"

"Then why did you say . . . ?"

"I don't think you've been thinking this through clearly. I agreed to allow Trey to spend time with you because you were right—you needed a friend. I was so worried you would slip into depression with Deborah and Harry no longer . . . in your life." She paused. "But if you manage to fix this timeline, your parents will be back and we'll be returning to life as it was before. Trey—well, he won't be at Briar Hill, based on what you've said. He took your slot at the school, correct? Trey is not going to remember any of this. He won't remember *you,* Kate."

I thought back to Trey's comment our first night on the porch— that I could just toss a sock or an earring on the ground, and he'd believe everything again. That might have been a good remedy several weeks ago when we had spent only a day together. But now? I would remember all of our time together and Trey wouldn't. Even if I did find a way to meet him again, it wouldn't be the same. That idea hurt a whole lot more now than it had at the beginning.

"Why can't he just be here when I make the jump?" I asked. "Like he was when I did the test jump? He'd be protected then, just like Connor and you are—and he'd remember, right?"

"Yes," Katherine answered. "He would remember. But I cannot allow that, Kate, for two reasons. First, it is a violation of CHRONOS rules—" She held up her hand as I began to object. "Please let me finish. It is a violation of CHRONOS rules to disrupt the timeline in that fashion. We are trying to repair the damage that Saul created and I cannot condone changing the timeline simply because you've allowed yourself to become so attached to Trey."

I narrowed my eyes. Katherine made it sound like Trey was a stray cat. "You said there were *two* reasons?" I asked, keeping my voice level.

Katherine nodded. "If you really do care about this boy, then you will understand my second point—even if you don't agree with the first one. Trey will eventually have to leave this house and when he does, he will have two entirely different sets of memories to reconcile. That's hard enough for those of us who have the CHRONOS gene," Katherine said, shaking her head slowly. "You said it was disorienting when he saw the picture of your father disappear. That was a few small memories that didn't coincide. Do you really want to subject him to that on a much, much larger scale? There would be thousands of points of disconnect—Connor and I really don't know what effect it might have on the boy. There could easily be a risk of permanent mental damage."

My heart sank. I hadn't thought at all about the possible impact on Trey.

"I'm not saying that you should end your friendship with Trey immediately, Kate. You still have a few days. Just enjoy the relationship for what it is—for what it has to be. Otherwise, you're going to end up much sadder than you need to be when it ends. Because it *will* have to end."

∞ 16 ∞

Despite my best efforts to replicate the sleek and sophisticated updo that was described step-by-step in the September 1893 edition of *The Delineator*, my hair was still down. I was used to tucking my hair up in a knot for school, but that was apparently too simple for women in the 1890s. The style required several side braids tucked into complicated loops of hair, all of it held into place by combs and heaven knows what else to form a gravity-defying swoop. I eventually gave up in frustration.

From the neck down, however, I was now in costume. The shoes that Katherine had ordered from an online costume house had arrived that afternoon, a few hours after the dress and undergarments were delivered from the seamstress. I helped Connor and Katherine slip tiny silver receivers of some sort into the fabric of the dress, the undergarments, and the boots to make sure they didn't disappear if I took them off. The receivers amplified the CHRONOS field—a setup similar to what Connor had rigged for the house but on a much smaller scale. This finally solved a question that had been bugging me for weeks. What was to stop a historian from snagging a Picasso sketch or stuffing her bag full of gold to bring back with her? It wasn't just respect for CHRONOS rules and regs. She wouldn't be able to sell the items because she'd be caught as soon as the stolen object left the protection of a medallion and the new purchaser discovered he or she held nothing but an empty bag.

The boots were made of a soft white leather. Katherine said they were kidskin, which I'm pretty sure means baby goat, and I tried not to think about that as I slipped them on. They fit okay, but it took forever to connect all of the buttons, even after Connor improvised a buttonhook.

And then there were the buttons on the *back* of the dress. "I could save everyone a great deal of agony," I remarked, "if I just sneaked some Velcro into one of the invention exhibits." Based on the books I'd been reading, everything from the automatic dishwasher to Juicy Fruit gum was being displayed to the visitors at the Exposition. "I could just slip a package to that guy at the fair who was demonstrating the first zipper—I'm sure he'd be delighted at the upgrade."

Connor raised an eyebrow. "Don't let Katherine hear you talking like that. She'll be convinced that you're too much like your grandfather to trust on a CHRONOS mission." His lip twitched slightly, as if he was repressing a smile. "History is sacred—like a nature hike. 'Leave only footprints, take only memories.'" His voice sounded like a cross between Katherine and a tour guide at a museum.

The doorbell and Daphne simultaneously announced Trey's arrival, just as I was starting on the buttons on the second shoe. When I finished, I left the library—a bit shaky on the unusually shaped heels—and began, very carefully, to descend the staircase. Trey was already seated on the couch, reading through his British literature assignment.

His face lit up when he saw me. "Well, good afternoon, Miss Scarlett."

I glanced down at the dress. The fabric was green silk, so I could see the comparison. The color was more vivid and closer to a dark emerald green, however, than the dress that Scarlett had created from recycled curtains in *Gone with the Wind.* The cut was narrower, too—and I was very glad of that fact, since it meant fewer hot, sticky crinolines. The bodice was fitted, with a square neck and sleeves that were puffed above my elbow and snug to the arm below, with ivory lace trim.

"You're about four decades off, Mr. Coleman," I replied in my very best Deep South drawl, holding a pretend fan to my face. "But flattery will get you everywhere."

He met me at the foot of the stairs. "Seriously, Kate, you look beautiful. The dress really brings out the color of your eyes." He glanced down at his school-mandated khakis. "I feel way under-dressed for the prom."

Prom. Another reminder of the world outside, where it was now approaching the end of the school year. Trey had mentioned finals a few times, but I hadn't even thought about the junior prom. I'd studiously avoided all school dances in the past, but with Trey, it might not have been so bad to dress up and dance under twinkle lights and crepe paper. "Briar Hill's prom . . . ," I began.

"Was last Saturday," Trey finished.

Last Saturday. The highlight of that evening had been a Scrabble game with the two of us versus Katherine and Connor.

"Don't even look like that," he said. "I wasn't planning on going before I met you, and while I'll admit that I would have been delighted to go with you, I was much happier here—*with* you—than I would have been there, *without* you."

I sat down on the edge of the sofa, remembering my recent conversation with Katherine. "Estella and your father probably hate me—you're spending so much time here. And I made you miss your prom."

"Which I wasn't going to *anyway.* Estella was beginning to hate *me* for not bringing you around. She was saying I'm ashamed of her—that she wasn't cool enough to introduce to my girlfriend—but all is forgiven now that she's fed you. And Dad just keeps giving me this little smile and shaking his head." He laughed. "You know, the oh-to-be-young-and-in-love . . ." He trailed off, both of us feeling a bit awkward.

"Anyway," he said, "once you fix the universe—in your Scarlett O'Hara dress—we'll make up for lost time, okay? You *can* dance, I assume?"

I elbowed him. "*Yes*, I can dance, although I wouldn't try it in this dress. It's not for dancing—it's daytime wear, believe it or not." I looked down at the ankle-length skirt and the absurd shoes, shaking my head. "It would be a lot easier to fix the universe if I could dress like Wonder Woman—or Batgirl."

"Ooh—I would love to see *that*." Trey smiled. "I can definitely picture you as Batgirl, kicking the villain upside the head. But her costume would get you arrested in 1893."

"Not if I stayed on the Midway," I replied. "I'd fit right in." We'd spent the previous afternoon looking through a variety of photographs that were taken at the fair, or, as it was officially called, the 1893 Columbian Exposition. While many of the displays had been staid, proper, and educational, the exhibits that pulled in the *most* money were located in a mile-long strip adjacent to the fair, which was called the Midway Plaisance, and included amusements like the giant Ferris wheel that Katherine had mentioned. Apparently there were other, less family-oriented entertainments as well—the photos included revealing pictures of a belly dancer known as Little Egypt, one of many exotic dancers who had performed to packed houses in the evenings.

"True. You'd fit in on the Midway," Trey acknowledged. "And I'm sure it would be more fun. But from what you've said, Katherine didn't spend that day at the fair hanging out with the belly dancers. So . . . when are you going? You're worried about it, aren't you?"

I shrugged. "Soon. My bonnet still hasn't arrived." *Bonnet.* That word was so not in my vocabulary. "I need to go upstairs and change . . . I can't breathe. Katherine needs to loosen this corset next time."

"*Corset?*" Trey laughed.

"Don't. Even," I warned. "There are more clothes under this costume than I would normally wear in a week."

Trey had rented a DVD, a recent Jonah Hill film. I changed into denim shorts and the "Self-Rescuing Princess" T-shirt he had given me for my birthday—rather appropriate, he said, under the circumstances—and then we made a couple of peanut butter sandwiches and some popcorn to munch on while we watched the movie. It was nice to spend a few hours in the twenty-first century, after days of focusing on the 1890s, and I was happy for an excuse to avoid thinking about the upcoming jump and what would come afterward. Maybe Katherine was right—I should just enjoy the time we had left. There was no reason to bring Trey down by discussing the inevitable.

Trey needed to finish an essay on Aldous Huxley for his British lit class, so he left a bit earlier than usual, just before dark. "I'll be online later," he said. "You said you've read *Brave New World,* right?"

I nodded.

"Good—then you can read the essay when I finish it to see if it makes sense." He gave me a concerned look. "You're kind of quiet tonight, babe. Are you tired?"

"A bit," I said, glancing down at my feet.

"Then maybe it's a good thing we have to make it an early night." He gave me a long, deep kiss as we stood on the porch and I watched as he headed down the sidewalk to where his car was parked. "See you tomorrow, okay?"

I smiled as Trey walked away, still enjoying the glow of his kiss. As I closed the door and turned to go upstairs to the library, however, I noticed his literature book on the table. I grabbed it, double-checking to make sure the medallion was around my neck, and dashed out the door. Trey was driving away as I ran through the gate, waving the book at him and calling his name. The brake lights flashed momentarily, and I thought for a second that he had seen or heard me, but he was just slowing down to round the curve in the road.

I had just turned to go back in and call him when someone appeared behind me, quite literally from out of nowhere. He grabbed my left arm, pulling it up sharply and painfully behind my back. My first impulse was to follow my self-defense training and twist toward him, kicking to throw him off balance, and to use the heavy textbook to whack him in the head—but then I felt his other hand reach under my T-shirt. He closed his fingers around the CHRONOS key and I froze.

"Drop the book and call for your grandmother." I recognized the voice immediately. It was Simon, my pudgy friend from the Metro.

Daphne had either smelled him—which I thought very likely since he seemed not to have bathed since our last encounter—or else she heard him because she began barking wildly from inside the house.

"I'm not playing around here, Kate. Just do it."

"Katherine, be careful!" I began, tossing the book onto the grass beside the walkway. My voice was little more than a hoarse croak. "Closer—we need to get closer if she's going to hear me over the dog." I was hoping that I could reach the maple tree that marked the boundary of the protective zone, but Simon yanked threateningly on the medallion. I shuddered, partly from fear and partly from revulsion at the feel of his arm against my bare skin.

Daphne's claws were raking against the door now, and a split second later Katherine opened it. I saw her make a quick motion with the hand that was still inside, pointing upward twice. Then she pushed Daphne back into the foyer and walked onto the porch, closing the door behind her.

"Who are you? What do you want?" Katherine asked.

"What do you *think* I want? Just bring your medallion here and I'll let Kate keep this one. She can go about her business and she'll be just fine, as long as she never forgets and takes it off in the shower." On the last word he rubbed his arm against my bare stomach again and I fought to keep from gagging.

I watched as Katherine removed the CHRONOS key from around her neck. The blue light glowed between her fingers as she clutched it tightly in her hand. She was still about a foot away from the maple tree, still behind the barrier. "She's taken it off," I said. "Let's go get it." I tried to move toward Katherine, but Simon pulled me back.

"No," he said. "I think she can bring it to me. Do it now, Katherine." I wasn't sure if Simon knew about the protective zone or if he was just obstinate. I suspected the latter, given his comment about me being safe as long as I showered with the medallion. Either way, he wasn't budging an inch.

Katherine took a step forward. "And why should I believe that you'll let her go?"

I could feel Simon shrug behind me. "Brother Cyrus just said to finish *you*. And Kiernan—well, he has a vested interest in this one." He leaned in and brushed the top of my head with the side of his cheek. "For obvious reasons." I yanked my face as far away as possible, and he chuckled. "I'd rather not cross Kiernan unless I have to."

Katherine glanced around as though looking for anyone who might help us. When she didn't move forward, Simon continued, his voice casual. "I can take her key right now and then come get yours. You can't outrun me, and we both know I can take care of my business here and be years and miles away before anyone hears you scream." He jerked at my medallion to make his point, yanking the arm behind my back upward with his other hand.

I clenched my teeth to hold back a scream. "He's lying, Katherine. He won't let me go."

Katherine caught my eye for a long moment and gave me a sad smile. Then she walked toward us, stretching out the hand holding the medallion.

After that, several things happened at once. Simon had to either loosen his hold on my arm, which he still had wedged against my back, or let go of my medallion in order to take the other one from Katherine. He made the mistake of releasing my arm, and I quickly used it to pin his other hand against my chest, thrusting my leg backward and leaning forward at the same time. The idea was to throw him off balance, flip him, and then fall against him, hopefully maintaining contact with the medallion.

To my surprise, the move actually worked—but it was a moment too late. Just as I bent forward, tugging on Simon's arm, I saw the medallion leave Katherine's hand and fall into Simon's. Out of the corner of my eye, as we fell, I saw Katherine blink out of existence.

"No!" I screamed, and Simon took advantage of my shock, flipping me over and wedging his knee into my stomach. I could hear Daphne behind the door—her bark, already frantic, climbed up three notches.

"Sorry, pretty Katie." Simon gave me a mean little smile as he stashed Katherine's medallion in his pocket, then reached behind my neck to undo mine. "I'm actually going to need this CHRONOS key, too—and the half dozen or so your grandmother has stashed somewhere in that house." I struggled, trying to pull my body and his along the ground far enough to reach the maple tree and the protective zone. I felt the medallion's clasp give way and changed strategies, trying now to grab Simon's own medallion, but my fingers slipped against the fabric of his shirt.

He pushed more of his weight onto his knee, pressing the breath from my body in a quick whoosh. "Or maybe I'll just take you with me. Cyrus would never allow a traitor like Kiernan to have you, not after his recent interference, but you and *me* could have a real good time . . ." He slid his hand suggestively along my inner thigh. His mouth was just inches from mine, his breath against my face, and I felt panic beginning to set in. My vision began to blur. The light on the porch, directly in front of me, faded in and out several times as I struggled to get even the tiniest bit of air into my lungs.

Then there was a loud whack. Simon's head snapped back and his body slumped to the left, a red line of blood swelling up on his right temple. I saw the blue light of my medallion, still in Simon's hand, arcing upward against the twilit sky as he fell away, and Trey standing behind him with a raised tire iron. I braced myself for nothingness, thinking only how very happy I was that Trey's face, and not Simon's ugly leer, was the last thing I would see before I vanished, just like Katherine.

∞ 17 ∞

But nothing happened. Trey reached down and yanked my medallion out of Simon's hand. "Are you okay?" he asked. He wedged the tire iron under his foot and leaned forward to put the medallion back around my neck. "Kate?"

I nodded, still unable to pull in a full breath, much less speak. Simon groaned as Trey scooped me into his arms and carried me to the porch. His jaw was tight as he turned back toward Simon and, from his expression, I'm pretty sure that the game plan was to grab the tire iron and finish the bastard off. If that was Trey's intent, however, he never got the chance. Simon was still sprawled on the lawn, but his hand reached up for his medallion and before Trey had moved more than a few steps, he was gone.

Trey stared at the spot where Simon had been for several seconds and then turned back to me. He looked stunned. "Did he hurt you?"

I shook my head, tears stinging my eyes. Trey sat down beside me, pulling me close. I breathed in his scent as I tried to fight back the tears. "Katherine . . ."

"I know. I remembered my lit book was on the coffee table—I was just getting out of the car, when she . . ." He paused, shaking his head in disbelief. "That's when I went back for the tire iron."

I glanced toward the curb. The bumper of Trey's car was just visible beyond the hedge. "I didn't even hear you pull up."

Trey shrugged. "Daphne's racket provided good cover. Thankfully *he* didn't hear me either." He pressed his lips against my hair and we sat there for a moment, trying to process the past few minutes. "I just don't understand why Katherine didn't wait—I know she saw me drive up."

The porch light dimmed again, then brightened briefly just before the bulb popped, causing both of us to jump to our feet. "Remind me to ask Connor where the lightbulbs are," I said in a small voice.

Trey nodded. "Yeah. And now that you mention it, where exactly *is* Connor?"

I don't know. I saw Katherine signal to him as she was coming out the door. Maybe we should go and check on him?"

I opened the door and immediately saw Daphne and Connor sitting at the top of the stairs. Connor's head was in his hands and Daphne's nose lay between her paws—a perfect study in dejection. They both looked up at the sound of the door, a confused expression spreading over Connor's face. "Kate? I thought—oh, thank God! I thought both of you—I mean, I saw Katherine . . . go . . . and when I looked back through the library window you were gone, too."

"If you saw Kate trying to fight that guy off, why didn't you try to help her?" Trey asked. Connor had started down the stairs but paused at the anger in Trey's voice. "Or Katherine? Where the hell *were* you?"

I put my hand on Trey's arm, shaking my head softly. "It's all right, Trey. Katherine told him to go up to the library. Right, Connor?"

Connor nodded, continuing down the stairs with Daphne beside him. "We could see through the peephole that you were outside the perimeter. She thought that trying to expand the safe zone with the third medallion was our best chance. But it didn't work. I still haven't figured out how to keep the damned thing from overloading the system."

I remembered the porch light dimming as I fought with Simon, then the surge popping the bulb a few minutes later. I gave Connor a sad smile. "It did work, briefly. Otherwise, I wouldn't be here. It just wasn't in time for Katherine . . ."

We sat down in the living room. I curled against Trey on the sofa. I was suddenly freezing and guessed that it was probably from shock. All of us, even Daphne, seemed dazed and the room was still for several minutes.

Finally, I broke the silence. "Can I fix this? I mean, if I succeed in stopping her murder at the fair, will Katherine be here when I get back?"

Connor gave me an uncertain look, but he nodded. "I think so. I mean, if she makes it to 1969, to New York, then everything from that point unfolds as it did before. She'd still exist in this timeline, so it really wouldn't matter whether she was holding the CHRONOS key."

"Then we do this. As soon as possible. There are just a few other things we need to figure out—it shouldn't take more than a couple hours."

To my surprise, Connor agreed. "You're probably right. I think the tricky part for you will be getting Katherine's attention without tipping her off about Saul."

"But why shouldn't Kate tell her about Saul?" Trey interjected. "Isn't he the one trying to kill her?"

"Not directly," Connor said. "Someone else will be doing the dirty work for him. Saul can't use the medallion any more than Katherine could. The version of Saul that's there with her in 1893 . . . he's rotten to the core, I'm sure, but he hasn't decided to kill her yet. And how inclined do you think Katherine is going to be to continue a relationship with him if she finds out his true nature?"

"It bugs me, too," I said. "Even though I know I have to keep quiet, part of me wants to warn her to run away, fast—I saw what Saul did to her face that night." Connor looked up, surprise and anger in his eyes, and I realized that Katherine might not have told him exactly how abusive Saul could be. "But if I do that," I continued, "it increases the chance that everything changes. No Mom—at least not one born in 1970—no me. And a lot of other differences in the timeline, too. So I can't tell her the full truth—just enough to prevent her murder."

"And then what?" Trey said. "Don't you think he'll try again—some other trip, some other day?"

"One step at a time," I said. "We need Katherine back. Eventually, we'll have to find a way to stop Saul—to prevent the rise of Cyrist International—and I'll be looking for any clues I can find on how to do it on this trip. But if I think too much about that, I'll never be able to focus on what's in front of me right this minute."

"So even when this is over, you're still in danger. How am I supposed to be okay with that?"

It was pretty clear that our conversation was headed down a more personal path, so I took Trey's hand and motioned toward the stairs. Connor's eyes were also red and watery, and he was running his hand through Daphne's fur in an absentminded way. I suspected that he would appreciate some personal space to deal with his own emotions. He was closer to Katherine than I was and he was even more alone now. My heart went out to him and I squeezed his shoulder as we walked past. "Get some rest, okay, Connor? We'll get up early tomorrow and start with clear heads."

Trey and I went upstairs to my room and sat down on the couch by the window. The moon, nearly full, was just visible through the leaves. I flipped my legs across Trey's lap, propping my bare feet on the sofa so that I could look at him, and traced the line of his clenched jaw with my fingers. Then I moved closer and kissed the side of his neck, tracing a small circle with my tongue—something that I knew, from recent experience, drove him just a little bit crazy. His arm tightened around me.

"I don't have a choice here, Trey," I said softly. "You know that, right? I'll be as careful as I can be—I promise."

He was silent for a moment. "I just feel . . . trapped, Kate. Not by you, no, just the whole damned situation. You're doing something impossibly dangerous and I can't help you."

I gave a slightly exasperated sigh. "Trey, you just cracked Simon's skull with a tire iron." I glanced down at my Self-Rescuing Princess T-shirt. "I didn't exactly live up to the title this time, did I? If you hadn't been there, I'd either be dead, or worse, he'd still have his smelly hands all over me." Thinking about Simon's arm against my bare skin made me shudder, and I felt Trey's body stiffen as well.

I reached up and kissed him again, a long, slow kiss to wipe away that memory for both of us. "Thank you."

Trey relaxed a bit, and then shook his head. His right hand was resting on my feet, and his thumb traced a nervous pattern across my toenails, which were painted a deep crimson. "The thing that's really killing me, Kate, is that I'm not going to *know* whether you fail or succeed. Tomorrow, when you make the jump, this . . . us . . . we're over, right?" He gave a bitter laugh. "Whether you save Katherine or you're both killed in the process, I'll just return to some version of my life before. At Briar Hill or someplace else, but either way, I won't remember *you*—I won't remember that I love you."

Neither of us had said it before, and my heart surged—despite everything, it was wonderful to have it out there, in the open, confessed. "I love you, too, Trey." He broke into a huge smile and then misery washed over his face again.

"When did you figure it out?" I asked. "I mean, not that you . . . love me, but . . ."

He shrugged. "Something in Katherine's expression the other night, at your birthday party, kept eating at me. Then today, as I was driving away, it sort of clicked into place. I turned the car around before I even remembered the stupid textbook."

"I wasn't as sharp," I said. "Katherine had to spell it out for me in big block letters. And I still tried to argue with her—why couldn't you be here? Why couldn't we let you remember?"

"And why can't I?" he asked, a bit of hope in his voice. "I can help Connor—you're one person short now."

I shook my head. "CHRONOS regulations, for one thing. We're trying to fix the timeline and that would be yet another alteration."

"Yeah, well, screw CHRONOS regulations."

"That's what I said," I continued, keenly aware of the role reversal. Here I was repeating Katherine's arguments with Trey's face and voice reflecting the very same emotions I'd felt—anger, denial, defiance.

"But the bigger issue is that it could . . . hurt you, Trey." I stared down at his hand, fingers laced through my own. "You remember when you saw the pictures disappear, right? That was your brain trying to reconcile two very small conflicting versions of reality. Multiply that thousands of times over if you stayed here tomorrow. You'd have to leave the protective barrier at some point, and Katherine doesn't know what it might do to you—mentally, emotionally."

"I don't care," he said.

"Maybe not. But I *do*."

We stared at each other for a while, seeing whose stubborn look would last the longest. Mine broke first, and I began crying. "I can't focus on what I have to do, Trey, if I'm worried that you're going to be hurt."

"And now you know how *I* feel. Damn it, Kate . . ." Tears were in his eyes and he held me for a long moment before speaking again. "Will you answer one question for me?"

I nodded.

"Who is Kiernan?" My face flushed, and I didn't respond. "I mean, I know he's Connor's great-granddad or whatever—the guy he showed me in the two photographs. But Simon was saying something to Katherine when I first pulled up—and then again when he was . . . on top of you. Exactly who is Kiernan to *you*, Kate?"

"He's no one to me, Trey." A small voice inside called me a liar, but I continued. I was determined to tell Trey as much of the truth as I could—as much as I understood, at any rate. "Kiernan told me to run that day on the Metro. He almost certainly saved my life when he did. And I've . . . seen his image in the medallion. He says we knew each other, in some other timeline."

Oh, and he kissed me, I thought, but didn't add, since that fact seemed likely to make Trey feel worse, rather than better. And I hadn't asked Kiernan to kiss me. Enjoyed, yes. Requested, no.

"He knew you well enough to stake a claim, from the sound of it." Trey's voice was bitter and hurt. "Simon said Saul would never let Kiernan have you *now* . . ."

I pulled his face toward mine and stared hard into his eyes. "Whoever Kiernan knew in that version of the timeline, Trey, it wasn't me. Neither Saul Rand nor Simon will be deciding who *has* me. *I* make that choice. *I* decide the person I love, the person I want. No one else."

I pulled my body closer to his and slipped my fingers inside his shirt, running my hand against his chest. "And I love *you*, Trey. I want *you*." I hesitated, looking for the right words. "I've never . . . with anyone . . . but I want *you* . . ."

Then his mouth was on mine, hard and hungry. His hands moved up the side of my body and I arched reflexively toward him. For several minutes, there was nothing else in the world, just the two of us, his body against mine—and then he broke away and sat up, staring down at the carpet.

"What's wrong?" I tried to pull him back toward me, but he shook his head.

I gave him a weak little smile. "Daphne's not here. No chaperone, see?"

He didn't respond. I was now thoroughly embarrassed and kicking myself for not letting him make the all-important first move. Biting my lower lip to keep it from shaking, I pulled away to the far end of the sofa and hugged my knees, staring at a different spot on the carpet.

After a moment, I felt his hand running gently down the side of my leg. I didn't look up.

"Kate. Kate? Look at me. Please." A tear was making its way down my cheek, the cheek he couldn't see. I closed my eyes tight, hoping my other eye wouldn't turn traitor as well. He got off the couch and knelt on the floor in front of me, brushing the tear away with the pad of his thumb. "Would you just look at me, *please*?"

I glanced up and he continued. "You *have* to know beyond any doubt how badly I want you." He chuckled softly. "I mean, really Kate, could it be any more obvious?"

I didn't answer, even though I knew he was right.

"At this very minute," he said, staring into my eyes, "there is nothing on this earth that I want more than you. But we both know that tomorrow or the next day, my memory of this night will be gone. You might remember, but I won't. And when we make love for the first time, Kate, that's a memory I want to *keep*."

∞

Trey didn't leave until nearly midnight. I don't know if he ever managed to write the Huxley essay. Probably not. He skipped most of his classes the next day, arriving on the doorstep just after noon with lunch from O'Malley's—lots of onion rings and three obscenely large sandwiches. He hadn't shaved and he didn't look like he had slept any more than I had.

"Ditching school again, Mr. Coleman?" I asked with a soft smile.

"My girlfriend is about to change this entire timeline. I can't imagine any scenario in which it actually *matters* that I left after my first class."

He had a point.

"What about your parents? Estella?"

"I told them that your grandmother took a turn for the worse yesterday, and that I needed to be with you. Neither of which is a lie," he added. "I expect the flowers my dad asked me to order will be here shortly."

We sat down to eat with Connor, who, despite his great love for corned beef on rye, didn't seem to have much appetite. The three of us reviewed the game plan as we finished lunch. "Try your best to follow her," Connor said, "but you also need to keep plan B as an option, in case Katherine disappears into the crowd. Because she probably will."

Connor was right. The fair attracted an average of 120,000 visitors per day between the time it opened in May and the time it closed at the end of October. That's about three times as many people as Disney World handles each day, and the Exposition was held on a much smaller plot of land. The odds of me being able to keep her in sight were pretty slim.

"I'll try to keep up with her," I said. "If I can't, she'll be with the mayor's group at the Ferris wheel at ten fifteen, and after lunch she'll be downtown at the place where they held all the big meetings during the Expo—the one that's the Art Institute now."

"Right," Connor said. "They called it the Auxiliary Building. But that's going to mean navigating Chicago's public transit. I know you've read CHRONOS notes on the era, but I'd feel a lot better if you stayed close to a stable point. If worse comes to worst, you can come back here and then take another stab at it."

He was right—we could roll the dice more than once. If I lost sight of Katherine entirely and simply couldn't find her, I could always return to the stable point and give it another try. A second jump would, however, mean multiple versions of myself walking around the fair, which would complicate things. I had a bad gut feeling about taking too long to accomplish this anyway, and both Connor and Trey felt the same. Katherine's house was relatively well protected by an alarm service, but we were totally unarmed. As much as I hate guns, it wasn't too comforting that Simon and whatever other minions of Saul's had weapons and we didn't. And, as Trey's dad had noted, Cyrists now had friends in very high places.

Connor and I had spent the better part of the morning going over Katherine's diary entries for the October 28th jump, gathering what details we could about her hotel and her itinerary on that trip. By the time Trey arrived, we'd had to admit defeat on one count— Katherine had failed to mention the hotel specifically, other than noting that it was near the fair. She had stayed at the Palmer House on the first jump for those dates, but that information wasn't much help since it was the slightly later version of Katherine who was targeted. There were several other bits of info that would have been really nice to know, and I mentally kicked myself for not having asked these obvious questions when Katherine was around to answer.

As I picked at my pastrami, it occurred to me that I could just make a jump back to the previous day and ask Katherine, but Connor quickly nixed that plan. "Can you honestly tell me you won't warn her?" he asked. "That you won't do something to ensure she doesn't walk out that door when Simon grabs you?"

I considered lying, but I finally went with the truth. "No, Connor—but so what? Why shouldn't I warn her? Or warn myself not to go outside? It's not like this is such a wonderful version of the timeline that it couldn't do with a bit of alteration, and I'm willing to risk having some out-of-sync memories."

Connor shook his head angrily. "Why in hell do you think she sent me upstairs, Kate? Our first priority has to be protecting you. No matter what. As much as it tore me apart to see Katherine vanish, at least I knew it was reversible—well, I knew it was reversible once *you* walked in the door, at any rate," he continued, his voice softening. "That's my point. Say we stop what happened yesterday—they'll almost certainly just attack the house at that point. If we change something and Katherine survives, but you don't—well, there are no mulligans without you, Kate. Then Katherine dies, Rand wins, and we just get to sit back and see what he does with the world."

I wasn't sure exactly what a mulligan was, but Trey was nodding. "Okay—that explains why she gave Simon the medallion even though she clearly saw me driving up. There was still a risk that he would pull your CHRONOS key before I could reach him. She was buying Connor some extra time to extend the barrier."

"And buying you some extra time to grab a weapon, although I don't know if she realized that," Connor added. "I just hope that slimy bastard is in a world of pain today."

∞

The floral arrangement from Trey's dad arrived later in the afternoon. It was beautiful—white lilies, lavender roses, and purple alstroemeria, with clusters of tiny white baby's breath. I hoped Katherine would eventually see it, and I was glad that there would, at least within this house, be some reminders of my relationship with Trey. Even though every little memento would hurt like hell, that still seemed better than what he was facing—no memories at all.

The flowers were followed within minutes by the delivery of a large hatbox. It contained a rather elaborate green bonnet, which I'd quite liked the idea of traveling without. So with the last of my costume in hand, we set a firm departure time of 6 P.M. and the three of us began final preparations for my jump.

An emerald-green parasol lay on the bed, next to the black handbag that Katherine had carried on her last CHRONOS trip. The bag was about forty years out of fashion for a trip to 1893, but it would have to do, as it contained several hidden pockets that would come in handy. I couldn't carry luggage, since I would emerge within the fairgrounds and there were no hotels on the premises. So the purse was stuffed with my spending money (all pre-1893, a coin collector's dream), one of the diaries, a vintage map of the Exposition, a hairbrush, a toothbrush and toothpaste, a tiny first-aid kit, a flask of water, and four energy bars.

Connor's inner Katherine had balked at several items in the bag, noting correctly that they were not historically appropriate, but this wasn't a typical research mission and I might not be able to stand in line for hours to get food or drink. I cut several paper bags from Whole Foods into rectangles so that I could wrap the energy bars in plain brown paper—they'd probably get hard, but at least I wouldn't starve. And I wasn't traveling without a toothbrush if I might have to stay overnight, even if that toothbrush *was* made of sparkly pink plastic.

At a few minutes after five, I went into the bathroom to change into my undergarments. Trey waited outside so that he could help me lace the corset. I felt a bit awkward when I walked back into the bedroom, even though far more of my body was exposed by the shorts and tank tops I usually wore than by the yards of white silk and lace in which I was now enveloped.

He raised an appreciative eyebrow and smiled as he took me by the shoulders, then turned me around to begin pulling the laces together. He didn't cinch it as tightly as Katherine had, but

I thought it was tight enough that the dress would fit. When he was done with the laces, he lifted my hair and pushed it over one shoulder, pressing his lips against the nape of my neck and adding several more very gentle kisses down my back until he reached the lace edge of the camisole. His breath was warm against my skin and I locked my knees to keep from melting into a gooey puddle on the floor.

"Promise me," Trey said, very softly, as he turned me around to face him, "that one day, I will have the pleasure of *un*lacing this contraption. I can see why you're not too happy with it, but there is something to be said for opening a gift very slowly."

I smiled up at him with a hopeful look. "You could just unlace it now?"

"No can do, pretty girl," he said, shaking his head. He sat down on the edge of the bed and pulled me onto his lap. "You have a job to finish. First, you're going to stay away from tall, dark strangers at the fair, especially ones who time travel." I blushed a bit at the veiled reference to Kiernan, but nodded. "I'd also prefer that you stay away from the guy who ran that World's Fair Hotel."

"No worries there," I said. "I'm going to have enough on my hands trying to prevent one murder, without taking on a serial killer. If I *have* to stay overnight, I'll follow Katherine's lead and catch a cab to the Palmer House."

"Okay—next, you're going to save Katherine and come right back here. And finally, you're going to *find me*. That shouldn't be too hard, even if I'm not at Briar Hill."

I held back the tears that were burning my eyes. "It won't matter, Trey. You won't know me."

"Correct," he said, and then flashed me a big grin.

"Then why are you smiling?"

"Because I know somethin' you don' know."

"And what is that?" My lips twitched, both at the *Princess Bride* reference and at the fact that I'd walked straight into his joke. "I already *know* you're not left-handed."

"It comes to this," he continued, the smile fading but never quite leaving his eyes. "I've been thinking pretty hard about the weeks since we met and I'm almost certain that I fell in love with you the moment you opened your eyes, right there on the floor in trig class. So does it really matter? You do what you have to do in 1893—I'm not even going to think about the possibility of you failing, because you won't fail—and then you *find* me."

"And exactly what am I supposed to say when I find you, Trey Coleman?"

He laughed. "Don't say anything. Or say, 'Wrong class,' like you did the first time. It won't make a bit of difference what you say. Smile at me, flip me onto my back with one of your wicked ninja moves, and then kiss me—even if I forget every single thing about you, I'm a guy, Kate. Believe me, I'm not going to push you away."

"Maybe not . . . but you'll think I'm crazy."

He shrugged and kissed my nose. "Thought you were crazy that first day, too, but I'm still here, right?"

I couldn't argue with that, and even if I'd had a viable argument, I couldn't bear the thought of taking the little glimmer of hope from his eyes.

The spare CHRONOS medallion was shining, bright and blue, on the nightstand. I tucked it into the lined, hidden pocket near the bottom of my petticoat, and then Trey helped me into the dark green dress and the annoying boots. We even managed to get my hair into an orderly, if not ornate, chignon and I arranged the bonnet on top.

It looked a bit ridiculous to me.

Trey, of course, said that I looked perfect—although something in his eyes told me he was still envisioning me in the white corset and petticoats that he knew were underneath. He fastened the bracelet that Katherine had given me around my wrist. The charm matched the dress perfectly—the ivory lace and green silk echoing the hues of the pearls and jade that formed the hourglass.

Connor was sitting in the kitchen when we came downstairs. He had been looking more and more uneasy about the entire jump as the day progressed. Judging from his expression when we walked in, I suspected that he had a full list of last-minute concerns to tick off. He glanced at the outfit and nodded once, however, which seemed to mean that I passed inspection, and then he turned toward Trey.

"Do you mind if Kate and I talk . . . privately? For just a moment? I hate to ask, but . . ."

Trey shook his head, although he looked a bit concerned. "No problem, Connor. Daphne's on the patio. We'll toss the Frisbee for a while." He leaned over and gave me a quick kiss on the cheek and then headed out the back door.

Connor watched him as he walked out. "He seems in a better mood than last night."

"I guess. What's up?" Connor didn't answer for a moment. I don't know if he expected some private confession from me about why Trey's mood had improved, but I just raised an eyebrow and waited until he finally spoke.

"You don't have to do this, Kate. We'll find another way. You're taking an awful risk and it just doesn't seem . . . right, to let you go."

I smiled at him and walked over to the coffeepot. It was still warm, so I poured the remainder into a mug. "If you were going to go all protective on me, Connor, couldn't you have done it before we buttoned up these horrid shoes? And the hair? And—"

"I'm serious, Kate."

I sat down beside him and squeezed his hand. "I know you are, Connor. But what choice do we have, really? I'm not willing to give up my entire family."

He motioned toward the backyard with his head. "And what about Trey? It's pretty obvious how you feel, Kate—and he's been head over heels since the first day you dragged him in the door. Are you willing to give him up?"

Having spent half the day either crying or fighting down tears, I wasn't a bit surprised to feel them rising to the surface again. "Again, do I have a choice, Connor? And maybe Trey is right. He's convinced himself that this won't matter—that I'll find him and we'll be together. I'll just have a few memories that he doesn't."

"I'm not trying to make things harder on you, Kate, it's just—" He broke off and looked down at the table, his thumbnail tracing a groove in the wood along the edge. "Katherine tell you about my kids?"

I nodded.

"I've always wished I had known what was coming—even if I couldn't prevent it, I could have prepared, said good-bye, you know?" He gave me a rueful smile. "But I didn't get the option."

He sighed and pulled an envelope out of his pocket. "Don't get mad at Trey—all he did was give him the address—he doesn't even know this arrived. It was Katherine's decision not to show it to you—said she didn't see the point in upsetting you. She was probably right, but . . . maybe you should know . . ." He pushed the letter toward me.

It was typewritten, but I recognized the signature at the bottom instantly.

Kate,

I remembered the name Briar Hill from the ID you showed me. I didn't remember your friend's last name, but fortunately there was only one Trey and one of the math teachers at Briar Hill located him for me. Trey gave me your address, but made it crystal clear that I'd better not hurt you again.

I never meant to hurt you at all, Kate. I hope you can under-stand my reaction. A lot of what you told me seems too incredible to believe, but I am convinced that you're my daughter or at least the daughter I would have had, if I'd ever known your mother.

If you decide that this timeline is where you belong, please call me. Do you need help? Do you need money, a place to stay? I want to know you—at the very least, maybe we can be friends?

Please call. Or write. I don't know how I'll explain this to Emily or the boys, but we'll find a way to make it work.

By the time I reached the end, tears were pouring down my face in a steady stream. At the bottom, I could see where he'd started to sign *Harry,* but he'd crossed it out. Instead, he had added the same signature I'd seen at the bottom of every birthday card, postcard, and note he'd ever written to me—*Dad.*

Connor looked uncomfortable. "I'm sorry, Kate. Maybe it wasn't a good idea to show you . . . I just . . ."

I could hear Trey laughing in the backyard, telling Daphne she'd made a good catch. Part of me wanted to view the letter as an omen, a sign that I should reconsider. But I shook my head.

"No, Connor, you were right to show me. Thank you. It makes me feel good to know for certain that my dad is a good person in any timeline. I kind of knew it already—I could tell he wasn't try-ing to hurt me—but it's nice to see that he wants to . . . be there for me, at least as much as he can be."

I leaned back in my chair and shook my head. "But this letter doesn't change anything, Connor—we both know that. Even if Saul were to back off and wasn't actively trying to kill me, I'd have to wear a medallion every time I walked out the door. So would you. My mom would still be gone and Katherine—your kids, too. And Harry still wouldn't be *my* dad. My biological father, yeah—but not my *dad.* I'll have all of my memories, but he . . ."

Connor glanced toward the door, and then quickly looked down at his feet. He didn't say anything, but I could follow his train of thought—the same would be true of my relationship with Trey.

"I know, Connor—but I've had a month with Trey and nearly seventeen years with Dad. And Trey seems convinced that all I have to do is kiss him and we'll magically be . . . *us* again."

"Princess Charming, I presume?" He gave me a halfhearted grin. "The only problem is that *you* seem less convinced on that point than Trey."

"Yeah, but letting him know that isn't going to make it any easier on either of us, is it?" I glanced at the clock. Five-forty-eight. The six o'clock deadline was obviously fluid—I'd be arriving early on the morning of October 28th, 1893, no matter what time it happened to be when I left the library. But every minute I waited made it more likely that I would lose my nerve.

"I'll meet you in the library in ten minutes, okay?" I gave him a shaky smile and walked to the back door, tucking the letter into my pocket.

Trey was seated on the low stone wall surrounding the patio, with his back to me. Daphne lay at his feet, happily chewing on the edge of her neon green Frisbee. The late-afternoon sun was low in the sky, and combined with the few remaining tears in my eyes, it created a soft golden aura around him. I stood there for a minute, just looking at him, wanting to cement this in my memory. He turned toward me and smiled, and I had to fight back a fresh wave of tears.

I bent down and called Daphne to me, delaying the moment when I'd need to look up at Trey. "You take care of Connor for a little while, okay, girl? I'm going to go get Katherine." The good-bye was more for me than for Daphne, since from her perspective, if everything worked out as planned, I'd only be gone a matter of minutes. She lifted her head and sniffed at my cheeks where the tears had been, giving me a soft lick before she went back to gnawing on the toy.

"What was that about?" Trey said, motioning his head toward the kitchen.

I sat down beside him and pulled the letter out of my pocket. He started to speak when he finished reading, but I smiled gently at him and shook my head. "It's okay, Trey. I'm glad I read it, although I'm still sorry that I interrupted his life. He seemed so happy there—but you know, he's happy with Sara, too. And with me."

I took his hand and laced my fingers through his. "And we don't know how any of this works; Katherine said that even in her era there was this huge debate about whether changing something would just spin off a new timeline . . . whether there could be an infinite number of different timelines all coexisting on separate planes. She said that maybe this timeline goes on, too, somehow, and some version of my dad will still be—"

"No," Trey interrupted, his voice resolute. "No. I don't believe that. This timeline *ends*." I realized with a pang that while the infinite-planes-of-existence theory had sounded pretty good to me, since this version of Dad and my two little half brothers might still exist in some cosmic sense, it had a very different meaning for Trey.

He shook his head, squeezing my hand tightly. "I don't want an infinite number of lives on different planes if even one of them means I'm not with you. You're going back to fix *this* reality, to make it right again so that we can be together. And it *will* be okay. Estella always tells me that you have to have faith to get through life—and I'm not sure I have the type of faith she's talking about, but I have faith in you. In us."

He pulled me to my feet and held me a few inches away, a mischievous twinkle in his eye. "What was it Westley said to Buttercup? 'This is true love—you think this happens every day?'"

"I just wish you were going to be there with me in this particular Fire Swamp."

"Me too," he admitted. "But you can do this. I know you can."

His optimism wavered a bit when we were saying a final goodbye at the front door. There were tears in his eyes when he kissed me. "I love you, Kate. Just find me, okay?" And then he was gone. I rested my forehead against the door, half hoping he would open it again and give me an excuse to change my mind.

After a moment, I heard his car start and pull away. Connor came up behind me and squeezed my shoulders. "Come on, girl. If we're going to do this thing, might as well get it over with."

I gave him a shaky grin. "Easy for you to say. Two minutes after I leave, you'll know if I succeeded. I'm the one who's going to have to chase Katherine around Chicago all day."

"You know I'd switch places . . ." he began.

"I know, Connor," I said. "Just teasing. I'm as ready as I'll ever be . . ."

So at exactly 5:58 P.M. I was in the library, my parasol and handbag in one hand and the CHRONOS key in the other. Daphne was barking downstairs in the kitchen, probably at her nemesis the squirrel, and Trey was in his car, headed home. Connor was in front of me, looking like he was about to change his mind again and tell me we'd find some other way. I leaned forward and gave him a kiss on the cheek and then, without pausing to think further, locked in the destination and closed my eyes.

∞ 18 ∞

When my eyes opened again, I was looking at a clear blue morning sky and could feel the faint chill of a crisp October breeze against my face. I'd gotten used to the sight of the lush green foliage at the stable point when viewing the location in the log, but it was a bit startling to have my other senses kick in as well. The island itself was quiet except for birds and chirping insects; I could detect the dull hum of a crowd in the distance. I caught the faint aroma of roasting peanuts and, much closer, the unmistakable smell of mud.

The local time was 8:03 A.M., one minute after Katherine and Saul's arrival. The gates of the Exposition had opened at eight, so it was still too soon for foot traffic to make its way to the Wooded Island near the center of the fairgrounds. I glanced around quickly. A dark-haired kid of maybe seven or eight years was energetically sweeping the sidewalk in front of a rustic cabin, and a bit farther away to the right I could see the retreating figures of Saul and Katherine.

Each time that I had viewed their arrival through the medallion, I'd seen Saul grab Katherine's elbow to help her up the small hill that provided cover for their sudden appearance on the island. The gesture had seemed like unnecessary gallantry, but I now realized that the soggy terrain, combined with decidedly unsensible clothing, was going to make it a lot more difficult to reach the sidewalk than I'd thought.

Sighing, I tucked the CHRONOS key into the hidden pocket in the bodice of my dress. I hiked up the long skirt with one hand and used my unopened parasol as a brace to pull myself up the incline. The ground was not as tightly packed as it looked and the tip of my parasol sank about six inches into the loose, damp soil and mulch, throwing me off balance. I caught myself and managed—just barely—not to fall flat on my face, but I made enough noise to attract the attention of the kid sweeping in front of the cabin.

My parasol was now streaked with dark mud and my gloves were ruined—so much for maintaining a ladylike appearance. I peeled off the gloves and stashed them in my bag, brushing the soil and stray leaves off the parasol as best I could before opening it, my hands shaking badly.

The shaking hands brought to mind my one and only time onstage, during a fifth-grade play. I had been desperately afraid that the curtain would go up, with dozens of eyes watching, and I would forget both of my very short lines. Even though the only eyes on me right now were those of the boy in front of the cabin, the feeling was the same. I took in a few deep breaths to calm myself, and then gave the kid a haughty look that I hoped would suggest he mind his own business. I turned to follow Saul and Katherine, who were now on the bridge that crossed the lagoon to link the Wooded Island with the main Exposition.

I could still see them clearly as I approached the bridge over the lagoon. Saul towered over Katherine's petite form, in her gray dress and purple hat topped with the lavender feather—just as I remembered from the many times I had watched them through the medallion.

I picked up my pace, still hoping to follow plan A and keep the two of them in sight. It wasn't, strictly speaking, a necessity. They would end up at the Ferris wheel around ten-fifteen, and—if that failed for some reason—I could always follow them downtown, where Katherine would be alone for much of the afternoon. But even if the version ahead of me was a half century younger than the grandmother I knew, and even if she had no idea who I was, I knew that I would feel much more comfortable if that silly lavender feather remained in view.

Plan A, however, was in jeopardy from the beginning. My ungraceful climb to the sidewalk had put me farther behind the two of them than I had planned. It would only take me a few minutes to catch up if I walked quickly, but there was trouble, quite literally, on the horizon. Although they were the only two people walking *away* from the island, about fifty yards ahead of them were the thousands of people who had arrived via the much more conventional route of the Sixty-Seventh Street entrance. Crowds were gathering around the various buildings in front of us and, unless Katherine and Saul turned to the right or left and walked along the lagoon surrounding the Wooded Island, they would be swallowed by the crowd before I closed the distance between us.

And then, to make matters worse, I heard someone running up behind me on the bridge. I glanced back over my shoulder and saw that it was the little kid from the cabin.

"You dropped this on the island, miss!" he said, a bit out of breath. He had a folded envelope in one grubby hand and a damp rag in the other. "And you'll want me to be helpin' you with that umbrellow—if you leave that mud to stay on it, the fabric'll be ruint."

I recognized the envelope at once and my heart rose into my throat. It was Dad's letter, which I'd stashed back in my pocket without thinking after Trey finished reading it. It must have fallen out during my stumble up the hill.

The letter had been stuffed a bit carelessly back into the envelope, and I suspected that the inquisitive eyes in front of me had at least glanced at it; although, he would hardly have had a chance to read it carefully during his run across the bridge—and that was assuming a kid his age could even read in this era. The postmark was clear on the envelope, but surely he would think it was a mistake if he had seen the date?

The boy reached up with the hand holding the letter to pull my parasol down and wipe the dark stain off the top. I let him have the parasol and took the letter, tucking it quickly into my purse.

"Thank you. I wouldn't have wanted to lose this . . ." I dug about in the small coin purse inside the bag, trying to decide what an appropriate tip might be.

"Int'restin' stamp," he said. "Must've come from a long way to cost forty-four cents for just sendin' a letter. And I ain' ever seen a stamp with a tiger on it like that. Looks like one of them tigers they have over on the Midway and the paintin' on it is real bright an' colorful. Don' guess you could let me keep it for my c'lection?"

I shook my head, glancing back over the bridge. Katherine was nearly out of sight. "I'm *very* sorry—but my sister collects stamps, too, and this is from our father, so it's already spoken for . . ."

He finished wiping off the parasol—I can't say that there was a noticeable improvement, other than the dirt being spread around a bit—and handed it back to me, shrugging. "S'okay, miss. Just real unusual, so I thought . . ."

"Here," I said, giving him my best smile. "Take this—a reward for returning the letter and a bit for your trouble." I handed him a half-dollar coin, hoping that it might take his mind off the stamp. "I really need to be going, however—I'm running way behind. Again, thank you."

His dark eyes grew very large, and it occurred to me that I might have been a bit *too* generous. A nickel or dime would have clearly been more appropriate. Running the numbers in my head, I realized that I'd given him the modern equivalent of about a twelve-dollar tip.

"No, miss. Thank *you*," he said, pocketing the coin and falling into step beside me. "What are you plannin' to see first? Do you have a map? If not . . ." He fished around in his pocket and pulled out a grimy, much-folded map of the Expo, clearly hoping that he'd be able to tap the rich girl for another buck or two before she got away.

"No, thank you, I have a map right here," I said, picking up the pace a bit. I tugged the official-looking replica of a Rand McNally Expo map out of my bag and craned my neck to see if Katherine's feather was still in view. It was, just a few feet into the crowd.

The kid was keeping up with me, step for step. "Don't you need to get back to your job?" I asked, although it felt a bit odd saying that to a kid who should be in about the third grade.

"Nope—I'm all finished there for the day. I don' have to be to my other job 'til later." He skipped a few steps ahead and then turned to look at me, walking backward. "Those maps are no good, y'know. Half of 'em was written before the fair was even finished so they could get 'em printed in time and some of the exhibits moved aroun'. What you need is a *guide*. A respectable young lady shouldn' be wanderin' the fair without an escort, anyway."

I raised an eyebrow at him. "I've seen plenty of women touring the fair without a male escort."

"Well, t'gether, yes," he admitted. "But not walkin' aroun' by their lonesome much, right? I c'n be your guide—I done it nine times already, once for a group of ladies all the way from London. I know ever'thin' about the fair, 'cause me dad worked here the whole time they was buildin' it."

He paused and drew in a deep breath. "For two dollars I can show you ever'thin' worth seein' here and ways to avoid the crowd and"—he blushed a bit—"where the ladies' necessary is, an' all that kind of stuff . . ."

I was about to ask what a necessary was, but then I considered his blush and put two and two together.

"So what d'you say, miss?" he continued, quickly. "You don' wanna be goin' around by y'rself. There's spots what ain' safe for a young lady to be in—there's some bad folk here might take advan'age of a girl on her own, y'know."

We had reached the middle of the avenue between the Mining Building and the Electricity Building. The gold dome of the Administration Building was just ahead, but Katherine's lavender feather was nowhere in sight.

Sighing, I glanced around and could see that he was correct—there were plenty of women in groups or even pairs, but I didn't see even one unaccompanied female. I had to admit that I would probably look less conspicuous if I wasn't alone.

There was also the fact that he had seen the letter. I still wasn't sure how much he had read, and I decided that it might make sense to keep the kid in sight and under my control until I was out of there. And it was pretty clear that the promise of additional cash would keep him close.

He could tell that I was mulling it over, so he stood quietly, stick-straight, with his hands behind his back—a small, grubby soldier awaiting inspection. It was apparently difficult for him to keep perfectly still, however, especially with such a major business deal on the line, and the excess energy had him bobbing up and down on his toes, like a pogo stick.

"I thought you had another job to be at."

"Not 'til a *lot* later," he said, shaking his head. "And that's just helpin' me mom at the booth t'night, and she'd much rather I was workin' somewhere else if I c'n bring in some extra. It's been tough since me dad . . ." Died? Left? He didn't finish the sentence and his face closed while thinking about it, so I decided not to press.

He was thin and his clothes were worn, and I suspected that his assessment that his mother would be happy to have a few extra dollars for the week was dead-on. He also seemed pretty sharp—which was a mixed bag, given that he knew more than I wanted him to about my arrival. The dark eyes were a bit mischievous, but his face looked honest and open.

"What's your name?" I asked.

"Well, they used t'call me dad Mick and me Little Mickey, on accoun' of us bein' Irish an' all. Only he's gone now and I'm not that little anymore, so you c'n just call me Mick."

"Okay, Mick—how old are you?"

"Twelve years, miss," he answered without a pause.

I raised a very skeptical eyebrow. "How old are you *really*? I'm not going to refuse to hire you because of your age—I just want to know."

"Nearly nine," he said.

"Try again."

"No really—I'll be nine in August," he said.

Given that it was October, he seemed to be stretching "nearly nine" to the breaking point, but at least that age seemed plausible. I tried to think up a story that an eight-year-old would buy, one that might keep him close and quiet until I was ready for the jump home. My mind flashed back to a book I'd read in middle school about Nellie Bly, the famous girl reporter of the 1880s who had traveled around the world on her own in seventy-two days. I was pretty sure she had been about my age when she started reporting.

"Okay," I said, bending down closer to his eye level. "Here's the deal I can offer, Mick, and it's *not* open for negotiation. I'm Kate—I'm a journalist, a writer . . . for a newspaper back East. I usually work with a partner, my photographer, but he's been delayed. I could use an assistant, but you'll have to do exactly as I say—no questions and no talking to anyone about this, because I'm working on an exclusive, okay?"

His brow creased a bit at the last part. I suspected that he wasn't quite sure what an exclusive was but didn't want to admit it. "A reporter? Followin' them other two, right? The man an' woman who came up before you? What's he then, a criminal or somethin'? He *looked* shady, he did—"

I gave him a sharp look and cut him off. "No questions, remember? Five dollars for the time I'm here," I continued. "I might be leaving today, but I could be here tomorrow as well, depending on how long it takes to get my story. I'll pay your expenses, too—meals and the like. And the first stop we make is to the *gentlemen's* necessary, and you scrub up—I want an assistant that's clean and presentable. Then you help me get to the Midway before ten o'clock."

He nodded again and grabbed my elbow, pulling me to the left, toward a cluster of large white fountains. "This way, Miss—"

"It's Kate," I repeated.

"This way, Miss Kate. I know the very bes' route."

∞

As we walked along, Mick flipped into tour-guide mode and it was soon obvious that he hadn't been padding his credentials. He really did know a lot about the Exposition and had memorized details about the various buildings and displays.

"This," he said, as we approached a waterway, one end of which was lined with enormous white fountains, "is what they call the Gran' Basin." Mick pointed toward the centerpiece of the fountains as we passed, a large classical sculpture of a ship. "Tha' one there is the Columbian Fountain—MacMonnies, the guy who designed it, tol' me it's s'posed to be a symbol for the country and how much progress we made since Columbus came. Those people rowin' are s'posed to represent the arts—y'know, like music an' paintin' an' stuff? The big guy there is s'posed t'be Father Time, steerin' the boat to the future with his big . . ." He paused for a moment, thinking. "Me mom always called it a *speal*—what d'you call it in English, the thing they cut hay with?"

"A scythe?" I asked.

"Yeah, tha's it," he said, pulling me slightly to the side to dodge a small pack of middle-aged women who, like me, were looking up at the statue and not paying much attention to where they were walking. "A scythe. I don' remember what the woman at the front is s'posed to be. Or those cupids. Maybe just decorations."

"Now that buildin' over there," he said, "is the bigges' buildin' in the world—the Manufactures Building. And that one we passed on the way over here? The 'Lectricity Buildin'? There's stuff in there you wouldn' believe even if you saw it. Got a frien' who works over there sweepin' an' he says there is this machine called a tel-autograph where someone can sen' a picture say from back East and that machine'll draw it for you here, just like you was gettin' a telegraph. He also says they have this new thing by Mr. Edison that makes pictures move so it looks like you're watchin' this guy sneeze, 'cept you're just lookin' into this tiny little box. An' just wait 'til you see it at night, that place is all lit up—you never seen anythin' so pretty. Like a million lanterns, but I looked at 'em in the daytime an' turns out they ain' nothin' but these little glass balls with a tiny wire inside."

It was odd to think that almost all of the magnificent structures Mick was pointing to were temporary buildings, made of a material slightly sturdier than papier-mâché. The exhibits would be removed and the buildings would be torn down or burned in a matter of months. Only a few buildings would remain, along with the gardens—which were amazing in their own right, since the area had been a swamp less than a year ago.

We walked around the edge of the lagoon, where several colorful gondolas were docked, boarding their first passengers of the day. Looking across the water, I could see the Japanese Tea House through the trees of the Wooded Island.

Most of the way, we kept to the sidewalks, passing the U.S. Government Building and the Fisheries Building, where Mick was delighted to give me a full and imaginative description of the huge shark that was on display. He then cut through the grassy area in front of the national exhibits for Guatemala and Ecuador, and I had to walk on my tiptoes a bit to keep the edges of the boots from sinking into the damp sod.

My right shoe was already beginning to rub a blister on my heel and I was increasingly suspicious that Mick's "bes' route" was not the most direct path to the Midway. I could see the Ferris wheel in the distance, and we seemed to be walking past where we should have turned.

"Yes'm," he said, when I pointed to the big wheel on the horizon. "But you don' wanna be usin' the necessaries over there. They ain' fit for a lady. The ladies from London were very impressed with the necessaries in the Fine Arts Palace. It's right up here, the very nex' buildin'. Said they were the nices' they ever seen."

"But the . . . 'necessary' . . . was intended for *you* to clean up. I really don't need to go right now." I was dreading the thought of trying to negotiate a toilet in my current dress, and had decided that it might be a good idea to just limit my intake of fluids for the rest of the day.

"Oh . . . sorry," he said. "I can use the ones on the Midway where you don' hafta pay the nickel, but . . . I thought maybe you just needed to . . . Some ladies won' say, y'know. One of the ladies from London never would say and she nearly—"

"Girl reporters aren't prissy," I said, giving him a little smile. "We say what we think. So if I need to go, I'll tell you straight-out." I glanced over at the steps leading up to the ornate portico of the building. "We're already here, so we might as well step inside. I'll just wait for you in the lobby."

We had a brief disagreement with the attendant at the gentlemen's lavatory. He took one glance down his long nose at Mick's attire and suggested he find another toilet. Mick argued with him for a moment and then I settled the dispute by handing the guy a quarter—well beyond the nickel charge for using the facilities. His attitude changed, but he still followed the boy inside, as though he was worried Mick might run off with the towels.

I sat on a black upholstered bench and looked around at the wide variety of statues in marble, plaster, and bronze. According to the clock inside the rotunda, it was only a few minutes after nine. We still had plenty of time, but I was too nervous to sit still, so I wandered over to examine a few of the works on display. One of the larger-than-life statues depicted a man who was about to punch an eagle that was attacking him. Nearby, a smaller bronze work with a French title showed a young child sitting on a riverbank. It was beautifully detailed, and I was surprised to see that the artist was a teenage girl from Boston, Theodora Alice Ruggles.

Mick emerged from the bathroom a few minutes later and had actually managed to remove most of the grime from his face and arms. His cuffs were a bit damp from his efforts to scrub them clean, but they showed a definite improvement as well. He had apparently made good use of the complimentary toiletries—his hair was now parted neatly down the middle. It was also slicked down with something that smelled like the bergamot oil they use in Earl Grey, and I was reminded of sitting half asleep in my dad's lap on weekends as a kid, while he read the paper and sipped his morning cup of tea.

The boy was again standing in inspection mode, so I gave him a quick nod. "Very respectable, sir. I think you'll pass quite nicely as a journalist's assistant."

He gave me a wide grin, and we left the Arts Palace. This was apparently not an area where Mick had much expertise, as he didn't say anything about the many statues and paintings we passed on our way outside, but he perked up again as we turned left on the sidewalk.

"The Midway's not very far at all, Miss Kate. So how do you know they'll be there at ten? What were they doin' over by the

Hunter's Camp anyway? I seen him there before, a coupla times. He's always comin' out of those bushes . . . I nearly tol' the cops, 'cause some ladies have been disappearin', but then I noticed it's the same woman with him each time. An' she's here at the Expo a lot. They got somethin' hidden in there?"

He glanced up when I didn't respond. "Oh, right. You said no questions. Me mom always says I'll get a lot further in life if I learn to button me lip."

"My mom tells me the same thing," I laughed. "I don't usually listen to her either. But it probably *is* good advice, you know."

He shrugged. "Yeah, but me *dad* said th' only way to learn is t' ask questions. An' it's hard to do that with buttoned-up lips. Anyway, I c'n tell that one you're followin' is a bad bloke. He has those eyes. He always give me the evil look when he comes up that hill, kinda like you did this mornin', but I could tell you was jus' scared. Not mean."

"I was *not* scared," I said.

"'Course you were," he replied matter-of-factly. "You're new here and followin' some bad guy. But you got a good guide now, so you'll get your story and then your boss'll be happy, right?"

It seemed pointless to argue with an eight-year-old kid, especially when he was essentially correct, so I just buttoned my lip and followed.

∞

The Midway Plaisance was already noisy, dusty, and crowded at nine thirty in the morning. The buildings weren't as immense as those in the main Exposition, but what they lacked in size they made up for in color and design. In the space of a few city blocks, we passed replicas of an early American log cabin, an Irish castle, a collection of Asian-looking huts, and a smaller version of a Turkish mosque.

We stopped at a small concession stand just past the German Village, where I bought two lemonades. After a few minutes, we found a spot on one of the benches in front of the buildings.

Unlike the rest of the fair, where the visitors were mostly white, the Midway looked more like a modern city, with a wide array of races and nationalities. I looked a bit farther down the street and watched a man in Arabic dress pulling a camel toward us along the main road. A middle-aged woman was sitting sidesaddle atop the camel's hump, clutching tightly to the edges and looking as though she was quite ready for the ride to end.

Mick followed my gaze. "That's Cairo Street, down there. You should come back here when they do the Arab wedding this afternoon. It's really—"

"Unfortunately, I don't think I'm going to have much of a chance to sightsee, Mick," I said. "I'm here on assignment and I don't have much time."

I was a bit surprised to realize that I *was* genuinely sorry about the need to rush, since there was a lot that I would have loved to see if this were a pleasure trip. I felt a surge of jealousy for Katherine's job, which had simply been to learn as much as she could.

"Too bad," he said. "You c'n spend a week here an' not see all of it. Not that you could really spend a week now, with it closin' an' all. It'll be cool to walk through here again when all the people have gone—like it was when they was buildin' it. I don' really like the big crowds. An' then ever'body here will get to start tearin' it all down, I guess, and then go home."

"Where's home for your family, Mick? I mean, before you came to America."

"County Clare—tha's in Irelan'," he said. "Town called Doolin. Pretty place me mom says, but the only work is fishin'. We been here since I was three or four. I kinda remember comin' over on the boat, but not Irelan'."

"So where will you go?" I asked. "I mean, soon there won't be much work here for you and your mom, right?"

He nodded, with a rueful twist of his mouth. "Lady at church is tryin' to talk me mother into movin' back to the big farm we worked at when we first came to America, and she's thinkin' 'bout it. I can tell she is."

"But you don't want to go?"

He shook his head. "It was clean and we had more space an' all, an' it was great workin' in the open air, but I don' wanna go back there. Me dad didn' wanna be on that farm—he didn' trust 'em an' neither do I. I'd rather stay in the city to work the fac'tries, even if it means bein' cooped up all day."

"What about school?" I asked, sipping the lemonade, cool and nicely tart, through a tall paper straw.

"Done with that," Mick said, rubbing a line in the dust with his shoe. "Went to classes for 'bout two years on the farm before the fair started and me dad died. I c'n read an' write just fine. C'n do my numbers, too. Anythin' else I need to know I c'n learn on me own. I'm old enough now to help earn me keep."

He lifted his chin proudly as he spoke and I was struck by how hard he was trying to be all grown-up. "When did your dad . . . ," I began hesitantly.

"Back in July," he said. "After the fair started and the buildin' work was finished, he got a job puttin' out fires. You get a lot of little fires in the rest'rants and some of the 'lectrical buildins. Then there was a big fire in the Cold Storage Buildin'—weird to have a buildin' with so much ice inside catch fire. Don' know what caught it, but the flames was huge. All of the firefighters workin' for the Exposition died and a bunch of those who came in from the city died, too. Took a long time, but they put it out, so none of the other buildins went up."

"I'm sorry about your dad, Mick."

"Yeah, me too. I miss him." He was silent for a moment, and then he finished off the lemonade, his straw making a loud slurping sound as he pushed it around the ice to get the last few drops.

"I'm really not all that thirsty," I said. That wasn't entirely true—the air was dusty and I would have happily finished off the last half of the glass if not for the looming specter of trying to navigate a bathroom while wearing a bustle and ankle-length skirt. "You can finish mine, if you'd like."

That earned me another grin. "You're nicer than me other boss. She only gave me a peppermint one time, and that was 'cause she said me breath smelled like onions. Which prob'ly was true." He quickly polished off the last few ounces in my glass and took the two empties back to the booth.

We worked our way down toward the Ferris wheel, which seemed even more enormous as we drew closer. It was easily five times as high as the one I'd ridden on at the county fair last year, and it cast a shadow far down the Midway. I sank gratefully down onto a vacant bench just around the corner of the next building, which afforded us a clear view of the ride's loading dock. The blister on my heel was becoming annoying and I really didn't want to stand about while we waited for Katherine's party to arrive.

"So we'll just sit here an' wait 'til they come? I c'n help keep an eye out . . . Are we gonna follow 'em when they leave an' see where they go, or what?"

He seemed to be growing increasingly impatient with the no questions rule, and I decided it couldn't hurt to lay out the basic game plan. "Well, I actually need to get close to the woman—the one who's with him? They'll be in a big group, about a hundred people, along with the mayor, so it shouldn't be hard to spot them."

"Oh," he said, nodding sagely. "It's a political story you're writin' then. The bad bloke's tryin' to buy off the mayor, is he?"

"No, no." I shook my head. "I'm not writing about the mayor. I just need to speak with the woman for a couple of minutes without the 'bloke,' as you call him, overhearing us."

"Okay, tha's easy enough," he said. "I'll get Paulie to put us in their wagon."

"In their . . . *what*?" I asked. "And who is Paulie?"

"The wagon on the big wheel," he said, nodding toward the carriages where people were now entering. "You said there was about a hundred in the group? Twen'y of 'em at leas' will be too chicken to ride, you'll see, an' the wagons hol' sixty people each. So it's just a matter of us gettin' on the right wagon."

I looked up to the very top of the wheel and thought he was probably right about the people who chickened out. The pit of my stomach tightened at the thought of going up that high in something that had been built in the 1890s, long before those comforting little signs that show a carnival ride has passed inspection.

"So Paulie," Mick continued, "he knows me—he can just shove us in wi' the rest of 'em. The ladies may all ride in one so the men can smoke, but if they're together, then I'll distract the bloke and you can have a chat wi' the lady."

"But I don't think there will be any children in this group," I said. "It's a lot of mayors and their wives . . ."

He shrugged. "Won' matter," he said in a conspiratorial tone. "I sneak on all the time withou' payin'. Lotsa kids do it—just gotta find a coupla ladies wi' big skirts an' sorta squeeze between 'em. Paulie don' care so long as nobody sees me. Most times, the ladies keep your secret when they do notice you, if you ac' like you ain' never been able to ride it before. An' if they do complain, Paulie'll just yell at me when we get off and call me a buncha names, maybe throw somethin' at me, so he don' get in no trouble."

"Well," I laughed, "at least you won't have to sneak on without paying this time." I handed him a dollar and a quarter. "Buy us two tickets and give Paulie the quarter as a tip for his help."

"Right." He hopped up from the bench. "You jus' stay here, since your foot's hurtin', an' I'll be back."

I had to give him credit for being observant. I hadn't said anything about the blister, and if I was limping, I wouldn't have thought it was enough that anyone would notice, since I was covered pretty much from head to toe.

Mick sprinted over to the booth and waited in the short line to buy the tickets, then paused for a minute to talk with Paulie, a boy about my age. They both looked in my direction, and Paulie gave a little wave, then Mick headed back to the bench.

"All set," he said with a grin. "If you're sure they'll be here at ten fifteen, we don' have but a coupla minutes, maybe five. When you see the mayor headin' this way, we'll go over and you just kinda blend in toward the end of the line. If there ain' no other kids, I'll keep outta the way 'til you start t' get in an' then slip in beside you."

It was as good a plan as any I could think of. "Even if they realize we aren't part of the mayor's group," I said, "they can hardly evict us once the wheel starts spinning, right?"

"I don' think the mayor would be too fussed," Mick said. "He likes kids. Tried to get the fair bosses to let poor kids in Chicago see the exhibits for free, but they said no."

"Buffalo Bill, though," he added, nodding off toward the end of the Midway, "was differ'nt. See those tents over there? That's his Wild West Show. He tol' the mayor he'd do it—had a waif's day where all the kids in the city got a free show, free candy, free ice cream. That was *some* day. 'Course," he noted with a serious look, "they make a lot of money over there—I bet the fair bosses wish they'da let Bill's show be part of the Midway. Said he was too 'low class.' But they got Indian shows at the Expo, too—just nowhere near as good as Buffalo Bill's."

He fell silent then, alternating between sitting on the bench and walking over to the corner of the building every thirty seconds or so to peer around the edge.

After the third or fourth trip to the corner, he sat down again and slid a bit closer. "There's a big group down just pas' the lemonade stand. It's them. You can never mistake the mayor; he's a big guy and he's got this hat—well, you'll see."

I did see, about two minutes later, when a tall, rather portly man in a slouchy-looking black hat rounded the corner and approached the ticket booth. Mick was right—he wore a professional suit, complete with the typical waistcoat and pocket watch, but Carter Henry Harrison definitely had his own style. All of the men wore hats—a wide array of bowlers, straw boaters, and a few top hats in the mix—but Harrison's hat had a slightly disreputable, cowboyish quality. It reminded me a bit of the fedora that Indiana Jones wore.

The mayor waved his hand toward the large delegation behind him and paused to hear something that one of the women was saying. Her hair was light brown with a few streaks of gray, and she wore a navy dress with a white lace bodice. She was an attractive lady, with wire-rimmed glasses, about my height and build. The mayor laughed heartily at whatever she had said and patted her on the arm before turning back to the crowd.

"If any of you are concerned, like Mrs. Salter here, let me assure you that the wheel is perfectly safe. The very first passenger was the inventor's own wife, and no, Mr. Ferris wasn't seeking to get rid of his good lady."

There was a polite chuckle from the group, and then Harrison continued. "I will just need a moment to speak to this kind person to arrange our passage, and then"—he motioned dramatically toward the top of the wheel—"the sky is our only limit."

Several of the women followed his arm upward with their eyes, and one of them, a plump middle-aged woman in a pale pink bonnet, gasped out loud. I don't know if she had actually not looked at the wheel until that moment or if the reality had only just sunk in, but she wrenched her arm away from that of the friend next to her. "I'm sorry, Harriet. I know I said I would go up with you, but there is absolutely no way that I am stepping foot inside that steel monster." She shuddered visibly and shook her head. "No. I'll wait for you here." She walked over to join a dozen or so women, and a couple men, who had gathered to watch their braver compatriots from the other side of the street. After a few seconds, her friend looked up at the wheel and, with a rather pained expression, decided that she, too, would remain on the ground.

Searching the crowd, I found Saul first, standing with a large cluster of men. A few seconds later, I spotted Katherine's feather, directly behind the woman in the navy and white dress who had just been talking to the mayor. They were near the center of the group, which, with the exception of these two women, seemed to have mostly separated by sex, with the women congregating on one side of the platform and the men on the other. Several members of the women's group were eyeing the two gender traitors, with tight-lipped expressions that made their disapproval quite clear.

I nudged Mick with my elbow. "That's her. I'm not sure about the other woman she's talking to. It might be the woman mayor they invited . . ." It seemed the most likely possibility, although I wouldn't have described the vivacious woman as "a meek little mouse," as Katherine had done.

"A woman mayor. If that don' beat all." Mick squinted a bit to try and get a better look, but both of the women were partially blocked from view by several of the men standing between us. "I'm gonna head over near Paulie, so you just slide into whichever wagon she goes an' I'll follow."

I moved toward the gender line demarcating the two groups and pretended to be looking through my bag for something as the men's group stepped aside and gallantly allowed the women to board first. I could pick out Katherine's higher-pitched voice among the lower rumble of the men's conversation. She was talking to the other woman, but I couldn't make out what they were saying, and as they made no effort to join the women's group, I hung back as well.

The door was closed on the first cart, and several women laughed and waved gloved fingers at the men in the delegation. I shifted toward the outside of the platform, near the back of the line. A few of the men gave disapproving looks to Katherine and her companion, and one gave a haughty sniff in my direction as well, as we moved toward the "men's" car and began to board. It seemed Mick was right. They'd been looking forward to a quick smoke and weren't too happy that they would now have to ask permission from the women on board.

I looked around the platform for Mick, hoping that he could sneak in next to my skirts, but it was soon clear that he had already boarded. Just as I stepped into the car, he let out a loud howl of pain and the woman in the navy blue dress burst from the back of car, dragging him by the ear. She was twisting hard, judging from the expression on Mick's face, as she pushed her way toward the men who were still lined up to enter the wagon. "We have a little stowaway," she said sternly, pulling up on his ear so that he had to stand on his tiptoes. "If you gentlemen could just step to one side, I'll toss him out."

I took a deep breath, hoping I wasn't making a colossal mistake. "He's not a stowaway, ma'am. I have his ticket right here."

I held up two ticket stubs, and everyone turned to stare at me, including Katherine. Her eyes were fixed on my upraised wrist, specifically on the hourglass charm that she had given me on my birthday. I caught her eye for a brief moment and then turned back to the woman who had the death grip on Mick's ear.

This was my first chance to get a close look at her and I had a sudden flash of recognition. The resemblance was still quite strong, although not as striking as it had been in the images on the stained-glass windows because she'd altered her hair color. And, up close, it was easier to tell that the eyes, now hidden behind wire-rimmed glasses, were a bluish-gray instead of green. I glanced down to look for the Cyrist symbol, but her hands were gloved, like my own had been until I managed to coat them in mud coming up the hill on the Wooded Island.

It was hardly the manner in which I'd expected to meet my long-lost aunt. I'd always envisioned her as the same age as my mother, so it was odd to meet this younger version. The gray streaks made her look a bit older to the casual observer, but now, on closer inspection, I doubted she was much beyond twenty-five. Her expression made it clear that she knew exactly who I was as well. Her eyes flashed briefly and then she slipped back into her character, a tiny, unpleasant smile inching across her face.

Mayor Harrison stepped forward. "Thank you, Mrs. Salter, but since the boy does have a ticket perhaps we should just . . ."

Prudence released Mick and pushed him toward me. "Funny," she said, narrowing her eyes as she continued to stare at me. "I don't remember you being part of this group."

"I'm not," I said. "I purchased the tickets this morning and we didn't realize this cart was exclusively booked." I nodded toward Mick. "He's my assistant . . . I'm writing a story, for my . . . my newspaper."

She sniffed and arched one eyebrow. "He's your *assistant*, all right, but you're not writing any story for a newspaper. Mayor Harrison, you might want to call fair security and have them evict these two from the grounds. They attempted to pick the pocket of a gentleman this morning as I was entering the gates. The young lady was distracting the gentleman so that this little tramp could do his work. If I hadn't rapped him across the bottom with my parasol, the two of them would have made off with the old man's wallet."

"That's a *lie*," I said vehemently. "That never happened, and you know it."

It was, however, a common enough ruse that it rang true for most of the people in the compartment, and I could feel the atmosphere shift. A few of them had seemed sympathetic a moment earlier, but now even Mayor Harrison was looking at me with a hint of suspicion.

"Why didn't you call for security then?" I asked. "If you thought we were doing something illegal—"

A soft voice from behind interrupted me. "What paper do you write for, miss?"

I turned toward Katherine with a panicked expression, and I stammered the first thing that came into my head: "The Roch . . . Rochester's *Worker's Gazette*. It's just a small weekly. We write mostly on labor issues."

"Oh, I *know* that paper," she said, stepping forward to stand next to me. "Your editor wrote an excellent piece on the complexities of dealing with child labor a while back. There was a short excerpt in the *Woman's Journal* just last month. Are you here to interview some of the younger workers at the Exposition?"

"Yes," I said, giving her a grateful smile. Her ability to pick up the tiny thread that I had dropped and weave a plausible story was impressive. "Mick knows a lot of young workers here, and he's been helping me. I thought I would take him on the Ferris wheel as an extra token of my appreciation."

"I always dreamed 'bout ridin' the big wheel," Mick added, looking down at his shoes with a plaintive expression. "But me mom needs all the money I c'n make." He glanced around at the others and then back at me. Those big brown eyes—with long black lashes that were going to make him a real heartbreaker in a few years—were all the more effective because they were still brimming with tears from the ear twist. "But it's okay, Miss Kate. I don' wanna make no trouble for you."

Mick was a convincing little actor, and I could feel the mood in the car shifting again as several of the people around me relaxed. Some of the men were glaring at Prudence, although I noted that they were generally the same bunch that had been looking unhappily toward her and Katherine as we'd entered.

"Dora," Katherine said, leaning forward, "don't you think it's possible you were mistaken this morning? Perhaps you misjudged the situation—it's *so* hard to tell what's going on when a place is teeming with so many people. I hardly think this young lady looks or sounds like a common thief . . ."

Mayor Harrison stepped in at that point. "Perhaps we could just ask you and your . . . young assistant . . . to take the next car? It seems like this was an innocent mistake, Mrs. Salter—and they do have tickets, as you can see."

Prudence knew she had lost the vote and shot an annoyed look toward Katherine as she huffed toward the back of the car. I paused on the pretense of slipping the tickets into my purse and whispered out of the side of my mouth to Katherine. "I need to speak to you alone. Today. And that's *not* Dora Salter."

Her eyebrows rose the tiniest bit and she gave me a small nod as I turned toward the door of the compartment, pulling Mick with me. Several apologetic smiles later, we were outside, and the rest of the men in the mayoral group, including Saul, boarded the car we'd just vacated. It was clear from Saul's face that Katherine hadn't exaggerated his motion sickness—he was already pale and kept glancing at the cluster of more timid souls across the street as though he might bolt at any moment. Paulie closed the door and shifted the lever to move the remaining cars into position for boarding.

"Thanks anyway, Paulie," Mick said as we entered the next car along with a throng of other passengers. We pushed toward the back of the car and Mick slumped against the side of the compartment, his face miserable.

"It's okay, Mick," I said. "I was only able to speak to her for a second, but she knows now that I need to talk to her later."

He didn't say anything and I bent down a bit to look him in the eye. "You did a good job. A *really* good job. I'm not sure they'd have believed us if you hadn't chimed in . . ."

Mick shook his head. "It ain' that, miss. I just got problems now." He closed his eyes for a moment, rubbing his temples with his fingers in a circular sort of motion. It was a very adult gesture, and somehow very familiar, although I couldn't quite place it.

I waited a moment to see if he would elaborate, but when he opened his eyes he just stared out the window at the gears of the giant wheel. A few seconds later we jerked upward again, after loading another group of passengers.

It tore at me to see a kid so young looking like the weight of the entire universe was on him. "So tell me about it. Maybe I can help."

He looked even more miserable and then shrugged. "Me mom's gonna be furious an' you're gonna hate me, and you prob'ly should. But I *like* you an' I don' really like *her* anymore."

"Your mom?" I asked.

"No," he said, clearly shocked at the thought. "No. I *love* me mom. It's that witch what pulled me ear. I didn't recognize her at firs' on account of how she dyed her hair to look older an' all, but it's her. She's me *other* boss."

∞ 19 ∞

My jaw dropped. "Your boss? You mean, from the cabin? On the Wooded Island?"

"Yeah," he said, his dark eyes imploring. "I'm sorry, Miss Kate. I shoulda tol' you, but I'm not s'posed to tell anybody, ever. Even me dad agreed wi' that part. And I was doin' the same as you, watchin' out for when those two showed up, so I thought maybe it would be okay, y'know, to join forces."

"And exactly *why* were you watching for them, Mick?" I asked. "What were you supposed to do?"

"I . . ." He shook his head and let out a long breath. "You won' b'lieve me, Miss Kate. There's this book? It belonged to me dad. It sends her a message. Me granddad give it to him, before he died, along with this round thing that glows. It lights up the space around it with words 'n' stuff when you touch it. They make all them inventions in the Expo look like cheap toys."

Apparently Saul had figured out a way to use the diaries that Connor and Katherine had missed. The boy glanced up at me, but I kept my face composed and nodded for him to continue.

"Well, I'd just finished doin' that—sendin' her a message— when I looked aroun' an' there you were comin' up the hill. An' then I saw the letter you dropped, an' . . ." He trailed off, and the gears roared loudly as the wheel, with its last passenger on board, began to rotate, lifting us high above the Midway.

"Is your boss the lady from the church that you were talking about?" I asked. "The one who wants your mom to move back to the church farm?"

He nodded but didn't say anything, so I pressed a bit further. "Why don't you trust her, Mick?"

"Because me dad didn'," he said fiercely. "Tha's why we left. The church brought us over—they paid our way on the boat all the way from Irelan'—so I think they 'spected us to work longer and for me to keep takin' their Cyrist classes, but me dad said we'd find another way to pay 'em back. There was a lot of arguin' when we left, an' me dad said we were done wi' that lot. He got a job on the construction, and me mom found work and some odd jobs for me. Ever'thin' was okay again, once we left.

"Then when the fair was all built, money was real tight." He looked at me out of the corner of his eye and continued in a voice so low that I had to lean in to hear him over the excited chatter of the crowd as we climbed higher into the sky. "Sister Pru, she found us here and she said she forgave me dad for leavin' the farm an' for all the bad stuff he'd said 'bout the Cyrists. She pulled some strings t'get him on wi' the firemen—an' I tol' you how that turned out."

His mouth twisted bitterly. "Me mom says she couldna known me dad would get killed an' I know *here*," he said, tapping his head, "that me mom is right. But here," he added, tapping his chest, "says she *did* know an' she foun' a good way to shut me dad up."

His lower lip trembled, and I gritted my teeth in anger. I couldn't say for certain whether Prudence *had* known that the Cold Storage Building would go up in flames and his father would be killed, but she'd certainly had the opportunity to know.

"I know it's stupid, but it's what I feel, an' I wish I didn' hafta work for her. Although," he said with a weak laugh, "I guess maybe now I *won'* hafta work for her. But oh, me mom is gonna be madder'n bloody hell."

It clicked then, with his last two words, and I realized why I'd had the touch of déjà vu earlier when he rubbed his temples. I probably would have recognized those eyes earlier, but when I had seen them before—both through the medallion and on the Metro—they had burned with a type of passion that the little boy in front of me wouldn't understand for several years.

He mistook my stunned expression for disapproval. "Sorry, Miss Kate. I ain' 'sposed to say that. One more thing me mom would be mad about if she knew I was cursin', 'specially in front of a lady."

I smiled at him. "No, it's okay, really. I told you, I'm not prissy." He didn't look convinced, so I leaned in and whispered, "Bloody hell. Bloody, *bloody* hell."

His mouth twitched and then he finally looked me in the eyes as a smile broke free.

I breathed in deeply and tried to decide what to do. My stomach lurched as I glanced downward at the now miniscule buildings below us, but it was hardly noticeable since my insides were already clenched in a tight knot. How much should I tell him? How much *could* I tell him without causing even more upheaval in the timeline? What if something I did now was the key to him being there to warn me on the Metro? Or if something I did now kept him from being there on the Metro? Bloody hell was right.

After a moment, I knelt down to his level and loosened the small pocket in my bodice, sliding the CHRONOS key out just a bit. His eyes grew wide and several conflicting emotions moved across his face—probably relief that I believed him, but mixed with a touch of what looked like fear. I realized that he associated the medallion with the Cyrists.

"I'm not a Cyrist," I told him quickly, taking his small hand in mind. "I don't like them, either. And I think you're right not to trust your other boss.

"What's your real name?" I asked, even though I knew beyond any doubt what his answer would be.

"Kiernan," he said. "Kiernan Dunne, same as me dad was."

"Kiernan," I repeated. "It's a nice name. Or would you rather I called you Mick?"

"No," he said. "I don' much like it, but ain' many people c'n be bothered wi' learnin' t' say me real name. Mick's easier for 'em, so I don' argue. Are you really called Kate?" he asked, with a skeptical twist of his mouth.

I nodded, deciding that, given his views of my aunt Prudence, he probably wouldn't want to know that Kate was actually based on my *middle* name. "What color is the light on the medallion for you, Kiernan? It's blue for me—a very bright blue, brighter than any sky you've ever seen."

"It's green for me, Miss Kate. A deep, pretty green like . . ." A blush crept over his face and then he looked back up at me. "Like your eyes."

"That's really sweet, Kiernan," I said, squeezing his hand before I let it go to tuck the medallion back into its hidden pocket. "So tell me, do you know what this medallion does?"

"It c'n make you disappear, at least some of the folks at the farm could do that. It's a holy object for the Cyrists. They said we were special, me and me dad, 'cause we could see the light and make the books send messages. Sister Pru wanted me to work on it ever' day, but it gives me a headache somethin' awful. Me mom ain' never been able to see it and there were a lot of others who couldn' see it either. Only a few of the people at the farm actually brung one of them—they call 'em keys—with 'em when they came to the farm. An' other than me dad, they handed the key things over to Sister Pru and the other leaders."

"Is that why Sister Pru and your dad fought?" I asked. "Your dad wouldn't give up the key?"

He shook his head. "I don' think so. She ain' ever tried to take it from me, either. Tol' me to keep it after me dad was gone."

The wheel jerked slightly as it began its second revolution, and I could hear the squeals from those who were now at the top, where the movement would have felt much scarier. I looked at Kiernan for a long moment and tried to piece all of what he had told me into the larger picture. I couldn't see any clear patterns, however, and eventually decided I would have to rely on my own instincts and give him just a basic outline.

"You don't have to feel bad about not being completely truthful with me earlier," I said. "I wasn't a hundred percent truthful with you, either. I *am* really called Kate, and I *am* really following the same two people you were. The man is really a bad guy—all of that is true—but I'm not a newspaper writer. I guess you could say that I'm a messenger of sorts. And you were right to think that the lady with him is in danger. That's what I'm here to tell her. But I've got to do it very carefully."

He nodded and then tilted his head to one side. "So the lady in the purple hat . . . why did she cover for us if you aren' really a writer? Or is that a real paper, that gazette you talked about?"

"No," I said. "I made it all up. She just . . ." I pulled the chain of the bracelet away from my wrist and held up the tiny hourglass charm. "I think she recognized this. She knows the lady who gave it to me."

"Oh, so it's like a signal she should trust you?"

"Exactly," I said, rising to my feet carefully as the wheel reached its highest point and then stopped, swaying slightly. I winced a bit as I caught my balance—the blister was clearly getting worse and it didn't help that these compartments were standing-room only. "I'd rather not try to talk to her again now, given that your boss—Prudence—is still there. But the good news is that I know where the other lady will be later this afternoon. Can I count on you to help me get there?"

He smiled, clearly relieved to know that he hadn't lost both of his jobs in one fell swoop. "Yes, Miss Kate. I'd be mos' happy to help."

I gave his shoulder a squeeze. "Why don't we enjoy the rest of the ride, then?" I said. "Afterward, you and I can find someplace quiet to sit down and figure out our next steps. And maybe we could make it a place where I can take off these bloody shoes?"

∞

The spot that Kiernan found was nicely secluded—a patch of grass just below one of the bridges that led to the Wooded Island, where I could not only remove my shoes but actually soak my feet. The water looked clean enough and felt wonderfully cool on the back of my heel, which sported, just as I had suspected, a very large blister. The only thing that kept me from hurling the stupid shoes into the lagoon was the fact that there was no Finish Line nearby where I could find functional replacement footgear.

I leaned back against the embankment to relax, glad the dress was green so that I didn't have to stress too much about grass stains. Kiernan had volunteered to go in search of some lunch, and I was happy to take him up on the offer. It wasn't quite noon yet, but I had forgotten about dinner in my own timeline, after the huge sandwiches from O'Malley's for lunch, and I was now starving.

Kiernan came back about ten minutes later with hot dogs, fresh fruit, and more lemonade. Having read Upton Sinclair's *The Jungle* in history class, I wasn't too keen on any hot dog from 1890s Chicago, but I took a few bites, mostly of the bun so that Kiernan wouldn't think I was too prissy to eat it. He seemed quite happy to trade off the rest of my hot dog for his apple. When we had finished, I pulled one of the energy bars out the brown paper I'd wrapped them in and offered him a piece.

"Not bad," he said. "Chewy and sweet, too. They sell these in New York?"

I nodded, washing it down with lemonade. That wasn't where Connor had bought it, but I was pretty sure they sold them in New York and pretty much anywhere else in the country, although definitely not in 1893. I wondered how much Kiernan knew about the CHRONOS key from his time on the Cyrist farm, and what his reaction would be if I told him he was eating something purchased by his great-grandson.

When we finished eating, I reluctantly drew my feet out of the water and propped them against a large stone to let them dry in the sun.

"Miss Kate!" Kiernan exclaimed, pointing. "What happened to your toes?"

"What?" I glanced down, half expecting to see a leech or a cut or some other trauma, but there was nothing odd. "What are you talking about?"

"Your toenails. They're all *red*—it looks like blood!"

"Oh," I laughed. "That's just nail polish. It's chipped off in a few places."

"It looks like paint." Kiernan sniffed disapprovingly.

I sighed. This was one of the anachronisms that Katherine would probably have caught as I prepared to leave. Did young women paint their nails in the 1890s? Had nail polish even been invented yet? I had no clue.

"Well, it is paint, sort of," I said.

"Me mom says . . ." He shook his head and fell silent.

"What does your mom say, Kiernan?" He didn't answer. "No, really, I won't be angry. What does she say?"

"She says only whores wear paint," he said, staring down at the grass. "They usually wear it on their faces, though. I never even heard of painted toes."

"Well," I replied, "what your mom says might be true in Ireland and maybe even in Chicago. I don't know, since it's my first time here. But in New York, all of the finest ladies polish their nails— toes *and* fingers. Some of them even glue tiny sparkly stones on the middle of their fingernails."

"Really?" he asked, sliding a bit down the bank to look more closely at my toes. "It looks like the paint is still wet. C'n I touch it?"

"Sure," I said with a laugh, holding out one foot toward him. "The polish is completely dry—it's been dry for days."

He reached out a tentative finger, touching the nail of my big toe, and I had a sudden vivid memory of Trey tracing the outlines of my toes as we sat on the couch in my room, just after Katherine disappeared. I felt a bit guilty—I'd promised Trey I would stay away from tall, dark strangers at the fair. Kiernan certainly didn't fit the tall part of the description yet, and there wasn't anything even remotely romantic about his interest in my toenails, but I was pretty sure that Trey would be jealous if he knew. So after a moment, I tucked my foot demurely back under my skirt.

I didn't have a watch, but since Kiernan already knew about the CHRONOS key anyway, I looked around to make sure that no one else was watching and then pressed the center to pull up the display. It was a little after noon. The mayor's group would be leaving the grounds of the Exposition around a quarter to one to take the train into the city, where the large Auxiliary Building was located. I pulled the Expo map from my bag and flipped it over, spreading it out on the grass in front of me.

"You don' need the map," he said. "I c'n find any of the exhibits . . ."

"What about in Chicago itself?" I asked, and he responded with a crooked grin.

"Prob'ly. I been there three times—all the way to the main downtown. Our room is closer here to the fairgroun', but I went in wi' me dad when he was lookin' for work las' spring."

"Do you know how to find the Auxiliary Building?"

"Easy," he said. "I been there once already. The ladies from London were here for some World's Congress for Women or somethin' like that, an' they wen' there t' listen t' speeches. That's pretty much all they do there—people stan' up an' talk an' then more people talk. It's no fun at all—but I s'pose that's where the lady wi' the purple feather is goin'?"

"You guessed it," I said. "I'm really hoping to avoid the trip into the city, if we can. The plan is to try and catch her before she gets on the train, but if I can't get a moment to speak to her alone, we'll need to follow them."

"There's a lot of differ'nt stations here, though . . ."

"They'll be at the Sixtieth Street station—the one closest to where they're having lunch."

He looked as though he was about to ask how I knew this, so I tried a bit of redirection.

"Can you go find a garbage bin?" I asked, handing him the wrappers and banana peels and other remnants of our lunch. "I'm going to see if I can squeeze my feet back into these blood-y awful hor-rid rot-ten shoes," I added, whacking the boots with my hand with each syllable. "Are you sure you wouldn't like to trade with me? Yours might be too small, but I bet they'd *still* be more comfortable."

He giggled and shook his head. "No, Miss Kate. I don' even think me mom would trade you—those boots are pretty enough if all you gotta do is sit, but not too practic'l for workin' or walkin' or stuff."

"Amen to that, kiddo."

"So why did you buy them?" he asked.

I felt a slight pang as I remembered asking my mom that same question about her heels the night we had dinner with Katherine. It seemed like an eternity had passed instead of only a little more than a month.

"They were a gift. I'd much rather have on my Skechers," I answered, holding up my hand as he started to ask the inevitable question. "And yes, those are something else they sell in New York."

I waited until he was out of sight to pull a small tube of antiseptic cream and an adhesive bandage from my bag—both of which were almost certainly not for sale in 1893, even in New York. After taking care of my feet, I pulled on my stockings and tackled the shoes. They took forever to get on without Connor's buttonhook thingy, and they were still uncomfortable. The long soak in the lagoon seemed to have reduced the swelling a bit, however, and a quick test proved that I could walk without too much pain.

The embankment where we had eaten lunch was on the side of the lagoon closest to the Midway, only a few minutes' walk to the Sixtieth Street station. We arrived a bit ahead of the expected twelve-forty-five departure so that we could, once again, find a place to sit relatively unobserved before Katherine's group arrived. I sent Kiernan off to buy us a couple of subway tokens, just in case we did have to board, and to find us a spot on a bench.

Meanwhile, I doubled back one block to visit the "necessary" that I had spotted on our walk over. The "Public Comfort Station" was much larger and more modern than I had feared it might be, although the multiple layers of clothing were still a royal pain.

I was rearranging my bonnet in the small dressing mirror above the sink when I felt a light tap at my elbow. It was Katherine. She grabbed my arm and yanked me around the corner.

"I thought that I saw you coming in here," she said in a low whisper. "*Mrs. Salter*—or whoever she is—followed me. She's in there." She jerked her head toward one of the stalls. "If you want to talk we need to leave now—we have only a few moments. I can't seem to shake that woman."

We dashed across the street toward the buildings that the various states had sponsored to parade their individual accomplishments, history, agriculture, and industry. The California Building was directly opposite the restrooms. I followed Katherine through the doorway and over to a gigantic tower made entirely of oranges, which I had to admit looked much more impressive in living color than it had in the black-and-white photos that I had seen. The display was apparently getting a bit overripe, however, as the unmistakable tang of molded citrus swirled in the air around us.

Once we were out of view of the entrance, Katherine held up my wrist to compare my bracelet to her own. The chains were different, but the charms were identical—a single jade and pearl hourglass, with a small chip in exactly the same place. "Tell me who you are, where you got this bracelet, and why you are here," she said.

"I can't answer the first question," I told her. "But the answer to the second question is that you gave it to me. And I'm here to tell you that you need to return to CHRONOS headquarters immediately. Go straight to the stable point near the cabin. I'll get a messenger to contact Saul—"

"But why? This isn't standard protocol!" she said. "I'll be back at the same time whether we finish our work here or not. CHRONOS doesn't interrupt the jump even for a family emergency."

"What is standard protocol if the historian is in danger?" I asked. "You *are* in danger, even if headquarters doesn't know it."

She didn't answer, so I continued, looking her directly in the eyes. "Listen carefully. I'm going to tell you as much as I can. I can't tell you everything without—well, you understand, right?"

"You don't want to mess up the rest of the timeline if you can avoid it."

"Right. Tell HQ that you're sick and cancel your next jump."
She started to interrupt again, but I held up a hand. "You're
creative—you'll think of something. A stomach bug might be
convincing given recent events. Oh, and keep that appointment
with your gynecologist, okay?"

Her eyes widened, and I continued. "Your suspicions about
Saul are correct," I said, and then paused, trying to decide how
much I could tell without changing her actions. "He's been bringing
medicines from your era back to this one. But you *cannot* confront
him about it until he returns from the next jump to Boston—the one
you'll be skipping."

"Why do I need to skip that jump?" she asked.

"Because I don't want to have to travel back, track you down,
and extract you again at *that* location!" I said, a bit exasperated.
"You need to stay put in your own time for the next few days."

I made myself take a deep, calming breath and continued.
"When Saul gets back, try to convince him to talk to Angelo—but
wait to tell him about the baby, okay? You've got a solo trip planned
next week, correct?"

She nodded. "To Boston, 1853."

"You do need to make *that* trip. It's . . ." I hesitated. "It's safe."
I didn't sound very convincing on that point, even to myself. The
image of Katherine's face after her fight with Saul floated before
me, and I couldn't help but remember her description of Angelo's
and Shaila's deaths, but I pressed on. "And it's *important*."

"Is that all?" she asked.

"Try to avoid Mrs. Salter?"

"Who isn't actually Mrs. Salter, according to you. A woman, I
might add, who looks quite a bit *like* you, beneath the superficial
differences in hair color and the glasses. Who is she? Is she the
reason I'm in danger?"

I shook my head. "I'm going to have to follow the lead of my mentor here and tell you that's strictly on a need-to-know basis, and—"

"And I don't need to know. Funny. That's the same line *my* mentor uses."

"Well . . ." I shrugged. "It's not exactly an original thought. Suffice it to say that if you can avoid her on the way back to the stable point, it would probably be for the best."

"That may be easier said than done." She narrowed her eyes slightly, and I could tell she was still trying to decide whether to trust me. "So tell me, how did that charm get chipped? The little hourglass?"

"An altercation between a carriage door and a starstruck young CHRONOS agent, as I understand it. Mr. Douglass is over at the Haiti exhibit, so you might want to avoid him as well—just in case he remembers the incident and asks you to return his handkerchief."

Katherine gave me a cool, measured stare. "I'm the only one who knows that story, so you must have gotten it from me . . . but I have a very hard time believing that I would have directed you to interfere like this. It's entirely against—"

"Yes," I said with a tight smile. "I know. Against CHRONOS regulations."

There was another long look and then she sighed deeply. "Okay," she said. "I'm going to tell Saul that I'm leaving. I'll make some excuse. He may want to come back with me, but I wouldn't be surprised if he doesn't, given his recent behavior."

"Just be sure that you don't let him know the reason why . . ."

"I won't," Katherine said. "I'm going to follow your instructions to the letter. Skip the next jump, keep the gyno appointment, and avoid discussing my suspicions about Saul's actions—and that's all they are, I would remind you, *suspicions*—until the 26th.

I'll make the jump on the 27th. I just hope you—or maybe I should say we—are doing the correct thing here."

I thought back to Connor's comments a few weeks earlier. "So do I. But as a good friend of mine—of ours, actually—recently told me, I'm pretty sure that what we're doing is *right*. Sometimes, right and correct aren't the same thing."

She didn't look entirely convinced, but she nodded and took a few steps toward the exit, before turning back. "Just in case we run into the ersatz Mrs. Salter, perhaps we should leave separately? She seems to have taken a rather intense dislike to you and your young friend."

I agreed, and Katherine headed toward the door. I don't know if it was a premonition or just that I was feeling nervous, but I only gave her about a twenty-second lead and then I headed toward the same exit that she had taken. As luck would have it, a large group burst through the door and I shoved my way against the tide of the crowd, which was almost entirely over the age of sixty. I muttered apologies and stood on tiptoe to look for Katherine over their shoulders as I pushed through the last few people and began to make my way down the steps in front of the building. One old woman rapped me on the leg with her walking cane. I really couldn't blame her, since I'd nearly knocked her down.

"I'm sorry, ma'am, I didn't—" I began, and then stopped short as someone shoved the woman directly into me. I stumbled on the first step and just barely caught her before she fell. I was busy trying to set her back on her now very shaky feet when her assailant put his palm against my chest and pushed hard.

I fell down the last two steps and landed ungracefully on my backside. The man's suit threw me off for a moment, since I'd previously seen him only in a ratty T-shirt and jeans. The jagged scar near his right temple was new, and it looked a bit like something that one might get if he were whacked very hard with a tire iron. He had added a truly pathetic little mustache, but there was no mistaking the face. I'd seen it too recently and much too closely for my liking.

"Hi, Katie," Simon said with a glint in his eye. "Imagine meeting you here. Catch you later, okay?"

And with that, he began walking at a rapid clip toward the Sixtieth Street station. Several members of the crowd I'd just pushed my way through came over to help me up, and one rather gallant gentleman, who was eighty if he was a day, tottered a few steps after Simon, shouting and shaking a fist in the air.

By the time I was on my feet, Simon was halfway to the station. A bit farther ahead I saw Katherine, who hadn't managed to shake Prudence. The two of them were approaching the platform where the mayor's group had assembled to await the train, which was chugging toward the stop. I raised my skirt and managed a weak imitation of a run, but it was clear that I wouldn't reach them before Simon did.

The only thing I could hope was that my voice would travel better than I could. I pulled in a deep breath and shouted, pointing directly at Simon, "He's got a gun! Stop him—he's got a gun!"

I'm not sure if the group at the station heard *me*, or if they heard one of the many fairgoers who screamed and repeated "a gun" in the chaos of the next few seconds. But the mayor's party all looked in our direction. Simon glanced over his shoulder once and then turned back toward the platform, his hand still in his pocket, as Prudence, with a maneuver worthy of a defensive lineman, tackled Katherine to the ground.

They both fell forward, Katherine's sleeve snagging against the wooden railing, ripping the cloth from shoulder to elbow, just before her head smacked the edge of the platform. The screams of the crowd were now mingling with the roar of the train as it pulled to a stop. Saul knelt beside Katherine, and Prudence jumped to her feet, scanning the faces in the station.

I rammed my way through the mass of people, trying to get closer to Simon, but I couldn't find him in the crowd. I didn't think that he would have been brazen enough to make a temporal jump in broad daylight with hundreds of people nearby, but then he had been perfectly willing to make a jump in a crowded Metro station after snatching the diary, so who knew?

Two men in matching suits were walking purposefully toward the mayor. A Columbian Exposition security badge was visible on one of their shoulders. "False alarm, everyone. False alarm—the young lady was mistaken. We have everything in hand."

Mayor Harrison walked over to talk to the men, shaking their hands and clapping them on the shoulders as he spoke. I couldn't help but wonder how this incident would affect him, just hours away from the moment when an assassin would show up on his doorstep, requesting a word. Would he be less inclined to let a stranger into his house without having someone at least do a quick frisk for weapons? Or was this type of scare a pretty routine occurrence in a Chicago that was only slightly tamer than the Wild West?

I spun around again, still searching for Simon, but there was no sign of him. Saul was holding a handkerchief against the side of Katherine's head. I could see a bit of blood on the white cloth, but it didn't look as though she was badly hurt.

Kiernan had now spotted me and was running toward the platform. I held up one hand and motioned for him to wait on the bench—the last thing I wanted was for him to be in the middle of all this. He nodded but flicked his eyes behind me in a worried fashion.

As I turned back toward the platform, I came face-to-face with the reason Kiernan looked so concerned. Prudence was directly in front of me, her eyes intense enough to burn a hole through the lenses of her wire-rimmed glasses. "I had this *covered*, Kate," she said in low whisper, grabbing my upper arm and squeezing hard. "Katherine would have been perfectly okay and we would have avoided a spectacle. You're meddling in things you don't understand."

I fought down the urge to laugh—she sounded like the villain in a *Scooby-Doo* episode. "What do you mean you had this covered?" I asked. "You're the one I'm trying to protect her from—you and your Cyrist thug. I need to find him . . ."

"Don't bother, you silly little cow," she said. "Simon is gone." She jerked her head toward the two large security guys who had spoken with the mayor. "I had men in place to grab the idiot. He would never have gotten near her. And if I had ever gotten two minutes alone with Katherine, she would have been back in her own time by now, with Saul none the wiser, and I might have actually had a chance to lure Simon over to my side."

I was thoroughly confused. "You're trying to *save* Katherine? But your group is the one—"

"You think this is for *her* sake?" Prudence asked with a harsh laugh. "Oh, no. This is personal. Did Saul really think I would give him that much power? Over *me*? All he has to do is yank hard on this damned medallion and I'd go out the same way she did."

"So you're going to help us fight them?" I asked. Having Prudence on our side would be an incredible advantage, and I could only imagine the joy on Katherine's face and my mother's if—

Her lip curled in a sneer, bringing my fantasy to an abrupt end. "I'm not *fighting* the Cyrists," she said. "I *am* the Cyrists. There would be no Cyrist International without me. I was willing to share power with my father, but if he thinks he can push me aside without consequences, he is sadly mistaken. This ends here.

"And you need to listen well, my little niece," she said, her eyes once more drilling into mine. "I'm letting you go for one reason only—your mother. Deborah had nothing to do with any of this, and it's possible that she values your life more than my mother valued mine, so—"

"That's not true, Prudence. Katherine tried to find you, but she can't use the medallion any more than Saul can."

Prudence's expression made it clear that she wasn't buying it even before she spoke. "You can drop the pretense, Kate. I know about the bargain she made with Saul. The funny thing is that I got the better end of the deal. Poor Deborah had to stay with *her*."

Prudence shot a glance back over her shoulder. The train was pulling away from the platform and several of the passengers were craning their necks to look out the windows, just in case the excitement wasn't really over. Katherine had gotten to her feet and Saul was leading her away from the platform, back toward the main fairground. We couldn't have planned it better if we had tried, since the minor injury gave Katherine a plausible excuse to terminate the jump early.

Prudence let go of my arm. "Damn it," she said. "I have to go. I haven't had a chance to talk to her."

"Wait," I called, running a few steps after her. "Don't bother. She knows—she's going back to HQ."

Prudence turned back toward me as I continued. "Katherine will skip the next jump," I said. "She understands what she needs to do—and not do—over the next few weeks in order to keep the timeline intact."

Her eyebrows shot up. "Well, maybe you're not *entirely* worthless," she said. "I just hope you didn't screw it up—otherwise it's going to be very difficult to get back in here to fix things, due to the mess you've made. I was trying to do a surgical strike and then you come through like a tank . . . There's no telling how many ripples this will create in the timeline."

It was beyond hypocritical for Prudence, who was working for a radical overhaul of history, to be lecturing me on the sanctity of the timeline, but I suspected that fine point would be lost on her. Rather than stick around and argue, I turned on my heel and headed toward Kiernan, who was still watching us from the side-lines.

Prudence grabbed my arm again, yanking me back to face her. I had an intense desire to flip her over my shoulder and see how pushy she would be when she was flat on her back, but I gritted my teeth and returned her stare.

"We're not finished here," she said. "I will keep Simon and anyone else from threatening Katherine on these jumps. Your existence and Deborah's and mine will be protected. *But.* Don't cross me again, Kate. You don't want to end up on the wrong side of history. You could have a nice, comfy little life if you play things smart. The Cyrists are the future and, given your obvious gifts with the equipment—"

"No." I opened my mouth again to elaborate, but there was really nothing more to add. So I just repeated it, shaking my head. "No."

"Suit yourself," she said, shrugging one shoulder dismissively. "You can't fight the Cyrists on your own, Kate. You can be one of the Chosen or you can line up with the other sheep to be fleeced and slaughtered."

I strongly suspected that she was right on the first point, but the casual way she referred to the destruction of those who were not "Chosen" turned my stomach. It also strengthened my resolve. No amount of power should be in the hands of a person who could say something like that with such conviction.

There was, however, little gain to be had in arguing with her. "Are you done?" I asked, my jaw set.

"Just one more little thing," she said, narrowing her eyes. "Stay away from Kiernan. He *will* be one of the Chosen—and he will be *mine.*"

I glanced over at the boy who was watching us nervously from the bench. "He's eight years old, for God's sake!"

"Now, yes. But he most definitely wasn't eight when I knew him. And not when you knew him, either," she added with a smug little smile. "But I guess you *lost* that bit of memory when the timeline shifted, didn't you? You're not the Kate he was in—in*fatuated* with. And I intend to make certain that it stays that way."

The fact that Prudence could remember a version of me that I would never know bugged me much more than I was willing to let on. Katherine had said I wasn't the same Kate she would have met if we'd been able to start my training six months earlier, and while I understood this on one level, it was an inconsistency that kept nibbling away at the back of my brain. If I understood Connor's explanation of the changing timelines, that other Kate shouldn't exist. Katherine's cancer would have been a constant in all versions of the timeline. And if so, I would always have started the training when I did and I wouldn't be listening to stories about this rogue Kate who was off somewhen having adventures I couldn't recall.

But I *had* glimpsed that other Kate's life briefly in the medallion. And Kiernan—the very much grown-up version of Kiernan on the Metro—was clearly thinking of that other Kate when he pulled the band from my hair and slipped it onto his wrist.

Remembering the expression on his face when he looked at me, I felt a sudden rush of empathy. How would it feel to stare into the eyes of someone you loved, someone who had loved you, and see no recognition, no love in return? I would soon know firsthand, assuming I made it back to my own time and found Trey.

I glanced back over at Kiernan. The trains ran on the half hour, and the crowd around the platform had now cleared out entirely, except for an older black groundskeeper who was using a large push broom to sweep bits of debris into a pile behind the ticket booth. Kiernan was still waiting, his face tense and his hands clenching the wooden slats of the bench. He had already been through so much at such a young age.

Despite my decision not to antagonize her, I couldn't ignore that issue. "What about his dad?" I blurted. "Kiernan said that you were responsible—"

"Kiernan is a little boy with a big imagination," she snapped, cutting me off. "He doesn't *really* believe I had a hand in his father's death. His mother most certainly doesn't believe it. And when Kiernan is all grown-up with"—she paused, giving me a suggestive little smile—"adult appetites, he'll be quite eager to follow me back into the Cyrist fold. Or anywhere else I want him to go."

Prudence reached into the bodice of her dress and tugged out a thick gold chain with a CHRONOS key at the end. She quickly scanned the area around us and then activated it. "Stay away from Kiernan and stay out of my way. If you can remember those two little things, you should be okay.

"Oh, and be nice to your mother," she added. Her eyes twitched down to the CHRONOS key and then she was gone.

∞ 20 ∞

The wooden bench was empty. Kiernan had been watching us intently, and I turned around immediately to see how he would react to Prudence's disappearing act. But he was no longer there. It seemed strange that he would have waited patiently for so long and then simply run off without saying anything.

The only person who had been there the entire time was the groundskeeper, who was putting his push broom back into a tiny alcove on the outside of the booth.

"Excuse me," I said. "There was a boy, waiting for me on the bench here. Did you by any chance see where he went?"

"Yes'm," he said, glancing up briefly, and then back down at the ground. "You mean Li'l Mick, right?"

I nodded, wondering exactly how many people at the Expo the kid knew.

"He took off that way mebbe a minute ago, miss," the old man said, tilting his head toward the Midway Plaisance. "He looked to be followin' a gen'l'man who come runnin' through from across the way—from over where the state buildins are."

My breath caught in my throat. "Do you remember what the man looked like? It's important."

"Well, I din look *real* close, miss—I was sweepin'," he said, his forehead creasing as he tried to remember. "But he looked young t'me, 'bout your age mebbe. Di'n' look like he worked out-side much, kinda pasty-lookin'. And di'n' look like he missed too many meals either, if y'know what I mean," he added with a low chuckle. "Mick'll be able to keep up with 'im, no doubt there. He's a smart li'l cricket."

"Thank you," I said, giving him a shaky smile over my shoulder as I ran toward the Midway entrance.

The description was too much like Simon to be a coincidence. Was Kiernan working with him? His older self and Simon had been on the Metro together. And they'd apparently been friends or at least compatriots at some point, based on what Simon had said when he attacked me in Katherine's front yard.

I had a hard time believing Kiernan was in on this, however. It seemed more likely that the boy had realized Simon was the one I'd pointed toward when yelling, "He has a gun!" Maybe he was still acting as my assistant, and trying to keep tabs on Simon for me.

Either way, his absence worried me. But what really baffled me was why Simon would be going to the Midway. If he'd come back to make a second attempt on Katherine's life, which was the only reason I could think of that he'd be back at all, why was he going in the opposite direction from the stable point on the Wooded Island?

And then I remembered—there were *two* Katherines wandering around the Expo today. That first trip was also in the diary that Simon grabbed when he took my backpack. Having been thwarted in his attempt to kill Katherine at the station, he had just moved on to the *next* logical target.

Connor's voice in my head was telling me to go back to the stable point, head home, and have another go at this after we'd had a bit of time to plan. But the idea of trying to tail Simon and, at the same time, avoid running into myself or anyone I'd seen that day, seemed fraught with even more problems than trying to find him here and now on the Midway. And he couldn't be *too* far away—I was only a minute or so behind him.

I just prayed that Kiernan wasn't with him. I really didn't think the boy would be helping Simon—it seemed too out of character— but I had to admit that I hadn't known Kiernan long enough to be completely certain. And if he was simply following Simon, I just hoped he would be careful, because I was pretty sure that Simon wouldn't hesitate to hurt him. Or use him as bait.

∞

The Midway was much more crowded and noisy than it had been earlier in the day. I had to veer off the sidewalk into the main street in order to avoid a large group lining up to enter the one o'clock showing at Hagenbeck's Trained Animals exhibit. Colorful banners over the entryway displayed a collection of elephants, lions, and tigers patiently standing on a pyramid of platforms, watched over by a ringmaster cracking his whip. The temperature had increased since the morning and the air around the building now had the stale, fetid odor that I remembered from the one sad little circus I'd attended as a child. That didn't seem to affect the enthusiasm of the people in the line, but in this era, I supposed that most of them had seen these exotic animals only in paintings and black-and-white photographs.

My eyes scanned both sides of the wide street for any sign of either Simon or Kiernan as I tried to recall everything Katherine had said or that I had read about the earlier jump. We had focused most of our research on the second trip. I'd just skimmed through the first one, mining it for background information about the fair itself. Katherine had said that the jump hadn't been connected to her own research—she was there to gather general impressions about the last days of the fair and the people's reaction to the assassination of Mayor Harrison, along with some background work for other CHRONOS agents.

I vaguely remembered her saying something about a camera, an African exhibit, and a beer garden. By African exhibit, she must have meant Dahomey Village, at the far end of the Midway. The beer garden was just ahead in the German Village, but I had no clue which day she'd gone where.

Rather than waste time trying to dredge the pieces up from memory, I paused in the shade of one of the viaducts that intersected the Midway and pulled the copy of the 1893 diary from my bag. After a few minutes of searching, I found the entry for October 28th and quickly scanned it. Katherine had spent most of the morning talking to young women at the International House of Beauty, a sort of global fashion show that was very popular—there was a long line outside both times I walked past, oddly enough with nearly as many men as women, although I suspected most of the guys were there to see pretty girls from around the world rather than to observe the latest trends in global fashion. Around noon, Katherine had walked back to the main Exposition, where she talked to some of the many workers who would be looking for new jobs in a few days when the fair closed its gates for the last time.

The next journal entry was the one I was looking for. It placed her at the German Village around 3 P.M. She didn't stay long, however, since she was there specifically to speak with the friend of a barmaid who had disappeared a few weeks earlier. The girl wasn't on duty until six, so Katherine decided to return that evening.

I leaned back against the brick wall of the viaduct and considered my options. Simon was also working with only the info from the diary, so he had no more clue than I did where Katherine would be between noon and three. His best chance of finding her, just like mine, was to stake out the various entrances to the German Village.

I could see one of the entrances from where I stood, but I wasn't sure if it led into the beer garden. Shoving the diary back into my bag, I decided to head over to the German Village to do a bit of reconnaissance.

Three little girls in native costumes were working their way across the street from the Javanese exhibit, holding hands as they crossed the Midway. I had just stepped toward them, thinking I would ask if they had seen "Little Mick"—he seemed to know everyone else at the Expo—when I saw the expressions on their faces transform all at once. One small brown hand flew up suddenly, as though its owner was trying to warn me.

I realized with a jolt of surprise that they weren't actually little girls at all but three tiny older women. The startled look on their faces was the last thing I remember clearly before I felt the sharp jab of a needle in my upper arm. The Midway began to melt into a kaleidoscope of random faces and body parts. I caught a brief glimpse of a man with a mustache and a black bowler, the colorful brocade fabrics of the Javanese costumes, and a small scuffed shoe as my knees buckled under me. Then, just shapes and colors. And finally, everything went pitch-black.

∞

For several seconds after I awakened, I thought I was in the small, cozy spare room where I always slept when visiting my dad's parents in Delaware. There was a slightly musty smell in the air, and as my eyes adjusted I began to pick out the intricate pattern of a crocheted doily on the nightstand next to the bed. I reached over to feel for the bedside lamp, but my hand bumped instead against a candleholder, knocking the stub of wax onto the floor. It rolled a few feet and then stopped, blocked by what I was pretty sure was a chamber pot.

This wasn't Grandma Keller's guest room.

I pulled back the thin blanket that someone had tucked in neatly around me. My green dress was missing. I was wearing only the white silk chemise and petticoats that Trey had so admired earlier. My right arm was unusually stiff and there was a small welt about six inches below my shoulder where the needle had punctured the skin. A red scratch marked the inside of my wrist, and the bracelet Katherine had given me was gone.

Everything was strange in the dim light, and I suspected that I was still feeling the effects of whatever drug I'd been given. Only the tiniest bit of sunlight seeped in through a dingy, grime-covered window about the size of my foot near the very top of the wall. A larger window, with closed curtains, was several feet beneath it to the right. I slid to the other side of the narrow bed and reached up to open the drapes, hoping to put a bit more light on my current situation.

But there was no window behind the curtains. The painted brick continued in an unbroken line to the opposite wall, where it was joined at an odd angle. There were no pictures, no decorations of any sort aside from the totally unnecessary curtains and the doily on the nightstand. Three holes had been drilled in the wall above the door, the first two no more than an inch in diameter and the third, the center hole, about twice that size.

I sat back on the bed and pulled my knees up to my chest. The movement triggered a memory of sitting in the same position, back in my room at Katherine's, watching DVDs with Trey. I glanced back at the non-window and then at the small holes above the door and my heart began to pound. I tried to tell myself that I was jumping to conclusions based on incomplete evidence, but I *knew*.

I was in the World's Fair Hotel, which meant that I had now broken two promises to Trey—although that was clearly the least of my worries.

How many women had Holmes killed in this room? How many had died on this very bed while he watched through the peephole?

My skin crawled at the thought and I stood up quickly. I was considering whether to try and open the door when it started to . . . well, *slither* toward the floor. I bit back a scream, and then a nervous laugh, as I realized the door was still on its hinges. The slithering was my dress, which had slipped off a coat hook.

I moved cautiously forward and picked it up, nearly tripping over the shoes that were underneath it. I was very glad to see the dress, but I had mixed feelings about those boots.

A movement caught the corner of my eye again, and for a split second I thought that I saw a flash of light in the opposite corner. I had the fleeting sensation of being watched, but when I turned it was still dark and no one was there. All that I could make out was the dim outline of a chair.

Sitting back down on the edge of the bed, I rubbed my eyes, hoping that the effects of the drug would clear soon. I spread the gown out beside me, feeling around for the hidden pocket in the bodice. I didn't really expect the CHRONOS key to be there, and it wasn't. That confirmed my suspicion that this hadn't been a random decision by Holmes to grab a girl who seemed to be traveling alone. That wasn't his modus operandi, and he was having plenty of luck luring young women here without resorting to abduction in broad daylight.

Somebody had convinced Holmes to take that extra bit of risk, and I was pretty sure that somebody was Simon. Why bother getting rid of me himself when there was a local serial killer who would be more than happy, probably for a ridiculously small fee, to keep me out of his way?

As that cheerful thought percolated in my head, the door opened suddenly. A soft yellow light spilled into the room from the gas lamps that lined the corridor. I tensed and was prepared to fight, but the figure in the doorway wasn't Holmes. The young woman was tall with wavy, flaxen hair. Her pretty, heart-shaped face creased with concern when she saw me.

"Oh, no!" she said, quickly setting the tray down on the night-stand. "You mustn't be standing yet. You're still much too weak. Here, let me help you get back into bed . . ."

"No," I said. "Where are my things? What time is it? I have to go . . ."

"You're not going anywhere. My name is Minnie. It's about dinnertime, and I've brought you some nice broth."

Minnie took me by the shoulders and in a very no-nonsense fashion led me back to bed. This had to be one of the wives or mistresses that Holmes had managed to charm, straight up until the moment of their deaths.

"You fainted on the Midway," she said, propping up the feather pillows and pushing me back against them. "It's very lucky for you that my husband was there when you passed out. He carried you back here.

"He's a *doctor*," she added, a note of pride in her voice. "And he says you need to rest.

"As for your things," she said, nodding toward the corner, "your hat is on the chair. That's all you had when my husband brought you in. I hope nothing was stolen at the fair—crime is really quite awful these days."

I couldn't argue with that, although I doubted that she realized how much of the recent crime wave was directly attributable to her spouse.

My first impulse was to tell her to get the hell out of Chicago before she ended up in the basement with the others. That didn't seem likely to increase my own odds of escape, however. The room was still semidark, but there had been enough light for me to see her expression when she was talking about her husband, the doc-tor. She was very clearly smitten with him, and I was pretty sure she'd run straight to Holmes, rather than checking for evidence first, if I started talking about lime pits, trapdoors, and skeletons.

"Where is Dr. Holmes?" I asked as she picked my dress up off the bed and returned it to the flimsy coat hook on the door.

Her back stiffened. "My *husband* is downstairs speaking with one of his business partners, so I decided to come up and check on you. I wasn't aware that you knew him." There was a noticeable change in her tone of voice, and she gave me a thorough appraisal as she turned to leave. Her eyes weren't nearly as friendly as before.

"I don't," I said.

"Then how did you know his name?" she asked.

"I didn't," I replied. "You said Dr. Holmes carried me back from the Midway, so I assumed . . ."

"Really?" she said, narrowing her eyes. "I'm pretty sure I never called him by name. You just stay in bed and finish your broth. The *two* of us will come up to check on you soon."

Hmm . . . perhaps she didn't trust Holmes fully after all. She seemed, at the very least, to be aware that her husband had a wandering eye, and she didn't like it one little bit.

The door closed firmly and I heard a bolt slide into place. I couldn't help but wonder why anyone would check into a hotel where the bolt was on the outside of the door, but judging from the three little holes at the top of the door, this was one of the "special rooms" where Holmes gassed his victims. It probably wasn't part of the typical guest tour.

I was once again in near darkness. How did the woman expect me to eat the broth without a lamp or candle? But it really didn't matter, since I had no intention of touching it.

When Minnie's footsteps had faded down the hallway, I pulled the covers back and ran my fingers along the inside of my petticoat. There was a brief, scary moment when I didn't feel anything—and then my fingers brushed against the thin metal inside the hidden pocket.

The spare CHRONOS key was there, on a thin silver chain, along with the extra bit of cash I had tucked away. Minnie was correct that I had been lucky. Not so much that Holmes had been at the Midway—I was pretty sure that luck had nothing to do with that—but rather that she had been here as chaperone. Having a jealous wife standing over him would certainly make even a total deviant like Holmes less likely to do a thorough check of an unconscious girl's undergarments.

Yanking my dress off the hook, I tossed it over my arm and, after a brief hesitation, grabbed the shoes as well. I wasn't going to bother putting everything on—Connor had seen me in less—but I would need the costume when I came back to fix this mess. Right now, however, I was going home. It would have been nice to get to a stable point, but given the way that Simon and Prudence had been blinking in and out like fireflies, it was pretty clear that Katherine's concerns were unwarranted. And either way, being captive in a hotel room with dozens of dead bodies in the basement had to qualify as good reason to invoke the emergency exit rule.

Holding the CHRONOS key in one hand, I pressed my fingers against the center. I'd pulled up the interface and focused on the stable point in the library and was just about to make the jump when the sound of footsteps running down the hallway broke my focus. The interface wavered and then disappeared.

The footsteps paused and I heard the bolt being drawn back. There wasn't enough time to pull the display up again, so I dropped the dress onto the bed, slipped the medallion down the front of my chemise, and moved to a defensive position behind the door. From the photographs I had seen, Holmes wasn't an especially large man, and I was pretty sure I could take him if he wasn't armed. And even if he was, I planned to put up a fight.

I came within about an inch of kicking my grandmother in the stomach. I pulled the kick at the very last second when the skirt clued me in that it wasn't Holmes. She swung her arm upward to ward off my foot with her handbag—the same bag that I had been carrying earlier.

It still took me a couple of seconds, however, to realize it was actually Katherine. She hadn't been joking when she said that the costuming department at CHRONOS did incredible work. If she had walked past me on the Midway, I don't think I would have recognized her. She had been aged about twenty-five years and my first thought was that it was my mom—which was odd because I'd never really noticed a resemblance between them before.

We both started to speak at the same time, and I stopped to let her go first. "Who are you?" she said in a hushed voice. Her eyes dropped to my chest, where the light from the medallion was shining faintly through the fabric. "Did HQ send you?"

I decided the truth was probably the quickest alternative. "Not exactly," I said. "I'm Kate—your granddaughter. We need to get out of here. But how did you find me? How did you get past Holmes?"

Her eyes scanned my face, confused. I don't know what she saw, but something there convinced her that I might be telling the truth. "I've been here on research twice before. There are only two rooms where Holmes could close someone in," she said. "I arranged a bit of a distraction—I tipped off one of his multitude of creditors to his current alias—and then sneaked in during the chaos." She turned to cast a nervous glance over her shoulder and then held out her right hand. "How did you get *this*?" she asked.

In her open palm was the bracelet. The chain was now broken, but the charm was the exact twin of the one that dangled from her left wrist. "You gave it to me," I said. "For my birthday. And yes, I know how it got chipped. Frederick Douglass, Susan B. Anthony, Sojourner Truth. You were watching them instead of paying attention to a carriage door. In 1860-something."

There was a pause and then Katherine gave me a small, pained smile. "Okay, I believe you. I never even told that to Saul." She stared at me closely again. I suspect she was wondering if I was *Saul's* granddaughter as well, but she didn't ask.

"When I saw that woman come out—is it Minnie or Georgiana? Minnie, I think. He went through companions very quickly," she said. "At any rate, I assumed it was *me* locked in here, that there had been some accident on a future jump or that Holmes had gotten wind that I've been asking questions about a few of the women he killed."

"But how did you know Holmes had—" I began.

"Some kid found me on the Midway and said that a lady wearing this bracelet had been taken to the World's Fair Hotel. He said he followed you here and that I needed to help you."

Kiernan. I had a sudden memory of the small, scuffed-up shoe I'd seen just before I fell. He must have snatched the bracelet when the crowd gathered around me. If I managed to get out, I resolved to give him every last penny I had and cover his little face with kisses.

"I could have gone back to HQ, gotten help, and come back in the easy way," she said. "There's a stable point on the third floor. But I couldn't shake that *kid*. I was afraid I was going to have to tie him up or knock him out or something, and then I remembered the financial dispute between Mudgett—Holmes, that is—and one of the gentlemen on the Board of Managers for the Expo."

Her mouth twisted. "It was all I could do to convince the boy to let me stop off to arrange the distraction, and then I wasted a good five minutes trying to get him to go back home. He finally agreed to wait in the alley. He wanted to storm straight in and see if you were okay, and I couldn't really tell him why that would be dangerous.

"He gave me this," she said, holding the bag out, "and a rather dirty parasol, which I ditched. This bag is mine, but with the exception of the key and the diary inside here, the rest of the stuff isn't exactly CHRONOS-issue is it? A pink plastic toothbrush?"

"No, those are not CHRONOS-issue." I sighed. "I was in a hurry, Katherine."

"Why? If you're not from CHRONOS, how can you use that key? And why do you have two keys? No one gets two keys."

"It's kind of complicated," I said.

That had been true from the beginning, but now it was even more difficult to know how much I should tell Katherine. I had no way of knowing whether Simon coming back to kill her meant that Prudence had failed in her promise to stop the attacks. He might simply have shown back up before she had time to force the issue. Things would have been so much simpler if I believed that Prudence would (or even *could*) keep her word, but I really didn't—there were just too many variables.

Given that her jump had originated from CHRONOS head-quarters, Katherine couldn't leave from anywhere other than the stable point at which she'd arrived, and I couldn't leave until I was certain she was on her way back to her own time. That meant my safe, quick, semidressed exit was out of the question. Resigned, I dropped the dress to the floor and stepped into the middle, pulling it up over my shoulders, and then turned my back toward Katherine. "Would you mind?" I asked, pointing to the laces.

She yanked the laces as I sucked in my breath. "We have to get you out of here," I said. "Holmes isn't after you, but someone else is—someone with a CHRONOS key. You need to go straight back to HQ. But—you can't tell them about me, Katherine. Believe me. Nothing is more important than this. Don't put this in your diary and don't discuss it with anyone, not even Saul. Convince Angelo to cancel your jumps for a few months. Take a vacation, or a sabbatical—whatever you have to do."

"I'm not sure that's possible," Katherine said as she started buttoning up the dress. "I don't run CHRONOS—Angelo doesn't even run CHRONOS. And I can't control other people's actions, only my own. Believe me. I've tried a few times."

She was clearly thinking of Saul. I rifled through my memory, trying to dredge up the dates. When had she become suspicious of Saul?

"I know that, Katherine, but I also know you're a very resourceful lady. You'll think of something." She finished the last button and I turned to face her.

"And . . . the concerns that you've had? That maybe Saul is not sticking to protocol as closely as he should? About his friends at the Objectivist Club? Check his bag when he returns from Boston. But—you can't confront him about any of this until April 26th. There will be an argument. You need to leave a message to let Angelo and Richard in on your concerns at that point. And you *must* be scheduled to take the jump the next day—on the 27th."

Her expression grew increasingly skeptical as I added each new complication to the plan. Katherine was a skilled actor—she had to be in her line of work—but could she really pull all of this off? And if she didn't, if she never made the jump to 1969? What would I find when I got back? Or would I even *get* back to my own time?

"Oh, and um . . . you're pregnant," I added with an apologetic smile as I sat on the bed and began to squeeze my feet into the boots. "You probably don't know that yet, because it happened after the New Year's Eve party."

Katherine looked a bit uncomfortable at the mention of that night, and I focused on the shoes again as an excuse to look away.

"You can't tell Saul about the pregnancy," I said. "Not until you know how he reacts to you finding . . . what you find in his luggage."

My fingers slipped on the buttons of the shoe and I cursed softly.

"But *you* already know how he reacts," she said, reaching up to pull a pin from the back of her hair. She bent the hairpin in two places with a quick twist of the hand and gave me the result—a makeshift buttonhook. "I'm smart enough to connect the dots. He's not going to respond in a reasonable way. But you expect me to go back, knowing all of this, and act like everything is fine for what, nearly two months? And to go through with an unplanned pregnancy that I could easily terminate at this stage?"

"I'm sorry," I said, bending down to finish the shoes. "I know this is asking a lot. But if you can't find a way to make this happen, exactly as I've said, I'm pretty sure that history is going to be rewritten on a grand scale. And, without giving too much away, you will not approve of the rewrite."

"I don't approve of *any* changes to the timeline," she said, pressing her lips firmly together as she retrieved my bonnet from the cane-backed chair next to the fake window. "That's what makes it difficult to believe what you're saying."

"Well, you've made an exception this time. At least, the Katherine that *I* know made an exception," I said, holding her eyes with a steady gaze. "In fact, she's spent most of the past twenty years trying to orchestrate this exception—even going so far as to arrange my parents' meeting on the off chance they'd produce *me*. And unless you follow her lead, millions—no, let's be honest, it's probably billions—of people are going to die well before their appointed time."

A long stare later, she let out a shaky breath. "Well, if that's the case, *granddaughter*, I guess we'd better go."

∞ 21 ∞

I really think we would have made it out of the hotel unnoticed if Kiernan had just stayed put on the sidewalk like Katherine had told him. Or if we hadn't taken a wrong turn at the second corridor, which turned out to be one of the blind hallways Holmes had thrown into the floor plan just for grins and giggles. If either of those things hadn't happened, Holmes would still have been in the office on the other side of the exit.

But both of those things *did* happen. The creditor Katherine had lured in to distract Holmes was downstairs, arguing loudly with Minnie, who was demanding that he wait for Holmes in the parlor. Holmes was on the landing between the first and second floors, holding a gun in one hand and the back of Kiernan's shirt in the other.

"Good evening, ladies." Judging from the pleasant smile on Holmes's face and the humorous twinkle in his blue eyes, he might have been planning to engage us in a casual chat about the weather. "Does this young fellow belong to either of you?" he asked.

Katherine answered "No" at the exact moment that I answered "Yes."

"He's my assistant," I said, giving Katherine an angry glance. "I'm a reporter covering the fair for the Rochester *Worker's Gazette*.

Your wife told me that you were kind enough to bring me back here when I fainted on the Midway. Thank you."

"Good," Holmes said. "That's exactly what *he* told me."

Even though I'm not a big fan of droopy mustaches, I could see why Holmes had found it easy to charm women. His eyes were almost hypnotic, and there were friendly crinkles—smile lines, my dad called them—around the edges.

I pulled my gaze away from Holmes to glance down at Kiernan. His face was pale and his dark eyes were wide and anxious. He mouthed the words "I'm sorry" silently, and I shook my head and gave him a look of sympathy. This wasn't his fault.

Holmes was still smiling when I looked up. He nodded toward Katherine. "And who might this good lady be?"

"My mother," I said. "She's traveling with me."

Katherine took her cue and stepped forward slightly, apparently deciding, as I had, that our best chance was to act as though the otherwise pleasant man on the landing wasn't holding a pistol. "Yes, sir," she said. "You have our deepest gratitude. I don't know what might have happened to my daughter if you hadn't . . ."

"No trouble at all, madam. In fact, it was my very real pleasure. Now if you and your 'daughter' wouldn't mind taking a few steps back?" He gestured with the gun and we backed up silently. He then reached down and hefted Kiernan under his arm, carrying him up the stairs to the second floor where we stood.

"I'd be delighted to stand here and chat with you lovely ladies," Holmes said as he reached the top step, "but I've had to leave my . . . wife to handle a rather distraught business associate and she's really not very good at these types of situations. So I'm going to ask you to return to your room, and we'll continue this discussion at our leisure later this evening."

He motioned again with the gun, and Katherine and I began to back toward the corridor.

"I think we'll move much more quickly if you turn around," he said.

We hesitated briefly, then reversed course, retracing our steps down the hallway. A few turns later, we were again in front of the door with the bolt on the outside.

Holmes tossed Kiernan at my feet as if he were a sack of potatoes and then held the door open as we filed inside.

"Please make yourselves comfortable. I promise I'll return just as quickly as I can."

Still smiling, he closed the door and slammed the bolt.

The tiny bit of daylight that had shown through the small window earlier was now gone. I could feel Kiernan's small body shaking next to me, but I couldn't tell in the dark whether he was crying. I knelt down on the floor and pulled him toward me, as much for my own comfort as his.

"I'm sorry, Miss Kate," he said. "I shoulda stayed in the alley."

Katherine gave a little huff as she sat on the bed, making it clear that he'd get no argument from her on that point.

"No, Kiernan," I said firmly, giving Katherine a dirty look, even though I knew she couldn't see it. "You were amazing—I can't believe you managed to grab my things right under Holmes's nose and bring help. But how did you find Katherine? I don't even think I'd have recognized her."

He shrugged. "It's just disguises. You get used to 'em on the Midway. She walks the same an' sounds the same. I seen her aroun' lotsa times this year. An' she always had on a bracelet like the one you're wearin'. The one you said was your special sign."

"You're incredibly observant for an eight-year-old," I said. "Are sure you aren't a grown-up in disguise?"

It was a lame attempt at humor, but he obliged me with a little laugh. I gave him a big hug and kiss on the forehead. "You saved my life, you know."

"I wouldn't be so quick to jump to that conclusion," Katherine said, "given our current predicament."

She then removed something from the pocket of her skirt. The glowing interface of a CHRONOS diary popped up a few seconds after she opened it.

"What are you doing?" I asked.

"I'm calling HQ for an emergency extraction. They can come in through the third-floor stable point and—"

"No," I said, snatching the diary.

"Do you have any better ideas?" she countered, attempting to grab the diary back from me. "Holmes will return eventually and I don't think he's planning an ice-cream social for the evening's entertainment."

"I told you no one at CHRONOS can know about this, Katherine. Have you thought about what happens to me if you pull in HQ? Or to Kiernan? Do you think CHRONOS will be willing to let him go, no questions asked, given what he's seen and heard?"

"He's only *seen* me open a diary, Kate, and *heard* a conversation that he doesn't understand in the slightest. And if you'd shut up and hand the book back to me, we can end that conversation so that he—"

"It's not the firs' time I seen one of those things, Miss Kate," Kiernan interrupted. "It's like the one of me dad's, the thing I used to send a message to—"

I yanked his arm a bit and he took the hint, but it was too late. Katherine reached into the handbag and pulled out the CHRONOS key I'd been wearing earlier. The glow from the key lit the room with pale blue and I mentally kicked myself for not thinking of using it as a flashlight earlier.

"What color is this?" Katherine asked, holding the medallion close to Kiernan's face.

"I canna really see it in the dark, ma'am," he answered, glancing up nervously at me.

Katherine's eyebrow shot up. "You're a smooth little liar, kid, but you're not fooling me." She grabbed his free hand and pressed it against the center of the medallion. The display wasn't clear—it was really little more than static, with the occasional visible word or button, but it provided her with the answer she needed.

"How?" she asked me. "How is he able to do that? They don't even start training kids this young."

"I can't really tell you that," I said. "It's part of what we're trying to correct."

That was a blatant lie and I hoped that my poker face was better than Kiernan's, at least in the dim light. A truthful response would have been that I was asking her to go back and start the very chain of events that would lead to Kiernan, myself, and who knew how many others being able to activate that equipment. But that chain of events was the one that I knew and the only one that seemed to promise any hope, however small, of stopping the Cyrists.

"So what do you suggest, Kate?" she asked, tucking the medallion back inside her dress. "I don't think there's any way out of this room, and our only other option is to sit here and wait for Holmes to return. It would be three against one, but one of us is pretty small, and I think the gun puts the odds slightly in his favor."

"There *is* a way for *one* of us to get out of here," I said. "And it only takes one person to open that bolt and get us all out. Your return trip may be restricted to the stable point on the Wooded Island, but mine isn't. I can jump to any stable point from here. Didn't you say there's one on the third floor?"

"Yes, but how can you—"

"I can't explain any further, Katherine." It was, admittedly, a bit of a kick to be the one restricting *her* knowledge on a need-to-know basis, but we really didn't have the time for a detailed discussion on the matter. And each bit of information I gave her was another string that she'd be tempted to pull, potentially unraveling the events that needed to transpire over the next few months.

"I only familiarized myself with the stable points inside the fair and near the entrances," I said, removing my CHRONOS key from the inner pocket and handing it to her. "I knew there were others, but—well, I didn't have a lot of time to prepare. If you can pull the location up on the key so that I can see it and lock it in, I should be able to make the jump and get back here in a couple of minutes. I'm just not sure how we're going to get out the front door with both Holmes and Minnie lurking at the bottom of the stairs."

"Miss Kate?" Kiernan said, tugging my arm. "Maybe we don' hafta take the stairs. Maybe we could take the ladder?"

"What ladder? There's a fire escape?" I hadn't even considered that possibility—I mean, really, what homicidal maniac would include fire escapes in the design plan for his torture castle?

"I don' know if you'd call it a fire escape, but there's a ladder from a window on the top floor, goin' down to the roof of the buildin' next door. I saw it when I was waitin' all that time in the alley. *Instead* of goin' home."

I couldn't help but grin at the note of sarcasm in his voice on the last sentence. If Katherine noticed, however, she didn't let on. She just reached over and took my hand, placing the activated medallion in my palm.

"The kid and I will put our heads together while you're gone," she said, "and try to see if we can figure out which window is most likely to lead to the ladder."

Positioning herself so that we could both see the interface clearly, she visually sorted through the various categories and then halted when a dark space came into view.

"Are you sure that's it?" I asked. "It's totally black."

"Yes," she answered a bit testily. "It's a linen closet. And it is nighttime. What do you expect?"

"I'm just not sure how you can tell this closet from some of the other dark closets you zoomed past. I could end up in Des Moines."

"I've never *been* to Des Moines. I've been here, however. Your first left and then your second left should get you from the closet to the staircase. And from there, you just need to retrace our steps back to this room."

I nodded and positioned my fingers over the controls, replacing hers. The display wavered for a moment and then sputtered out.

Katherine snorted in annoyance and pulled it up again. "Focus this time, okay?"

"Fine," I said. "I like you better as an old lady. You need time to mellow." It was true, but I reminded myself that it had been a pretty stressful day for her as well. She'd just learned she was pregnant and that the father probably wasn't what he was pretending to be, and she was smart enough to realize that her world was about to change in major ways. That was a lot to digest, even without threats from a serial killer.

The display flickered again briefly when Katherine moved her fingers to make way for mine, but I was able to pull the image back.

"Okay. I've got it. Thanks, Katherine.

"Kiernan," I said, keeping my eyes locked on the display, "I'll be right back. Only a couple of minutes. Katherine's really not as nasty as she seems."

"I'll be all right," he said. "Be careful, Miss Kate."

"And Katherine?" I added in a lower voice. "If something happens, I'm trusting that you'll *get him out* of here. I know for a fact that he is not meant to meet his end in this hotel. You'll tell CHRO-NOS he saw nothing and he knows nothing."

"My God, Kate. What do you think I am?" she hissed. "The kid has been a major pain in my backside today, but I wouldn't *leave* him with that monster."

"So I have your word on that? You'll do everything you can to get him to safety if I don't make it back?"

"You'd *better* make it back, since you seem so convinced that the fate of the world depends on it. But yes—you have my word. Would you just *go?*"

I focused on the very middle of the black rectangle that Katherine claimed was the third-floor linen closet and blinked.

∞

I'm not a fan of small, dark spaces, so I was relieved that the arc of blue light from the medallion illuminated most of the closet. Apparently CHRONOS hired only very thin historians, however, because the stable point was a tight fit even for my slight frame. My shoulder collided with a shelf as I turned, tumbling a large stack of linens to the floor. The stench of chemicals and something more earthy and pungent underneath assaulted my nose.

Out of habit, I bent down and started to pick up the sheets that I knocked over, but the smell was stronger near the floor. Fighting back a wave of nausea, I decided I really didn't want to know what was under the stack of linens and pushed the door to my right. It wouldn't budge and there was no handle on the inside.

I moved back two steps to see if I could get enough room to kick it in. That's when I felt something round and hard poking my spine.

I bit back a scream. Then, after a few seconds of nothing happening, I glanced behind me and saw that my attacker was the doorknob to another, larger door. Relieved, I opened it and escaped into the hallway. I had no clue where the first door led, and given that the smell was stronger in that direction, I was very glad that I didn't have to find out.

The light from the medallion was again very useful, since the gas lamps in the third-floor hallways weren't lit. The corridors were confusing enough without having to feel my way along the walls in the dark. The entire floor seemed deserted, but I couldn't shake the memory of the things that had happened behind some of these doors.

Of course, Katherine's instructions were *wrong*. The first left did take me to a main hallway, but the second left along that corridor was one of Holmes's amusing little dead ends.

Coming back toward the main hallway, I passed a door that, like the second-floor room where Katherine and Kiernan were waiting for me, had a bolt on the outside.

I knew Katherine would screech that I was violating the timeline—and she was undoubtedly correct that anyone in there probably wasn't supposed to escape—but I really didn't think much of the CHRONOS ethical guidelines on that front. I yanked the bolt back and opened the door.

I heard a scuffling sound from inside, but it could very easily have been a mouse and I didn't have time to stop and investigate. "If there's anyone in there, the door is open," I whispered. "Holmes has a gun, though, so be careful."

I didn't wait for an answer, just turned right at the main corridor, and then tried the next left. Thankfully, that one did lead me to the stairs.

I paused at the top of the open stairwell to listen. The muted noise of an argument drifted upward, but it didn't sound like the man from the bank.

" . . . not leaving you here with . . ." That voice was clearly Minnie. I couldn't make out the entire response, but the other voice was low and calm, and I was pretty sure it was Holmes. I picked up the phrase "back at the flat," and "business" as I moved slowly down the stairs, but that was all I heard.

When I hit the second floor, I took off quickly through the hallway. No wrong turns this time and the gas lamps were easier to travel by than the dim light of the CHRONOS key. It was still a confusing maze of twists and turns, but I reached the room a few minutes later. I unbolted the door, and a very relieved-looking Katherine and Kiernan rushed out.

As we hurried back toward the stairway, I took all of the cash that I could find at the bottom of the handbag and crammed it down the front of Kiernan's shirt. It was at least ten times the salary we'd agreed upon and he started to protest.

"You've earned it, kiddo. And," I said softly, "if we get separated, you may still have a job to do. Get Katherine back to the Wooded Island—the spot near the cabin."

"I know how to get back to the Expo, Kate," Katherine said. "I've spent plenty of time here."

"Yes, but I'll wager you don't know the back ways as well as he does. And based on what I've seen, he's friends with half the people who work at the Expo. I'm willing to bet they'd help him—no questions asked.

"Kiernan," I added, "take every back alley you know and keep an eye out for the guy you were following earlier. The pudgy one. He's still looking for Katherine, probably on the Midway."

"What about you?" he asked.

"I'll be okay—I can jump straight home from here—but I won't see either of you again for a long while."

Katherine had just turned a corner. I held Kiernan's arm to keep him back so that she couldn't hear our next exchange.

"If you get out, you don't come back, okay? I'll be fine." I tapped the medallion hanging from my neck and spoke quickly. "Is yours at the cabin?"

He nodded, and after a moment's hesitation, I slipped the spare medallion around his neck and tucked it into his shirt. "Never take it off, okay? Never. Prudence is going to demand your dad's key at some point, and I think there's a good chance you won't remember any of this if she does. You might not even remember why you don't trust her, and I really don't think that's fair, do you?"

His eyes were solemn. "No, Miss Kate. I don' think that's a bit fair." The chain was very long on him, well below his waist, and he rearranged it as we turned the corner, wedging it into the waistband of his trousers.

I again had the eerie feeling that I was being watched and spun around to look back down the hallway we'd just left. But there was no one in the corridor—just the flickering shadows from the gas lamps.

Katherine, who was now approaching the stairwell, looked back impatiently over her shoulder. I turned back to Kiernan, putting my finger to my lips and flashing my eyes toward Katherine, hoping he'd understand both that he needed to be quiet and that she didn't need to know about our little exchange. He nodded and gave me a little smile.

There were no voices in the stairwell. A few lights were still burning in the pharmacy, but Holmes's office was dark. I crossed my fingers that he had stepped out to help his wife find a cab to take her home, but I had a bad feeling.

I led Kiernan toward the inner edge of the stairs and we crept upward to the dark third floor of the hotel. When we reached the landing, I gave Kiernan's shoulder a little squeeze and moved the two of us in front of Katherine.

"What are you doing?" she asked, in a barely perceptible whisper. "I'm the one who knows which way we're going."

"Do you have martial arts training?" I snapped. "If not, we stand a better chance if I go first. Just in case. You take the rear, Kiernan in the middle. If we all stay close, you can nudge me when we need to turn."

She made a slight face, but nodded once and pulled back against the wall so that I could inch out in front of her. "It should be the second left."

After my last experience with her thinking it was the second left, I was tempted to ask if she was sure it wasn't the third, but I decided it was best to keep chatter to a minimum.

We crossed to the other side of the hallway and were just about to make the turn when two gunshots sounded from behind us. All three of us jumped and ducked as we ran around the corner, but the shots were clearly on a lower floor. The good news? Holmes was nowhere near our current location. The bad news? He was most definitely still in the building. And from the sound of things, that bad news had probably been much worse news for someone on the first or second floor.

"Come on," I said. "At least now we know he's in the building, but not close by. We just need to find that window."

"But he doesn't shoot anyone tonight," Katherine said.

"You know that for a fact?" I asked, my voice tense. "He killed a lot of people here."

"I just hope he hasn't killed someone else because of us," she said. "Someone who wasn't supposed to die."

"I do, too," I said. "But there's not much we can do about it now, is there? We need to keep moving."

There was a rapping sound behind me and I whipped the CHRONOS key around to look down the corridor, bumping into Kiernan as I spun around. For a split second, I saw a tall shadow in the very middle of the hallway and then it was gone.

"Did you see that?" I asked Katherine.

"No," she said. "What are you talking about?"

"I thought . . . ." I shook my head. It clearly wasn't Holmes, and I'd had very little sleep in the past forty-eight hours. "Nothing. Just jumpy, I guess."

We ran down two more corridors, including the one where I'd paused earlier to unbolt the door. The door was open a good deal wider than it had been when I left, and I wondered whether the occupant had escaped the frying pan only to land directly in the fire.

And that's when I smelled the smoke.

∞ 22 ∞

I don't know how long we spent in those hallways. It was probably less than ten minutes, but they were easily the longest ten minutes of my life. The place was, for all intents and purposes, a maze, designed to disorient anyone unfortunate enough to get lost in the middle.

We had just passed the door I had unbolted earlier and the stable point in the linen closet for the second time. Every time we were forced to backtrack after encountering a dead end, I was terrified that we'd come face-to-face with Holmes. To make matters even worse, the smoke was getting thicker.

"I know there was a window, Miss Kate. It was on *this* side of the buildin'." It was the second time we'd walked all the way to the end of this corridor and tears were now pouring down Kiernan's face.

"Well, there's no window at the end of the hall and no rooms on this side of the hallway," Katherine said.

I stopped for a moment. "Unless . . . there's a hidden door? He used trapdoors, didn't he? I remember something about him walling up a shipment of furniture—building the room around it—so that he could claim it never arrived and avoid payment. Maybe . . ."

"What are we supposed to do then?" Katherine asked. "Start kicking in walls at random?"

I didn't answer her, just tore down the hallway, back to the linen closet. Ignoring the fact that something back there reeked foully, I gave the closed door inside the closet a hard kick with the side of my foot. It opened about an inch and I had to put my arm over my mouth and nose to keep from vomiting.

I kicked again, trying not to think about what I was dislodging. With the third kick, there was a soft thud and the small door swung inward.

I bent down to look inside and could just barely see the window at the very end of a long, narrow room that stretched the entire length of the hallway. If there was a moon out, it was behind a cloud, because only the faintest hint of light was coming in through the glass. I couldn't see a ladder, but Kiernan had said he didn't think we'd be able to see it from the inside, since the rungs began just below the window's edge.

I turned to Katherine and Kiernan, who were standing at the entrance to the linen closet. "You were right, Kiernan. This has to be it."

"What is that god-awful smell?" Katherine asked.

"I think we both have a pretty good idea," I answered. "I guess Holmes didn't manage to get all of the victims to the pit in the basement. Just hold your breath as much as you can—and be careful to duck as you enter. The doorway is very low."

I held the CHRONOS key out into the room, hoping for enough light to pick a relatively clear, corpse-free path to the window. As I began to move away from the door, my skirt brushed against something solid. I really didn't want to know what it was, so I just kept inching forward.

"Are you okay, Kiernan?" I asked, reaching back for his hand.

"I'm okay, Miss Kate," he said, but he slipped his hand into mine. "We need to hurry. I mean, if he set the fire, then this is prob'ly his escape route, too . . ."

I moved forward as quickly as possible with only the CHRO-
NOS keys for light to guide me. The room was mostly empty, aside
from some stray items of furniture, but it was only about four feet
wider than the broom closet had been.

We passed several shadows that looked like cots along the left-
hand wall and I was pretty sure that the long, thin object dangling
from the edge of the second one had once been someone's arm. I
heard a quick intake of breath from Katherine a few seconds later,
and when I looked down at Kiernan's face his eyes were tightly
closed—he just clutched my hand firmly and blindly followed my
lead.

We'd covered another five yards or so when a shuffling noise
came from behind us. A quick glance back revealed nothing. I told
myself it was probably just the body that I'd shoved away from the
door slumping the rest of the way to the ground. Or a rat. Normally,
either of those ideas would have freaked me out, but right now they
were a source of great comfort.

But the sound came again. And then again. Either the body
was following us or it was a very *large* rat. Even more likely, it was
Holmes.

He obviously knew we were in here. If I could hear one person
moving stealthily behind me, he could definitely hear the three
of us. Holmes must have known we were in here before he even
entered—otherwise, why no lantern? We had a slight advantage,
in that he could not see the light from the CHRONOS keys that we
were using to find our way forward. He had a much better idea of
the territory, however, since he'd designed this nightmare.

"Go," I whispered, still moving forward. "Keep low and stick
to the side so you aren't silhouetted by the window. If it won't open,
smash it. Don't stop for anything. You both know what you need to
do once you're out of here. I'll see you—eventually."

Kiernan leaned in toward me for just a moment and clutched my hand. I was afraid he was going to argue, but he didn't. "Bye, Miss Kate. Be careful."

I gave him a quick kiss on the top of the head as they moved past me. Pulling myself as close against the wall as possible, I listened, trying to separate the sounds of Katherine and Kiernan on my right from the less obvious movements to my left.

Inching over a few feet, I positioned myself across from the two cots I'd seen earlier. The room was, at most, six feet across, and with the obstacle of the cots on the other side, Holmes would have to pass directly in front of me in order to get to the window. I fought the temptation to tuck the medallion back in my pocket. There was no way he could see the light, but it still made me feel exposed—a bright blue beacon pointing out my location.

I took a few slow, deep breaths to try and steady my pulse and then stole a quick glance at Katherine and Kiernan. I couldn't see them clearly, just the glow from Katherine's CHRONOS key ten, maybe fifteen yards away from the window. *Please, dear God, let this be the window with the ladder,* I thought.

Holmes was still advancing from the left, but it was very hard to gauge his exact distance. His breathing was jagged—as if he'd recently been running or had inhaled a lot of smoke.

Another quick glance at the window. I couldn't even see the blue glow anymore; Katherine must have slipped the key back into her dress.

I was about to turn away when the faint outline of the window shifted slightly. There was a loud creak as the frame resisted, but the gunshots were even louder.

Holmes fired twice in rapid succession. I don't know where the first shot landed, but the second shattered a section of the window. I twisted toward him just as the third shot went off and was able to pinpoint his location—he was almost on top of me. In fact, if he hadn't been staring at the window when he fired, I'm pretty sure he'd have caught a glimpse of me in the brief light of the explosion.

I stood up, my back pressed to the wall. The blue light gave an unearthly glow to Holmes's face that would have been sinister enough without the long-barreled revolver he was clutching. He had stopped in order to take a more careful aim when I kicked upward. The goal was to hit his arms, which were holding the revolver at chest level, but the skirt limited my movement and the blow caught him just below the belt of his overcoat.

Holmes doubled over, his finger squeezing the trigger of the gun as he did. The shot went wild; the vibration in my feet suggested it had lodged in the floor. Catching my balance, I pulled my knee up sharply into his face. I heard a crunch, but it wasn't enough to stop him; his hand lashed out and snatched the foot I was standing on out from under me.

As I fell, I could see Kiernan's form visible in the window from the chest up. I couldn't see Katherine; she was either standing out of the light of the window to avoid being a target or she was already on the ladder.

My head smashed against the floor. I pushed myself up to a sitting position, my back against the wall, as quickly as I could, but I was disoriented. There were dozens of little blue lights when I opened my eyes and I remember thinking that must be what they mean by "seeing stars."

There was a noise to the left of me, so I pulled my legs in and kicked again. One foot clipped him, in the knee, I think, but it was more of a glancing blow than a direct hit.

"You have an impressive kick for such a little lady," he said. "But it's no match for a gun." He was moving the gun slightly from side to side with one hand as his left hand fumbled in his jacket pocket.

My heart pounded in my ears as the gun swept past where I was huddled. *He can't see you, Kate, he can't see you,* I reminded myself. And there had already been six shots—two downstairs, and four up here. I didn't know a lot about guns, but I'd seen a few Westerns, and the one in his hand was a "six-shooter." That meant the gun should be empty. Unless, of course, he'd stopped to reload before entering the linen closet.

He hadn't reloaded, but it didn't matter. His hand emerged from his pocket holding a single bullet.

As Holmes clicked the round into the chamber, I turned sideways and centered the medallion in the palm of my hand, wedging my arm against the wall to keep it steady so that I could pull up the kitchen at Katherine's house.

He took a couple of steps backward, probably to give himself a wider view to catch any movement, his left hand stretched behind him to feel his way. His legs buckled when he bumped into one of the cots. There was a clank of glass against glass, and Holmes cursed softly, then stopped in mid-profanity to laugh.

I don't know what instinct caused me to turn away from that laugh. It meant breaking eye contact with the medallion and I had already locked in the kitchen—I was just pulling up the date and only needed a second more, two at the most. If I hadn't turned away, however, the liquid would have caught me square in the face.

The acid was pure flame, scorching my neck and scalp. I screamed—there was no way to avoid it even though it gave away my location. I held my breath, waiting for the shot, but I heard a different loud noise instead. It sounded like he had tripped over the cot, but he was soon on his feet again, moving toward me.

He was just playing it conservatively, I thought—with only one bullet he wanted to be certain of his target. I crawled along the floor as quickly as I could, away from him, back toward the linen closet, trying to keep from whimpering as each tiny movement worsened the blazing pain on the side of my head.

The smell of smoke was growing stronger, battling with the stench from the decomposed body just ahead. Holmes had only one escape route from the fire—the window. With any luck, he would think that was my only way out as well and maybe, just maybe, leave me to my presumed fate in a burning building. If I could keep moving and avoid slipping into shock, however, all I had to do was get out of this room and find a spot where I could concentrate and use the CHRONOS key.

The doorway had to be close. I struggled to my feet so that I could move faster. I was still seeing the little blue stars, so I leaned against the wall to steady myself before taking a step. I couldn't see Holmes, but I heard movement from behind me.

My hand finally found the opening in the wall and I lowered my head to step through and enter the tiny linen closet. I shoved open the door to the hallway and sucked in a mouthful of air—smoky, but at least without the underlying stench of decaying flesh. Running as fast as I could in the general direction of the stairwell, I whipped around one corner a bit too fast and caught the heel of my stupid boot in the hem of my skirt. The rip echoed through the hallway—the auditory equivalent of a big red arrow pointing Holmes in my direction.

I ducked into the third corridor on the right and then darted across the hallway, taking a left at the next intersection. Hopefully, the doctor would assume that I'd taken the quicker, easier turn to the right. He had stopped to light a lantern—I could see it casting shadows against the walls as he ran.

At the third room down, I jiggled the knob on the off chance that it had been left unlocked. No luck. The footsteps grew louder and I pulled myself as close to the door as possible. Taking a deep breath, I pressed my fingers to the center of the medallion.

I didn't think there was time to pull up a location and lock in the date—I was just going to pick a spot and blink. I remembered Connor's caution about landing in the middle of a highway, but if the other choice was a mass murderer armed with acid and a gun, a possible collision with a semitruck sounded like a bargain.

I tried to steady my hands so that I could focus and pull up the display, but it was hard to concentrate. The display wavered and then disappeared.

As I prepared to try again, I saw a faint light from the corner of my eye. The doctor turned briefly into the right corridor—then the lantern swung around and he headed straight toward me.

And then the door behind me opened and I fell backward into the room. A large hand covered my mouth, trapping the scream before it could escape my lips. Another hand, holding a white folded cloth, moved toward me.

∞ 23 ∞

The man yanked me to the right of the doorway. The white cloth was sopping wet and he pressed it against the side of my face, his arms holding me close against his body.

"Kate!" It took a moment for the familiar voice, soft but urgent in my ear, to cut through my panic. I looked up into the man's face. It appeared strange in the blue light from our medallions, but the dark, worried eyes were the same ones that I'd stared down into only a few minutes earlier.

"Kiernan? But how—"

"Kate, please. You have to focus. I've pulled up a stable point, love." The display showed a small, dimly lit room with blankets in the corner. "Just slide your fingers over it and go. I'll be right behind you. I promise."

I don't know if it was his voice or just the knowledge that I wasn't alone, but amazingly, my hands steadied as I reached for the CHRONOS key. It flickered only the tiniest bit and then it was clear. I blinked and pulled in a huge lungful of fresh, smoke-free air, before I collapsed onto the dirt floor.

I faded in and out of consciousness for a while. Kiernan's voice would pull me to the surface for a few moments before I slipped back under. The clearest memory I have was the sensation of water being poured in a steady stream on my neck. It hurt, but the pain was far worse when the water stopped. He forced me to sit up at one point, his hands gentle, and made me swallow a few capsules. My eyes closed again and I slipped back into the fog.

It was daylight when I fully woke. Kiernan's sleeping face was the first thing that I saw, his long dark hair damp against his skin. He was sitting with his back against the corner of the cabin. I was wrapped in blankets, my head resting on his thigh, his fingers laced through my own. The smell of smoke was strong and pungent in his clothing. I pulled my free hand up to the right side of my neck and felt a large swath of gauze, held in place by medical tape. Several bottles and containers of ointment were scattered around us and the remnants of a fire were smoldering in the fireplace. My green dress lay in a crumpled heap, with the damp dirt floor showing through the numerous spots the acid had dissolved.

My body was stiff and I needed to readjust my position. I moved slowly, reluctant to wake Kiernan, but his eyes flashed open at once. "Kate? Are you all right?"

I tried to nod, but that wasn't a pain-free option, so I stopped and gave him a weak smile. "Yes. It hurts, but I'm okay. This is the cabin—on the Wooded Island, right? But *when* are we?"

"Around 5 A.M., I think—it's just the next day," he answered. "There's no one here—there won't be many people here at all today. The closing ceremonies were canceled because of the mayor's assassination. And it was easier for me to set everything up here. I'm—it takes a lot out of me to jump long distances. Little jumps are easier, but I've been making a lot of them lately—I didn't want you to be too far away, just in case I had to walk here to reach you."

"Holmes? And Katherine, did she . . . ?"

"Holmes escaped, just as he was supposed to. He's probably on the train to Colorado today. The fire wasn't supposed to happen for a few more weeks, but I don't think it will change anything with his eventual capture and trial. And yes, Katherine and I made it to the stable point. I took her by a back route and we didn't run into any problems."

I sighed, relieved to know that at least that much of the plan had succeeded. "Tell me how you knew, Kiernan. Why did you come back? How did you know to be in that room?"

He stared into my eyes for several moments before he spoke. "It took me a long time to put the pieces together, Kate. You were always there, at the back of my mind year after year, but I never knew for certain whether you made it out of the hotel. I went back that night, after taking Katherine to the Wooded Island, and the place was in full blaze—the firefighters said there couldn't be anyone alive inside. There wasn't anything I could do but go home.

"I did as you told me. I never removed the medallion. I even kept my hand on it when I bathed. We moved back to the Cyrist farm—there really weren't many options once my mother took ill. I let them teach me to use to the CHRONOS key. I'm not as good with it as many of the others, but that never mattered much to Prudence," he added with a bitter laugh, "and she generally determined who would be given privileges."

"She didn't—" I broke off, hesitant to say what I was thinking. "You were so young."

"Oh, no. Nothing like that. She wasn't that much older than me most of the times she came to the farm. About your age, maybe, the first time I saw her as a young woman. I was only sixteen—it's very hard to say no to a willing girl at sixteen, Kate."

"Didn't you know that she was—well, that you knew her when she was older? And when you were younger . . ." I shook my head and then winced as the bandages shifted against the burn. "I mean, you seemed convinced that she had something to do with your dad."

"Yeah . . . but that was Pru when she was older, y'know? I don't know what she did later—I still don't have any proof one way or the other—but none of that had happened for *her* when she was eighteen."

"Christ, that makes my head hurt," I said. "It doesn't make you crazy? Thinking of an older Prudence knowing you when you were younger and then the two of you, together as teenagers?"

"I keep forgetting that you're—how do you say it—a 'newbie'?" Kiernan said with a teasing grin. "You'll get used to the twists and turns soon enough. At eighteen, Pru was just a confused kid, not entirely sure of what Saul wanted her to do or of her place in all of this. She wasn't a bad person, then, from what I could tell. After a while, I decided it wasn't fair to judge her on the basis of something she wasn't—or at least wasn't yet. Does that make sense?"

"No," I said. "I mean, I understand, but I can't say it makes any sense at all. None of this does."

"I'm not proud of that relationship," he said. "I'm not sure I would say that I *used* Pru—at least not any more than she used me—but my feelings were complicated by my past. I mean, if I never looked at her eyes when we . . . well, she reminded me of you. I was just a kid when we were here together, but I never forgot you, Kate." He paused for a moment, tracing my lower lip ever so softly with his finger, and a shiver ran all the way through my body. *No, Kate,* I thought, *no, no, no. You're exhausted and grateful and . . . yes, damn it, incredibly attracted to him. But* no.

"Then, a year later when I was seventeen, you *were* there, Kate—not you, not this you, but a different Kate. My Kate. A little older than you are now—so beautiful, so intent on convincing me to fight the Cyrists. We were so much in love, Kate, but you had no memory of an eight-year-old boy, no memory of the Expo. I could never understand that.

"And now, even though I understand why, it's hard to imagine a Kate who doesn't remember that year we spent together. I think you were in Boston 1905 more than you were in your own time and place. It's a miracle you didn't collapse from exhaustion— you'd tell Katherine you were going downstairs for coffee and then jump back to spend all day with me, popping back in ten seconds after you left. They were always so much easier on you, the jumps. They . . . drain me, and we had to be careful to hide things from Prudence."

"You were still . . . with Prudence?" I asked, wincing a bit as I pushed myself up to sitting. I tried to keep the totally irrational note of jealousy out of my voice, but the pleased little smile on Kiernan's face told me that I had failed.

"No, Katie. Never again, not *that* way. Not after I found you." He sat in front of me and took my hands in his.

"Pru was madder'n hell when she found out, and that's when she swiped Dad's key. Well, not her directly, it took three of her Cyrist goons to get it off me, but they had no idea about the spare you gave me. Pru gave the key back a few months later after they'd made the changes, and I played along—she's never realized that I know the whole truth.

"But then . . . you stopped coming," he said. "And I finally realized that wherever you were, you hadn't been protected by a key. Something had changed. The entire resistance we were trying to put together had never been started. I just, well—sort of lay low, waiting. They teamed me up with Simon to watch you—it was Pru's idea of a little joke, I guess, to put me so close since she thought I had no memory of you and you wouldn't know me from Adam."

I shivered, pulling the blanket tighter, and tried to sort out all that had happened. "I'm not so sure any of this was her idea, Kiernan. Or if she was in on it at the beginning, she changed her mind." I gave him a brief rundown of my conversation with Prudence and her belief that killing Katherine was a power play designed to get her out of the way.

Kiernan chuckled. "She finally put two and two together, I guess. I don't know that he was planning that specifically—but Saul doesn't tend to think that the normal rules of morality should apply to him. And she's been pushing to run things her way for some time now. He may well have decided she's more trouble than she's worth."

"You've met him?"

"Oh, sure. Several times." Kiernan helped me turn around to lean my back against the cabin wall and then poured a bit of water into a glass from a large jug. He shook two very modern-looking pills into his hand and gave them to me.

"Pru was always secretive about our destination—she'd lock in the coordinates on my key without giving me any idea of where or when—but Saul often summons the people he and Pru consider part of the 'inner circle' to meet with him. I doubt I'll be invited again, however. He doesn't know about this—that I helped you get away from Holmes—but he does know that I warned you that day on the subway."

I remembered Simon's comment about Kiernan's interference. "They're angry, aren't they? They'll be looking for you."

He shrugged. "Probably. But I'm good at fading into the background. They'll have some idea of *when* I am, but not where."

"I'm sorry, Kiernan. You're in all of this because you chose to help me."

He didn't speak for a moment and pulled in a deep breath before looking back at me. "It wasn't a choice, Kate. There was never a choice. When I saw you on the train that first day, the day you were trying to destroy the diary?"

"I wasn't trying to destroy it," I said. "Just testing it to see what it was."

He smiled, but his eyes were as sad as they'd been that day on the Metro. "I knew before we arrived on that train," he said, a tiny break in his voice, "that you were different. I knew everything about my Kate. Hell, I knew her soul. She knew mine. No secrets. And when you looked at me and there was nothing in your eyes . . . you didn't know me. That life had never happened and you weren't *my* Kate—but you were still Kate. I still . . . loved you. I had to find a way to protect you. Do you understand?"

"Yes," I said, thinking again about Trey. The next time I saw him he would still be Trey, but he wouldn't be *my* Trey. No matter what happened between us in the future, I would never see that Trey again. "I do understand. I'm so sorry, Kiernan."

He sighed and shifted to sit beside me against the wall, putting his arm around me very carefully to avoid hurting me. "But here's the real kicker," he said. "I didn't get the full irony until I learned about the plot against Katherine. You are *also* my Kate, my *first* Kate—the girl with the funny painted toes who gave me the medallion, who was willing to risk her life to be certain that an eight-year-old boy got out of that hotel. And I realized then that I really didn't know what had happened that night—and that I had to find out."

"So that's why you were there tonight? Watching?"

Kiernan clenched his jaw. He looked exhausted—there were dark circles under his eyes and he'd clearly skipped the razor for at least a few days. Scruff looked unbelievably good on him, and I fought the urge to run my fingers along the side of his face.

"I've been to that hotel dozens of times, Kate. I've spent every possible minute in that hellhole for the past month. I've watched from every position, every angle, every vantage point." His arm tightened around me. "I came so close to just killing Holmes, just strangling him there in the dark and tossing him down one of those chutes straight into the lime pit in the basement, just like he'd done with so many women. But you—my other you—were adamant that we could only change the bits of history that Saul and the Cyrists had disrupted. Holmes's trial—that was worldwide. What kind of ripples would it cause if I killed him?

"And there were only a few seconds where I could act," he continued. "If I made a wrong move, I couldn't take it back—all I could do was add on. I mean, if I tripped him that first second and the gun went off and shot you, I couldn't undo that, aside from coming back earlier and stopping myself from tripping him. I also couldn't risk interfering until Katherine was fully out of the window."

He let out a long, slow breath and closed his eyes. "I watched you die over and over again, Kate. I watched him shoot you point blank fourteen times before I could see any way to change it."

"The lights!" I said, sitting up fully. "Oh my God—that was you? I thought . . . my head—I hit it really hard when I fell. I thought that's why I was seeing little blue flashes. But it was you!"

He nodded. "I finally did trip him, to slow him down, but he had the acid—I thought at first that he was getting it from the bottles near the cots against the wall. I was pretty close to one of those cots and I think he'd used acid on the woman who died there. But he had the bottle in his coat pocket. I thought it was the sound of his foot against the glass that reminded him he was carrying it—I even removed the bottles once, to see—but I guess it was just being there, where he'd used it once before that triggered the memory. I had to time it just right. The first four times I tripped him you were still facing forward. The acid caught you full in the face; two of the times your eyes were open."

I flinched, remembering the scorching pain when the acid hit my neck and realized how very much worse it could have been.

"I'm sorry," he said. "Part of me said to keep trying until I got it entirely right and you left there without injury, but . . . I couldn't keep going. I'm pretty sure you'll have a scar on your neck, but I don't think it will be very bad. I've put an advanced hydrogel on the burn. I put three more tubes in your bag."

"My bag!" I said, looking around. "I didn't . . . ."

"No," he said, reaching over to his right. "But I did. You dropped it when you fell. The hydrogel inside is from 2038, so you won't get anything nearly as good in your time. I just wish your hair had been down—it would have shielded you a bit more."

I smiled gently, thinking of the way he'd pulled the band from my hair in the Metro. "You always wish my hair was down, if I remember correctly."

"Guilty as charged," he said. "It reminds me of that time when we were at . . ."

Kiernan's voice trailed off, and then he closed his eyes, shaking his head slowly. After a moment, he opened them again and gave me what he clearly hoped would be a cheery smile. "So who is this Trey person?"

"Trey?" I looked down, unable to meet his eyes. "He's a friend—or he *was* a friend before . . ."

"Kate." Kiernan's voice was soft and so full of understanding that tears rushed to my eyes. "You called his name in your sleep, love. He's more than just a friend, I think."

It was *so* unfair for this to make me feel that I was betraying Kiernan. But it did.

He tilted my chin up ever so slightly and I looked into his eyes, as wet with tears as my own. "You cannot hide from your heart, Kate. It always finds you. And, sadly, I cannot hide from mine."

He pulled me into his arms and kissed me—softly at first and then with a passion that shook me to my very foundation. I was carried back to the wheat field just as clearly as I had been when I first looked into the medallion. There were at least two blankets between us, not to mention clothes, but the memory of the earlier kiss was so strong that I could almost feel his bare skin against mine. A slow delicious burn rose from deep inside me as I kissed him back, wrapping my hands in his long black hair.

I'm not entirely sure who broke the kiss, but I don't think it was me. I turned away and just sat there for several minutes, eyes closed, face flushed. I was stunned, confused, angry at myself, angry at Trey, angry at Kiernan, and all of that was competing with the very strong temptation to pull Kiernan's mouth back over mine and forget everything else, if only for a little while.

I could feel his eyes on me, but I couldn't make myself look at him. Finally, he pressed his lips to the top of my head and held them there. "Ah, Katie," he whispered, his breath warm against my skin in the cool morning air. "I'm being selfish. You have to go back—you need rest. I was so afraid you would go into shock last night. I kept the fire roaring so high it's a miracle I didn't torch the cabin. And I can't stay here much longer either—I've pushed myself to the limit already. Even these short hops are a strain."

I knew he was right. One half of my mind was screaming that I needed to get back, to see what had happened, to find out if Katherine was there, to find my parents, to find Trey. The other half was completely terrified of the prospect because there were so many ways that it could have gone wrong. Here and now was safe; the calm after the storm. There and then was simply unknown.

"Are you sure you can get back?" I asked. "You were worried about doing another jump . . ."

"I'll be fine, love," he answered. "If I can't make it right away, I'll rest up a bit. Going back home is never as hard as trying to leave. I feel like there's a physical . . . anchor, I guess, dragging me back there."

"Then I should go." I met his eyes for the first time since we kissed and tried to muster up a smile. "But—you spoke about a resistance. Are you still in? I mean, even if Prudence gets Saul to back off and they don't go after Katherine again, this isn't over. I don't know exactly what it is they're planning . . ."

"I have a pretty good idea," Kiernan said, leaning back to rest his shoulders against the bare wood of the cabin wall. "They refer to it as the Culling, necessary to save humanity and the planet. It will be pitched as an environmental accident of some sort. They've floated the idea of both airborne and waterborne, so I'm not sure.

"There's no specific date, as far as I know—the general plan is to wait till they have about one-quarter of the population under their thumb and they'll do whatever tweaking of the timeline they need to in order to make that happen. Cyrist members—or at least a good portion of them—will be given the antidote, along with a select few outsiders. People whose skills their experts have targeted as being vital for rebuilding."

"So—it's like the Creed they chanted at the temple," I said. "'As humans have failed to protect the Planet, the Planet shall protect itself.' Except the Cyrists assume the role of 'Planet' and kill off those they consider unworthy?"

"Yes," he said. "But don't dismiss the appeal of their message so quickly. They make a compelling argument when you're in the fold, y'know. There was a time when what Saul said made sense to me. You take someone from my time, a young kid who's just learned to use the CHRONOS key and show him select scenes from say, the 2150s. Jump him around and give him a firsthand view of a nuclear disaster or two. Tell him about a society where your future is planned before you're even born—written into your very DNA. Give him a few glimpses of modern war and the full extent of man's inhumanity to man and the Cyrist solution doesn't sound quite so evil."

"So you think they have a point?" I asked.

"Don't you?"

I didn't answer for a moment. "Yes—okay," I eventually admitted. "There's a valid point somewhere beneath the layers of insanity. But most of the things you described are . . . incremental evils, if that makes sense. The mistakes of one generation build upon the mistakes of the next and you get a society that no one really wanted. Saul is talking about massive, *planned* evil, however, and assuming that you end up with a better society as a result. Morality aside, how is that logical? It seems to me that they're gathering the greediest and most power-hungry of all, and I don't think they'll play nice together when the smoke clears. Prudence is one of those designing this brave new world and she actually told me I could either join them or line up with the other sheep to be fleeced and slaughtered."

Kiernan snorted. "She could at least try for originality. That line is one she stole straight from her papa. But yes, it was precisely that kind of callous disregard for those who chose *not* to follow the Cyrist Way that caused my dad to leave." For a moment he sounded like his eight-year-old self—*my dad* was almost *me dad,* and the same anger simmered beneath his voice.

"So you ask me if I'm in?" he said. "Of *course* I'm in. I'll do anything I can to bring them down. But Kate, I was serious when I said that my abilities are limited now. They're much weaker than they were just a few years ago, especially when I've been using the key so regularly. I doubt I'll be able to do much more than a short hop out of my timeline for the next month. Maybe more."

"But you have knowledge that we lack, Kiernan. You can give us the information we need to get started. Let me know how to get in touch with you," I said, squeezing his hand. "You don't have to go anywhere. I'll come to you."

I felt him stiffen slightly. I wasn't sure what I'd said, but I would have given strong odds that I had stirred up the Ghost of Kate Past.

"I'm in," he repeated after a long pause. "When you need to reach me, there's a stable point in Boston. It's a corner in the back of a tobacco shop near Faneuil Square. It's stable from 1901 to 1910, but I'm going back to July 17th, 1905. Anytime after that, Jess will know where I am. He's a friend. He's the only one who's ever behind the counter, and he won't be surprised if you walk out of his storeroom—you've done it plenty of times in the past. You can leave a message with him and I'll leave my location with him, too, once I've settled on a new place."

"So—did we have a game plan? Before, I mean."

"Yes," he said. "And we'd actually made some progress before you . . . disappeared. It's conceptually pretty simple. We just need to go back and convince the CHRONOS historians to steer clear of Saul and Prudence and give up their keys."

"And if they won't?"

"We take them anyway," he said with a crooked smile. "So far, you'd persuaded twice and stolen twice."

I gave him a weak chuckle. "So I get to play repo man? Great."

"You once said you were going to get a T-shirt printed with 'CHRONOS Repo Agent' on the front."

"Poor Kiernan. Listening to me must be like being around my dad's uncle—he never remembers he's told you the same joke a dozen times."

"I don't mind," he said. "It's interesting to see you from a different . . . angle, I guess. And a lot of what we were doing was really more detective work than repossession work. The first few were easy—Katherine already knew exactly when and where those historians landed."

"Why do you remember all of this, and Katherine doesn't?" I asked.

"You'd have to ask her," Kiernan said. "But I'd think the only logical answer is that something happened when she wasn't under the protection of a medallion."

"Was she still alive in my other timeline? When I was eighteen?"

"Yes," he answered. "And aside from a touch of arthritis in the winter, she was quite healthy."

"That's . . . ," I began.

"Confusing," Kiernan finished. "I know. Katherine's cancer isn't a given in the timeline, even though you'd think it should be. Another thing to puzzle out after we've both gotten some rest."

I nodded and started to get to my feet, but Kiernan pulled me back down. "Probably not a good idea, love. I'll get your things. That medicine I gave you is pretty strong stuff and I doubt you've had much to eat."

He was right. Even the slight movement had left me a bit dizzy, so I leaned back against the cabin wall. Kiernan walked over to the pile of cloth that had been my dress and held it up for my inspection. I wrinkled my nose. It was clearly a lost cause. "I do need to get the little booster cells that Connor put in the pockets and hemline—he might be able to reuse them, I guess." Kiernan removed several small silver rectangles and stuffed them into my bag.

"Anything else?" he asked.

I shook my head. "If the dress doesn't disappear when I leave, toss it in the fireplace."

The boots, unfortunately, seemed to have survived without a scratch. He placed them and the bag in my lap and then knelt down in front of me. "I'm sorry—I know you had a bonnet, but I couldn't find it."

"I'm not worried about a stupid hat," I laughed. "You were trying to get me out of Hotel Hell in one piece. And I don't think I ever really said thank you."

He gave me a sideways grin and squeezed my hand. "Actually, love, I believe you thanked me very thoroughly just a few minutes ago. But I wouldn't say no to a second round."

A blush rose to my cheeks and I looked down into the bag in my lap, trying to avoid his eyes. I fished out the CHRONOS key and had just pulled up the interface when he touched my wrist, breaking my concentration.

"This Trey," Kiernan said, his voice rough. "Does he treat you well? Does he love you?"

"He does . . . or at least he did," I amended, my mouth twisting into a wry half smile. "He seems convinced that he will again. That all I have to do is smile at him or something and everything will be as it was."

"But you're not convinced?" he asked.

I shook my head, and looked up into his eyes. "Can you re-create the same magic the second time around? I don't know."

Kiernan stared at me for a long moment and then leaned over, kissing me gently on the corner of the mouth. "But you have to try, right? *Slán go fóill, a stór mo chroí.*"

I didn't have the slightest idea what the words meant, but it was clearly a farewell. He squeezed my hand one last time, and then I looked down at the key and closed my eyes.

∞ 24 ∞

I caught a glimpse of myself in the reflection of a computer monitor a second before Connor even realized I'd arrived, so I fully understood his look of shock. The entire right side of my neck was bandaged. There were two red patches just above the hairline. Several other red marks dotted my shoulders and there were even a few holes in the petticoat.

Connor stared at me for a moment and then his lower lip began to quiver. I couldn't tell if he was about to laugh or cry and I'm not sure that he could tell, either.

"We simply can't send you out to play in nice clothes, can we, Kate?" he said finally. "What on earth happened to you? Are you—"

Whatever else he was going to say was drowned out by a crazed volley of barking from downstairs, followed by the sound of the doorbell.

"You," he said, pointing. "Do not move."

I knew it was Katherine before Connor reached the door. That wasn't Daphne's stranger bark. It was her welcome-home bark, the one with a little "I missed you" whimper in the middle.

Katherine's voice drifted up the stairs. "How did I end up in the yard without a CHRONOS key, Connor? Or a house key, for that matter?"

I lay back on the floor and closed my eyes.

The next thing I remember was waking up in my bed. The floral arrangement Trey had sent to Katherine was on my dresser. It seemed an eternity ago, and yet the flowers looked as fresh as when they'd first arrived. Daphne was curled up on the rug next to my bed and Katherine was sitting on the sofa near the window, reading what appeared to be a historical romance—the sort my mom sometimes referred to as a bodice-ripper or lusty-busty. It was the first time I'd seen Katherine reading anything that wasn't on a computer screen or inside a CHRONOS diary.

She glanced over after a few minutes. "Oh, Kate. I'm glad to see you're awake, dear. I was beginning to worry."

"The little blue pills," I said, my head still quite fuzzy. "In my bag. They're . . . nice."

"I see," Katherine replied, a hint of a smile touching the edges of her mouth as she sat on the side of my bed. "And where did you *get* the nice little blue pills? Connor filled me in on the day before you left. I've told him what I *now* remember from our adventure at the Expo. But neither of us know what happened to you after I climbed out that window."

My lips were very dry and I asked for a glass of water first. After a few sips, I put the glass back on the nightstand. "Kiernan," I said. "He gave me the medicine. He got me out of the hotel."

"But how?" she said. "He was a very bright little boy, but I don't see how that hotel could possibly have been standing when he got back. All of the historical accounts that I read—"

"He *was* a remarkable little boy," I interrupted. "And he's a remarkable young man."

I gave her a brief synopsis to fill in the missing pieces, having to pause repeatedly to keep my brain on track. It felt like I was reaching through fog to find phrases to string together, and they never came out quite the way I'd planned. I must have dozed off for a few minutes at some point, because when I opened my eyes,

Katherine had returned to the couch and was again reading her book.

"Where was I?" I asked.

"You were explaining Kiernan's plan—or was it your plan?— for repossessing CHRONOS keys, when you drifted off between words," she said, setting the book aside on the sofa. "After what you've been through the past few days, I was a bit afraid you might decide that you were done with us. You've got your life back for the most part and Prudence seems to have given you at least a limited degree of—immunity, I guess. You could walk away, you know."

The thought hadn't really occurred to me, but now that she'd spoken the words aloud, I was surprised that it hadn't. I could return to my life before Katherine showed up with the medallion. Mom was back, Dad was Dad again—

"Charlayne?" I asked.

Katherine looked confused for a moment and then shook her head. "I haven't checked, but I'm pretty sure nothing has changed for her."

I asked her to bring me the computer, and after a brief search I pulled up the same wedding photo, the Cyrist emblem clear and distinct against Charlayne's dark skin. Saving Katherine had fixed my life, but whatever happened with Charlayne's family was entirely separate.

I pushed the computer to the side and looked back at Katherine. "Connor's kids? They're still gone, right?"

She nodded.

"Then you're wrong—I really *don't* have a choice." The truth was, even if no one I cared about was personally affected in this timeline, I knew that I could never just sit by and watch as the Cyrists drew more converts and moved closer to some sort of mass genocide. Walking away wasn't an option.

"So—what about you?" I asked, shifting slightly in the bed. The medicine was fading, which was both good and bad—words were less slippery, but the pain was also returning. "Do you remember anything from the day after the shift . . . after Simon?"

"I remember holding out the medallion to that foul cretin. And Trey . . ." She stopped, giving me a sad smile before continuing. "Trey's car had just pulled up. I didn't see any choice other than to have faith. Faith that Trey would move any mountain he had to in order to save you from Simon. Faith that Connor would work his magic with the boundary. Faith that you would be able to fix this timeline. I've never been good at that—at giving up control to others—but it seems to have worked this time."

"But you remember being in the hotel and running from Holmes . . . and everything that happened that night. Isn't that . . . disconcerting? I mean, you have two sets of memories."

"It *is* a rather odd feeling," she said. "But all of that happened so long ago. I do remember wondering whose daughter you would be—Deborah's or Prudence's—when the two of them were small. My bet was on Prudence, given the resemblance, until she disappeared."

Katherine fell silent for a moment and then asked, "Prudence wasn't in on it, then? She was trying to save me?"

I debated lying to protect her feelings, but I knew it wouldn't serve much purpose. "She was saving you in order to protect herself, Katherine. And maybe to protect Mom. It definitely wasn't out of any sentimental ties to you, or to me, for that matter. I got the feeling she thinks you traded her off in some sort of a custody battle. But I do think she'll keep them from going after you again—at least until she finds out I'm still trying to stop the Cyrists."

Katherine bit her lip but nodded. "Which means we're going to have to move very carefully this time."

"Yes," I agreed.

I was quiet for a moment, not sure how to broach the subject that was nibbling away at the back of my mind, but I finally just decided to tackle it head-on. "You handled it okay, didn't you?

Having two different sets of memories? So how can you be so sure that Trey wouldn't have handled it, too?" I could hear the petulant tone in my voice and didn't really like it, but it was hard not to feel a bit cheated.

"I can't know anything for *certain*," she admitted. "But Trey doesn't have the CHRONOS gene. And with me, we're not talking about recent memories. Even something as vivid as being trapped in a burning hotel with a serial killer hot on your heels fades after a while, so it's not quite the same as two conflicting sets of memories. It's more like reading an old diary and remembering things you'd forgotten you knew. Or remembering both the truth about an event and a lie you've told so many times to so many people that both versions seem equally real. Does that make sense?"

"No," I admitted. "Not really. But I've kind of gotten used to things not making sense. I've decided the only way to stay sane is to just roll with the punches."

"I'm afraid that reconciling the past month will be a more difficult task than reconciling the distant past. Connor and I have been talking about the best way to adjust our own little slice of the timeline. The only reasonable thing is to have you go back to the day of the time shift—otherwise, your mom and dad are going to be very worried."

Mom. Dad. It felt unbelievably good to hear those words and be reminded that I was back in a world where I had parents again.

"You've been gone for over a month in this timeline, at least from *their* perspective, and this way, we can spare them that agony." Katherine traced her fingers along the edge of my bandage. "I took a peek while you were asleep and applied a bit more of the hydrogel to the two spots on your scalp. The burn on your neck is pretty deep, but I don't think the scar will be major after a few weeks. It would have been a very different situation if Kiernan hadn't been prepared. So any ideas for a cover story that your parents might buy?"

I thought about it for a moment. "Maybe we could pass it off as an idiot with hot coffee on the Metro? I could tell Mom that I just had a cab bring me here, rather than trying to find Dad on campus. And you took me to an urgent care . . . ?"

"If we give it another day or maybe two, to heal, I think that might be plausible," she said. "And then, once you're settled with them, I think it might be best if Connor and I made ourselves scarce for a few weeks—fewer points of overlap for you and for us. We'll tell Harry and Deborah that there was a last-minute opening with an experimental drug trial in Europe."

"I'm going to tell Dad everything, Katherine. I mean, he'll be living here, so we'd be lying to him constantly. I'm not good at that, so we can tell Mom the cover story, but—"

I broke off suddenly. Her comment about a drug trial had finally reached my brain, and it reminded me of my conversation with Kiernan. "You're cancer-free in the other timeline, Katherine. Kiernan was certain of it. Can you think of any reason why you'd be sick in one timeline but not in the other? I know that there are some environmental causes for cancer, but they don't develop suddenly, do they? I thought something like that would take years to develop."

"It should," she agreed, looking a bit stunned. "The only time I was outside of the protection of a medallion after Prudence disappeared was during a hospital stay when they were doing a biopsy. I was adamant that I needed to keep it on me at all times—I told them it was a religious medal. But when I came to, the medallion had been placed in the plastic bag with my other belongings."

She was silent for a moment and then shook her head as though to clear it. "Just one more thing to think about when Connor and I go on our little vacation, I guess. Do you think you could keep an eye on Daphne for us?"

Daphne thumped her tail once at the sound of her name and then went straight back to her nap. I laughed. "I don't know,

Katherine. She's a real handful. Of *course*, we'll watch her. Dad won't mind staying here on the nights I'm with Mom. The kitchen might actually get some real use for a change."

Just the mention of food started a rumble in my stomach. "Speaking of food . . . I'm starving. Is there anything to eat?"

"I saw half of a large deli sandwich, if that sounds okay?"

"Yes," I said, thinking that Connor must have already raided the fridge at least once if all that was left from O'Malley's was *half* a sandwich. "That sounds amazing. And chips. And a banana or anything else you can find. It's been at least twenty-four hours since I've eaten."

Katherine started toward the door and then turned around, crossing back to the couch. She opened the cover of the book she'd been reading and took out a computer disk. It was sealed in a white disk envelope, with my name in large letters across the flap.

"I found this on the porch, right next to the door. I'm guessing it's from Trey?" She walked back over to me and placed the disk on top of the computer. "I really *am* sorry about Trey, Kate. But I still think it was for the best."

I closed my eyes until I heard the door shut behind her and then picked up the disk. I was pretty sure it was just the Cyrist financial information that Trey's dad had promised to give him, but I held it against my lips for a moment before opening it. My hands weren't very steady as I opened the envelope and placed the disk in the drive. I expected to see a file directory, but after a couple of seconds Trey's face popped up, and my breath caught in my throat. He was wearing the same shirt that he'd worn that last night. His gray eyes were a bit red around the edges, and he looked dog-tired, but he smiled into the webcam.

"Hey, pretty girl. If you're seeing this, you've successfully saved the world, just like I knew you would. And if you're seeing this, I'm probably only a few miles away, but totally oblivious to the fact that I made this video and that the most beautiful girl in the world is watching it. But I'm missing you, Kate. Even if I don't know it, I'm missing you."

He took a deep, shaky breath and then continued, looking down at the keyboard and typing in a few strokes. "So—what follows is a brief video compilation of Trey and Kate's greatest hits. All those nights when I'd come home and then we'd end up on a video chat for half an hour or more? Well, I saved them, all except that first time, 'cause I didn't have the software yet. I don't really know *why* I saved them. It's not like I ever had a chance to rewatch them, since I was always with you. But they're all here, on my hard drive. I'm going to burn them to disk, along with a couple videos I took on my phone and the ones we recorded at your party. Everything I can find. Oh, and if you check out the file directory, the stuff Dad promised is there as well.

"The DVD was Connor's idea, so if it helps, we owe him big. It didn't even occur to me, but he told me that anything I left there, with you, would be protected, just like the books are. You need to make a copy, once you're back here, in the present. Or past, I guess. Ask Connor. He can explain it better than I can. I think this could work, Kate—this would be pretty hard to fake. I mean . . . I'd have to be incredibly dense not to recognize a message from myself, right?

"Here goes then—Lawrence Alma Coleman the Third, also known as Trey. If you have any doubts that this is you talking into the computer, I know what you did that Saturday afternoon when you were thirteen and Mom, Dad, and Estella went to that art gallery opening over on R Street. Never told anyone about that, did you?"

I smiled and made a mental note to ask him, one day, exactly what he'd done that Saturday.

"The girl who gave you this disk is Prudence Katherine Pierce-Keller, aka Kate the Time-Traveling Ninja. She has a few memories that you don't. Maybe these videos will help bridge that gap. But really, all you need to know is this—she has the prettiest green eyes in the universe and very ticklish feet. She's a sucker for *Princess Bride* quotes, onion rings from O'Malley's, coffee—but not if Connor made it—and you're so in love that you cannot imagine life without her.

"Now, back to you, Kate," Trey said. "Find me, kiss me, and make sure I get this message. In that order. And hurry, okay? I love you—and I miss you already."

He was still staring at the camera as the video faded out and shifted to one of the webcam shots, with my face in the big screen and Trey's in a smaller inset window in the upper right-hand corner. We weren't talking about anything, really—just an excuse to be together for a few more minutes before sleep. I clicked through quickly, knowing that I would go back later and watch every single minute. They were all there, in chronological order, as best I could tell. Every conversation, every silly joke, me painting my toenails while we talked, Trey offering me a bite of ice cream and dripping chocolate syrup on the camera.

I was laughing and crying at the same time when I heard a soft knock at the door.

Connor cracked the door and stepped in, carrying a large tray. "Should I come back?" he asked.

"No. You have food," I said. "Don't you dare leave." I moved the computer to the other side of the bed and slid over to make room. "In just a minute, I'm going to start shoving that into my mouth as fast as possible, and it wouldn't be polite to talk then, so let me say thank you first. For everything, but especially for giving Trey this idea. This is why he was able to let go, isn't it? Why he stopped fighting me about staying here when I made the jump."

"I suspect I would have had to evict him bodily otherwise, and he would probably have still camped out on the porch." Connor smiled, shaking his head. "I thought he'd tell you himself, but maybe he didn't want to jinx it. You're going to need to make a copy of that disk—once you go back to before the last time shift. Make it here, at the house, and it should be okay. It'll be a video from this time, but the disk—that will be in the same timeline as Trey, so . . . you should just be able to give it to him."

I had the sandwich unwrapped and was already eating. "It won't vanish? Or be blank?" I asked, with my mouth half full.

"Not as long as you make a copy," he said. "I'm not positive, but I can't see why it wouldn't work. The diaries still work, right?"

I glanced down at the sandwich in my hand. "You'd better be glad that I'm too happy to be mad at you," I said between bites. "This is Trey's roast beef. Did you eat my pastrami?"

"Didn't know if you were coming back," he said. "Shame to let a good sandwich go to waste."

∞

I spent the next few days sleeping, eating, and recording everything that I could remember about the past month. Then I saved the files in a CHRONOS diary to give to Katherine and Connor, and backed everything up on a DVD to give to Dad and eventually, I hoped, to Mom as well.

By day three, the burn on my neck had faded to the point where a scalding cup of coffee actually could have been a possible cause. I dragged my Briar Hill uniform from the back of the closet and very gingerly pulled my hair back, being careful to hide the few bare spots near the nape of my neck.

I retrieved my ID holder—now short two photographs—from the dresser drawer. I'd eventually add new photos of Mom and Dad, but for now I put in a photograph that Connor had taken of me and Trey in the backyard with Daphne, and the picture of me with Charlayne, our arms around each other, grinning from ear to ear with our new belts—mine brown and hers blue—tied around our white jackets.

Both of those photos would vanish if I ever took them outside of a CHRONOS field. If Connor's theory was right, I could always make copies later—and a vanishing photo might come in handy. Either way, the CHRONOS key was going to be a permanent accessory from now on. That was kind of annoying, since one of the reasons I'd agreed to this insanity was because I didn't want the constant worry of what might happen if something separated me from the medallion. But given everything I'd been through over the past few weeks, being stuck with an odd piece of jewelry seemed like a small price to pay for a little existence insurance and an emergency exit option.

There were a few other items I couldn't leave behind—like the necklace and T-shirts Trey had given me, even though I knew that I could never take them out of Katherine's house if I wasn't wearing them. I shoved the items into Katherine's handbag along with the *Book of Prophecy* and the DVD that Trey had made.

It seemed a bit silly to be sad about saying good-bye to Katherine and Connor when I'd be seeing them in just a few minutes, but I was. They wouldn't be the same Katherine and Connor. Our relationship would have to be rebuilt, and I could tell that they were thinking the same thing. I kissed them both, and gave Daphne a pat on the head. At least with her, I was pretty sure everything would be the same if I threw in a couple of dog treats and a few minutes of belly scratching.

And then I pulled up the stable point for Katherine's foyer, set it for 9 A.M. on April 7th, and went back to my life.

∞

Connor was surprised, to say the least, when I appeared without warning in the hallway. He was just coming out of the kitchen, wearing the same jeans and plaid shirt he'd been wearing when he'd rushed out to pay the cab driver after my backpack was stolen.

He yelled for Katherine, and she came hurrying down the stairs in her red bathrobe. And then we all sat down on the couch, and Connor made the bad coffee. But instead of Katherine telling me her story, I told them mine—or at least enough specifics that they could play their parts for a few days. And Connor passed me the entire box of gingersnaps, instead of three measly cookies this time.

I borrowed Katherine's phone to call Mom and tell her about the accident—nothing major, I said, just a scald. But I'd lost my backpack in the confusion. Of course, I started crying the moment I heard her voice on the other end of the line, but she mistook the tears for worry about the backpack.

"Kate, sweetie, it's no big deal. I'll cancel the credit card; we'll get you a new phone and iPod. We'll pay for the books. I'm not angry about this, so you don't need to be upset."

"I know, Mom. I love you."

"Do you need me to come there, Kate? You sound really shaken."

"No, no. That's okay, Mom. I'll see you tomorrow."

Then I called the Briar Hill office and asked if they could give Dad a message—I'd had a minor accident and wouldn't be in trig class, but I'd see him back at the cottage.

Connor drove me to the cottage a few minutes later. My hands shook as I slid the key into the lock, just as they had when Trey was waiting on the steps. There was no *#1 Grandma* mug. Dad's wok was in its usual place on top of the cabinets. I rushed to the fridge, and saw the jambalaya on the second shelf.

There would be plenty of time to tell Dad everything when he got back from class. For now, I just sank down on the sofa and closed my eyes. Home.

∞

Telling Dad was a multistage process, and the fact that I broke down into tears the first time I saw him didn't help to expedite matters. At least Dad understood what was going on after a long conversation with Katherine and Connor and a few demonstrations with the CHRONOS key. He and I agreed that it was probably best, for now, to keep this between us. So Mom didn't have a clue why I hit her with a waterworks display and extra long hug when she walked in the door after classes on Wednesday evening. That's really not our typical style of interaction, and I think she was seriously considering scheduling another session with the shrink. I talked her into dinner at O'Malley's instead. Extra onion rings.

Most pieces of my normal life fell back into place over the next few days. I returned to my typical routine of Mom's house, Dad's house, and school. The only major changes were packing up some of my things for the upcoming move to Katherine's house and having to remind myself that there was no Charlayne for me in this timeline.

And I kept putting off the very thing I'd promised to do first.

The freshly printed DVD was in my new backpack. I'd scanned the photo of the two of us for safekeeping, and I was pretty sure that the original I'd tucked into the ID holder would vanish as soon as I handed it to him. I'd watched the DVD at least a dozen times and even left a copy on Dad's kitchen counter when I went to class on Friday, just to prove to myself that it wouldn't disappear and that the contents would remain the same. It was still there when I returned, and it was still Trey's face that greeted me when I inserted it into the computer. There was no logical reason to put this off, but the knowledge that Trey would look at me and see a complete stranger terrified me.

Finally, on Sunday afternoon, when we were clearing away the dishes from a wonderful spinach lasagna, Dad suggested gelato for dessert. From Ricci's, near Dupont Circle. Just a few short blocks from Kalorama Heights. Walking distance to Trey. My stomach sank.

Dad watched me a moment and then shook his head. "You can't put this off forever, Kate. You said you made the boy a promise. Even if it isn't exactly the same as the relationship you remember, it isn't fair to Trey or to yourself not to give it a chance. And," he said with a grin, "I'm getting tired of hearing you play that DVD. Did you two ever talk about *anything* remotely substantive?"

I snapped the dish towel threateningly in his direction, but I didn't argue. He was right. I missed Trey. And there wasn't any chance at all of getting him back if I couldn't muster up enough courage to make the first move.

∞

I sat on the front steps, staring at the neat border of grass that ran along the walkway between the house and sidewalk. I realized I was chewing on my knuckle about the time I heard the door open behind me and I tucked my hand underneath my jeans to hide the bite mark. The early-evening breeze picked up the faint, familiar scent of his shampoo, so I knew it was him before I even looked up to see those beautiful gray eyes with their tiny flecks of blue. His smile was as open and friendly as it had been that first day when he followed me across the soccer field. And suddenly I wasn't nervous. This was Trey, my Trey. He just didn't know it yet.

"It's Kate, right?" he asked, sitting down next to me on the front step. "Estella says you're with the Briar Hill welcoming committee? I'm Trey, but I guess you already know that."

"Hi, Trey," I said.

And then I kept my promise. I leaned forward and kissed him, long and slow. He was startled at first, but he didn't pull away—and he most definitely kissed me back. It was totally unlike our first kiss, which had been shy and hesitant on both sides. This time, I knew what he liked and I threw everything I had into that kiss.

"Whoa—what was that for?" he asked when I finally drew back.

"Just keeping a promise," I said.

"Okay." He looked a little stunned, but he smiled at me again. "I think I like Briar Hill's idea of a welcome."

"Well, I *am* at Briar Hill, but this is more of an unofficial welcome," I said, holding out the picture and placing it in his hand. It was very clearly Trey, with his arms wrapped around a girl, who was very clearly me. I kept my fingers on the photo long enough for him to get a really good look, long enough for the inevitable question to creep into his eyes, and then I pulled my fingers away and watched the picture vanish.

I grabbed his hand and placed it on the CHRONOS key, holding it between my own two hands. His face had the same pale, pained look as before. "I'm sorry," I said. "I know that's uncomfortable for a minute, but . . ." And then I kissed him again, a soft kiss on the side of his mouth.

"Who *are* you?" he asked.

"I'm Kate. And I love you, Lawrence Alma Coleman the Third. I'm not some crazy stalker girl. There's a DVD in this envelope, videos that *you* made, that will explain everything. The disappearing picture, the reason I'm holding your hand against this weird piece of jewelry—do you feel okay now?"

He nodded, but didn't speak. I stared into his eyes for a long moment. I saw confusion, doubt, and all the other things I'd expected to see, but behind all of that there was a light that I'd seen before. It wasn't recognition, it wasn't love, but it also wasn't the blank stare of a stranger. There was a connection between us and I felt a surge of hope that Trey had been right to have faith, right to believe that we could rebuild *us*.

"The videos will explain everything." I placed the manila envelope in his lap and leaned forward, kissing him once more. "Bye, Trey."

I was halfway down the sidewalk before he called after me. "Kate! Don't go. How do I get in touch with you?"

I smiled back at him over my shoulder. "Just open the envelope."

Acknowledgments

Every historian I've known has imagined having a time machine. Not to *change* history, but just to see how events actually unfolded, without the varnish or bias that gets added to historical accounts. But would we be able to resist tweaking things just a bit to create a better world? I'm not so sure.

That was the idea that launched *Timebound*; and here at the end, I'd like to take a moment to thank some of the people who helped along the way. With the exception of taking a few liberties with dates and events, the description of the Exposition is largely based on actual history. I spent many hours digging through the Internet Archive, a vast treasure trove of photographs, recordings, and first-hand accounts of the Exposition. The Urban Simulation Team at UCLA has created a truly incredible online simulation of the 1893 Columbian Exposition that made me feel as though I'd actually strolled the sidewalks of the Wooded Island, toured the Palace of Fine Arts, and explored the Midway Plaisance. Finally, a large body of work on serial killer H.H. Holmes, aka Herman Mudgett, including Erik Larson's wonderful book *The Devil in the White City*, and several detailed documentaries provided background information that brought the horrors of the World's Fair Hotel into gruesome focus.

Thanks go to my sisters for listening to me when I needed to vent, and to my parents and brother, along with many other friends and family, who helped to get out the vote when *Timebound* reached the finals for the Amazon Breakthrough Novel Award. I'd also like to thank my nieces and nephews for giving me glimpses into the lives and Facebook statuses of young adult readers. (Amanda, you're old enough to read this now.) Conversations with Gareth and Ariana helped to flesh out the Cyrists, and Mary reminded me many times of that illusive quarry of every writer, the "suspension of disbelief."

I am also indebted to the many friends, colleagues, and students who have (with various levels of good grace) stuck with me through this project. Gigantic bear hugs to my beta-readers—Ryan, Donna, Pete, Ian, Teri, Joy Joo, Savannah, and Mary Frances—and an extra big hug to those of you who had the patience to comment on multiple drafts. My two favorite Goodreads groups—YA Heroines and Time Travel—provided much needed moral support and insightful commentary on the earlier draft, as did a wide array of book bloggers and fellow writers.

Additional thanks go out to everyone at Skyscape and Amazon Publishing, especially Courtney Miller, Terry Goodman, and Tim Ditlow. This has been a wild ride and you've all been very patient with a newbie author. And an extra big thank-you goes to my developmental editor, Marianna Baer, for her insight and commentary. To all of you: if I didn't incorporate some of your suggestions, please remember that I'm stubborn, and you were probably right. Your advice and feedback were invaluable and I owe you mega.

And even though I've mentioned a few of you already, I've saved for last the group that I can never thank enough—my wonderful family. You guys rock.

About the Author

 Rysa Walker grew up on a cattle ranch in the South. Her options for entertainment were talking to cows and reading books. On the rare occasion that she gained control of the television, she watched *Star Trek* and imagined living in the future, on distant planets, or at least in a town big enough to have a stoplight. These days, when not writing, she teaches history and government in North Carolina, where she shares an office with her husband and a golden retriever named Lucy. She enjoys yoga, über-dark chocolate, Galaga, and Scrabble. She still doesn't get control of the TV very often, thanks to her sports-obsessed kids. *Timebound* is her debut novel.